THE LIGHTNING ROD

TONY J FORDER

A DI Bliss Novel

Copyright © 2022 Tony Forder

The right of Tony Forder to be identified as the Author of the Work has been asserted by him in accordance Copyright, Designs and Patents Act 1988.

Republished in 2022 by Spare Nib Books

Apart from any use permitted under UK copyright law, this publication may only be reproduced, stored, or transmitted, in any form, or by any means, with prior permission in writing of the publisher or, in the case of reprographic production, in accordance with the terms of licences issued by the Copyright Licensing Agency.

All characters in this publication are fictitious and any resemblance to real persons, living or dead, is purely coincidental.

tonyjforder.com
tony@tonyjforder.com

Also by Tony J Forder

The DI Bliss Series
Bad to the Bone
The Scent of Guilt
If Fear Wins
The Reach of Shadows
The Death of Justice
Endless Silent Scream
Slow Slicing
Bliss Uncovered
The Autumn Tree
Darker Days to Come

Standalones
Fifteen Coffins
Degrees of Darkness

The Mike Lynch Series
Scream Blue Murder
Cold Winter Sun

The DS Chase Series
The Huntsmen

This book is dedicated to my father, my grandfather, and my uncle Sean. These three men were the most influential in my life, and I miss them more than I can ever express. I want to thank them for their words of inspiration and the creative spirit they instilled in me, lighting a flame in my imagination that still burns brightly to this day.

ONE

Driving north west out of the city towards the small village of Ufford, Bliss focussed on the car's stereo system. All too soon, his head would consume itself with grotesque imagery floating in the pool of inky-black darkness left in the wake of a fellow human being. Until then, he was happy to be in the company of Danny Wilson. A largely unheralded eighties band from Scotland, Bliss found their first album a source of inspiration.

Lost in vibrant melodies and layers of sound, he got stuck behind a vehicle moving so slowly his paternal grandmother might as well be driving it – and she'd been dead for decades. He spotted a clear stretch of road ahead and floored it. As he blew by the other car, he glanced across, smiling to himself when he saw an elderly woman behind the wheel. Her face was little more than a mask of desiccated flesh stretched tight over a skull, but somehow her ruby red lipstick made it work.

It was unusual for Detective Inspector Jimmy Bliss not to be somewhat inebriated at approaching 8.00pm on an off-duty Saturday night, but he'd started late and had put away only a single beer when Penny Chandler called. Attending the scene of a probable murder-suicide was an unappetising prospect at the best of times, but when she mentioned three young victims among the dead, it almost brought bile up into his throat. Not for the first time, Bliss asked himself how many more scenes of extreme violence he could visit without suffering lasting emotional damage. As had been the case more often than not in recent years, he reckoned there was no way to unring that bell.

During his brief exchange with Chandler he had wondered – but hadn't enquired – why DS Olly Bishop wasn't taking responsibility for the scene, given he was on call for major crimes all weekend. Until recently, Bishop had been working his way towards promotion and becoming a novice Senior Investigating Officer. He had, however, decided to detach himself from the promotion programme and at the same time withdraw from the role of acting DI. It was a resolution he'd not managed to sell to his wife, who was both unhappy and unsatisfied with his explanations for doing so. Evidently, she reminded him of it often, and as a result the burly DS had been a little off his game over the past few weeks.

Bliss saw the crime scene emerging out of the dusk long before he laid eyes on the property in which five people lay dead. *Five Friendly Aliens* happened to be drawing to a close when he spotted the array of emergency vehicles and their attendant pulsing lights. The sight sucked all enjoyment out of the music, which he immediately snapped off to reclaim the silence.

As he parked up on the roadside verge, he noticed his colleagues grouped together outside the front door wearing dour expressions and angry scowls.

Bliss exited the car, exchanging a blanket of chilled air for a wall of moist heat. The day had topped out at only 75 degrees, but he doubted it had dipped much at all since, even with the sun fast disappearing over the horizon, leaving behind a vivid blood-orange afterglow.

Bishop and Chandler approached somewhat sheepishly as he signed the record of attendance handed to him by a PCSO, before making his way up the short driveway towards a rambling chalet-style bungalow built in the shape of an L. 'What's with the sour faces?' he asked. 'You both look as if your mothers sent you to bed with no afters.'

'Sorry for the call, Jimmy,' Chandler said, offering an apologetic shrug. 'Hope I didn't ruin a glorious evening of fun and frolics.'

Bliss left that alone while Bishop also expressed regret at having called his boss in on one of his rare evenings off. 'I'm sure me and Pen could have handled this until tomorrow morning, but your mate Abbott was insistent.'

This gave Bliss pause. Abbott was the lead forensics investigator, responsible for all the city's crime scene management. 'Neil? Believe me, he's no mate of mine. And since when does he get to dictate who attends his crime scenes?'

'Since he started banging on about the prospect of potential bias at this one,' Chandler said with some venom. 'And that's despite me insisting I had nothing to be biased about.'

'Biased? I'm not with you. What exactly am I missing here, Pen?'

'I'll explain,' Bishop said, taking a step closer and lowering his voice. 'SOCO thinks this crime scene has too many similarities to a previous one for it to be a coincidence.'

'So what if it does?'

'We investigated it a few years ago, not long before you came back to Peterborough. We resolved it as a murder-suicide. He's seeing a similar MO here, which concerns him.'

Bliss caught the implication immediately. 'Because if it is the same, then chances are your murder-suicide was murder only.'

'Precisely.'

'Even so, explain to me how Neil gets from there to where he refuses to allow you inside.'

'He's concerned about how it might look. He's worried others may second-guess our reaction once we realised we'd got that previous one wrong. Further on down the road, people might wonder if we fudged a few things here at this scene, perhaps trying to make sure the two cases were not conclusively linked.'

Bliss felt a vein pulse in his left temple. 'The cheeky bastard,' he said, unconcerned with who might overhear. 'What right has he to question your integrity?'

'I don't think he actually believes we'd do that,' Chandler swiftly interjected. 'More a case of him wondering how it might be viewed in retrospect by the big cheeses. I reminded him I was working down in London at the time, so wasn't even part of that investigation. Didn't seem to matter, though. He insisted on speaking to somebody with more rank.'

'And was okay with that person being me? That's unusual for him. Neil usually complains about me treating his crime scenes with disrespect.'

'I'm sure it was more a question of how much grief he might get if he demanded the presence of somebody more senior than a DI.'

Bliss sighed and gave himself time to reflect. He ran a hand across his face, then looked up at Bishop and said, 'Any chance the unit got it wrong back then?'

The big man shrugged, chewing on his bottom lip. 'You know how it goes, Jimmy. Of course we could have got it wrong. We didn't think so at the time, but anything's possible.'

'What I mean is, do you remember having any doubts at the time? Any bones of contention? Any disagreements among you?'

'No.' Bishop shook his head adamantly. 'None of that. Fact is, it was one of those cases where everything was cut and dried. It looked exactly what it was. We had no other suspects, and reason enough to believe it all went down as we thought.'

'Then I don't see the problem. Either Neil's suspicions are wrong now, or it was called wrong in the first case. Shit happens. We'll deal with it and move on. At the moment, what's inside this home is both my priority and my only concern. I noticed you two chatting with Gul when I pulled up. Is she the only other member of the team we have here on scene besides the pair of you?'

Bishop nodded. 'I didn't feel the need to call in Phil or Alan until I knew for sure what we were dealing with.'

'That's fine. I take it Gul worked the other case with you?'

'She did.'

'All right. First of all, I'll have a word with Neil. Technically, it is his scene until he calls it or allows us access. I'll see if he's happy to let you and Gul inside provided I'm on site with you. That is, I'll persuade him not to be a dick about it. Do you know if he's given Nancy a bell?'

'Not as far as I'm aware.'

Bliss gave himself a moment to consider. Nancy Drinkwater was the lead pathologist for the area, working out of the city hospital mortuary. She would most likely have carried out the post-mortem on the previous victims, in which case Neil Abbott might want her to take a look at the fresh bodies and offer her opinion on any comparisons he was seeing.

'Okay,' he said eventually. 'Before I talk to Neil, tell me more about the first case.'

'It was a pretty standard situation,' Bishop said, scratching his chin. 'Wife and two kids stabbed multiple times, clearly murdered. Husband took his own face off with a shotgun. No stab marks on his own body, and the discharged weapon by his side suggested he was responsible. Prints and GSR looked to have confirmed it. We didn't stop there, though. We were thorough.

What we learned from family and friends told us the couple had their problems, and he was under some financial pressure. He also did his fair share of drinking, and was known to fly off the handle when provoked. Apparently, the wife was the type to push his buttons. No suggestion either were having an affair, they didn't owe money to any wrong'uns, weren't into drugs, and had no known enemies. We didn't have a single alternate suspect.'

'Was it his shotgun? All licensed and above board?'

'Yep.'

'Then it sounds as if you did your job. But if Neil is right, can you think of anything now for us to even consider? Anything at all that, if we do discover it was murder all round, you could point to and in retrospect realise was out of place.'

Bishop vigorously shook his head. 'Jimmy, I've thought of little else since my conversation with Abbott. There's nothing. If we missed something, I genuinely don't know how. Nor can I imagine what it might be.'

'Then don't let it get to you, Bish. You did your job before, no matter what. Who are our victims here tonight?'

'The Sperling family.'

'Okay. I'll sort out the access we need. And you… stop second-guessing yourself.'

Bliss marched towards the front door, fearful of what lay beyond.

TWO

Bliss and Neil Abbott faced each other across the threshold leading into the kitchen. 'You'll get no apology from me,' the crime scene manager said defiantly. 'I'm not having my forensic work here discredited because some twat from the CPS further down the line dismisses it as having been tainted by police officers with an agenda.'

'Is that all we are to you, Neil?' Bliss asked without malice, already squirming uncomfortably inside the lilac Tyvek forensic suit he'd been forced to don. 'Just a bunch of coppers traipsing around your fiefdom with no self-regard, no professionalism? I know you have your issues with me because I prefer to be on the plot too early for your liking, but you've known Penny and Bish for years. Gul, too. Do you genuinely have so little respect for them and what they do?'

Abbott rolled his eyes. 'See, now you're making it all about me. It isn't. It's about the evidence. The evidence and those who outrank us all when it comes to pointing the finger. You must acknowledge how it might appear, Jimmy.'

'I do. Of course I do. But you're missing something blindingly obvious.'

'Oh, really? And what's that when it's at home?'

'Neil, if my team are to be treated with suspicion, why haven't you recused yourself? The other scene you're so concerned about was yours every bit as much as it was ours.'

Abbott churned that over before shaking his head and blustering defensively, 'The difference being, Jimmy, I know my only agenda is to get it right. I'm not going to cover anything up to spare my own blushes.'

'Precisely. And you know my people, Neil. You know them well enough not to pre-judge them.' Bliss held up a hand to forestall another comeback. 'However, let's put that aside for the time being and get on with our respective jobs, eh? Now, is there any part of the scene you'd be willing to free up for us to eyeball?'

'From a distance?'

'If that's the best you can offer.'

'I'll lay down some additional footplates, and provided you stick to them I'll let you have a look at the dining area. I can't give you access to the bodies until tomorrow morning, but if you want to get a sense of it now, I'm willing to indulge you.'

Abbott wasn't usually so obliging. Bliss guessed the man was feeling a little guilty about denying the others entry. 'Before you do that,' he said quickly, 'tell me about the MO and its similarities to the other case.'

'I have several concerns. First of all, the spread and density of gunshot residue is not just similar, it's identical. Would two different men of two distinct shapes and sizes intent on suicide hold the weapon in precisely the same way, aiming into their own face at precisely the same angle? Possible, but unlikely. Secondly, the number and the pattern of stab wounds, while not identical, are too similar to dismiss as unconnected. In addition, the binding around the wrists and ankles matches. Finally, the bodies were clustered together at the dining table as if preparing for a meal. Just like before. It's a chilling sight, Jimmy. Not one I'd seen previously, or since… until today.'

Experience in working murder scenes was both a gift and a curse. The latter meant those who did the job required no imagination. If Bliss closed his eyes, he'd still be able to see mutilated bodies. If he was struck deaf, he'd still be able to hear the screams of victims, despite not having been present at the time of their murders. There was no need for him to cast an eye over this particular grisly tableau in order to appreciate the carnage.

He would, though.

It came with the warrant card.

Abbott ordered one of his technicians to distribute additional footplates, while he and Bliss surveyed the scene from the far end of the dining area. 'The real horror – the bodies and the blood – is confined to this dining room,' he explained. 'Our victims were all subdued somehow, forced to sit at the table, where they were stabbed. Other than the husband, who was blasted with both barrels of the shotgun. No doubt in my mind this entire scene was made to look like a murder-suicide. As I must now presume the other incident was.'

Behind his mask, Bliss drew saliva into his mouth while he absorbed the horrific details. The bodies of the wife and three children were slumped, heads lolling as far forward as their necks would allow. The husband lay in the exact opposite pose, thrown back into his chair and remaining there long after the blast had shredded his face to a series of grotesquely unrecognisable pieces. Blood pooled around the dining table, thick spatters splashed across the table and chairs like some lurid poster for a horror movie. A number of thinner trails reached the wall behind Mr Sperling, together with blotchy clumps of matter Bliss didn't even want to contemplate.

He cleared his throat and asked the first question that came to mind. 'Tell me truthfully, Neil. If it wasn't for the other case back in 2017, would you have seen anything here that screamed something other than a murder-suicide?'

'Probably not,' Abbott admitted.

'And in truth, didn't you believe the first one was?'

'I did, yes.'

'As did the pathologist, Nancy.'

'True. Eventually. There were a few concerns because no genuine motive was established, but all the evidence pointed to it.'

'So why give my people a hard time tonight? If they missed something, then so might you have.'

'I didn't. We didn't. My team and I.'

'And yet you were perfectly happy to assume my lot couldn't handle it. You threw suspicion over them without a second thought.'

Abbott turned to confront him. 'You're way over the fucking line here, Jimmy. It's my job to secure the scene for evidence. To keep it unspoiled. There's nothing more to it than that.'

'You just don't see the hypocrisy, do you?'

The crime scene manager scoffed and flapped a hand in his direction. 'You're taking it far too personally. Take a step back and consider it for a second. Bishop and Ansari attended the original crime scene. I'm not for one moment suggesting they would tamper with this one, but I had to avoid that accusation being made at some point in the future. I apologise if I didn't make that clear to them.'

'Tell *them* that. I'm not the one you need to say sorry to.'

'I bloody well did it as much for their sake as mine. And to protect the investigation. If you can't see that, then you're not the copper I thought you were.'

'Maybe. But you're exactly the bellend I thought *you* were.'

The two men were silent as they eyeballed each other, anger causing them both to pant and flex. Then Abbott turned away to slam the side of his fist against a wall.

'Shit! Sorry about that, Jimmy. I may have been the one who overreacted.'

His outrage spent, Bliss shook his head wearily. 'No, I'm the one who should apologise. You were right – you were doing your job by protecting the scene and the investigation. I should have thanked you, not bollocked you.'

A CSI tech hovering close by muttered something about them both getting a room.

'Fuck you!' they said in unison.

'And the horse you rode in on,' Bliss added.

A moment later, Abbott pulled a pained expression and said, 'Is this going to be a shit show, Jimmy?'

'You mean if a wrong call on a murder four years ago allowed a killer to go free and strike again now?' Bliss snorted. 'Yes, Neil. If you're right, this is going to get very ugly indeed.'

THREE

Bliss was the last to arrive in the conference room on the third floor at Thorpe Wood police station. He was a couple of minutes early for the 10.00am management meeting, but disliked being the final body through the door. As he made his way around the table to find the first available empty chair, he felt all eyes upon him. The presence of one pair in particular took him by surprise. Seeing David Benning – in post as the area Police and Crime Commissioner for less than three months – gave Bliss pause.

'Apologies,' he said as he sat down. 'I was delayed by an update from SOCO.'

'Fresh information, Inspector?' Detective Chief Superintendent Feeley enquired.

Bliss shook his head. 'No, sir. It was just a quick call to let me know the victims are all with pathology and CSI will be at the scene until later this afternoon.'

'Very well. Now that you are here, I can complete my introductions. DI Bliss, our PCC you'll be aware of, but the man to my left is Superintendent Giles Pickford.'

'We've actually met before.' Bliss offered a thin smile. 'Good to see you again, sir. Still at Bedford HQ?'

'You, too. And yes, I am. I suspect they'll have to cart me out of Woburn Road in a box.' He turned to Feeley. 'Jimmy and I worked a few cases together when he was with the NCA.'

'Successfully, I trust?'

'Completely.'

The DCS cleared his throat as if disappointed by the answer. 'Good to hear. Okay, so most of you are probably wondering why Superintendent Pickford is with us today. Perhaps when I tell you he is also a PIP 4 investigator, the penny will drop.'

It did for Bliss. Level 4 investigators from the Professionalising Investigation Programme were called in for only the more complex reasons, which in this instance immediately sent alarm bells ringing.

'There's going to be an urgent case review,' he said. 'And DSI Pickford is here to smooth the waters ahead of it.'

'Spot on, Inspector. Given the information coming in from Ufford, I had no alternative but to ask the ACC to request a formal case review relating to the Armstrong family investigation. He spoke with the Chief Constable, who in turn discussed the matter with the PCC yesterday evening. We'll be casting the net wide, but to keep down the costs it'll probably be DSI Haskel from Northants who carries out the review. That's yet to be decided. For now, Superintendent Pickford has been good enough to give up his Sunday to listen to what we have to say, and to offer advice accordingly. I thought this might be of some help when the actual case review begins. That way, there will hopefully be fewer surprises.'

'I take it that means you've already decided a case review is absolutely necessary?' Bliss said.

It was Benning, the PCC, who responded. 'Naturally. Do you see a problem in that, Inspector Bliss?'

'Only that it seems oddly premature at this stage. Other than whatever Neil Abbott has come up with, what else do you have? Anything specific to confirm his instincts as yet?'

He already knew the answer. Abbott was good at his job, and if he believed the scene had all the hallmarks of the earlier case, then it probably did. What troubled Bliss was the rush to organise a case review. It felt almost prejudicial.

Benning demurred to Feeley. The PCC, an ex-uniformed constable whose views on the previous Police Authority were well known, having voiced his concerns on many occasions as a Liberal Democrat councillor, sat back and folded his arms.

'Nothing solid, no,' the DCS admitted in response to Bliss's question. 'But I have had a quiet word with DS Bishop, and he agreed the scene was too similar to disregard. You must realise there's no avoiding a review. I'm merely buying some time for you in getting a head start.'

'I see a number of concerned expressions around this room,' Benning said, appraising everybody at the table. 'Suspicion, too, on some faces. Please don't worry. I'm sure you have nothing to fear provided you've done nothing wrong.'

Pickford nodded furiously as he interjected. 'I've been there, so I have a perspective from both sides. A case review at this level leaves a bad taste in the mouth. Let me assure you, DI Bliss, these reviews are not about blame and finger pointing. They exist so that we can learn from them and hopefully make improvements. They are also necessary in order for us all to have a better understanding of where, how, and why things go wrong during an investigation.'

'Or if they went wrong at all,' Bliss said sharply. 'Let's not begin the process with any preconceived ideas.'

'A good point, Inspector. In my experience, very few investigations are completed without error, but of course there are exceptions. Now, I'd like to hear from Superintendent Fletcher first, please. Beginning with an outline of the initial case.'

Fletcher opened up a folder and scanned its contents, refreshing her memory. Bliss knew it would be a hard copy version of the policy book for that operation. 'This is from June 2017,' she said after taking a sip of water. 'A local businessman by the name of Kevin Armstrong, his wife, and their two children, were found dead in their home. Mrs Armstrong and the kids had each been bound to dining room chairs before being stabbed multiple times. The carving knife used in the attack had been removed from a block in the kitchen and was left behind on the dining table. Mr Armstrong, who died from gunshot wounds to the head, had been neither bound nor stabbed as far as anyone could tell. A Benelli under-over shotgun licensed to Mr Armstrong was found on the floor by his side. The only prints on it were his. Forensics found GSR traces on his skin and his clothing. It looked like the scene of a murder-suicide to everybody who attended. No verifiable evidence was discovered at the scene to suggest anybody else had been inside the house at the time.'

'Prints on the carving knife?'

'Two sets, belonging to Mr and Mrs Armstrong.'

'Thank you,' Pickford said. 'And the SIO on that case was…?'

'That would be me,' DCI Edwards said, raising a finger. It had been a while since Bliss had seen his old boss, and he was alarmed by how exhausted she looked. It showed most of all around her sunken eyes, but the flesh seemed to hang awkwardly on her face, creating pouches beneath her chin. 'And I have to agree with Marion. Murder-suicide was the first thought that went through my head when I saw the scene for myself. Nothing about the subsequent investigation altered that impression.'

'Is there a danger in forming an opinion so quickly? Could your immediate gut reaction, and that of your team, have created a straighter and less cluttered path for your investigation to follow?'

'You mean did we hear hooves and decide on horses rather than consider zebras? No. Absolutely not. Sir, with respect, a proficient police officer will look at a scene and draw some initial conclusions. You'll know as much from your own experiences. Most of the time those first impressions are proven correct, but that doesn't stop us from considering all other angles.'

'That's very true. And DCI Harrison? He ran the case as your deputy SIO.'

'He did. Sadly, it was the last we worked together. His wife fell ill shortly afterwards, at which point he took an extended leave of absence. He resigned the following year, having never returned to the unit.'

'You're telling us you had two Chief Inspectors working the same op?' the PCC said brusquely. 'That seems unnecessarily top-heavy.'

'I understand why you'd think that. But things were upside down here at the time in terms of staffing. We'd had a DI transfer out, and his replacement failed to materialise. We did consider bringing in an inspector from the outside, but ultimately we decided we could cope with what felt like a straightforward case.'

'I wasn't here, so I'm not about to second-guess the merits or otherwise of that decision,' Pickford said, taking charge of the conversation once more. 'But DCI Harrison essentially ran the ship with you at the helm, and he had no qualms when it came to concluding a murder-suicide at the end?'

'No, sir. We were in complete agreement. We all were. DS Bishop was very much a part of the decision-making process. If he'd had doubts, he would have spoken up. As SIO, all final policy decisions were mine alone, but we worked it as a team and there were no dissenting voices. I feel I should point out that of the current unit, only DS Bishop and DC Ansari worked that first investigation. DS Short was also in that team, but as I'm sure you know, she was later killed on active duty.'

Pickford drew in a deep breath. 'I am aware, and my condolences to you all. But if I may, you came across as a little defensive there, DCI Edwards. I'm sensing an undercurrent of tension in the room, and this is not even the case review proper.'

'With respect,' Bliss said, 'it doesn't feel that way.'

'Then let me make myself clear. I'm a friend to this team, here at the request of your Chief Superintendent and the PCC. My role is to expose you to the rigours of an actual review, and to perhaps round off a few of the sharper edges. But it's also essential for you all to realise something: when a PIP 4 investigator arrives here from another area force, he or she will not be your enemy. Their sole responsibility is to report on their findings. They're not looking for scapegoats. They will analyse the case, they will speak to each of you who was involved, they will draw conclusions from what they learn, and they will deliver their verdict along with a list of recommendations for this host force to accept or not.'

'Which, because their report is deemed disclosable material in any connected trial, this force would have to have very good reasons to disregard,' Bliss argued. 'In other words, what this outsider says, goes.'

Pickford frowned at Bliss. 'I wouldn't put it quite like that. But you're right, your CC will look foolish if he agreed to funding a case review only to ignore the outcome of the report he paid for. And I do understand how you must all feel, believe me. As I mentioned earlier, I've been there and it wasn't a good time for any of us. However, there is no enmity involved. Certainly not from the perspective of the PIP 4 investigator.'

Bliss huffed, and the DSI's eyes narrowed. 'You doubt me, Inspector?' he asked.

'It's not that, sir. Of course I believe *you* believe what you're saying. But this investigator, though highly qualified and experienced, is still only a human being. People have their own agendas, their likes and dislikes, and occasionally other people get caught up in the middle of all that.'

'You clearly have strong feelings about this, Inspector. And yet you were not even here at the time of the original case. It's not your work about to be scrutinised.'

Bliss felt himself flushing beneath the collar of his polo shirt. He was doing all the talking and setting himself against the leaders in the room. He steadied himself before responding. 'I realise that, but members of my team were part of that investigation. Are you suggesting they'll be completely unaffected as we attempt to work this new op? Human nature doesn't work that way. I can already see DS Bishop second-guessing himself, and I don't doubt DC Ansari will be doing the exact same thing.'

'Would you rather a different team took over the case?' DCS Feeley chipped in.

'No, sir. That's not what I'm saying, and it's not what I want. And for the record, I'm not trying to be difficult here. But let's be honest… it's one thing to stand on the sidelines and give the official version of how things will be, but quite another when reality bites. I appreciate you asking DSI Pickford to help us prepare. All I'm suggesting is that if we're going to do that, then let's do it properly. Let's have it, warts and all. My colleagues need to know what to expect when it comes to the case review, and the rest of us need to know what to expect when it comes to any overlap with the case we're working now.'

Feeley and Pickford exchanged glances. The former paused for a moment to reflect before giving a single nod. The DSI breathed through his nose and relaxed back into his chair. 'Fair play, Jimmy. You're right, of course. No sugar-coating. I've told you all how this review ought to go. Now let's discuss the ways in which it can easily go wrong.'

FOUR

By the time he made his way back down to Major Crimes, Bliss had won a further important concession, in addition to the agreement for the unit to continue working the case provided they liaised with whichever PIP 4 was eventually brought in. Feeley had suggested the unit begin their operation with a full-strength team starting on Monday morning, given the op was not yet officially classified as a murder investigation. Bliss had argued otherwise.

'I'm sorry,' he said, sounding anything but apologetic. 'But you know how critical the golden hour can be. Also, if you insist our new case is suspicious enough to warrant an urgent review of the 2017 operation, then it surely demands as many officers as we're able to bring in at short notice today. Irrespective of the impact on overtime budgets.'

The 'golden hour' to which he referred was in fact not an hour at all, rather an unspecified passage of time during which material evidence was often more readily available immediately following an incident. During this period, the police threw everything at building the foundations of their investigation. Bliss was happy to have won the argument, as it meant he and his team would not be forced to sit idly by as the clock ticked down.

An hour later and only Gratton remained absent. He had called in to apologise, explaining he had gone away for the weekend to Wales and wouldn't make it back in time to join his colleagues that day, even if he drove at record speeds. Bliss accepted his absence as one of those things, but was nonetheless pleased to see the major crimes room almost full. He began the first briefing by providing details of the case and his earlier meeting. By prior arrangement, DS Bishop then stood to provide his perspective. He shuffled from foot to foot awkwardly, constantly adjusting himself in rare off-duty clothing.

'I apologise to those of you who were not part of the investigative team on the Armstrong case. By the sound of it, this unit will be operating under a cloud because we might have got it wrong in 2017. I'm sorry about that. Neither Gul nor I can imagine what we missed first time around, if we missed anything at all. But it was our op, and now five people, including three kiddies, are dead. If it is the same killer in both cases, that won't sit well with either of us.'

'Don't beat yourself up, Bish,' Chandler insisted. 'Nobody else pulled a rabbit out of a hat, did they? Sounds to me as if you reached the only logical conclusion based on the evidence presented. But that was June 2017, and here we are fifty months later. If they are related, the work of the same man, then why nothing in between?'

'Pen raises a good point,' Bliss said, running a hand through his recently trimmed hair. 'I've been wondering the same thing. We'll need to query HOLMES to see if there are similar incidents elsewhere. Perhaps in a different region of the county, maybe further afield. To look at this rationally, if a handful of people hadn't worked both cases, we'd probably still be in the dark. Four years ago, the deaths of Mrs Armstrong and the two children were recorded as murder at the hands of Kevin Armstrong, who then went on to take his own life. Without any evidence to the contrary, this Sperling incident would almost certainly have taken the same route.'

'You were at both scenes, Bish,' DCI Edwards said. 'As was I. Your overall impression was the same as mine, wasn't it?'

'Yes, but we both know impressions aren't enough to make a judgement call,' Bishop replied testily. 'I worked the first case, but only got a glimpse of this one from the sidelines. From what I could see, it looked much the same. It looked like a murder-suicide.'

'It did to me as well,' Bliss said. 'We may peek around corners when we investigate, but we also take stock of what's directly ahead. Neil Abbott admitted much the same thing. This fresh case will be investigated as a murder scene because of its similarities to the Armstrong case, not because the evidence for murder is so overwhelming. In fact, as things stand, there is none. I spoke to him earlier today, and although he's not yet done with it, he's so far not found anything out of the ordinary. And this time his efforts are working at paranoid levels.'

Detective Chief Inspector Diane Warburton, who stood arms folded close to Bliss, coughed into a hand and stepped forward. 'I realise you'll all be troubled at this turn of events. You might also be wondering why DCI Edwards has joined us today. Quite simply, Alicia was closely involved with the Armstrong operation and she's here to offer her valuable insight. So, this team will work the current case. The case review investigator will study the previous one. Whatever overlap there is comes only one way. By that, I mean you will not reinvestigate the Armstrong killings. You are not to go anywhere near it. If our PIP 4 has relevant information pertaining to both, he or she will share whatever it is with this team. You will ensure *that* aspect is a two-way street. I won't tolerate any of you holding anything back. Your sole task here is to solve this case, irrespective of what happens with the other one. Are we clear?'

The response was muted but generally agreeable. Nobody enjoyed the added pressure, but the decision had been made at the highest level and they would have to accept it.

'I understand the desire to keep us from going anywhere near the review, but what if the new case takes us back to the old one?' Chandler asked uneasily.

'In what way?' Warburton wanted to know.

'What if we find something else connecting these two families? We're basing our entire op on there being a connection between them in the way they died. If there was also one in the way they lived, then we'll have no option but to refer back to that case. Possibly even reinterview everybody involved at the time. Perhaps even a full TIE strategy.'

Bliss slowly nodded as he weighed up his partner's words. The Trace, Interview and Eliminate protocol would certainly necessitate his team reinvestigating the previous case in terms of anybody who made a statement. On this occasion, because of what they now suspected, it would branch out with a complete focus on uncovering new suspects.

'Pen is bang on,' he said. 'We could end up all over it, and that could get messy.'

Warburton said nothing for a moment, before eventually nodding. 'You're both right. And in fact, you could say those of us at a more senior level are approaching this in the wrong way. The case review will mainly concentrate on how the team ran the investigation. Clearly, they'll assess the case itself, but their report is aimed at identifying the procedure and decision-making process. There's room for you there to slide in if you must. But only if it can't be avoided. Agreed?'

They did. His DCI's change of heart was one of the reasons why Bliss enjoyed working with her so much; she could never be accused of digging her heels in when alternative suggestions were put to her.

'To that end,' he said, 'I want to talk about strategy for a moment. By late briefing tomorrow, the post-mortem results will be in, plus the highlights from forensics. Either or both might tell us everything or nothing at all, so we should prepare ourselves for all eventualities. There's plenty for us to get our teeth stuck into before then, though.'

He noticed a raised hand. 'What is it, DC Virgil?' he asked.

'Just a thought, boss. I'm sure you've probably got this covered, but it occurred to me that we already have a new overlap with the previous case. Potentially, at least.'

'Go on.'

'It's the evidence. You mentioned forensics, and that's a potential source of overlap right there. Because now we can have them run comparative tests on samples taken from both scenes. Hair and fibre, for example. If they get a match, then we'll know for certain what we're looking at.'

Bliss would have thought about the possibility soon enough, but was impressed with the eager young rookie detective's speed of thinking. 'Not for the first time, let's give a hand to DC Alan Virgil,' he said, applauding. 'And your reward for volunteering a bright idea is…?'

Everybody in the room laughed, some slapping Virgil on the back as he groaned and said, 'The snacks are on me?'

'Yes, they are. Mine is a Yum-Yum, please. And as punishment for not getting there ahead of you, DC Gratton can make or fetch the drinks.'

'Get a mixed box from Krispy Kreme, Tiger,' Bishop said. 'You can get them delivered.'

The nickname triggered further laughter. DC Virgil went through a lot of orange Tic Tacs. He had a habit of carrying them in his trouser pocket, so when he ran or even trotted, they rattled in their plastic casing. Chandler had initially christened him 'Rattler', but after Virgil complained that it didn't sound tough enough, Gratton happened to mention how deadly the tiger rattlesnake was, and the name had stuck.

Glad of the break in routine, Bliss continued with the meeting. 'Alan's right. Evidence comparisons can now be made between the scenes, and we can only hope for a lead or two arising from that. Meanwhile, if we look first at the victims themselves, let's get into their social media accounts. Assuming Mr and Mrs Sperling had mobiles, pull their data. Land line, too, if they had one. Financials as well. Neil says if you ask for something still at the scene, he'll do his best to clear it for you. Inspector Hope was duty officer yesterday and has arranged the door-to-door, though the home is detached in an acre or so of grounds, so no obvious close neighbours from what I could tell last night. We should also look hard at the lives both parents led. Did either of them have enemies or do anything to provoke this? That leaves family and friends to interview. I want to know if the Sperlings were just a normal couple, or if either or both of them did something to bring this into their home. Questions?'

'How about those possible links to the Armstrongs, boss?' Ansari asked.

'I was coming to that. We're unable to get too close to the previous case from the outset, but if they were all murders and no suicides, then we need to know why. Is there some nutjob out there who enjoys inflicting carnage on innocent families, or were they specifically targeted and murdered for reasons yet to be established? So yes, anything connecting the two families is of significant interest.'

'We'll do all we can for today,' Warburton interjected. 'Hopefully some progress with HOLMES, exploring the family's social media presence, getting the ball rolling with RIPA requests for phone data, and perhaps set up interviews with family members, friends, and work places if relevant.'

The DCI then exchanged a few more words with her CID counterpart, Edwards, before summoning Bliss, Chandler and Bishop into a smaller meeting in her office. She had requisitioned and repurposed what had once been a small break area rather than take her appointed room on the third floor, explaining that she preferred being close to her team. It was another thing Bliss admired about her.

'Nobody likes having their work critiqued,' she began. 'But I'm relying on you three in particular to lead the way here. A case review can put people off their game, but we still have an ongoing murder inquiry on our hands. I need everybody to be at their best. Bish, keep an eye on Gul. She will probably feel the pressure more than most, given she worked alongside you on the Armstrong case. Don't allow her to become sidetracked.'

'I think we all know what's at stake here, boss,' Bliss said. 'I'll keep an eye on Bish, he'll keep one on Gul, and we'll make the best of a bad deal. I'm sure any case review is going to conclude the same thing this team did in 2017: nothing was missed.'

'DCI Edwards has only one serious concern, and that's DCI Harrison. He was evidently not his usual self at that time, and a number of allowances were made as a result of his personal circumstances. As SIO on that case, she has the most to lose if the review report discovers missed opportunities to spot a murderer. She's worried that Harrison might not have had his finger on the pulse. That something important slipped through the cracks. I must stress, she's not blaming him in any way, and fully accepts she was in overall charge and therefore the outcome was her responsibility.'

'I genuinely don't think she has anything to worry about,' Bishop said, chomping down on a finger of Twix, smudges of melting chocolate on his lips. 'I'm anxious about the review, but confident in our case. If we got it wrong, we did so because we lacked the evidence to arrive at any other conclusion.'

Warburton nodded. 'Yes, and that's the exact same fear we have about the current investigation. If it also leads us to conclude murder-suicide knowing full well by that stage that it can't be, then we have a much greater problem on our hands than the result of a review.'

'We'll have an elusive killer who leaves nothing for us,' Chandler said softly. 'What a nightmare.'

'The worst kind,' Bliss said, his features solemn.

'How so?' his partner asked.

'Because with this one, there may be no waking up from it.'

FIVE

After lunch, Bliss decided he and Chandler ought to reacquaint themselves with the scene of crime to get a better appreciation of the place in daylight. It was yet another in a long line of hot and humid days, and he was glad of the loose-fitting polo shirt. His colleague wore a claret t-shirt and black denims, her hair pulled back and fixed with a toothed clasp. As usual, she looked both radiant and cool.

'You're so bloody irritating,' he complained, driving a railway spike through their contemplative silence.

'Me?' Chandler protested, a hand to her chest. 'What have I done?'

'What you've done is look both serene and relaxed. As if you don't find the heat oppressive, as if you don't perspire at all. You sit there all neat and tidy and perfect. Me, I'm sweating like a glassblower's arse and my clothes feel too long and too large, but at the same time too tight in all the wrong places. My balls are literally slick enough to have been dipped in olive oil and tossed in a salad shaker.'

Almost choking on her laughter, Chandler said, 'I can do

nothing about those nuts of yours – you're on your own there, as it sounds totally gross. As for the rest, exercise more. Teaching kids how to box a couple of times a week clearly isn't doing the trick at your age. Although I wouldn't say you are badly out of shape.'

'Really?' Bliss ran a hand over his stomach.

'Not at all. Not if the shape you're trying for is round.'

Bliss growled. 'It just annoys me how you always manage to look so refined and untouched by the climate or any shit going on around us. If you and I were a swan, you'd be the half gliding effortlessly on the water, while I'd be the legs padding furiously beneath the surface.'

Her laughter this time erupted with a snort. 'I take care of myself, Jimmy. I watch what I eat and drink. I go to the gym. I'm also a docile person, which you could never claim to be. Plus, I'm a fair bit younger than you.'

'Yeah, don't rub it in. I watch what I eat and drink, too… all the way down my gullet. Ah… forget about it. The heat always makes me grouchy.'

'Life makes you grouchy, come rain or shine, heatwave or frost. Death, taxes, and Jimmy Bliss having the hump are the only things we can rely on in life.' Her face lit up. 'What setting did you find the Bliss Pissed-Ometer at this morning?'

What she had described amounted to nothing grand. A cardboard sheet charting his emotional state, none of them placid. An arrow pinned to its centre pointed towards one of the prescribed moods. He'd removed it a couple of times, had even bent it in half and stuffed it in the bin on one occasion. Yet it had survived, and Bliss had no idea who sneaked into his office to move the arrow. Though not today.

'The arrow's missing,' he told her. 'Can't find it anywhere.'

'You think somebody took it?'

'I reckon someone half-inched it in order to wind me up. I also suspect they did so having been wound up themselves. Perhaps even a certain rookie who will feel my boot up his arse later.'

'So you're telling me that in a police station full of coppers, a copper stole your arrow and tampered with your ometer?'

'Where better than the shovel?'

A bright smile illuminating her face, Chandler nodded. 'I got that one. It's "shovel and pick", right? Rhyming slang for nick.'

He nodded. 'You're getting better. But seriously, where else are you going to find a building stuffed to the rafters with so many people who know everything there is to know about skulduggery?'

'That's so true. Coppers always make the best crooks.'

'Yeah, bloody tea-leaves. Oh, and let's not pretend you're as meek as you claim to be. Of the two of us, which one chinned a priest while we were in Ireland visiting my mum?'

Chandler rolled her eyes. 'He was not a priest, as well you know. He was a con man, and he deserved to be decked.'

Bliss chuckled, squirming in his seat. It was good to see his closest friend seemingly relaxed. Detective Sergeant Penny Chandler had been less than her normally effusive self in recent weeks. Her daughter, Hanna – or Anna as she was now known – had returned to Turkey to be with her father, who had recently been diagnosed with cancer. Having been estranged from the girl for so many years, Chandler's obvious concern was that Anna might not return to her studies at Cambridge. Today, she seemed back to her old self, and Bliss was glad of it. He had allowed his DS to vent on numerous occasions, knowing how precious Anna was to her. But Chandler wasn't the kind of person to be cajoled out of a slump; she had to find her own way, so he'd also given her room to breathe.

He took the A47 west, turning north shortly before reaching the A1. As they approached the Sperling family bungalow, he looked beyond the property and saw a row of houses some 200 yards away in the distance. He wondered if anybody living there had heard the shotgun blast, or had perhaps passed by during the attack. After all, if the murderer came from outside the home, they had to have travelled there. Their vehicle could have been spotted by somebody driving by. He'd not yet read any reports coming back from the door-to-door officers, but thinking about the possibilities gave him hope.

'What do you think?' he asked Chandler, gesturing around them as they climbed out of the Mondeo.

After completing a full 360-degree turn, she hiked her shoulders and said, 'I'm not sure. It's not exactly cut off from the rest of humanity here, but the closest neighbouring properties are some distance away. Mind you, if that shotgun is fired in the dead of night, I reckon they hear it. But afternoon or early evening, there's probably too much going on for it to be noticed.'

Bliss glanced at the blue sky, feeling the sun toast his flesh. 'It was a nice day, remember? Just as it is now. Bound to be somebody barbecuing or just chilling in their garden. You can fit a couple of football pitches between this place and those houses across the field, but a blast like that might just have stood out.'

'I suppose,' Chandler agreed. 'Which reminds me... who called it in?'

'An Amazon delivery driver. Apparently, this is a fairly regular stop for him. If nobody answers, he knows he has to go around the side and leave the packages in the utilities cupboard. Only, as he was passing by the dining room, he happened to peer in and saw the family at the table. Initially he tried to get their attention by rapping his knuckles on the window, but then he looked more closely...'

'You want to talk to him?'

'Let's look at his statement first. If there's anything not covered, I'll send Dumb and Dumber.'

As they signed in to enter the property, Chandler chuckled. He'd recently started referring to DCs Gratton and Virgil in this way; his limp-witted take on both men being so bright.

Neil Abbott was back on site, having left his most trustworthy techs to continue working while he grabbed a few hours' sleep. He told the two detectives they had the run of the house, with the exception of the dining room. It was the last – and most important – area still being investigated, so neither argued with him. As was their usual practice, they took the rooms together, Bliss pausing momentarily on the threshold of each to take in its entirety.

He paid most attention to the office and the parents' bedroom. In his experience, these were the most likely to be holding secrets if there were any to be found. The office space was decked out in rosewood furniture, the lacquered timber in stark contrast to the plain grey walls on which hung a range of framed pictures depicting transport-related cartoons.

Bliss knew going in that Donald Sperling owned and ran a large haulage company. He came across nothing in the desk drawers or filing cabinets to suggest the business was anything less than legitimate, with no side ventures either, as far as he could tell. The worst effects of the pandemic had led to an economic downturn, but Sperling had reacted swiftly with the effective use of reduced rates and increased routes. No debts, no staffing issues or competitive wrangling. At least, none the two detectives were able to uncover.

Ever the sceptic, Bliss turned to Chandler and said, 'That's the surface done, the parts we're meant to find if we came looking. I want to dig deeper, though. Let's have the techs dive into his browsing history and check his computer devices for hidden or locked folders.'

'Hark at you getting all techy on me. I thought you were a committed Luddite.'

'With bells on. But a few of our recent cases have shown me a thing or two, so I'm not going to ignore it deliberately. I understand its uses.'

'We'll make a modern man of you yet.'

'Sod that! We old farts can still teach you freshly scrubbed rubes a lesson here and there.'

They both smiled, enjoying the ribbing. It was a part of their relationship Bliss hoped they would never lose.

'The family looks pretty clean to me,' Chandler observed.

'That's exactly what I was thinking. I'm hoping we're both wrong.'

'Why's that?'

'I want there to be a good reason for someone taking the lives lost here. It was brutal, much of it witnessed by those who were attacked last. If it had to happen, I'd rather it did because of a grievance. The thought of some fruitcake just getting it into his head to do this on an impulse is something I don't want to think about.'

Chandler shuddered. 'Me neither.'

The main bedroom proved to be equally free of skeletons. The closer Bliss looked, the more frustrated he grew. Throughout the decades of his career, he had rarely come across killers acting without logical motive. It did happen, and he had investigated such people, but they were by no means the norm. In the vast majority of cases, there was a motivating factor, even if it only made sense to the person themselves. More often than not, the reason became obvious, something Bliss could understand, though never condone.

Yet he was already having doubts. His first thought was to wonder if they were looking for more than a single suspect. Subduing five people, albeit three of them children, was no easy feat. He could see how it might be done: the killer taking the family by surprise and immediately threatening the lives of the most vulnerable of them. This would render the two adults fearful and compliant, willingly subjecting themselves to anything rather than have their children harmed. Even so, it would take only one parent to react without caution to cause sufficient distraction. Better to have an accomplice than tackle the job on your own. It was something to throw into the mix when arriving at a hypothesis.

By the time he and Chandler had searched the rest of the property, Bliss was more confused than he had been when stepping inside. This appeared to be the home of a happy, well-off family who lived a comfortable life without excessive or unnecessary superfluities. No pool in the back garden, no gold-plated fixtures and fittings, no media room complete with cinema-style seating. Tasteful living as opposed to showy opulence. If there was any dark mystery here, Bliss was not seeing it.

But that didn't mean it wasn't there, nor that it couldn't be discovered.

'What do you make of it now?' he asked Chandler.

'It's idyllic. Stylish, charming, and relaxed. No sign of any sadistic sexual paraphernalia or depraved porn. No evidence of dark paintings or drawings hidden away by the children, nor any hint of abuse or neglect. The Sperlings come across as a perfect family.'

'You reckon?'

'Yes. Why, don't you?'

'I'm not sure. I did notice a Jamie Cullum CD in their collection. That's not normal, surely?'

Chandler laughed. 'And I saw one by that awful Steely Dan you like, so what does that say about you?'

He held his hands up. 'Okay. You got me there. As for this lot… a little too perfect?'

'Perhaps. Or is that just us being cynical?'

'That's us speaking from experience, Pen. I've yet to encounter the unblemished family, but these are as close as you can get. If I remove them from the equation when it comes to motive, then we're looking at a psycho. I'm not prepared to call it that way.'

'I'm not sure if I agree, Jimmy. Look, I know what we were told, but I'd really like to compare the Armstrongs to these, see how they match up.'

Bliss licked his lips, pondering. He straightened his back and said, 'Me too. So, if we were to find something on them or the Sperlings, what do you think it might be?'

'My guess is it would have to involve money. Large sums of money. That's the only reason you take out a whole family like this.'

'Or we have a crazy on our hands.'

Chandler nodded. 'Although that could still be exactly what this is.'

'I'm not close to calling it that way, Pen.'

'How come? Given what we know.'

'I still think these people have to have a wrinkle or two. We'll find them. And when we do, we'll know if it's enough to have sucked this nightmare into their lives. Or if they were just plain unlucky.'

'I'm still leaning towards the latter.'

'I hope you're wrong,' Bliss said, glancing over at the dining area and feeling his stomach clench. 'I really do.'

SIX

Bliss sat on the wooden bench in his garden, chomping his way through a chicken tikka kebab. With every other mouthful, he broke off a piece of pitta bread and passed it down to the animal lying by his feet. He'd recently taken Max in as a rescue dog from the Wood Green animal shelter in Godmanchester. The four-year-old Golden Lab had settled in well, its benign nature not entirely tortured out of it by the previous owner, the kind of man Bliss would like to find alone at night in a dark alley.

Though not a pure-bred dog, Max was enough of a Labrador to remind him of Bonny and Clyde, the two he and his late wife had bought as pups. He'd missed them terribly after having both euthanised within three months of each other, but for a myriad of reasons had not replaced them in either his life nor his affections until five weeks ago. He put his change of heart down to concluding he was destined to live out the rest of his days alone, and while he loved his fish, what he felt he was missing most was a companion.

The Koi basked in the gradually fading sunlight, goldfish swarming around them like an entourage to the star attractions. He washed his food down with a bottle of Oranjeboom lager, relaxing with every sip, admiring the shapes and contours of his Zen garden. The acers were thriving, some changing colour almost before his eyes. Standing stones faded into the background as the sun died. As ever, he felt at peace in this spot.

Until the dark shadow of his latest case fell over him.

The office meeting prior to quitting for the day had been illuminating. Two of the five post-mortems had been carried out, and senior pathologist Nancy Drinkwater had brought the reports over to Thorpe Wood. Bliss asked her if she wanted to read them out at the briefing, which she had. Esther Sperling, she told them, could have died from any number of her wounds. The six-inch blade of a carving knife had pierced vital organs, including the lungs and heart. However, Drinkwater listed exsanguination as the ultimate cause of death, the woman bleeding out having been stabbed or slashed seventeen times in total. In her husband's case, the COD was far more obvious.

'Mr Sperling received no stab wounds. As for the impact, angle of delivery, prints, and gunshot residue, all are consistent with a self-inflicted firearm discharge. If it were not for the Armstrong case in 2017, I would have no hesitation in recording suicide in his case. Unfortunately, everything I am seeing with these victims I saw back then. I can't in all honesty regard any of them in strict terms of their individual deaths. The likelihood of a murder-suicide like this being replicated so precisely is infinitesimal. My final report, therefore, will say I made a mistake with the Armstrongs. Despite the physical evidence, there's no doubt in my mind these two family slayings were the work of someone other than the male adults.'

While the pathologist's statement only confirmed what they already believed to be true, it was nonetheless a moment to draw breath and reflect. Bishop, in particular, reacted badly.

'Damnit!' he cried, slamming his teeth together and hunching over his desk, bellowing through his nostrils like a bull.

DC Ansari slipped a comforting arm around his shoulder. 'Take it easy, Bish. This was not our fault. We did our jobs.'

'Did we?' he breathed without looking up. 'Because if so, then we must be shite at it, Gul. Five fresh victims tell us that much.'

DCI Warburton threw a worried glance at Bliss, who nodded in reply. 'Bish!' he said sharply. 'Look at me. Look at me, Sergeant.' When the big man pushed away from the desk and turned, Bliss continued, an index finger pointing at himself. 'See this mug of mine? Old before its time. You know why? Because of the hours I've spent doing precisely what you're doing now. Wasted hours they were, too.'

'Are you saying dragging that anger in on yourself doesn't work?' Bishop said. 'That it's never turned an investigation in our favour?'

'That's exactly what I'm telling you. Because you have to know the difference. Worrying over something you missed, or a decision you might have got wrong, is one thing, but beating yourself up over something out of your control is where the waste comes in. The truth is, you can't miss something that's not there, Bish. And you can't reach a proper conclusion without having all the facts.'

'But we got the Armstrong investigation wrong, boss. There's no denying that now.'

'Agreed. What I'm saying to you is, not every case is going to reveal the truth of itself to you. We've all known ops in which not everything gave itself up to us. Sometimes that one telling and vital piece of evidence simply isn't there. On other occasions a witness fails to come forward, or doesn't even recognise the significance of what they saw or know. All you can do is your best. Did you do that, Bish? Did you and Gul and others do your best?'

Bishop extended his chin and put his shoulders back. 'Yes. I did. Gul did. We all did.'

Bliss nodded. 'Then you all did your jobs. You screw yourself into a knot of anxiety over something like that, you'll end up with a craggy old boat like mine ten years before your age alone has earned it.'

His colleague took a deep breath and sagged. Good enough for Bliss. He turned his attention back to the pathologist. Drinkwater seemed somehow smaller out of her scrubs, less authoritative away from her own domain. Her charm and enthusiasm remained the same no matter what the environment, and he had never not been smitten by her smile. 'Thanks for prioritising these, Nancy. A couple of further questions, if you don't mind?'

'Of course. Go ahead.'

'Was Mrs Sperling sexually interfered with in any way?'

'I don't believe she was. No trace of semen, nor lubricant. No vaginal bruising associated with a rape or molestation.'

'I have to ask... how about the daughters, Virginia and Elizabeth?'

'Sorry, I haven't got around to the children. But no obvious sign at first glance. I'll let you know if that changes when we do the PMs, of course.'

Bliss nodded his thanks. 'How about toxicology? Anything in their systems we need to be aware of?'

Drinkwater grimaced. 'I don't have answers for you, I'm afraid. I won't have results back until tomorrow. Is there any particular substance you'd like me to look for?'

'If one man subdued this family, then perhaps the parents were more compliant than you might otherwise expect. It's worth knowing one way or the other if they were sedated.'

'I'll get it ordered.' She hesitated, eyes drawn to her own feet before adding, 'I was asked if I wanted to attend the scene prior to the bodies being released by the crime scene manager. It wasn't a request to assist, more a consideration towards me. I gave it some thought, but felt my time was better served carrying out the post-mortems. I can reflect on the Armstrong case at my leisure, though I fail to see how we could have all got it so badly wrong at the time.'

Bliss reached out to rub Drinkwater's arm. 'That's okay, Nancy. You don't need to explain yourself to us.'

'I realise that. I just wanted you all to know I take this matter seriously. As seriously as any of you. I think my head would have been cluttered had I attended the scene, that damned other case crying out in the back of my mind. I hope I made the right decision.'

'You did. And for the right reasons.'

She smiled, squeezed his hand and left them to it.

A few minutes later came a message from the crime scene, telling them they would have full access the following morning, with Neil Abbott confirming the connection to a previous case as part of his report.

Door-to-door enquiries had provided no useful intelligence or potential leads. Nobody had heard the firearm, nobody had seen anyone near the Sterling home that day. CSI had turned up no unexpected evidence, though they still had to run print and fibre tests and now make comparisons to the Armstrong investigation. Bliss asked if unexplained tyre tracks had been discovered on the drive, but the answer came back negative. As the information was disseminated among the gathered team members, realisation of the monumental task ahead soured the overall disposition in the room. That was a signal for him to call time on the day's work.

As he felt his own mood starting to sour once again, Bliss drained the remains of his beer and set the bottle down on a small glass-topped table by his side. He breathed in through his nose, out through his mouth. Bringing himself back down, doing his best to make the most of this moment. In all likelihood, it would be his last opportunity to sit and chill for quite some time. Max stirred by his feet and whimpered, perhaps sensing his discomfort. Bliss ruffled the dog's pelt and told him he was a good boy while the Goldador lapped from his water bowl before settling down once again.

From the living room, the sound of a mellow Larry Carlton playlist helped set the tone. On warm summer evenings such as this, it was hard to imagine the atrocities being committed elsewhere. Bliss had come to appreciate the peaks of life, having spent too long wading in the murky depths of the troughs. He was still seldom able to switch off completely, but he was better at it than he used to be.

For some reason, although his mother had passed away more than three months earlier, he still half expected the phone to ring and for her to crack a joke at his expense or to say something outrageous to make him laugh. He missed those conversations. More than he allowed himself to admit. Other than the odd uncle and aunt and a fair number of cousins – none of whom he saw or had remained in touch with – he had no close family. Both his parents had now died following the kind of massive heart attacks from which no recovery was possible. He looked down at the remains of his kebab and reminded himself he was not keeping his own ticker in ideal condition.

'Fuck it,' he whispered to himself. He was not ready for a complete change of lifestyle. He'd leave all that guff for when he retired – if he made it that far.

For a few more minutes he lost himself in Carlton's smooth bluesy-jazz guitar tones, the man's fingers on the neck of a Gibson .335 as slick as fresh dog shit off a hot shovel. He craved another beer, but was too comfortable where he was. He understood that if his late wife, Hazel, had not been murdered, his life now would be dramatically different. Kids, possibly, however they were acquired. Perhaps still in the job, maybe not. Definitely not living in Peterborough. In fact, he'd never have moved to the city in the first place, and would not have known the pleasure of Penny Chandler's friendship and company. You couldn't miss what you'd never had, but the thought of never having known Penny made him question the vagaries of life.

As for his mother passing away, its suddenness had knocked him for six. It had been the same way with his father, whose own death had also occurred out of the blue. The effect ran deep, but it had undoubtedly prepared him for the loss of his other parent. His propensity for dwelling on grief and exposing himself to maudlin thoughts was a thing of the past, and he believed he had coped well since his most recent loss. That didn't mean he never felt its sting or the residual pain every so often. But he could think of her now with a smile on his face while burying the aching sadness in his heart.

In the process of dozing off, Bliss was startled when his phone started ringing. He checked the caller ID and debated answering it. He changed his mind twice before sliding the green icon. He glanced down at Max, but the dog had barely raised his head this time.

'Hi, Sandra,' he said. 'How are you?'

Sandra Bannister was a journalist with the city's local newspaper, the *Peterborough Telegraph*. The two had worked together on several previous occasions and had somehow found their way to an understanding in terms of how much either was willing to help the other.

'Oh, sorry to disturb you,' she said. 'I was hoping to talk to Jimmy Bliss. Is he there?'

'It's me, you muppet. What are you banging on about?'

'I do apologise. It's just that you asking me how I was completely threw me. I'm not sure you've ever asked that before.'

'And if all I get in response is earache, I won't be bothering to ask again.' He smiled at her joke, though in retrospect she probably wasn't wrong.

'Okay, okay. I'll get on with it. Sorry to disturb you on a lazy Sunday evening, but I'm guessing yours hasn't been quite so relaxed.'

'Why? What have you heard?' He knew there had been no media briefing to date.

'Something going off in Ufford. Big police presence last night, still some there today, and mortuary vehicles. Gossip has it that a local businessman by the name of Sperling murdered his family and then blew his own head off.'

Bliss cursed silently. The bloody Amazon delivery driver. Had to be. Unless one of the officers at the scene had earned himself a bit of cash by spilling his guts. If the *PT* reporter had this much, she wasn't about to let it go. He had to make a swift decision, and for once opted for discretion.

'Let others run with that if you like,' he said. 'My advice to you is to keep your powder dry. I'm expecting a media release tomorrow. The moment I get wind that's definitely happening, I'll feed it to you first.'

'Okay… what are you not telling me, Jimmy?'

'More than you'll ever know, Sandra. But for the time being, wind your neck in. The official announcement will reveal something else entirely.'

'Ooh, sounds intriguing.'

'For you, yes. For us, a pain in the proverbial.'

'Fair enough. I shall wait with bated breath. Meanwhile, how are *you* doing?'

'I'm okay, as it happens.'

'In your garden?'

'Of course.'

'Okay. Well, give my love to the Koi.'

'I'll let them know you were thinking of them.'

On a whim, he called Chandler when he was done talking with Bannister. He knew her boyfriend was away on business and thought they might enjoy a few drinks together at the Charters bar, a barge moored by the town bridge virtually opposite his partner's apartment building. She declined, explaining how much she had to do around the flat and getting her clothes washed and dried before the working week.

That's fine, he thought to himself afterwards. No problem at all. *Alone has never meant lonely for me. I can be with people or not, and either just as happily.* It was something he had told himself time and again over the past two decades.

One of these days, he was actually going to believe it.

SEVEN

Enjoying a sloppy cheeseburger in the city centre Five Guys, Bliss stopped chewing long enough to ask his partner if she thought an op they'd heard about from Essex police might be connected to their own. HOLMES had spat out a few results relating to their query regarding similar crimes, and he'd spent much of the morning on the phone with the investigating DCI. Collegially enough for someone who nevertheless kept mentioning how busy he and his team were, the man had led him through various aspects of the case not found in the stark language of databases.

At first glance, it had all the appearances of a murder-suicide; a husband strangling his wife before hanging himself. But the pathologist had noticed peculiar marks beneath those caused by the rope wrapped around the victim's neck as he hung down from a balcony banister rail in the couple's home. The pattern and wounds, he concluded, had been made by a thinner type of cord shortly before the husband supposedly hanged himself. And while the length of rope matched a sample coil discovered in the attached garage, no cord had been found anywhere on the property.

'If we ignore the specifics of the MO in our case,' Chandler replied, 'the essential incident is the same. In both, a murder was made to look like a suicide. There's no dining room staging as there was in ours, and the method is also entirely different. But it's still homicide disguised as something else, with no witnesses and no evidence of note.'

Bliss was of the same opinion. 'And as with the evidentiary comparisons between our two cases currently being made, so we can now throw it open to Essex police and their CSI people to make comparisons with whatever we have to offer. Unidentified hairs and fibres at most, I'm guessing. But something rather than nothing. Any match at all and we'll have a significant development on our hands.'

The pair went on with their meal, but Bliss continued to outline potential approaches. 'If our victims are connected, we'll find the link,' he said assuredly. 'The only reason one hasn't already been discovered is because nobody was looking for it. But we are now, so that's our route in. The real problem comes if they're arbitrary murders. Victimology works either way, but at a different pace. If the killings are random, then whatever draws our killer to his prey won't be as obvious. In fact, chances are we won't discover the answer unless we get to question him. For all we know, he makes his selection by throwing dice or drawing a card.'

'That's hardly encouraging,' Chandler said gloomily around the paper straw she was sucking on.

'Reality seldom is. But even if these are all haphazard acts, they're not entirely so. Think about it: even if he chooses the location by throwing darts at a map, and the victims by drawing names he found on the electoral role out of a hat, he elects to kill them in similar ways. Even if that's the only non-indiscriminate aspect, it's still one we can use against him. The psychology of it will reveal something about him.'

'But you still say it's the victims who will tell us more?'

Bliss paused. He'd made quick work of the burger and was rapidly demolishing his stack of fries. He wedged a handful into his mouth and washed them down with a long sip of chocolate and peanut butter milkshake. He brushed salt and oils from his hands and wiped his lips with a paper serviette before responding.

'I do. I have to, Pen. I can't dwell on the possibility of some deranged lunatic picking off these families just because the voices in his head told him to. I have to be more positive than that. The fact that we, SOCO, and at least two pathologists are coming up with the wrong answers tells us whoever is doing this is cunning and clever and not at all hurried. But there's still the pattern of his actions, and in trying so hard to make these murders look like the work of a demented father and husband who then goes on to take his own life, that says to me there has to be a reason behind it. I believe that reason lies with the victims themselves. One of them in each case, at any rate.'

Chandler acknowledged this with a shrug. 'HOLMES might help us out there. The more cases we can link, the more likely we are to spot similarities. He only needs to cock up once, and it looks as if he already has.'

'Very much so. In the Essex case, he for some reason used two different kinds of noose, removing the first from the scene. Our Armstrong and Sperling crime scenes were identical. He repeated himself, which is something I suspect he never intended to do. Even if he did, he thought of himself as invulnerable because we'd never make the connections. Maybe he's becoming cocky because he's been getting away with it. If so, that's how we'll find him.'

Bliss liked the symmetry of that idea. It meant they weren't waiting for him to make an error, and there was no need to search for one, because at least two were already staring them in the face. Their killer had unwittingly drawn attention to himself, due either to conceit or pure oversight and negligence. Bliss suspected the former. Their unidentified target struck him as somebody who didn't make mistakes of neglect or inattention to detail. But vanity? Overconfidence? Yes, he could see that. It had been the downfall of many a criminal in the past.

As they headed back to Thorpe Wood, neither Bliss nor Chandler were their usual talkative selves. He found himself growing increasingly anxious. The parallels between the three cases were such that he believed HOLMES would spit out more. If their killer was on a spree, he was too good for these to have been his first attempts. The murders in 2017 were far too competent to be the work of an inexperienced killer. The Essex case was a year old. Logic insisted there were others, possibly closed and never brought back into the light for re-examination. If it was a spree, then there could be several. That was an unappetising notion. And yet what else might explain these slayings?

'Know your victims to understand your killer,' he muttered, as much to himself as his companion.

'What's that?' Chandler asked, turning her attention away from the side window.

'I keep coming back to victimology. I have a feeling that's the way to go here.'

'Okay. In other words, the more we dig into them, the closer we get to why they were killed, and therefore who killed them.'

'Precisely. I read a study undertaken by Radford University in the States. It said that only 31% of serial killers did so for enjoyment; those who murder for the pure pleasure they get from the act itself. Almost as many did so for financial gain. Top three methods: shot, strangled, stabbed. There's nothing there for us to get our teeth into if our suspect is of that ilk. But when it comes to our victims, the percentages tell us there are more reasons than our man being the type who just fancies killing. I'm saying we dig down into the database to see if there are more victims, and then we drill deeper into each one we find. Something tells me our way in lies with them, not with whoever is doing this.'

Chandler regarded him for quite some time before breaking out into a happy smile. 'Your mind is so uncluttered right now, Jimmy. You think when you look back, you'll regard these as your true halcyon days? Everything must seem so bright and clear to you at the moment.'

'Are you saying I was a fucking hopeless investigator before?'

'Not hopeless. Just piss-poor.'

'It's a fair cop. But a lovely bloke for all my faults, eh?'

She shook her head. 'Sadly, not even that. Tolerated. Because you're the boss.'

'You jest, but I have questioned myself in recent years. Could I have been sharper? Could I have sussed things out quicker? Might one or two people not have suffered if I'd truly been on my game?'

'Might politicians have integrity and unicorns fly around excreting chocolate doughnuts in enchanted forests? You were born to worry, born to be self-critical, born to ask that eternal question: what if?' Chandler jabbed a finger in his direction. 'That, my friend, is the final stage of your transition.'

'You think so?'

'I know so. I also know it's a transition you'll never complete. Like I say, it's who you are. The real Jimmy Bliss. And you know what…? We can all live with that. So can you. It's fundamental to how you operate.'

He shooed away her words as if they were flies dancing around his face. 'What utter tripe.'

'It's not tripe, Jimmy. And I'll tell you something now: it's infectious. It's rubbed off on all of us. Look at how Bish reacted yesterday. He didn't just shrug it off, he was bloody annoyed with himself. You're a better copper for having that streak in you, and you've improved us along the way. That'll be your true legacy. Not only what you managed to do in your career, but also what you helped others achieve.'

Bliss blinked. 'Wow. That was some speech. How long have you been working on that?'

'Every day in the bathroom mirror for the past year.'

'That must have been tough on you, having to stare at that ugly mug.'

'It was awful. But I persevered.'

'And you saved it for this little pep talk?'

'Now seemed like as good a time as any.'

He smiled and nodded. 'I take it you are aware it goes both ways? I'm better at what I do because of you lot. I learn from everybody. The good, bad, and bloody ugly. I've worked with all types, taken orders from them as well. You hope the good sticks, and the bad you tuck away somewhere, but keep with you so's you won't repeat the mistakes of others. As for the ugly, some of the clobber you wear fits the bill.'

He didn't mind the not-so-gentle punch to his arm. But as his thoughts returned to the investigation and the myriad questions that remained unanswered, Bliss couldn't help but imagine dark clouds overhead in what was, in reality, a clear azure sky. As ever, it didn't matter what the weather offered, nor what mood he was in. Inhumanity had a bad habit of stripping all of that away, leaving only the cold touch of murder and chaos in its wake.

EIGHT

Bishop and Ansari trudged along a public footpath, emerging from the cover of trees into open land behind the village cricket ground. The DC pulled out her mobile and shot video footage as she turned a full circle. She also took a handful of stills before pocketing her phone.

'You can't see the Sperling home from here,' Bishop said, peering off into the distance. 'The woods block the view of the bend in the road.'

Ansari shook her head. 'I don't think our man came this far. He didn't need to. But he may still have parked on the footpath closer to the road.'

The pair were in Ufford following an earlier call from Bliss, who had suggested they search the area around the Sperling property for somewhere close enough to the home for the killer to have hidden a vehicle out of sight but within easy walking distance. The footpath felt right. On that same side of the road, a pavement ran alongside a low stone wall right up to and beyond the house. Less than a five-minute stroll – though, admittedly, out in the open, the exposure bothered Bishop.

'The path rules out a car, but allows for a bike or a motorbike. It's a risk, though, as is the pavement. The bike could be discovered by somebody else using the footpath, and he'd be seen by any vehicle travelling along the road.'

'Okay, so maybe he used the cover of the trees. If he was on two wheels, his ride would be easy enough to tuck away out of sight, and he could have remained concealed all the way through to the Sperling home.'

Bishop took a breath before spinning and heading off back down the path. 'Come on, then,' he said. 'Let's do just that. We'll duck into the tree line and make our way to their place. Then we'll see what difficulties our man might have encountered.'

'Shouldn't we call out forensics?'

'We will if it's necessary, Gul. The chances of us taking the exact same route are slim to none, so we won't be trampling all over any evidence. Still, keep an eye out. You spot any tyre indentations or footprints you mark them and skirt around them.'

It wasn't hard going. Undergrowth grew wild and dense, and the trees were plentiful but with distance between them. This left plenty of room to navigate a pathway with some comfort. Bishop also noticed how simple it would be to remain hidden from the road or pavement. They found no indicators suggesting a cycle had been pushed into the wooded area, nor that anybody else had taken the route they'd forged.

'If our killer just drove right up to their front door, then this woodland adventure has all been a waste of time and effort,' Ansari grumbled.

'Yeah, but what if he didn't?' Bishop said, deliberately bumping his partner off her stride. 'What if he came this way and we're about to find a vital clue?'

She bumped him back. Tried to, at least. Ansari was no irresistible force, but the big man could be an immovable object when he put his mind to it. 'You're starting to sound like Jimmy.'

'I'll take that as a compliment.'

'It wasn't meant as one.'

Bishop winked at her. 'Yes, it was, and you know it.'

A few minutes after setting out, they arrived at the property boundary, traversed easily by stepping out onto the pavement and taking a few steps before ducking inside the entrance leading to the driveway. Virtually no danger of being spotted, let alone encountered.

'These homes can't all have been this easy to reach without risk of exposure,' he said to his partner, thinking of the incident in Essex and others he felt sure would come to light in the coming days. 'I'm trying to think back to the Armstrongs' place. That was surrounded by trees as well, wasn't it?'

Ansari nodded. 'I remember driving downhill towards it. You couldn't see their home from the road at all. We had to pass through gates and drive some way along the gravel path before the house came into view.'

'Those gates weren't high, though. You could ride up to them, lift a bike over the top and then jump over without breaking sweat.'

Ansari reached out a hand to grasp his. 'The dog,' she breathed, her voice almost a whisper. 'Remember their dog?'

Bishop shrugged, eyes narrowing. 'No. I can't say that I do.'

'That's because it wasn't there. They did have one, though. Only it wasn't at home with them the night they… well, the night they were all murdered.'

He snapped his fingers. 'Yes, you're right. We spotted its food and water bowls on the utility room floor, saw the lead hanging up, found its grub in a cupboard. Turned out it was at the vet. Not sure we ever discovered why.'

'There was no need. We knew what had happened. What did it matter why the dog wasn't at home? Only now I'm wondering if it did matter, after all. If our killer wanted the dog out of the picture…'

'We can find out. Can't be too many vets in that area. If the killer slipped the dog something poisonous to make sure it wasn't around when the home was invaded, that would make perfect sense.'

Ansari scrunched up her face. 'Which would have been nice intel to have at the time. But now? Does it help us at all? We already know the suicide was staged.'

Bishop realised she was right. Only by now another thought had occurred. One he had hoped would not rear its ugly head during this investigation. Was the absent dog the vital clue they had missed? Should one of them have suspected the animal's absence to be germane to the operation they were running? Or had the scene painted such an obvious picture for them that alternative canvases were never given due consideration?

*

He sat alone, watching the woman and her two young children playing together in the park. Their mood was joyous, laughter raucous and unbridled. He observed the energy of their movements as they ran without restraint in attempting to 'catch' the one who was 'it'. They larked about with abandon as if the world around them did not exist. As if it contained no living nightmares such as him.

Certainly the woman could have had no idea he was watching her, his eyes unseen behind the opaque dark lenses of his sunglasses. And because she was unaware of being observed, she took no precautions. Her green vest top hung low when she leaned forward. And although she wore a bra which concealed her nipples, her ample bosom provided many desirable views of cleavage and soft, rounded temptation. The same could be said of her denim skirt, which was short and allowed him full view of her long, tanned legs. Full calves and muscular thighs, with the occasional glimpse upskirt of red underwear as she playfully wrestled with her kids on the grass, aroused him as he sat back on a nearby fallen log and sighed deeply to himself.

She was a natural beauty, even on only semi-display as she was here. But indoors was a different matter entirely. In the bedroom, as she changed her clothes or flung off her towel after a hot shower, she abandoned any pretence at covering up. Naked with a soft sheen, she was every man's desire. He longed to run his tongue over that velvety skin, to caress and cup her full breasts, to part her legs and explore the hairless cleft between.

Tonight.
I'll have you tonight.
I'll make you cry out in the darkness.
I'll make you scream.
More times than you would believe possible.

Having become fully engorged at the thought of her opening up to him, he had to wait several minutes before rising to his feet. Looking across at the woman, he raised a hand to catch her attention. She waved back.

'Time to go, sweetheart,' he called out. 'You, too, you mad things.'

His wife and children stopped playing, and with exhausted smiles, came running over to him. His son and daughter rushed breathlessly into an embrace. His denim-skirted wife kissed his cheek. He removed his sunglasses, winked, and gave her backside a gentle tap. She raised her eyebrows. He nodded. She cast her eyes down to his groin and he saw them widen. He smiled, hooked an arm around her shoulder, and together they walked home, their kids skipping happily beside them.

NINE

Bliss studied the sheets of hard copy printout handed to him by DC Ansari. He could see why she was excited by the discovery lying within the HOLMES database. A case on the south coast had been investigated and ruled a murder-suicide after a man had first beaten and then strangled his wife to death, before hanging himself in their garage.

Nobody would have thought twice about it were it not for a remark overheard by a family liaison officer who'd been tasked with sticking with the wife's grieving parents. According to the report provided by the FLO in question, the deceased woman's brother had been in conversation with other members of the family when he mentioned the husband's alleged connection to a major face in the illegal drugs business.

Hugh Worsley worked as an accountant for a reputable firm of solicitors. His wife, Lynda, was an administrator for the same company, which is where the two had first met. Nobody had a bad word to say about either of them. And by all accounts, the Worsleys were enthusiastic and hard-working employees. Between them, the couple enjoyed a comfortable life with no known issues in their personal lives or professional capacities.

Why, then, had Lynda Worsley's brother uttered his off-the-cuff remark linking Hugh with a high-ranking London criminal?

Following up on the FLO's report, the man was subsequently interviewed by investigating officers. He initially made light of it, claiming he'd made a terrible joke at the expense of a man known to be staid and practical. When pushed, however, he revealed the remark had been based on a relatively detailed rumour. Subsequent investigations exposed further evidence to suggest Worsley and the drugs kingpin had been spotted together on numerous occasions at a bar in the Hilton hotel on Park Lane in London.

A full forensic investigation into the couple's finances eventually uncovered an offshore bank account into which annual payments of £250,000 were made, each originating from separate shell companies known to be used by Marty Reid, a ruthless gangster. This fresh evidence led to the reopening of the Worlsey murder-suicide case, this time the focus on trying to prove that Hugh had also been a victim of murder. The case remained open, though with no additional leads.

Bliss thought it through. Except for the methods used to kill, this case bore all the hallmarks of the two carried out in the Peterborough area. The methodology was, in fact, far more common in such cases. A beating and strangulation committed in a fit of rage by an angry husband, followed by the man taking his life, having realised the full tragic consequences of his actions. To Bliss it had all the appearances of another op in which the most obvious explanation had been taken for granted. It could yet still be the case, but equally it might be the work of their man. When he was done, he looked up and raised his eyebrows.

'Any joy out at the Sperling place earlier?' he asked.

'None, boss. No sign he approached via the back or from either side.'

Bliss nodded, then indicated the information his DC had brought to him. 'This is good stuff, Gul. What caught your eye about this case?'

Ansari beamed at him, clearly delighted to have found useful intelligence. 'Hugh Worsley wouldn't be the first person to be taken out by a heavyweight looking to clean up after themselves. We know there are many peripheral figures doing straightforward jobs for all kinds of gangsters. In this case, I'm thinking Worsley did the accounts for Marty Reid's legit businesses. Maybe he skimmed, or became superfluous. Reid had him killed, and the killer chose to make it look like something other than murder. It's actually not such a half-baked idea, because it takes the subsequent investigation down by several notches. I just thought we might find a way to see our own investigations in the same light.'

'I like the way you think,' Bliss told her. 'In fact, I like it enough to take it to the team.'

The major incident room was in full flow, conversations taking place on phones and between team members, computer keyboards rattling in the background. Bliss called everybody together before stepping back and handing centre stage to Ansari. After they had listened to the DC talk her way through the documents she and Bliss had read and explaining the inferences she had drawn, DCI Warburton was the first to respond.

'If this is the work of the man who also took out our two families – with help or not – then it's fair to assume he's doing so on the orders of the same gang leader: Marty Reid. If that is the case, where might Kevin Armstrong and Donald Sperling fit in with this serious drug dealer? Any thoughts?'

'Sperling ran his own haulage company,' Bishop informed them. 'Perhaps Reid paid for his services to ship merchandise around the country. Maybe further afield. Sperling could even have used his vehicles to smuggle the gear in from Europe.'

'Kevin Armstrong and his wife ran a chain of florists,' Ansari followed up. 'Hiding merchandise in plants or bouquets makes for a decent cover. It's been done before.'

Bliss scratched at the small scar on his forehead. 'Okay. We're fishing here, obviously. But these are sound suggestions. From what I read, there's not much coming out of the reopened investigation. I can have the relevant SIO send us over their case files, but they've been on it for a while now without much success beyond the initial discovery. There's enough distance between this Marty Reid face and the offshore banks used to pay Hugh Worsley for the CPS to have no further interest. So I think it's best we focus our attention on the Armstrong and Sperling murders, the latter more specifically. If we can connect Donald Sperling and his haulage company to Marty Reid or any other known faces, then we'll have a much better idea of what we're dealing with.'

'I'm waiting for responses to our requests for mobile data,' Ansari reminded him. 'I doubt we'll find anything incriminating, but I'll follow up on that later on.'

DC Virgil raised a hand before speaking up, prompting a few chuckles and some gentle ribbing. New to the team, he still acted like it. 'The laptops and pads are with tech support over at Hinchingbrooke, boss. I'll give them a bell when we're done here and let them know the kind of thing we're looking for. If Mr Sperling was using an offshore account, he probably did so on one of the devices we found.'

Bishop and Ansari then outlined their ruminations when assessing the killer's entry and exit strategy. Chandler voiced her concern about the theory. 'If it's the same killer, then these murders are spread far and wide. A bicycle is surely a local mode of transport. I mean, I know cyclists cover long distances, but it's inefficient for these purposes.'

'So maybe it's the secondary method,' DC Gratton suggested.

'He travels close to the location in a car or van, the bike inside or strapped on, followed by a much shorter distance to the family homes from wherever he parks up.'

Murmurs of agreement rippled around the room. Bliss smiled and clenched a fist. 'I'm loving what I'm hearing, people. Great minds at work here. I can't fault any of it. Of course, it could all turn out to be a complete load of bollocks. There may be no connection at all between our victims, and the killer might just as easily arrive and leave in his own motor. But if we're only partially right, this has been a productive day so far.'

'Agreed,' Warburton said. 'But we need some actions if I'm going to start a policy book.'

Bliss was prepared. 'Pen and I are on the Essex case. We'll try to arrange a Zoom conference with their team and have them look harder at their victims for a similar connection. We'll also start digging into this Marty Reid's life, see if we can find connections that way. I'm thinking Bish and Gul can access CCTV and traffic cameras closest to the Sperling property. I realise it'll be limited, but we might get lucky with the bike or a vehicle transporting a bike. Phil and Alan can pick up the slack on mobile data and the tech info coming back from HQ in Huntingdon.'

The DCI was happy with that. 'I'm meeting with the Super and media management immediately following the evening briefing. First up, what do we want going out to our journos?'

'Nothing about these possible connections or anything negative regarding the victims,' he said firmly. 'I'd say go with the bare minimum for now. We're treating the incident as murder-suicide until and unless evidence shows us otherwise.'

'What if they've already picked up chatter relating to the case review?'

Bliss huffed. Gave it a beat. Warburton was right to raise the prospect, and it was hard to explain away without the matter gaining traction. Any reporter with even a modicum of common sense would sniff something out if they became aware of a case review focussing on a similar investigation by the same team.

'When is that being finalised?' he asked.

'At my meeting later on. I'd expect a PIP 4 to be in place tomorrow. Wednesday at the latest.'

'Then stall. Just for today. Tell the media it's something not on the books – which won't be a complete lie.'

'I'm sure the three of us will come up with something suitably vague. So, in terms of strategy... what am I telling Superintendent Fletcher? Do we have a firm hypothesis? And by that I mean one you want to hang your hat on?'

Bliss shrugged. 'I'm not sure we're there yet, Diane. We're making a number of assumptions at the moment. They're based on sound logic, but although we're going to throw the kitchen sink at this specific notion, I'd hardly register it as a complete working hypothesis. You can give the Super everything we have to date, explain why we're following up on what essentially came up by accident in another case. Thing is, while we agree it's an avenue worth exploring, we also have bugger all else to go on right now.'

Warburton smiled. 'I might leave that last bit out.'

'Probably for the best. Look, I realise this seems like a long shot at the moment, but we only need to find one more connection between our victims and criminal enterprise of any sort for me to go all out. I know our assumptions don't tick all the boxes in our ABC guide. We're assuming too much when we should be assuming nothing. We're believing a throwaway conversation overheard by an FLO when we shouldn't believe anybody at this stage, but we will check the hell out of this before we take any significant steps. Give us tomorrow and we can take a fresh look at what we have then.'

'Done. Everybody happy with that?'

The team were used to working under such pressure, mainly because they knew the first few days of a major operation were critical to its eventual outcome. First assumptions and theories often proved either closely related to or bang on in terms of case direction. They had something here, and Bliss could tell they were feeling the early stages of the thrill of the chase.

'They are,' he said. 'We are. If we're nowhere by five-thirty tomorrow evening, then you stick your SIO hat on and we'll follow your lead.'

Warburton's lips twisted as if she'd bitten into something sour. 'If the case review does begin in the morning, it's likely they'll want to talk to Bish and Gul. Do you want me to delay that for as long as possible?'

'Very much so. I need them both concentrating on this new case until late briefing at the very least. Buy us as much time as you can, please.'

'It might be out of my hands, but I'll do my best. Oh, and by the way, your case is now Operation Insulate. Make of that what you will.' The DCI held his gaze. 'You and your team have done excellent work today, Jimmy. If you all bring your A games tomorrow as well, I'm confident we'll have enough to convince the Super.'

'I share your confidence, boss.'

'I knew you would. And one last thing: Superintendent Fletcher wants to see you first thing in the morning. Thirty minutes before briefing. No excuses.'

'Do you know what it's about?'

'No clue, I'm afraid.'

Bliss didn't like the sound of that. If it was operational, Warburton would most likely have been involved in the decision-making process. That left few other possibilities, and he was left deep in thought long after his DCI had left the room.

TEN

Those same thoughts stayed with him overnight, growing darker and more reflective as the hours wore on. Some downtime with Max had alleviated his mood to a certain degree, but it wasn't until he gave the dog his morning walk that he finally managed to get a grip of his emotions. Even so, by the time he walked into the Superintendent's office, he was both pensive and fearing the worst.

'Thanks for arriving promptly, Jimmy. Please, take a seat.'

Fletcher had been struggling in her personal life lately. Her mother had passed away shortly after his own had died, but he didn't also have a father suffering the early stages of dementia to further weigh him down. Fletcher was working hard to manage the crisis, but not doing a great job of it. She'd missed days, missed ops, missed meetings. Fast approaching a chat with Feeley and human resources, the DSI had decided to give the situation one last crack before finding a care home for the ailing man. Bliss had subsequently made allowances for swift changes in mood and unbalanced behaviour of the kind all humans experienced in times of immense emotional stress. He had no idea what to expect on this occasion, but he was ready for anything.

He pulled out a chair and sat, saying, 'To be honest with you, ma'am, I usually avoid this office like the plague. But this time I didn't even bother to find other things to do.'

Detective Superintendent Fletcher gave a wounded look, prompting him to continue. 'No reflection on you. It's just that more often than not, my visits here end up in a bollocking, so I tend to put them off as long as I can. Am I in trouble again? I've been playing nicely with the other boys and girls lately. Behaving myself generally, as it happens.'

Her eyebrows rose and fell. 'If you say so. And how about we stick with Marion and Jimmy for this meeting?'

Bliss was intrigued. Being summoned to the Super's office was nowhere near as rare as rocking horse shit, but the outcome seldom ended in his favour. He dipped his head and spread a hand as if allowing the more senior officer to go on.

'You're working your last year on the job,' she said. 'Before compulsory retirement, that is. What I know about you, Jimmy, tells me you won't exactly be happy about that. In fact, I'd be astonished if you weren't considering a two-year extension.'

'I can't say it hasn't crossed my mind, ma'am... Marion. But an extension is something I have to apply for. Would there be any point in my case?'

The question needed asking. Senior officers tended not to be huge fans of his, and DCS Feeley had already put him on notice following an incident of insubordination.

'The requisite forms come to me once you've completed them, so I'll tick and initial every box before signing off on it. But that's me, Jimmy. And as you are well aware, any contract extension request eventually lands on the desk of the Chief Super. What do you imagine his response will be?'

Bliss snorted. 'You mean other than hysterical laughter?'

'And that's if you catch him on a good day. So, we're agreed any such approach would be hopeless as long as DCS Feeley is in charge.'

'That's why I asked if there was any point in going ahead.'

'Okay. Well, there may shortly be some news on the Chief Super's post. Between you and me, rumour has it he's looking to move elsewhere, which may or may not help your situation. But if we assume the status-quo is maintained, I might have found a healthy compromise. Interested?'

'I'm here, aren't I?'

'You're here because I ordered you to be.'

'True. In which case, I'm intrigued enough to hear you out.'

Fletcher feigned gratitude. 'How kind of you. Okay, then. I've been analysing some of your higher profile ops, and one thing that became abundantly clear to me is how often you end up rooting into past cases. In fact, the more I look, the more I'm convinced of how good at it you are.'

Bliss shifted uneasily in his chair. He thought he knew where this was headed. 'Your solution is not to ship me off to work unsolved cases, is it?'

'Not immediately, no. You'll remain with major crimes until your retirement day. What we're talking about here is what comes afterwards. If your extension forms come with a request to move over to Hinchingbrooke to work cold cases, I believe DCS Feeley might regard that as a win-win. See, the thing is, Jimmy, while he's not a fan of you, he is a fan of your results.'

'Then let him be a fan of the results I get in major crimes.'

'He is. But in your current post, the chance of you once again becoming a thorn in his side remains a distinct possibility. Switching across to cold cases, however, removes you from his purview, and he can continue to bask in the warm congratulatory glow when you solve a few.'

With a huff, Bliss said, 'Okay, I'll think about it.'

'Good.'

'I've thought about it, and the answer is no.'

'That's it? Well, at least you gave my suggestion all due consideration. Thanks for that.'

Bliss took a beat before responding. 'Marion, I'm grateful to you. Really I am. If I've not said it often enough, I greatly appreciate the support you've given me. You and Diane are the reason I still have a job here at all. You're a great boss, and I work better knowing you are in my corner.'

'So why not take time to consider my suggestion?'

'Because it's just not for me. I know some people say the job is all I am, that without it I'm nothing. But the truth is, major crimes is all I am. I'm nothing without major crimes, not the wider job. When we're working a case, I don't need coffee in the morning to get me going. The work is all the buzz I need. And without the buzz…'

Fletcher was silent for a few moments before nodding. 'I understand what you're saying, Jimmy. For you, it's all about the desire to act, to resolve, to save, and to see justice served. But wouldn't solving a previously unsolved case give you some of that?'

'I don't think it would, no. For starters, if it's unsolved then it's probably cold for good reason. It may be unsolvable.'

'Not all major crimes cases are solvable, either.'

'True. But with the majority of them, we manage to find a way. And while we don't always see justice served, we do so often enough to make it worthwhile. I admit, not so long ago, I thought achieving real justice was a thing of the past. Dead and gone the way of dinosaurs like me. But now I regard justice as being more what people say it is, deserved or not. Even if part of me still believes it doesn't actually exist, knowing we got a result and that some lives are better off for it is still what drives me. The idea of poking around in some old case long forgotten by those who first investigated it is never going to produce that same rush.'

'It might not give you the same end result, but how about the victims? Or their families?'

'Give me a for instance.'

'I will. Rikki Neave. Remember how we assumed the bastard who murdered him had got away with it? We knew it was him, but we could never find the evidence to prove it. We had to let him go, and even the Chief Super at the time said we were not looking for anybody else. But we know what continued to happen behind the scenes. Tell me, Jimmy, how would you have liked to have been the one who broke that case?'

Bliss processed the question quickly. The thrill of landing the man who thought he'd got away with murder for the better part of twenty-eight years had spread across the entire region. And most likely far beyond. He had to admit, he'd envied those involved in finally nailing their suspect and watching him thrown behind bars. The major crimes unit in Cambridge had taken it on as a cold case, with a completely fresh investigation team running the show. This had led to the first arrest of James Watson in 2016. The man subsequently fled to Portugal, but was rearrested and, despite the original CPS decision not to prosecute due to lack of evidence, they eventually buckled following a Victims Right to Review appeal.

'You make an interesting point,' Bliss finally admitted. 'Even if you're a bit slippery using that case, given how much it means to us all in this area.'

Fletcher smiled. 'I'm not wrong, though.'

'No, you're not. You think Watson will go down?' he asked her.

'You can never tell with a jury, but yes, I'm expecting him to be found guilty of murder. By this time next year, he'll be serving a life sentence. I'm convinced of it.'

'Which is terrific. No doubt about that. But how often does one of those come along for a cold case investigator?'

'Not often, I'll grant you. But I'll make sure you're still working major crimes only. The difference being they won't be active.'

'Would I get to partner up with the team from time to time?'

'Provided they didn't work the original investigation, I see no reason why not. Obviously, it depends on their existing caseload, but I'm sure we can work things out. You'll still carry a warrant card, so technically you won't need to be with anyone else. But if you need a hand, I'm all for it.'

He shifted in his chair. Uneasy with the notion of leaving the MCU in a downward move, but uneasier still with the idea of moving on entirely when he hit sixty. He'd long been of the opinion that there would be nothing for him when he left major crimes, but Fletcher's suggestion was not without merit.

'I really will consider it this time,' he said. 'And thank you. Will you be going for the job again if the DCS takes up another post?'

'Absolutely. I want that promotion, Jimmy. I damned well know I've earned it. If I eventually have to leave the area to achieve it, then that's life. But I would much rather remain here. And before you ask… if I should happen to be in the post at the time your extension application form crosses my desk, I will, of course, be accepting it.'

'Then, for reasons other than wishing you well, I hope it works out like that. But if not, then I'll come back to you about the cold case idea.'

'You do that.' Fletcher clasped her hands together on the desk. 'Now, then. How are you feeling about having a PIP 4 carrying out this case review? I get that you weren't with the unit at the time, so there are no personal axes to grind. But knowing you as I do, I suspect you're getting a tingle right now about how much this might affect the team. Bish and Gul in particular.'

'I won't pretend I'm not on edge. We had a good day yesterday, even if the progress made was all circumstantial and theoretical. We need an even better day today, and I'll admit I have concerns about DSI Haskel nosing around.'

'She was an excellent choice for this specific job, and I know her to be scrupulously fair. So if you find yourself tripping over her toes, or she yours, come to me rather than attempt to interfere personally. Use my rank, Jimmy. I will voice any doubts you may have.'

'And if she doesn't listen.'

'She'll have no choice but to listen to me. If I don't like what I hear, then I boot it up the chain. However, we invited her in to carry out this necessary review. We extend her all courtesies. None of us like it, but it's where we are. So we deal with it. Understood?'

'Of course.'

'Let's not pretend we both don't know how you can be sometimes.'

'Wouldn't dream of it. But I see the big picture. My team has its own focus, and we have no intention of fighting any theoretical battles.'

Superintendent Fletcher raised her eyebrows. 'I'd heard about this new, more sanguine Jimmy Bliss. I think I'm seeing him for the first time.'

He inclined his head. 'I've changed. A little. But at my core, I'm still very much the same man. Provided she stays in her corner, I'll stay in mine. If she moves into our lane, all bets are off.'

'DSI Haskel and I are due to meet shortly,' Fletcher said, glancing up at the clock on her wall. 'I'll apprise her of your thoughts, Inspector.'

'Back to rank so soon?'

She smiled and waved him away. 'Go to your team. Let's have that good day you promised us.'

'I will,' Bliss said, rising to his feet, nowhere near as confident as he sounded. He'd barely slept the previous night, which had worked out well for Max who'd enjoyed two lengthy walks. But this was already day three of the investigation, and although they'd made progress, it was slow going. Worse still, something told him that wasn't about to change.

ELEVEN

'What did Marion want?' Chandler asked when Bliss walked into the major incident room assigned to Operation Insulate.

'To talk about my future,' he replied.

'That must have been a short conversation.'

'Longer than you might think, sarky arse. Though probably shorter than the topic deserved.'

'What did you do wrong this time?'

He pulled a pained expression. 'Why does everybody – including me – assume I've done something wrong whenever I get summoned to the Super's office?'

'Because more often than not, it's true.'

Bliss puffed out his lips. 'Well, not on this occasion. I'll tell you more over a drink after work.'

Bishop and DC Virgil were standing closest to them. It was the latter who looked up sharply. 'Something wrong, boss? Anything we can do to help?'

The latest recruit to the unit, and still technically on loan from CID, Virgil had the makings of a first rate detective. Bliss was keen to make his position on the team more permanent, and he liked the way the man immediately looked to become involved. The officer he had temporarily replaced, John Hunt, was the complete opposite in that respect.

'It's fine, thanks. Nothing I can't handle,' he said, then strode towards the front of the room. 'Heads up, people. Detective Superintendent Haskel is here at HQ today. DSI Fletcher is going to ask her to tread lightly for the first twenty-four hours. She will want to discuss the case review with DS Bishop and DC Ansari, but that won't be until tomorrow at the earliest. So, game faces on boys and girls. We have until our office meeting this evening to find some traction on this notion that our victims were murdered at the behest of a drugs kingpin.'

'And if we can't?' Chandler asked.

'Then we at least need to be closer than we are now. Otherwise, DCI Warburton is going to lay down other paths for us to follow.'

'If she can find any.'

'I got the impression her day will be mainly concentrated on that very subject. She's trying to find alternatives, while at the same time hoping we're correct. I have to say, if it were only the adults who were being killed, I'd probably be more confident. But killing the children, especially the way he does it, bothers me enormously. Even if taking their lives is all part of the plan to make it seem like a murder-suicide, the stab wounds are… frenzied. The problem being, I don't see our killer as the kind of man to lose control.'

'Have you considered the possibility of him being a bit of both?' Ansari asked. 'He may be being ordered to take out one or both of the adults, which explains his presence and the action he takes. But he might also enjoy his work, resulting in him killing the others just for fun.'

Bliss nodded and wagged a finger at his DC. 'Yes, Gul. That's a great thought. You could be spot on. Ostensibly, he's there to do a professional job, but gets his personal jollies at the same time.'

'I'd say Gul has something there, boss,' Bishop said. 'It feels right.'

'It does. Okay, so let's steer that course for the time being. We have a couple of probable cases in addition to our own two that we know of. My money is on HOLMES spewing out more. The crack through which we might slip in and force this whole thing wide open is the potential link to our known villain, Marty Reid. Yesterday evening I alerted detectives in Poole to our interest in their op, and they're sending over what they have. They're also going to reinterview Hugh Worsley's brother-in-law. As previously mentioned, if we can find one further case with some connection to Reid, or any other criminal for that matter, then we'll have a working hypothesis to follow.'

'What do we know about Reid?' Bishop asked.

'He's the real deal. The man runs an empire, but never gets his hands dirty. There are cells within cells within cells… highly organised, in other words. The Met has a huge amount of intel on him, tugged him a few times, too. But he's too far removed from the actual foot soldiers to have had charges laid against him.'

'And I don't suppose anyone further down the chain will grass him.'

'No chance. Thing is, anybody thought to be in his orbit who has been arrested, charged, and even convicted, are not even sure if Reid is pulling their strings. The higher up his people are, the fewer arrests are made. The man is in his fifties, and he's been at it a long time. But people know not to talk, because they've seen what Reid is capable of when it comes to how his thugs treat their opposition.'

'Is it time to widen this, Jimmy?' DC Gratton asked. 'Bring more bodies into it. The actions are only going to start mounting up from hereon in, and we could do with delegating a number of them.'

'Already in hand, Phil. As people come aboard, we'll spread the load. But we're not exactly overflowing with staff, so I don't yet know how much we'll be able to ease the burden on the team. I might not have to account for every penny, but those above me do, and they're always happy to remind me when I overstep the mark.'

Disinclined to debate budgets and staff shortages any further, Bliss stopped himself from going off on a full-blown rant. It did none of them any good, and often resulted in more harm being done. These days, PCCs had a tight grip on the reins, and every area force needed a strong Chief Constable to stake their claim for extra staffing and overtime in addition to all other necessary resources. The strain of being overworked was felt by every member of the team, and he saw a plea for understanding in his colleague's eyes.

'Look,' he said, softening his tone and taking in the faces turned his way. 'I don't want this same conversation to be part of every op. I don't enjoy standing here banging on about a lack of resources. Like the rest of you, I hear about a superintendent being asked here from another force to review one of our old cases, and all I can think about is how much that's costing and what else we could do with that money. It is what it is, though. Now, you might be sick and tired of hearing me say that, but I'm not wrong. We have murders to investigate, so let's do what we do best. I won't be asking any of you to put in a single hour of unpaid overtime, and whatever budget we are allowed will be allocated on a voluntary basis only. You with me?'

Bliss was happy enough with the nods he got back in return. They weren't the most enthusiastic, but knowing his team, they would have already decided the murder of a family, including three children, deserved their best efforts. He was about to add something when the door to the incident room was yanked open and in marched the PCC, accompanied by a woman Bliss did not recognise.

Once again, he was caught unawares. The previous Police and Crime Commissioner seldom mixed with the rank and file, rarely straying far from their comfortable offices inside the Hinchingbrooke police headquarters at Huntingdon. Bliss wondered if David Benning's time as a uniformed constable had something to do with his venturing out across the area. The former Commissioners had both been ex-forces, and he suspected their lack of police experience had kept them behind closed doors, safe from being challenged on protocol and procedure.

Benning thrust himself forward, hand outstretched. 'Detective Inspector Bliss, I felt a personal introduction to Superintendent Naomi Haskel was warranted under the circumstances. Naomi will be responsible for the urgent case review.'

'My pleasure,' Bliss said, remaining wary as he shook hands with them both.

'Can we talk in your office?' the PCC asked.

'Of course. It'll be a bit crowded, but I'm happy to remain standing.'

A short walk down the corridor from the incident room, the major crimes area was quiet. Bliss's office quieter still. It was too small for the desk and filing cabinets, let alone three bodies, but they made do.

'Thing is, Inspector,' Benning began. 'I also wanted to have a word about this review process. Both DCS Feeley and your own Super were keen to put you at your ease. Which is all well and good, and I'm not here to interfere in that aspect of your communications. However, this is the first case review under my leadership and I want to make sure it goes off without a hitch.'

'Of course.' Bliss nodded. 'You're not alone in that wish, I assure you.'

The PCC smiled and raised a finger. 'Ah. Now, that's just it, you see. It may be your wish, Inspector, but it's my desire. In fact, I am insistent upon it.'

Bliss frowned. 'I'm not quite sure what you mean?'

'Then I'll simplify it for you. I demand full transparency. My job is to ensure the people of Cambridgeshire feel not only safe but also that the police will stop at nothing – whilst adhering to all elements of PACE, of course – to ensure their own back yard is spotless. If mistakes were made in the case being reviewed, they will be exposed, given light, because the public must trust that we will do everything in our power to prevent those errors from happening again.'

Bliss kept his attention on the man's eyes. 'I understand. In other words, throw to the wolves those at fault, because whatever did go wrong did so under the stewardship of a predecessor.'

Bristling indignantly, Benning said, 'You don't believe blunders require correcting, Inspector Bliss?'

'With all due respect, that's not what I said. If mistakes are made, then we learn from them. You can't do that if you're pushed out into the cold. None of us are infallible.'

'Are you not the exception?'

Bliss shook his head. 'Far from it, sir. Like every other copper, yourself included, I suspect, I've made the odd lapse in judgement along the way. But I learned and I improved. And I took that improvement into the job, which benefitted from it. It's the nature of how we function… if you recall.'

'Lapses in judgement are one thing. Errors leading to the subsequent deaths of others, quite another. That's something you ought not to be given the chance to repeat.'

Bliss felt anger rising deep inside. He was better at managing it than he once had been, but that didn't stop him from feeling his flesh tighten. 'I see. So I'm to ignore what was said in yesterday's management meeting, am I? When I was assured this was not going to be a witch hunt, that was just bullshit, was it?'

Anger flashed across the PCC's eyes. 'The rumours about you are true, Inspector.'

'And what rumours might those be?'

'That you're prone to sudden outbursts of candour. That you have a tendency towards insubordination. Why on earth would I stand for any of that?'

'Your staffing remit ends with the Chief Constable,' Bliss snapped back.

Benning stood his ground. 'My remit is first and foremost to secure an efficient and effective police service for this area. And in setting my policing and crime objectives, Inspector, I made it clear I was going to enforce accountability. Did you not get that memo, or did you simply not care what it said?'

'No, I read it. I subsequently filed it under "things people say but don't really mean", and then promptly forgot all about it.'

'Then let me assure you, I meant every word. When I say there will be transparency, that is precisely what I expect. Superintendent Haskel has been briefed by both myself and the Chief Constable. They also know what I demand of them. Now it's your turn. Of course, there's bound to be some overlap between the case review and your current investigation. But you will operate within clearly defined boundaries. If you need to reinvestigate any part of the case in review, you will run it by Superintendent Haskel first. If she allows you access, you will step in and you will then step out again as quickly as you are able. You will not – and please don't test me on this – you will not seek to influence the outcome of the review in any way, shape, or form. Anything you discover, you will pass over to the review. And I do mean anything and everything. Is that understood?'

Bliss struggled to keep himself in check. The PCC was obviously gunning for blood in what he pompously assumed would be a result in his favour. For a moment, neither man said a word. Their eyes remained locked. DSI Haskel stood mute by the door, looking as if she wanted to melt into the wall. Eventually, Bliss composed enough to answer.

'I understand you,' he said. 'You want to make a name for yourself, without any regard for the careers ruined in the wreckage you're looking to create.'

With a snort, the PCC said, 'Then you don't understand me at all. Accountability, Inspector. That's what I'm about. Your kind of feigned hyperbole is not what's called for here. The situation demands critical thinking and honesty.'

Bliss was far from done. 'I also happen to believe in people being accountable for their actions and their decisions, sir. And for me, integrity is not just a word. I wasn't around when the case was investigated, but some of my closest colleagues were. I refuse to stand by while you destroy them in the name of making front page news.'

Benning chuckled humourlessly. 'I was told you were yesterday's man, Inspector. Now I've learned that for myself. We don't just feature in newspapers these days. No, no. You're ignoring the rise of social media. That's where the influencers have their roots and their sources. Look, I have a job to do. Naomi here has a job to do. Stay out of her way. Stay out of my way.'

'Or what?'

'Or you get swept up by the machine, Inspector.'

Bliss sneered. 'You won't need to sweep me up. I promise you that. You go gunning for my team or our unit leadership and I'll resign.'

'And what makes you think that's a threat?'

'Because if I'm forced to step down, I will not go quietly.'

'And what does that mean, exactly?'

Turning away, Bliss said over his shoulder, 'Believe me, if you value your shiny new position, you don't want to find out.'

TWELVE

Bliss accepted Superintendent Haskel's surprise invitation to lunch. He only ever left the rear of the Thorpe Wood building, and always by car, yet still he had to nudge their way through two stubborn lines of animated TV and newspaper journalists gathered outside waiting for quotes, before finally puncturing the human barricade they had presented and slipping out on the road.

Over a drink and a sandwich they discussed the case review. A tall woman with a slender build, she had a long neck accentuated by the low cut of her summer dress. Behind crimson-rimmed glasses her eyes were wide and took in everything around her. She wore two necklaces and several bangles on each wrist, but no rings. Her accent placed her as having grown up somewhere around the Nottingham or maybe even Stoke-on-Trent area further to the West Midlands.

'Please don't make the mistake of lumping me in with Benning,' was the first thing she said after they had settled into their seats. 'Your Commissioner clearly has his own agenda, and apparently doesn't mind who knows about it. That conversation back in your office should never have taken place with me present. I imagine he did it to show me who was boss. But I'm my own person, Jimmy. That's not about to change now. The review goes where it goes. I won't be led, badgered, coerced, or blackmailed. Not by anybody.'

'That's good to know,' he said, appraising the DSI. He imagined she was the type to sit back and absorb, speaking only when she had something valuable to say. 'You'd think somebody who was once one of us would understand the vagaries of investigations.'

'Perhaps in his case it works against him. He may be one of those who believed he was capable of offering more, given the opportunity.'

Bliss shrugged. He sensed Haskel knew more about Benning than she was willing to admit. 'Whatever his professional issues, he should know better than to make them ours.'

She took a sip from her glass of Chardonnay, taking time to carefully weigh her words. 'He's new and looking to make his mark. I'm also guessing seventy grand a year plus expenses is something he'd like to cling on to for more than the statutory four years.'

'That's a possibility. So how do you avoid bending to his will?'

'By following procedure. It's both as simple and as complicated as that. I'm here at the request of the area force as a whole, not the PCC. I've been in this situation before, only usually they want to influence me into finding nothing. In this case, the taint goes with his predecessor.'

'Only you can't be influenced. Right?'

Bliss couldn't tell if she was amused or disappointed by his tone, but her expression altered slightly. 'You sound sceptical, Jimmy. But no, I can't be. I review, I analyse, I report on my findings. If I do stumble across investigative errors, they'll be mentioned. If I don't, the absence of error will be equally obvious. Mine is merely an independent review of the case.'

'And when our paths cross, as you know they are bound to?'

'That depends. How often do you expect that to happen?'

'I can't be certain, Naomi.' They had agreed on informality during the short car journey to the Woodman pub close to the station. 'Our current lines of inquiry, as you know, impact the outcome of the case you're reviewing. That doesn't only affect our investigation, of course. You've also got to consider the coroner's verdict, pathology findings, and forensics. Without evidence to suggest foul play, and with everything pointing to a murder-suicide, that is where we ended up. I've looked over the policy book and the HOLMES case file, and without going deeper I can't say I'd've drawn any other conclusion.'

'And yet if obvious mistakes were not made, then the chances are good that something was overlooked.'

Bliss angled his head, his gaze narrowing. 'Now you're being premature. Just because we got it wrong doesn't mean we overlooked anything. There might just have been nothing for us to find.'

Haskel smiled. 'You're taking it awfully personally for someone who wasn't even stationed here at the time.'

'That's because I know the Super, I know DCI Edwards, I know DS Bishop, and DC Ansari. Then you have SOCO and the pathologist. You couldn't ask for better people. If anything had been there to find, one of them would have spotted it.'

'Now who's being premature?'

It was his turn to grin. He scrutinised her over the top of his glass. 'Look, I get the impression you're one of the good guys. You tell me your report is independent, I believe you. Provided you stick to what you find, I'm sure my colleagues will be cleared. As to how often we clash, the more time ticks down the more I suspect we're going to have to take a close look at the case you're reviewing. I'm talking evidence, pathology, witnesses, the victims themselves. If, as we suspect, at least one member of each family was targeted, then the chances are they are connected somehow. I'm fully prepared to take the review case and start all over again. Now,' he held up a hand to forestall any complaint. 'I will do everything in my power to make our case on Operation Insulate alone, but if we need to move into your line of vision then so be it. No holding back.'

'Didn't the PCC insist you had to ask my permission first?'

'He did. And are we suddenly taking notice of what he said?'

The Superintendent sighed. 'You know what? Let's play it by ear. Working at cross purposes won't help either of us. I get the impression you're a stubborn man, and I'm not known for taking a step back against my will. So let's just see how it goes, and we'll iron out any wrinkles as they appear.'

Bliss agreed. 'Where will you begin?'

'With Superintendent Fletcher and DCI Edwards.'

'Marion and Alicia won't throw up barriers. The DCI and I haven't always been on the same wavelength, but she's great at what she does. As for the Super… I'd go as far as to say she's the best I've ever worked with. One thing I can guarantee is they will be honest with you.'

'Good to know. Over the next few evenings I'll review the file and all available information. Starting tomorrow I'll want to speak to those closely involved with investigating the case, which includes DS Bishop and DC Ansari.'

'I rely heavily on Bish and Gul. Please don't tie them up any longer than necessary.'

Haskel laughed, regarding him quizzically. 'You're an unusual man, Jimmy.'

'Oh?'

'In my experience, those running investigations rarely admit to relying on anybody else. Usually every break in the case is due to their own good work.'

'Well, I can't speak for others. But you know as well as I do that no case is ever solved by one person alone. When I say it's a team effort, I genuinely mean it. So, you won't keep them tied up, then?'

'Only for as long as I need to. How about yourself, Jimmy. What's your next move?'

As he was about to reply, Bliss's work mobile rang. He answered, spoke for a few minutes, then ended the call. 'Interesting. That was DCI Moran from Essex. They had another look at the victims in their case. They found nothing to raise an eyebrow on the male adult. His wife, however, has a bit of a past. Nothing to suggest she moved in circles occupied by Marty Reid, the drugs heavyweight we're keen on, but they did discover a link to an organisation run by another serious villain by the name of Church. Evidently, the victim ran one of his nightclubs.'

'Hmm, that's quite a development. And it's also your op, Jimmy, not mine. I'm still assuming our paths will cross over the next few days. All I ask is that you treat me fairly.'

'That's the least I can assure you of, Naomi,' Bliss told her. 'And I'm more than happy to agree to it.'

THIRTEEN

Bliss offered to drive Haskel back to Thorpe Wood, but she declined, hoping to clear her thoughts by taking a walk prior to continuing with her work. They had more than cleared the air by the time she left. He also believed he could trust her to do as she had promised.

He was in the process of draining the remains of his pint when a woman slid in to occupy the space in the booth recently occupied by the Superintendent. Bliss put her at around his own age, and something about her was familiar enough to send a tingle down the back of his neck.

'If you're not Jimmy Bliss, I'm going to seem like a right berk,' she said, her voice as full-on cockney as his could be when he didn't rein it in. Her wide smile was more certain than hopeful.

'You have me at a disadvantage,' he said carefully, gradually overcoming the suddenness of the woman's appearance across the table from him. 'I feel as if we know each other, but unfortunately I can't place you.'

The woman reached out a hand to pat his own. 'Don't worry about it, sweetheart. It's no big deal if I wasn't memorable enough for you. I'm only happy not to be going off my rocker.' The woman paused to pout, though the humour never left her eyes. 'Mind you, given the nights you and I spent together, I can't say I'm not a teensy bit disappointed you don't recognise me.'

But then he did. In an abrupt burst of clarity, memories began rushing in. The passing of time flushed through his senses in a flash, leaving him with a deep sense of melancholy.

'Pam?' he breathed, doubting himself though he knew he had to be correct.

Her smile returned, now switched to full beam. She laughed right in the back of her throat and clutched a hand to her chest. 'So you do remember?'

'How could I forget?'

How could he? Pamela Daniels may not have been his first sexual partner, but she was his first love. It had to be forty years since he had last laid eyes on her. Just shy of four decades that had been kinder to her than to him if looks were anything to go by.

'You look… amazing,' he said, pushing himself back into his seat. 'What on earth are you doing here?'

'I'm in Peterborough for a conference. Just up the road at the Holiday Inn hotel. I was told the lunch was better here than whatever buffet delights we were going to be served up. Imagine my surprise when I saw a familiar face sitting at a table all on his jack.'

'Well, their loss is my gain. I'm surprised you recognised me, but as you did, I wish I could stay and have a natter. Unfortunately, my own break is over and have to get back to work.'

'Oh, that's such a shame. You still Old Bill?'

Bliss frowned. 'How did you know? You and I split up before I joined.'

Her smile was everything he remembered it to be; warm and inviting, crinkling her eyes. 'Did you really think I wouldn't keep tabs on you afterwards, Jimmy? After what we had going?'

'I did the same with you,' he admitted. 'For a while.'

'That makes me feel a bit better. At least you didn't instantly forget me. So, you married? Kids?'

'No, to both.'

Her eyebrows arched. 'A bachelor? Jimmy Bliss? I always booked you as a man who would settle down at an early age and have a bunch of saucepans biting ankles.'

He wasn't about to get into an in-depth discussion about his late wife, or their lack of children. He shrugged it off with his own question. 'How about you?'

For the first time since she'd sat down, Pam's features clouded over. 'Ah. Well, I was married for a while, but that was a long time ago now. But I do have a son. Angus.'

'I'm sorry. About the marriage, I mean.'

'Thanks,' she said, leaning forward, peering directly into his eyes. 'It's okay, Jimmy. You can ask.'

'Ask what?'

'Really, it's all right. You know how old I am. It's the next logical question to ask now that you're aware I have a kid.'

Bliss laughed, but shook his head. 'I won't. It wouldn't be chivalrous.'

'Fair enough. I should've expected that from you. I'll just put you out of your misery. I *am* also a grandmother. Just the one at the moment.'

'Congratulations. You certainly seem happy with your lot. Content. I'm pleased for you, if that's the case.'

Pam pursed her lips. 'We're old style, my friend. People like you and me. We make the best of things and carry on regardless.'

'That we do. Look, I'm really sorry. I'd love to stay and chat some more, but I've got something fairly major on, and I have to get back to my team.'

She seemed dejected, but nodded anyway. 'Of course. I understand. What are you these days… Chief Superintendent?'

With some reluctance, he got to his feet. 'No, no. A humble DI. Mostly by choice.'

Pam also stood, leaned across the table, rested a hand on his shoulder, and pecked his cheek with warm, soft lips. 'Yeah, I can believe that. You always did like to be in the thick of the action, no matter what you were doing. Listen, I'm here until the end of the working week. I understand you're a busy man, but maybe we can get together for dinner and a drink. It would be lovely to catch up.'

Bliss said nothing for a moment, poised awkwardly, trying to avoid her gaze. Their relationship had lasted far longer than they had actually dated, having known each other since they were kids. But the past was just that, and going back seldom did any good.

'Please,' she said.

The single word and the pleading expression did the trick, breaking through any emotional barriers he had erected. Anything they'd had ended four decades ago, and their time together was as teenagers. Their lives since had taken them in entirely different directions, and for all he knew they might now be radically different people to the two who were attracted to one another in the first place.

'If I can, I'll call,' he said. 'What's your room number?'

She gave it to him, adding. 'Seriously, it would make my week if we could spend a couple of hours talking over old times. There's a lot to catch up on.'

When he left the pub, Bliss wasn't certain what he would do, but he felt surprisingly open to seeing his old girlfriend again.

FOURTEEN

Detective Superintendent Fletcher removed her glasses and rubbed her face several times before pausing with fingers steepled beneath her chin. Her flinty gaze fell upon Bliss, and he braced himself. She tended to deliver her wrath more by rapier than bludgeon, but he knew he deserved either. Or both.

'This has to be a personal record, Jimmy,' she said in a soft voice imbued with displeasure. 'Only a few short hours ago, you and I discussed your future. We agreed you were a changed man, one who had learned how to keep his head down and his nose clean. Yet already you've pissed off the PCC during the most difficult time the unit has known in terms of evaluation. And while David Benning has no direct influence over extending your employment beyond compulsory retirement age, he will still be the Commissioner and his opinion will therefore carry significant weight.'

Bliss looked up, determined to stand his ground one more time. 'I accept that, ma'am. It doesn't change what's right and what's wrong.'

'Jimmy, as PCC, all he has to do is whisper in the ear of the Chief Constable and that's you done on the day you turn sixty.

Why, today of all days, with my endorsement still ringing in your ears, would you put that at risk?'

'I'm guessing he didn't feed you the whole story. His part in our disagreement, at least.'

'The man was puce with rage. And from what he told me, with due cause.'

'Again, that suggests he held one or two things back. So, I'll tell you exactly what he said and you can make up your own mind. And for what it's worth, Superintendent Haskel heard the entire thing.'

Bliss spent the next few minutes describing the conversation in full. While he was talking, he noticed Fletcher visibly relax. When her anger finally resurfaced, it was not directed at him.

'You're telling me Benning *is* looking for a scapegoat despite everything he said?'

'No.' Bliss shook his head. 'I'm saying he's looking for scape-*goats*. Plural. I have no doubt the buck will stop with you as opposed to your boss at the time. But Benning also wants the scalps of DCI Edwards, DS Bishop, and DC Ansari. Any current officer connected to that op, in fact.'

Fury pinched her cheeks. 'The two-faced bastard. Now I understand why you reacted the way you did.'

'I thought you might. He couldn't. In his small mind, I wasn't here at the time, which means I shouldn't give a crap what he's trying to do. He's new in the job and perhaps wants to show he's in charge. But he's also one of us, and should bloody well know better.'

Clearly dismayed, Fletcher said, 'Word coming back from those who worked with him in the trenches suggests he had a bit of a chip on both shoulders. He was a nine-to-fiver, no more, no less. But he never bought into the grunt work, had a poor attendance record, and colleagues apparently didn't have much time for him.'

'So now he wants to make a name for himself by taking down officers who might have screwed up an investigation.'

'Hmm, the problem being he's almost certainly right.'

Bliss shook his head. 'As I keep telling people, ma'am, I'm not so sure about that.'

'I'm no longer annoyed with you, so I think we can go back to you calling me Marion. And while I'm grateful to you for your support, the facts point to us having cocked up.'

'Only if you all missed something. I agree in terms of responsibility and accountability. And yes, we got the wrong result. But you have to take the broader view of this. If the evidence wasn't there to be found, if nothing was missed, then nobody got it wrong. I'll keep on saying this until I'm blue in the face or somebody acknowledges it's true.'

The Super raised her hands. 'I hear you, Jimmy. I do. But let's not be naive. You, of all people, know the difference between reality and perception. If the PCC wants blood, all he has to do is kick off about us getting the wrong result. How we got there is clearly irrelevant to him. Which reminds me… did you actually threaten to resign and more if he pulled this stroke?'

'I did. And I meant it. You honestly think I'm going to sit by while that man destroys the careers of good coppers?'

'No, not for one moment. But he is the Commissioner.'

'Yeah, and he fucked up, Marion. He assumed Naomi Haskel would follow his lead. She said nothing when he spoke, but made it clear to me afterwards how she felt about the matter. I not only think her review will be clean, I also reckon she'll back me up if I tell my story. He'll have less leverage if her report doesn't point fingers, and he might just be shrewd enough to realise she won't play his game.'

'Unless he exerts pressure beforehand. Prior to her delivering the report.'

'That's a genuine possibility. Perhaps you could have a word in her shell-like. Pledging support in the name of a legit finding.'

'Even if it blames me for poor leadership?'

'It won't. But yes, even then.'

Fletcher drew in a deep breath and let it out slowly. 'I'll speak to her. I'll make sure she knows she has backing from this corner.'

'Good. Then let's hope it's enough.'

*

Olly Bishop seemed to be in a better mood when Bliss entered the incident room. The big DS was holding court about the Armstrong case and how he and Gul Ansari had found it odd working under two chief inspectors with conflicting personalities. He could be a wonderful raconteur when he wanted to be, and the outcome of his stories ensured laughter all round. Bliss joined in at the conclusion of this particular anecdote.

'Shame you weren't with us at the time,' Bishop said to him. 'We could probably have used a different perspective. Still, I think we're making inroads. HOLMES has coughed up three new cases for us to look at. Only one is a presumed murder-suicide, but after looking at all questionable ops involving whole family casualties, we have another two likelies.'

'Sounds good. Give me what you have so far.'

Bishop rubbed his hands together. 'All right. Peckham in south London. That's the murder-suicide. We ran the adult victims' names and got no joy. But Gul noticed one of their kids was almost 19, so we looked hard at him and found connections to a dubious outfit from the Elephant & Castle. Drugs, pros, protection… you name it, they had a hand in it. Not big time, but enough to make a noise.'

'Sounds promising. Go on.'

'We've got a supposedly accidental fire. Wiped out a family

of three. That's still open and ongoing from last year. No evidence of arson, but the op suggests the investigating officers aren't happy. They suspect the fire was lit deliberately but can't prove it. Anyway, the father was a known face. Worked with a crew in Birmingham.'

'Another interesting one. And the third?'

'This one is the most speculative so far, boss. Last summer, a family of four touring the Derbyshire peak district were reported missing after they failed to arrive at the home of a relative. They seem to have vanished off the face of the earth. No trace since last September. No activity on their bank account, debit, or credit cards.'

Bliss considered it, but shook his head. 'Stick it on the bottom of the pile. I'm not feeling that one at all.'

'Any connection to crime?' Chandler asked.

Bishop tipped his hand from side to side. 'A bit iffy. The wife's ex-husband is doing a long stretch in Frankland, County Durham. Armed robbery, second conviction.'

'Hmm. It's a maybe, but I think we have stronger cases to follow.'

Nodding – as much to himself as to anybody else – Bliss said, 'All right. So what do we reckon we have here, chaps and chapesses? A hitman who takes the path less trodden? We're categorically saying somebody ordered hits on these people, but that our offender attempts to disguise the murders as something else? Am I right or wrong?'

'That's what I get from this,' Chandler told him. 'I thought we'd already agreed on that?'

'We had. That's definitely what it looks like. But appearances can be deceptive, and the victims still bother me. Some of the links to crime are tenuous. And as yet we haven't established that connection in the case of the Sperlings. Nor the Armstrongs, for that matter. So it's iffy, but let's say we're right. Why would a firm, or several firms as it now looks to be, take out people at this level?'

'Sounds to me as if they're cleaning house,' DC Virgil said.

Bishop jumped in on that suggestion. 'Yes. Remember in the late seventies and early eighties how many rogues upped sticks and buggered off to Spain? Costa del Crime and all that? Some of the real hardened villains did a similar thing prior to fleeing. Peripheral faces were turning up dead left, right, and centre. There wasn't any extradition at the time, which is why Spain became such a popular destination, but those with a lot to lose didn't take chances with some of the poor sods they were leaving behind to take the heat.'

'It's a thought,' Bliss admitted. 'But it's been going on for a while now. Perhaps as long as four years. It feels like a bigger shift than cleaning up behind them.'

'We can't be certain the Armstrong case was part of the more recent spree,' Chandler pointed out. 'Our killer might have been at it for some time for all kinds of reasons.'

'That's true. Good point.'

'Maybe there's more going on in the underworld than we realise,' DC Gratton ventured. 'Gang wars. Takeover bids. Even just closing business down because it's become way too risky, or they're retiring and taking no chances.'

'Do gangsters really do that?' Ansari asked, looking directly at Bliss.

'The lesser of them, usually not. They have to earn and take all the risks to keep up their lifestyles. It's the ones you hear only rumours about who need to be watched more closely. They're the faces with the capital to just close the doors and move on.'

Ansari chewed on her bottom lip. 'What about the ones you don't hear of at all? Those at the top of the food chain who keep themselves so detached we only get to know about them when somebody wants to strike a major deal.'

'There aren't any supergrasses about these days, are there?' Chandler asked.

Bliss nodded. 'Yeah, they're still around. Earlier this year, one of the most notorious in recent times went into hiding. There are fewer than there used to be, though.'

'Why is that?'

'Because they get murdered. At least five in the past four years. Not only that, but their families are often included in the revenge hits.'

Chandler frowned. 'How do you know all this shit, Jimmy?'

He tapped the side of his nose. 'Because I keep this close to the ground. I have friends in high and low places, remember?'

'All right,' Bishop said, 'but even if that's what's going on here, this is no ordinary hitman we're talking about. Today's hard bastards are just as likely to murder and chop up their victims as they were forty or fifty years ago. What we're seeing here is murder by stealth. That's a whole new type of hitman.'

'A super villain,' Gratton said.

Bliss disagreed. 'They're no more super villains than we are super coppers. We're all so drearily normal. But our killer this time is bright and thoughtful, and worst of all, patient. He takes his time. Not because he has to, but because he chooses to. It's probably why he was chosen to carry out this type of work. I suspect he's a hitman-come-fixer. Someone a bit more cerebral than your average thug.'

'Any chance of your contacts in the NCA having something for us?' Chandler asked him.

After spending more than a decade working for both the National Crime Agency and its predecessor, Bliss had built up plenty of goodwill with his ex-colleagues who still tackled organised crime on a daily basis.

'I'll make some calls. See what's what. Meanwhile, what do we have on our victims' finances, social media, and phones?'

Ansari referred to her notebook. 'Sperlings first. Nothing out of the ordinary on their computers. Finances are as we might expect, with no suspicious income or expenditure. Little social media. Mrs Sperling had the largest presence, but mostly with friends and family discussing fairly banal stuff. She also had a WhatsApp group with shared messages between friends, but nothing to see there, either. To be honest, the Armstrongs are no different. If they had skeletons, they were well tucked out of sight.'

'Who checked out vets local to the Armstrong home?'

Virgil raised a finger. 'That was me, boss. Their dog was taken in the day prior to the killings. Poisoning, not considered deliberate at the time.'

'I don't believe in those kinds of coincidences,' Bliss said flatly, looking around at his team. 'So our killer does his homework. He made sure the dog wouldn't be at home to interfere. But rather than just kill it as well, or even make it disappear, he tried to make it seem like a natural event. He really does like to cover all the angles. Any mention of dogs at the other scenes?'

'I'm not sure. I can check.'

'Do that,' Bliss told him. 'But dogs only. Cats will either just yawn and lick themselves or scarper while their owners are being mutilated.'

DC Virgil chuckled and made a note for himself. 'How about fish, boss? A likely deterrent?'

'Depends. A piranha might be up to the task.'

'I'm starting to get an uneasy feeling about this man,' Chandler said.

Bliss snorted. 'You mean other than him being a stone-cold killer?'

'Actually, yes. This one is careful. Too careful for my liking.'

'And yet he made a mistake.'

'He did?'

'He did,' Bliss said. 'He used the same MO in the same area. Had he used that MO anywhere else in the country, he'd most likely have got away with it. But Neil Abbott spotted it, Bish and Gul confirmed it. As did Nancy Drinkwater. He could have walked away from both clean as a whistle. Instead, he now has us hunting him down. Other area forces, too, if we're right about this. Essex being a prime example.'

'And if he fucked up this time, he probably did so before,' Ansari said excitedly.

Bliss smiled and took a breath. Nodded and winked at his DC. 'Precisely.'

FIFTEEN

Pam Daniels was in the year below Jimmy Bliss at school. He'd noticed her around, but it wasn't until he closed in on his 16th birthday that he realised he was attracted to her. A week later, he took the plunge and asked her out. A friend had managed to cadge spare tickets to see Dr Feelgood at the Canvey Island youth centre, and to Bliss's delight, Pam was as crazy about the band as he was. Throughout the long drive to the coast, the pair of them belted out their own wild versions of *Back in the Night* and *She Does it Right*, as well as John Lee Hooker's *Boom*. On the return journey, their heads were buzzing, ears ringing, lips meshed together.

That night out was the first thing Pam reminded him of when they dined out later that evening at an Italian restaurant in Stamford. The memory exploded inside his head, taking him back to a time when he wore his hair long and harboured a genuine desire to be a musician in the same vein as Wilco Johnson of the Feelgoods. These fragments of the past coalesced to wrap around him like a comfort blanket, dispersing his anxiety and reminding him why he had called her room earlier.

Prior to that, his mind had been so focussed on the case that he'd not given his old flame a second thought until the team were winding things up for the day. Knowing he'd be back at it later at home, his thoughts turned to food, and only then to Pam. He felt like a teenager again when he called, tentatively asking her out – *not on a date, no strings, no ulterior motive, just for some grub and a catch up chat.*

He had to admit, she was stunning in a low-cut crimson dress. While it was not short, it didn't need to be to show off her great legs. He remembered them so well, though other men – envious friends mainly – had lusted after her ample chest. Even at school, she was developed beyond her years, and didn't seem to mind flaunting it. She now looked at least half a decade younger than her true age and held herself upright at all times. Her poise had set her apart from other girls at school, and Bliss imagined it stemmed from self-confidence. In some ways, Pam reminded him of a more recent woman in his life; Emily Grant. Both women were sensual, intelligent, and funny. They oozed sex appeal and left him feeling way out of their league.

To his astonishment, the pair slipped into the same kind of verbal exchanges they'd enjoyed while dating. They shared common attitudes, and the same sense of humour, and having old ground to cover didn't hurt. Her laughter was infectious, so much so that he encouraged it at every opportunity. Unlike so many other evenings spent with various women in recent memory, Bliss felt relaxed, able to be himself and enjoy their limited time together.

Time passed by in a flash. Uninhibited conversation had a way of making that happen. He eventually got around to telling Pam about his late wife and her murder. It was not a topic he liked to dwell upon, preferring to remember Hazel as she lived her life rather than how brutally she had died. Pam listened, seeming to understand his reluctance to continue beyond the stark facts. After a while, Bliss deliberately eased them away from the subject, mentioning his Zen garden, the fish pond, and finally Max.

'You have a dog?' she said, her eyes widening.

'You seem surprised.'

Pam wolfed down a forkful of profiterole and wiped her lips with a serviette before responding. 'I am. I'm not sure why. I suppose I never saw you as an animal lover.'

'Perhaps I wasn't at the time you knew me. We didn't have any pets when I was a kid. Hazel and I had a couple of Labs, but they died many years ago.'

'Doesn't… Max get lonely? You must be gone a fair bit.'

'No. I learned my lesson with the other two. There's an agency here in the city. They put dog lovers together with dog owners, so I always have people to take care of him when I'm not there. Not all the time, obviously. But when I'm on duty I have scheduled care, plus if I'm out or working late or even away, it's easy to make ad-hoc arrangements for someone to go in and make sure he's okay.'

'That sounds like a lot of your door keys floating about out there.'

'True. But I trust them. I am a copper, remember?'

When the flow of conversation drifted back around to his job, he gave up only as much as he felt able to. He'd always found it difficult to explain to an outsider precisely what the work entailed. As for describing the horrors he had encountered over the years, that was never going to happen. He eased himself out of that exchange and slipped into one about her life, her job, her family. Pam ran her own fashion chain, which she enthused over and was happy to elaborate about whenever he posed a question. Although she refused to dwell on her marriage, she spoke with great enthusiasm about her son and grandson.

'How about your old man?' he asked during a brief lull.

She both nodded and shook her head. 'Yeah, the old goat is still with us. Barely. Not for much longer, though. Liver disease. Not a great deal they can do for him now but make him comfortable when the time comes.'

'I'm sorry to hear that.' Bliss recalled Pam's father as being a bull of a man, strong and fearsome.

'Yeah, I bet you are.'

He also remembered her father as a villain, running a gang of blaggers out of nearby Stratford. In those days they hit armoured cars and jewellery stores, plus the odd bank and wage heist. Pam's father had served a ten-year stretch for armed robbery, but that was long after she and Bliss had broken up. He'd obviously not approved of a young Jimmy Bliss, whose father was a police officer. And that same police officer had not approved of his son dating the daughter of a known face. Some mixing of coppers and villains was allowed, but Dennis Bliss drew a line when it came to people who carried guns and other weapons and hurt innocents in the pursuit of money. Ultimately, this divide proved to be insurmountable.

'I never wished him any harm,' Bliss insisted. 'So, yes, you have my sympathies. Both my parents are gone, my mum just a few months ago, so I can imagine what you're going through.' Pam had lost her mother to a road accident when she was still quite young, and it sounded as if she was about to be orphaned, like him.

They continued to talk the evening away. To his surprise, Bliss found himself enjoying her company as much as he had when they were teenagers. There was no sense of melancholy, no wondering what might have been. Just a pleasant evening reacquainting themselves with one another.

Until the time came to drop her off at her hotel.

'Do you want to come up for a coffee?' Pam asked him. There was nothing in her voice to suggest there was anything other than a hot drink on offer. Even so, Bliss wasn't so out of touch that he didn't know how the offer could be construed. Or misconstrued.

He made a show of checking his watch, even though the time was clearly visible on the car's media and control screen. 'I don't know. I've really enjoyed myself, and I've loved getting to know you all over again, but I have a lot to do before I turn in for the night.'

Pam shifted in her seat to face him. She reached out a hand to clasp his. 'Jimmy, I'm not a kid anymore and I no longer blush when I have an adult conversation. It may not be the same for either of us, but I'm completely unattached and it's been a long time since I invited a man to my bed. We'll probably never see each other again after this week, so I'm telling you I'd like you to come up with me. And I hope you will. A night doing what men and women do. Where's the harm in that?'

One-night stands were never his thing. But Pam was right – men and women with no other emotional attachments did this sort of thing all the time. This was no long-term commitment, just two human beings coming together for perhaps the most human reason of all.

*

Bliss didn't check his phone until he got home shortly after midnight. He found no updates on the case, only two puzzling texts. The first was from Chandler, all in caps, which implied either urgency or anger on her part.

WHAT DO YOU THINK OF THAT DISPLAY? IS HE A MORON OR LOOKING FOR HIS 15 MINUTES?

Olly Bishop's text also left him wondering.

Do you believe that idiot? Why would you make an announcement like that? Did you have any idea he was going to do this?

Bliss felt his stomach starting to clench like a fist. He'd obviously missed something while he was at dinner and… afterwards. His imagination immediately took him to the PCC. Was Benning the idiot? The moron? He couldn't imagine who else it could be.

It was too late to reply, so he opened up Chrome on his phone to run a local news search. He stopped when he noticed he had a voicemail, wondering if either Penny or Bish had followed up their texts with a call. He played the message without checking the source, which turned out to be Sandra Bannister.

'Tell me, Jimmy, did you fuck me over or did Benning fuck you over? Has to be one or the other. Even if you're the one getting reamed, how come you didn't let me know? You could still have insisted I didn't run with it immediately. Now I'm looking as if I don't know my own patch, and that really pisses me off. I know we haven't always seen eye-to-eye, but I would have expected something from you. Even if it wasn't the entire story. If you have an explanation, call me back. If not, don't bother. We're done.'

A second voicemail notification intrigued him. He played it, though he was still reeling from the previous one. It was Bannister again.

'Jimmy… I'm sorry. You know me. I let my temper get the best of my emotions. Of course we're not done. And of course I don't expect you to come running to me every time you have something juicy. I'm disappointed, that's all. I'll get over it. Again, my apologies. Please do call me when you get a moment. Thanks. Bye.'

Bliss tapped a question into Google and moments later a series of relevant headlines popped up on screen. They all featured an image of a dour-looking David Benning. Clicking on a link to a video clip, Bliss puffed out his cheeks, set the phone on the kitchen counter and got himself a Peroni from the fridge. Max accompanied him, hoping for a treat. But Bliss was too far gone to even consider it.

What have you done this time, you dick? he thought to himself, focussed on the PCC's media address. Three minutes later he closed his eyes, drained the bottle of beer, and silently cursed the treacherous prick running the area police force.

Not only had the Commissioner announced the undertaking of an urgent case review, he had also referred to the victims by name. Furthermore, he'd stared boldly into the cameras trained on him as he made clear his determination to bring to book those officers whose incompetence had failed the victims in both local cases.

The knots inside Bliss's stomach unravelled, replaced by a swelling of anger he might not have been able to control had Benning stood before him at that moment.

'Fuck!' he roared, slamming the bottle down on the counter. 'Fuck you, you twisted shit!'

Reacting to the outburst, Max yelped and fled to his basket. Tail thrust between his legs, he curled up and lay there shaking. Cursing himself, Bliss got down on his hands and knees and slowly crawled across the kitchen floor making soothing noises. Easing out a hand, he ran his fingers across the dog's head and then sat stroking him for a few minutes. Having spent so many years alone, Bliss was unused to reeling in displays of anger within his own four walls. Conversely, Max was all too familiar with such behaviour. And the violence that often followed verbal outbursts. It took a while, but the fussing eventually settled the animal. While he continued to sit and pet Max, Bliss turned his thoughts back to the PCC.

This was the Commissioner's direct response to Bliss's challenge. Informing the media of a case review was, in itself, not a major problem. But in telling anybody who cared to listen the particulars of the case, revealing the surname of the victims in that specific investigation, he had either forgotten about or deliberately chosen to ignore one crucial factor: his audience might well include their killer, in which case that individual would now be aware that the police suspected a connection between the two operations. Not content with this, Benning had committed himself to punishing those who investigated the Armstrong murders just as soon as the review reported back on any errors made. The consequence of this revelation would of course put Superintendent Naomi Haskel in a bind, but it also left Fletcher, Edwards, Bishop and Ansari exposed to all manner of media hounding – including the social kind.

Bliss didn't have accounts with Twitter, Instagram, or Facebook, and had only a basic notion of what TikTok was. The one thing he did know was few people got a fair hearing on these platforms. Ignorant rabble spat poison and spread fear with abandon, requiring no evidence or facts to back up their claims. At a time when the police were already classed as fair game for such toxicity, Commissioner Benning might as well have thrown his officers to the baying mob.

SIXTEEN

Her face held a rare beauty, he decided. Early morning dew beaded her silken skin. A high, round cheekbone drew his glance across its gentle slope, down to a chin jutting prominently as if in one final surge of defiance. She lay at an odd angle, head turned sideways. Much of her hair remained dry, though the end curl of the ponytail lay fully submerged beneath the surface of the stream.

The first jagged claws of dawn revealed her to him almost in slow motion as they sliced their way across both unblinking green eyes. Sunlight's touch left in its wake an echo of radiant life, even as he heard the gentle morning breeze snatch up her final breath. He imagined it coiling into the air, each tendril alighting somewhere different and far away. One perhaps brushing against a young man's cheek like the softest of kisses, before dispersing entirely and becoming lost for all time.

She continued to stare sightlessly up at him as he crouched close by, ripples of blood staining the trickling stream as it sluiced over pebbles surrounding her prostrate body. He would have preferred her to be naked in this moment, but her attire was sufficiently thin and brief to excite him. The wet material of her strap top and shorts clung to her full and enticing form; perhaps made more alluring now that she was dead. Beguiled by the impossibly angled limbs broken and crushed by her fall, he released a gentle sigh of pleasure.

'You've got to love what you do,' he whispered. The mantra had been driven into him by his father throughout his boyhood years. 'A man who enjoys his job never has to work a day in his whole life.'

Of course, his old man had stolen the saying from an ancient Chinese philosopher. The prick never had an original idea in his entire miserable life. But the feeble-minded bastard had been right about this: he did enjoy his job, and it had never once even come close to feeling like a chore.

Women made such a fuss over the purely biological act of bringing new life into the world. Just let them feel the overwhelming sensation of ending one. Then they would truly know how it felt to walk in the shadow of God.

The 'accidental' fall had been simple enough to plan and arrange. The route the young woman ran through the woods took her on a narrow, broken path thirty feet above the brook. From the very beginning he had counted on the element of surprise working in his favour, leaving her no time at all in which to react. He had imagined the point of impact many times before putting it into motion. As he sprang up out of a coiled crouch from behind a twisted knot of abundant shrubbery, he slammed into her at full force. He knew precisely what he was doing and had prepared himself for every eventuality. If the thirty-foot plunge down the steep hillside pockmarked with rocks, large stones, and thick tree stumps failed to do the trick, he could always race to her side, taking a path he had previously mapped inside his mind. There he would finish her off by holding her head face down in the stream and pushing her mouth and nose into its silted bed.

He was glad it hadn't come to that. Having to touch her again while she was alive would have spoiled everything. From the moment she smashed her head against the first rock, he knew she would not survive. Her arms had not reflexively shot out to protect herself when she splashed into the stream, and her only strangled cry had occurred as he clattered into her thirty feet above. By the time he reached her side, she was immobile and in the process of expiring.

Do you see me? he wondered briefly, as her life drained away into the flowing water. *Do you see me and realise as you die that I am the man who robbed you of your future? Or do you see only a bright light, far away in the distance, yet at once welcoming and enticing? Perhaps you are asking why? Why did I do this to you? If it was by accident, why am I not attempting to save your life? Why am I sitting here allowing it to ebb away? And if I sent you crashing down here deliberately, why did you deserve this fate?*

He smiled to himself, caught out by the phrase flickering through his mind. *Does anybody really deserve to die? And if so, for what reason? Who decides? And who decides who decides?*

Questions like these, he had come to understand, had no reason to be asked. They were existential. There were no good answers, after all. And even if there were, would that change the way he regarded his purpose? Would they have any influence at all on the final outcome?

If he was ever drawn to wondering, at least he had the presence of mind never to ask. These people presented a threat. It was his job to protect those he worked for from those threats. Taking a life did not come without its moments of agonising soul-searching. The path he had chosen led to only one place when his time was over. But he absorbed the hits so that they didn't have to. And if, as in some cases, he took time to savour his work, then so be it.

Nobody had to know.

And he did not have to share it with anybody but the dead themselves.

SEVENTEEN

Bliss arrived at work earlier than usual on the fifth day of the investigation, but was still beaten to the punch by Superintendent Fletcher. She was waiting in his office, gazing out of the room's only window with her arms folded. A pale rising sun cast shadows over the creases of her face.

'We need to talk, Jimmy,' she said, turning to him.

'That doesn't sound good.' He closed the door behind him, puzzled by her sour expression.

'It's not. Diane won't be with us for the rest of the week, perhaps even longer. All I am able to tell you is one of her children is unwell.'

'I'm sorry to hear that. Is it bad?'

'I don't have any more details than I gave you. Anything else you want to know will need to come from Diane herself, unless she informs me and instructs me to pass along an update.'

'Okay. I won't bother her with a call at a time like this, so I'll just shoot her a text later on.'

'Whatever you decide. You'll report to me directly while she's off. Also, Naomi Haskel wants to interview both Bish and Gul tomorrow. She has a general understanding of the Armstrong investigation, having pored over the case files and rummaging through HOLMES.'

'I don't suppose the PCC's outburst the other night helped matters.'

Fletcher raised her eyebrows. 'That was unfortunate.'

'It was idiotic, Marion. Interference of the highest order.'

'Naomi has her head screwed on. Benning has no influence over her because she comes to us from another area force. The man's a peacock, but when the dust settles, his bluster will be seen for what it was.'

'Did Naomi give you any indication which way she's leaning on this after having familiarised herself with the case?'

'No. And I'd be disappointed in her had she said anything at this early stage. Her review is still in its infancy, but don't worry. When she's finished with all her other interviews, it'll be myself and DCI Edwards who finally get to have our say. I'm happy with that arrangement.'

'Okay. Unless there are any surprises waiting for me at briefing, it's probably time for us to look harder at the Armstrongs. How much will I need to run by Naomi first?'

'At the very least, find out who she has left on her list to speak to. If you want to run background checks on their lives, that won't be an issue. But if you extend that to interviewing friends and family, you're going to need to coordinate with her.'

'No problem. But we have priority, yes? Ours is the ongoing and current investigation.'

'You mean you want dibs?' Fletcher smiled.

'If you like. Yes, I want dibs.'

'Then dibs you shall have. I'll make sure she knows. But speak with her, Jimmy. Give her that courtesy.'

'I will. I was going to without that rebuke, thank you.'

She held her hands up. 'Okay. I apologise if I went too far. As for everything Benning said, have a quiet word with Bish and Gul today. They both might be struggling with the burden of carrying that extra weight after his media outing.'

'I'll speak to them. Don't worry. And how's DCI Edwards taking it?'

'Alicia's fairly laid back about the whole matter. She's confident the review will support the conclusions of the team. Returning to Operation Insulate, I take it yesterday was somewhat of a disappointment?'

It had been. The unit had worked tirelessly following up on leads, setting and resolving actions, but still an entire shift had passed by without them seeing any significant progress. Bliss had decided against travelling anywhere, though he had kept in touch with developments in every area in which a relevant op had occurred. Across the course of the day, his feeling for the case had drifted from 50-50 to 70-30 against. But Fletcher didn't want to hear that, not when there was so much at stake.

'We take it on the chin and move on, ma'am,' he said. 'Today's another day.'

Fletcher raised an amused eyebrow. 'Ever thought of giving all this up in favour of philosophy, Jimmy?'

'You think I'd be any good at it?'

This time, she laughed. 'No, not really.'

At briefing, each member of the team laid out where they were with on-going actions. CCTV and ANPR sweeps had come up with nothing obvious regarding the night of the Sperling family murders. Phone data and social media scouring also proved to be a dead end. Additional information was still coming in from each of the areas in which potentially connected crimes had been committed. Meanwhile, DCs Gratton and Virgil were sifting through further HOLMES records in the hope of spotting something useful.

The connection between the Dorset victim, Hugh Worsley, and a London-based drugs baron, sucked Bliss in. He made actions for himself and Chandler to speak with both the National Crime Agency and the Met's drugs unit to see if they had any other intelligence linking the dealer, Marty Reid, to Mr Worsley. He'd also ask the same teams to find out if Reid was behaving erratically of late, perhaps acting as if he might be considering closing down his business in the nation's capital and moving on.

As his mind sought different pathways ahead, Bliss's thoughts turned once more to the case out in Essex. Another error from their killer – by now he was convinced it was the same man. The unique approach to taking people out revealed a lot about their quarry, but he was still only a human being. Which meant he was flawed, prone to making mistakes like everyone else. Bliss wondered if there was more to be gleaned from that particular case than had so far been uncovered. It continued to nag away at him.

He was, at best, a restless man. At his worst, he could become almost too much to bear. He knew this about himself, but put it down to human nature. To say he was currently disgruntled would have been an understatement, and he did not hide his frustrations.

The majority of murder investigations he'd been involved with were resolved within a day or two, the killer found quickly because their motives were easily identified. Most murders were not the well-planned actions of a psychopath. In his opinion, they had already tumbled to the motive here, as well. Only this time, that was as far as they had got. Even if all roads eventually led back to Marty Reid on the most circuitous of routes, that still didn't give them their killer. Or any evidence to prove Reid paid for the contracts.

Bliss closed the briefing with a niggling sense of frustration. He wanted to sniff things out in Essex, but also pull a few strings down in Poole; to go wherever these leads took them. But today was for bedding down, especially without DCI Warburton in the office. A period of consolidation was necessary for every case that reached this stage with no suspect identified. As he had told many officers in the past, taking a step back to look at the larger picture was never a bad thing. Often it was the point at which something telling was spotted.

Maybe he ought to consider philosophy after all.

Before sending DS Bishop and DC Ansari off to continue with their actions, he took them aside to discuss the Commissioner's Tuesday evening media briefing.

'I should have had a word with you both yesterday, but the truth is, I forgot all about it. I hold my hands up to that, and I'm sorry. I realise it's easier for me to say than you to do, but please try not to think about Benning and his venting the other day. He's puffing out his chest, that's all. Making himself look good in the eyes of the people who see him on TV or read about him in the news. The voters, in other words. That message was more for his and their benefit than it was to assist with our case. Focus on the simple fact that if Superintendent Haskel submits the report I expect from her, then Benning will be left unarmed. No stick with which to beat any of you involved with that op. Understood?'

They both responded by muttering the right things, but he knew he'd only papered over the cracks. The millstone was around their necks, not his. In their situation, he'd feel it in much the same way. The PCC was a fool, but his authority carried with it the power to wreak havoc – if only until he was proven wrong.

'So you and I are left to mix it up with the Met and the NCA today,' Chandler said to him afterwards. Knowing it was going to be a long day, she'd fetched them both lunch from the canteen to give them some fuel to burn. 'That'll either be exciting or like walking in treacle.'

She wasn't wrong. Bliss's own experience of both organisations led him to the exact same conclusion. If they were happy to include you and take you into their confidence, they could be a pleasure to work with. Equally, if they dragged their heels and left it all to 'channels', it might end up like pulling teeth.

'Sooner we get to it, the better,' he said, biting into his sausage sandwich. 'Either way. I'll start the conversation with both, you back me up and run any associated checks. Okay?'

Chandler nodded amiably. He smiled. His partner was game, no matter what the hindrances of trying to work with other authorities. For some reason, her attitude made him feel more positive about their prospects than he had only thirty minutes ago. Some days, it was enough to be just knuckling down to work, because it at least gave the illusion of making progress. There was still one dark cloud hanging right over their heads, however.

The Police and Crime Commissioner.

'We're going to have to watch some backs, Pen,' he said, after looking around to make sure they could not be overheard. 'Even a prick like Benning won't throw the book at everybody involved in that first investigation. My gut tells me he'll choose one from the top and one from the bottom.'

'You mean rank?' Chandler asked. When he nodded, she huffed and said, 'In that case, it'll be Fletcher for certain. She and the DCS don't get on, and I'm sure Feeley will have fed that upstairs to the Chief Constable.'

'That may be true, but Benning isn't necessarily going to run it by anybody before he makes up his own mind. Obviously he'll eventually discuss it with the CC, but possibly only after he's already reached his own conclusions. And of course, it also depends on whether he has friends or allies waiting in the wings to fill a specific void. Would you put it past him to give Fletcher the big E if he happened to have a superintendent mate looking to come in and snap up that vacancy?'

'Sadly, I wouldn't. So the same goes for Bish and Gul, I'm assuming.'

'Less so, I'd imagine. Might be a coin toss, but top and lower ranks will bear the burden.'

'I still can't believe he screwed us like that.'

More than a day later, Bliss was also recovering slowly from the move. 'It's one thing to come in and start bashing cops for making mistakes. But to reveal the name of the victims in the review case? That's utter madness, and completely reckless. Which reminds me: I've not said anything until now because it never felt like the right time yesterday, but I sent an email of complaint to the CC.'

Chandler turned her head so fast he thought it might swivel all the way round and spin right off her neck. If she'd been drinking at the time, she would have spat out her hot chocolate. 'You did what?!' she exclaimed. 'Jimmy, what the fuck?'

He pushed aside his own drink. 'I didn't think I had a choice, Pen. Effectively, Benning put our investigation at risk. He's laid it all out there, and if our doer hears about it he'll either go to ground or will, as we speak, be covering his arse. To my mind, that was something the CC needed to thrash out with the man.'

'And you reckon our Chief Constable is up to the task?'

'Actually, I do. He has a bit of steel about him. He came up the long and hard way. I can guarantee he has no time for the Commissioner, and will be only too happy to have a sharp stick to prod him with.'

'Except Benning has all the power.'

'He does for now, yes. But if he alienates the very people whose job it is to implement his policing strategies, then he's going to be a one-term man at best. I think that gives the CC some leverage. Enough to make a point, at least.'

'Perhaps.' Chandler nodded sullenly. 'But the damage is already done. Honestly, what did complaining achieve, other than adding another nemesis to your list? Jesus, you must have more arch-enemies than all the Avengers put together.'

'You mean John Steed and Emma Peel?' Bliss said, feigning confusion. 'What have they got to do with it?'

Chandler pulled a face and stuck out her tongue. 'Yes. Bowlerman and Catsuitwoman. Had to be those Avengers I meant. Nothing from this century for an old git like you, obviously.'

'Did you know you scrunched your nose up when you get haughty?' he teased.

'Oh, really?'

'There you go again. You look like a pug with flatulence.'

Chandler gave him two bug eyes and a matching number of fingers, signalling the end of that particular discussion.

Bliss regarded his partner fondly. She was good for him. Not only could she always make him laugh, even during the toughest moments, but she also made him work hard for every advantage. Chandler pushed him like nobody else ever had or could, her influence making him both a better detective and a man. But at what cost to her own career? It was something he'd been asking himself for some time.

EIGHTEEN

The morning passed by in a blur as the team pulled and prodded at the threads of their operation, unable to gather the various strands together with any degree of satisfaction. For Bliss and Chandler, their time was spent successfully engaging both the Met and the NCA, though neither bore any fruit.

The Met's drugs unit had a lot to say about Marty Reid. A Glaswegian by birth, Reid had come across the border as a nine-year-old when his father got a job working in the print for a major newspaper group. Less than a year later, the trade suffered the largest cull in its history, and to make ends meet, Marty's father took on odd jobs for a variety of south London villains. A tough and battle-scarred brawler, Billy Reid gained considerable notoriety in the late eighties and all the way through the nineties. Eleven months into the new millennium, he met his match by bringing only his fists, elbows, knees, and forehead to a gunfight. According to intelligence reports, Marty soon followed in his father's footsteps, earning himself a reputation as a vicious and ruthless bastard on his journey to the top.

The conversation ended with Bliss's Met contact insisting they would look into connections between Reid and each of the names

Bliss had provided. They would also talk to their informants to find out what the word was on the street concerning Reid's near-future plans. As far as the Met officers were concerned, Reid was thriving and showing no outward signs of jacking it all in and moving on.

Nobody Bliss spoke to from his old agency was able to provide more information than he already had. They matched the Met's promises and told him they would pass everything up to the agency's Serious and Serial Crimes team. Knowing the agency as he did, he anticipated a response within the week. The one thing he hadn't expected was an appearance from the head of the SSC later that same day. The moment Bliss laid eyes on him, he knew his operation had stumbled upon something significant.

The first thing most people noticed about Frank Rogers was the unsightly scar that ran the length of his entire face, missing his eye by the smallest fraction. The first thing Bliss noticed, however, was how much the man had aged since they'd last met. The NCA head of department had been shown up to the conference room after receiving his visitor badge on a green lanyard. Bliss marched over to shake the man's hand as he stood patiently facing out of the glass walls.

'It's good to see you again, Frank.'

'You too, Jimmy. Been a while.'

'Too long, pal. How're Laura and Debbie?'

'Both well, thanks. Laura is still in treatment, but she's getting there.'

Frank's estranged wife and son had been murdered, his daughter abducted. At the time, he ran his own debt collecting agency, but having been an ex-detective, his friends on the force were not shy in plying him with information from the outset of the manhunt. Then the abductor upped the ante by insisting he would deal only with Frank, and leaving his first murder victim as a gift for those on his trail. In pursuit of his daughter, Frank had almost been overcome by the depths of darkness he'd needed to wallow in to establish a rapport with the man who had taken her. As he made a final desperate bid to free his child, his face was sliced open with a blade. Bearing the ugly five-inch weal was a price he was more than willing to have paid.

Although physically unharmed, psychologically his daughter remained locked away inside her own head for long periods of time. Debbie, a friend of the family, stepped up to become part of that reduced household. Frank had once confessed how much the new woman in his life had held him together as his entire existence crumbled to pieces. Bliss was happy to hear the couple were still an item, the pair working hard to keep Frank's daughter from falling apart.

'Are you seeing genuine progress?' he pushed. The two men were not close, but in brushing up against each other in the past, they had each felt a kindred spirit in the other.

Rogers nodded emphatically. 'It was always going to take time,' he said softly. 'What she lost, what she went through, what she saw, what she imagined… you can't survive horrors like that with your psyche untouched. I wear the physical scar of that conflict, but Laura carries the mental ones inside her head and has to confront them each and every day. Me, I can choose not to look in the mirror. She can't switch it off. Even now. But she's getting better at managing. She's learning to adapt, using the skills taught to her by a number of excellent therapists. They are all confident she can turn her life around. They tell me the darkness will never go away entirely, but with hard work, she'll eventually spend more time in the light.'

Bliss could only imagine what each day in the hands of a psychopath had done to the then twelve-year-old Laura Rogers.

But if she was anything like her father, she had a better than even chance of making it to the other side.

'And so to why you're here,' he said, gesturing towards a chair.

Rogers refused with a shake of the head. Not a big man, his presence nonetheless dominated the area beyond whatever space he occupied. 'The drive up gave me a sore arse and an even more painful back, so no thanks. I wonder I don't have piles as it is. Plus, I think you know why I'm here.'

'I'm hoping my conversation earlier threw up a red flag or two.'

'It certainly did. Thing is, Jimmy, you're not the only one to have spotted this particular MO. I've been mulling over a few cases in recent weeks, wondering if they are more than they first appeared to be.'

Bliss felt a warm glow of satisfaction. He and his team looked to have been on the right track, after all. 'That's interesting. Are these the same investigations we've been looking into?'

'Some of them, but we have one or two different cases that took my eye. I've been analysing them with three other agency officers. So far, we've mostly stumbled into dead ends. But we've also picked up some intel we were not aware of before we began.'

'Such as?'

'You ever heard of the Lightning Rod?'

'I'm aware of what a lightning rod is and what it does. But I'm guessing you mean something quite different.'

'Indeed I do. Fact is, we're picking up on street chatter suggesting there's a human form out there somewhere. Evidently, he's some kind of invincible fixer-come-hitman. Did you ever see a TV show called *Ray Donovan*?'

Bliss shook his head.

'It was set out in the States, but when I first heard about our Lightning Rod, it reminded me of this Ray Donovan character. A fixer who does everything in his power to protect those who employ him. Essentially, he protects them from other villains as well as the police. The difference in the possible reality we're facing is that in the show, everybody knew Donovan existed. Friend and foe alike. Our man is a ghost. If he exists at all.'

Bliss was sceptical. 'Sounds like it could be some kind of urban myth.'

Rogers nodded. 'That's what we thought at first. But there were other whispers, and they didn't all come from the same direction.'

'Nobody at the Met mentioned him to me.'

'I've not told the Met about him.' Rogers spread his hands. 'You know what it's like, Jimmy. You never can tell who is trustworthy and who isn't. Who might be on the payroll of a face, who might be taking money from journalists? I'm sharing it with you because I think we're after the same man. I came here today to discuss an exchange of intelligence. I'm not suggesting we team up as a formal joint task force, but let's make it easier on ourselves by having all the information to hand. You've already provided us with several leads to think about. Now I'm giving you the Lightning Rod.'

Bliss regarded him with interest. 'You're putting a great deal of faith in rumour, Frank. That's unlike you.'

Rogers ran a hand across his face. 'Look, this position was offered to me on the back of the work I did on my own daughter's abduction and the killing spree that monster Swain went on. I made psychological connections I never imagined I had in me during those dark days. I might even have become more of a pure psychopath than the sick fuck I was hunting. Part of what I do now is to overlook the obvious, search for the… what was it you called them… the anomalies?'

Nodding, Bliss said, 'Yes. When time is getting away from us, while my team works through the actions, I peer around the edges. So I know what you mean. You heard mention of this Lightning Rod and got a glimmer of interest.'

'To the point where I can't let go until I've run it down as far as I can. I think he's our man. Only, as of right now, I have absolutely no idea who he acts as a lightning rod for.'

'The name Marty Reid came up in our investigation,' Bliss said.

Rogers decided to take a seat after all. He sat down heavily with a grunt. Winced before speaking. 'I saw that in the notes I was given. The connection looks to be shaky. What credence do you give it?'

'Enough to still be interested. But we're agreed about the way our man works, right? When he has a contract to fulfil, he tries his level best to make it seem like something other than murder.'

'Absolutely. That's why these cases have not been on our radar until now. Accidents and murder-suicides don't attract the same attention as ongoing murder investigations. Accidents in particular slip by us, and for good reason. Except some accidents now seem as if they were deliberate acts. And while the murder aspect of murder-suicides draws teams like your own, the killer in those cases is also dead, so the investigation can't push by the incident itself. You can examine it, look at what led to it, but there's no next play to consider because there's no suspect to go after. It stymies an operation, and in some cases the investigating teams can become a little lax.'

Bliss jerked his head up. 'I assume you're aware of the case review we're undergoing? And the over-reaction of our PCC? Were you talking about my team just then, Frank?'

Rogers regarded him with surprise. 'No. Not at all. I didn't aim that remark at anybody in particular. It's a perfectly natural thing for a team to do.'

'Yeah, well, in our case, nobody got lax. Nobody fucked up. The evidence for murder by an outsider simply wasn't there.'

'Then why are we even talking about it?'

The two men paused, then smiled at each other. 'Sorry,' Bliss said. 'I react badly when I think someone is having a pop at my unit.'

'I'm very glad to hear it. Loyalty coming back down the line is virtually a thing of the past. Now, Jimmy, what do you say to this intel exchange I suggested. You up for it?'

'I'll have to run it by our Super, but as deputy SIO, I'm all for it.'

'Where is your SIO in all this?'

'DCI Diane Warburton. She's absent due to a family illness.'

'Okay. Well, can you have a word with Superintendent Fletcher now? If she agrees, we can put our heads together and provide a briefing for your team before I go back and have words with my own.'

Bliss jabbed a finger at him. 'You already had the name of my Super. I'm betting you also knew my immediate boss was DCI Warburton.'

Rogers chuckled. It brought colour to his ashen face. 'I didn't have time to find out everything, Jimmy, but I wasn't going to drive up here completely blind.'

'I'd forgotten how wily you were.'

About to say more, Bliss was interrupted by the ringing of his work mobile. He accepted the call. Closed his eyes as he listened, hardly daring to breathe. He felt his hand shake a little as he ended the conversation and replaced the phone inside his trouser pocket.

'We have another one,' Rogers said, reading his face accurately.

'Looks like it. A young girl out jogging yesterday morning fell down the steep side of a rocky hill, smashing her body to pieces before ending up lying in a stream. She didn't make it.'

'What about that is of interest to us? Aren't we looking for families?'

'Yes, although the alert request also stipulated suspicious deaths of any kind. This was brought to our attention because of its peculiar nature and the MO.'

'So the locals are saying it was staged?'

Bliss blew out his breath before nodding. 'It *was* staged. It was murder. And this time we know for sure because we have a witness.'

NINETEEEN

SINNINGTON SAT ON THE edge of the North Riding National Park in North Yorkshire. The river Seven passed through the village, feeding many tributary streams, including the one in which twenty-three-year-old Taylor Sweeting had died the previous morning.

Though the path she had taken around a spinney rose high, it was wide enough for two people to pass comfortably by side by side. Bliss was blowing hard by the time the slope levelled out. His vain attempt to conceal it led to a coughing fit. To his chagrin, neither his partner nor Frank Rogers seemed unduly affected by the climb.

The witness had pointed the police in the right direction. More than twenty-four hours after the incident, the path was useless to them in terms of evidence, but photos provided by local CSI revealed definite scuff marks traversing the rutted lines created over time by many thousands of pounding feet. The spot had remained taped off, encompassing a break in the foliage from which the killer had emerged. Crime scene investigators would have combed the area for footwear impressions and discards, such as cigarette ends, gum or sweet wrappers, bottles, ring-pulls;

anything a person might thoughtlessly dispose of while they waited. Bliss knew if items had been found, they had not come from their man. The killer had made mistakes, but being careless with minor details was not in his makeup.

Rogers turned slowly on the spot, scanning high and low. He appeared to be getting a visual impression of their surroundings, but probably doing more thinking than anything else. Having turned a full circle, Rogers nodded to himself.

'Care to share your early thoughts now that we've seen the SOC?' he asked, looking at both detectives in turn.

'We've seen only half,' Bliss reminded him, turning to gaze down the steep drop. 'But my first thought was to wonder how our killer knew where and when Taylor ran.'

'He had to have been waiting for her, knowing she'd pass by at some point,' Chandler said.

'Correct. Which means he knew her route, her approximate timings. Also that she exercised alone. What does that tell us?'

'That he's a patient man,' Rogers said. 'He must have watched her on at least two previous occasions, possibly more. He couldn't have been certain of those details otherwise. He was spying on the victim, stalking her. He clearly had a plan and stuck to it. His was no impulsive move. He waited for the precise moment to strike.'

'What did he do next?' Bliss asked Chandler, who immediately checked her phone.

'According to the witness statement, the man stood in place for a minute or so after Taylor went over the side. He glanced around on a couple of occasions to make sure nobody else was on the path, but mostly he gazed down at her.'

'And where was our witness while all this was going on?' Rogers asked.

Chandler pointed across to the wooded area rising up in staggered stages on the other side of the stream. 'The witness is a twitcher. Birds are fairly active early on in the day, and he wanted to get settled into his hide before they went scavenging for food.'

'Was he able to describe the man he saw?'

'Let me see… yes, but it's pretty generic. Taller and larger than average, but the witness was mostly drawn to the poor victim. He described the bloke as a hiker.'

'Skin colour?'

'White.'

'Okay. So our killer slams into the girl, watches her as she tumbles down, then hangs around to survey his handiwork. Most likely, he took time to see if she moved at all once she'd finished falling. Then he made his way down to the stream, where he crouched close to the victim's body. Remind me, did he scramble down the side or take the pathway back?'

Chandler read from her phone screen once more, scrolling through pages. 'Back along the path, then through the trees and walking on the rocks out to the edge of the stream. Our bird man watched him all the way. He didn't dare call anybody while the killer remained close by. The man crouched by his victim's side for about ten minutes before finally leaving.'

'Did SOCO get any decent footprint casts?' Bliss asked. He waited patiently while his partner navigated her way to another file.

'They got a few, but nothing they consider fresh enough to be our man's. Up top, the marks were too vague, and due to the rocks and stones lining the stream, our man didn't need to walk along any patches of damp soil.'

'This is an ideal spot for a kill,' Rogers said. 'If you're dressed as a hiker, you blend in. The clothing helps disguise your appearance. You can pause anywhere, go anywhere, and nobody will think twice about it if they come across you. All you have to do is secrete yourself away once you reach the right location, wait for your target to approach, make sure nobody else is around to see or hear, set yourself, and then act decisively. Checking on her afterwards down in the stream took some neck.' He turned to look at Chandler. 'Penny, what does our witness have to say about it all? Was he convinced it was intentional from the very beginning?'

'Actually, no. When the two first collided, he couldn't be certain. But then the man stood there doing nothing to help. Neither did he seem remotely agitated about what he'd done. Our Twitcher said he'd been about to call out when he realised he might have witnessed a murder and not a tragic accident.'

Bliss could see the NCA officer's brain ticking over. It was in the eyes, the way they narrowed and stared off into the distance even when looking directly at someone. Rogers came with a reputation. He'd been an outstanding cop, but his work on the investigation into his wife's and son's murder and the abduction of his daughter had elevated his status to a whole new stratosphere. Having subsequently accepted an offer to head up the new Serious and Serial Crimes team at the NCA, he'd gone on to use his gifts to tease out at least three serial-killers that nobody else had been aware existed. The two had previously met on several occasions, but having never had the opportunity to work alongside the man who was by now a genuine legend, Bliss was happy to take a step back to observe him at work.

'This man we're after has a blind spot,' Rogers said, following a lengthy pause. 'He planned this meticulously. He took time to get to know Taylor Sweeting, and he executed his plan ruthlessly. And yet, for all that, he made no allowance for our bird watcher. On my way up to Peterborough, I phoned a colleague and had him read me out one or two examples of other potential murders we suspect this man of carrying out. In the case of him hanging his target victim to make it look like suicide, it was only after completing his job that he realised the cord was a little thin and fragile to work as he'd intended. It did the job when manually pulling it tight, but if the pretence was going to work, the cord was too insubstantial for dropping the male victim off the balcony. He was alert enough to make the necessary correction, but by then he'd already dropped a bollock. Likewise your two cases. Using the exact same MO in an area covered by the same investigators, CSI, and pathologist, is poor on his part.'

'So, what's his blind spot?' Chandler asked.

'Hubris. At least, that's my preliminary conclusion. His sureness exceeds his competence. Chummy's determination to steer us in a different direction in all these examples gives him a sense of pride, leading to an over-confidence he simply can't live up to. He's human – they all are, after all – yet doesn't allow for human weakness, human oversight, human lapses.'

Chandler let out a low whistle and said, 'Wow! It's almost like listening to a certain DI who goes by the name of Bliss. Except he'd throw in a bit of slang to try confusing all of us who weren't born within the sound of Bow bells.'

Frank Rogers laughed for the first time since they'd been in his company. He was not a tall man, yet he was nonetheless imposing. Broad and fit, with lean features, the premature ageing revealed itself most of all in his hair and skin tone. Bliss continued to be impressed by him.

'Oh, I revert to type myself when I'm not on the job,' Rogers said, his shoulders still heaving. 'By the way, those bells are not in Bow itself, which is in the heart of east London. It refers to St Mary-le-Bow, a church on Cheapside in the city of London itself. You might hear them on a good day with a favourable wind from where Jimmy and I were born, but it's doubtful.'

'Doesn't stop him from using all that "apples and pears" and "dog and bone" cobblers,' Chandler said, throwing Bliss a look of distaste.

Rogers narrowed his gaze. 'And neither should it. Slang was the language of the streets where we were raised. I've learned to tune it out professionally, as I found too many senior officers looking down their noses at me.'

Chandler gestured towards her boss. 'Ah, well, there you go. Vive la différence. You cared what they thought. Jimmy never has.'

'Enough lip from you,' Bliss told her with a wry grin. Then he looked across at Rogers. 'And how do you happen to know where I was born and raised? I don't recall ever discussing that with you in the past.'

'I told you before, I used my travel time wisely,' Rogers told him. 'I don't go into something where potentially I will team up with fellow investigators without knowing a bit about them.'

'What do you know about me, then?' Chandler challenged him, hands on hips.

'You, Penny, are a puzzle.'

'Really? What makes you say that? I've always thought of myself as an open book.'

'You may well be in your personal life. But you've been a DS far longer than your career path would imply. I can find nothing in your records to suggest you were held back by senior officers for something you did wrong, which leads me to conclude it's self-inflicted. You haven't sought promotion to DI or beyond, and I find that curious.'

'I've been telling her that for years,' Bliss said, waving a hand at his colleague. 'She had it in her to go all the way, but for some reason she's happy working as a sergeant.'

'Because it's we sergeants who do all the bloody work,' Chandler said defensively. Then she hiked a thumb in Bliss's direction. 'Mind you, when you have this one as a mentor and inspiration, it's hard to believe the low standards required of a DI these days.'

'It's not for want of encouragement,' Bliss said to Rogers, ignoring the barb. 'She ought to have moved on and up many moons ago. We had this conversation not so long ago. I just can't seem to persuade her.'

Rogers gave a crooked grin. 'Perhaps you're not trying hard enough, Jimmy. After all, who would want to lose a DS of Penny's experience and calibre?'

'Please don't make her head any bigger, Frank. We'll have to widen all the doorways back at the factory. And where's she going to get a decent hat afterwards? Believe me, there's nothing I'd like more than to shift her out of my team. She takes no notice of me whatsoever, and you've heard the way she talks to me.'

'Sounds to me as if you two have the ideal partnership. You want the best for each other, but you work so well together you don't want to let go. It's admirable in these trying times.'

Bliss threw his arms up in the air. 'Seriously, I urge her to sign up for the courses. I had another DS in mind to take over the unit when I finally handed in my card, but he's withdrawn. There's no one I'd rather have doing so now than Pen. She would have been my first choice all along, but I know how she feels about stepping up.'

With a non-committal grunt, Rogers said, 'Time will tell, I suppose. She may just surprise you one day.'

Chandler threw both of them a look of disgust. 'Do you two mind not talking about me as if I wasn't here? And can we please move off the subject?'

'You're right, Penny. That was mean. And given what you said last, I suggest we take a look down below before heading off to York.'

'What's in York?' Chandler asked.

'Pathology,' Rogers replied. 'It's where Taylor's body was taken for the PM.'

'You certainly do your research, don't you, Frank?'

'I find it pays to, yes.'

'We could also do with asking a few questions of the Taylor family and the investigation team up here,' Bliss said. 'Looks like we're having an overnighter. That okay with you, Frank, or do you have to get back?'

'No, I'll stay on with you two. I'll give my wife a call a bit later with the good news.'

'I just need to have somebody look in on my dog. How about you, Pen?' Bliss asked. 'Shrek going to be all right with you spending the night with two red-blooded males?'

Chandler made a show of peering around. 'I see Frank here, but is somebody else joining us?'

He laughed.

'I mean it, Jimmy. I still haven't got over that time you mentioned your ball sack being filled with dust. I doubt there's any red blood pumping through your system at all now.'

Rogers joined in with the laughter. 'You two are a riot,' he said.

'You have no idea,' Chandler replied. 'Oh, and thank you, Frank. You're a gent.'

He frowned. 'For what?'

'For not calling me Pen.'

TWENTY

The pathologist's report gave them little more than they knew or had already surmised. Taylor Sweeting had suffered catastrophic injuries during her fall. In addition to broken blood vessels, numerous shattered bones, multiple skull fractures, dislocated joints, and a fractured hip, the young woman had also received a collapsed lung and unsurvivable damage to her brain. Cause of death had yet to be declared, but the pathologist who carried out the post-mortem told them it could have been any of two or three different injuries.

Bliss was of the opinion that the rest of their working day would be best spent in conversation with the investigation team, leaving their victim's family until the following morning, when their grief might be more bearable. Taylor had still lived at home with her parents, who were naturally taking the news of their daughter's murder extremely hard.

When they left York hospital, they'd headed straight up the A19 to Northallerton, arriving at the relatively new area police and fire HQ shortly before its Major Crime Unit team was due to clock off for the day. The operational Senior Investigating Officer, Superintendent Krish Laghari, volunteered to stay on in order to brief his visitors. A proud Sikh, Laghari sported an official police turban, complete with the badge of the area force he served with pride. Introductions made, he outlined the current status of the case.

'Due to the sheer good fortune of having a witness, a Mr Sampson, who described a murder and not an accidental fall, we were able to get a full forensic team on scene soon after the incident occurred. Our Major Crime team followed up immediately by questioning the man. The victim had ID on her, which was another stroke of luck. For us, at least. I'd say those fortuitous breaks gave us a healthy lead on what might otherwise have been a protracted process. By all accounts, had it not been for Sampson, we would never have known we were looking for a murderer.'

'What, if anything, were you able to glean from Taylor's family?' Bliss asked.

'We have an FLO with them, of course. Other than a couple of brief questions to ascertain if Taylor had been threatened, or had any known enemies, or if the family members had noticed any strangers around or suspicious vehicles on the street, we've given them time and room in which to mourn. Our FLO tells us nobody in the family has so far mentioned anything of interest to our investigation. It clearly came as a shock, entirely out of the blue. By all accounts, Taylor was a popular young lady, unknown to us, didn't appear to associate with the wrong crowd. She studied at the university of Hull, but was living back home for the summer break. She is – sorry, was – a competitive runner at both 800 and 1500 metres. Evidently, she runs that particular path because of its slopes and uneven surface, believing it gave her an edge in terms of endurance on the track.'

'So, she ran the same one every day,' Frank Rogers said.

'Actually, twice a day. It's a circular route of about two miles in total, so she ran approximately four miles a day.'

'Always in the same direction? If it's circular, I'm assuming she could choose clockwise or anti-clockwise.'

Superintendent Laghari raised his eyebrows. 'I must confess, I don't know the answer to that question. If it was asked by a member of my team, then it will be in the case file which I can send across to your email addresses.'

'I can't imagine it not being asked. Taylor would, of course, have still passed by the spot where she was attacked, no matter which direction she chose to run. The difference in her time of arrival at the spot where he hid would be considerable, though.'

'If it's not in the notes, I'll have the relevant officers asked about it first thing in the morning. If it wasn't asked, I'll make sure they do so.'

'No need,' Bliss told him. 'We'll be speaking to the family ourselves tomorrow. I'm assuming that's okay with you?'

'Of course. I offered our full cooperation, Inspector. You have complete access to our unit and their investigation. The family is part of that.'

'Thank you. I'll make sure to run it by them if we don't find it in the case notes.'

'I take it you're still convinced this is the work of the man you're looking for?'

Bliss paused for a moment to consider. 'Convinced? No. I do think it's highly likely. However, there's one thing we have to ascertain and one issue still bothering me.'

'And they are?'

'Those deemed to be the primary target victims have links to criminal organisations. At first glance, it's hard to see where Taylor Sweeting fits in with that pattern. What also bothers me is why her family is still alive. In the past, we've seen others taken out alongside the true target. That doesn't mean she isn't another victim of the same killer, but it would suggest we need to expand our search parameters. If he's taking out individuals when he feels that's appropriate or best fits his planning, then there might be a whole range of potential victims we've not yet considered.'

*

Upon arrival at the home of Mr and Mrs Sweeting the following morning, the first thing Bliss did was to chat with the Family Liaison Officer. For reasons he was unable to fathom, the public had many misconceptions about the role of an FLO. They were assumed to be junior in terms of experience, whose responsibilities stretched no further than keeping the family company and making them cups of tea. In fact, over the years, the role had become a critical function of serious crime investigations. All such officers were skilled investigators, gathering evidence and intel from the family members, while at the same time relaying information and acting as the first line of support beyond the immediate family. It was a taxing job, requiring compassion, sensitivity, tact, and diplomacy; a job Bliss knew he would fail to do well.

DC Wayne Peacock's brief report had nothing further to add to the details in the case file. In compliance with the family's wishes, he'd not stayed overnight with them. Instead he'd returned early, but only ten minutes ahead of Bliss, Chandler and Rogers. Neither Mr and Mrs Sweeting nor their now only child, Phillip, had any night-time revelations to share with the police. As far as they were concerned, the attack on their daughter had to be the unprovoked work of a madman.

'Do they know what we suspect?' Chandler asked.

The North Yorkshire officer shook his head. 'We felt it was unnecessary to pass on that information. They have enough to contend with.'

'A good decision,' Rogers remarked. 'I take it you've been briefed about our suspicions?'

'I have. Can't say I see it right now, but I suppose people can surprise you.'

'Explain that to me, please.'

'Your victimology involves vague connections to criminal enterprise. I can't see that in the case of Taylor. There's nothing I've seen or heard to even suggest it.'

'That may be because neither her parents nor her brother were aware of it,' Bliss said, though his own thinking had been along the same lines. 'They can't discuss something they're unaware of.'

Rogers nodded along. 'Inspector Bliss is bang on. I'm inclined to think her connection – if there is one – has nothing to do with her home life. There's bugger all in this neck of the woods anywhere close to being big enough. No, my guess is we ought to be looking towards Hull, where she's being educated and where she spends a good amount of her life.'

In the discussion that followed with Taylor's parents – their son having been dismissed from the room – it was Bliss who steered them towards Taylor's time at university.

'Did Taylor share student accommodation with anybody?' he asked.

The couple sat close together on a sofa, knees touching. Old before their time, made vulnerable by grief and sudden loss. It was Carl Sweeting who looked up to answer. 'She was one of four renting out a property close to the main campus. Her BSc was in Sports and Exercise Science, and at least one of her housemates was on the same course.'

'Are the student accommodations co-ed?'

Sweeting shook his head. 'No. Female only.'

'Did Taylor get along with those she shared with, as far as you know?'

'Yes,' he said. 'With the possible exception of one girl. I think her name is Rose. The way Taylor spoke about her suggested she could be quite difficult.'

Bliss eyed his colleagues before continuing. 'In reference to what?'

'The girl was clearly troubled. Troubled and privileged.'

'I take it she came from money?'

'Yes. I mean, we're comfortable enough, but this girl's parents were known to be one-percenters. Evidently, she dabbled in drugs and Taylor believed she was spending far too much time with different men.'

'Are we talking about a healthy interest in sex or something potentially more unlawful?'

In the pause that followed, Christine Sweeting sniffled, dabbed her eyes with a tissue, before saying, 'There was some talk about her possibly being an escort. I've seen photos of her, and she was quite stunning to look at. In a tarty sort of way.'

Bliss wet his lips. Now they were getting somewhere. Here was a potential link to a crime family turning out escorts. He'd had plenty of experience of dealing with these low-life elements. A young student lured first by drugs and then being blackmailed into something far more invasive was not unheard of. Yet he had to remind himself this was a fellow student, not Taylor herself.

'Did your daughter ever express deeper concerns about this girl, Rose? Was she worried about these unsavoury elements drifting into her own life as a direct result of her housemate's proclivities?'

'I don't think so, no. If she was anxious about that, she never spoke about it. Taylor didn't dislike her. Not at all. She was just… different.'

'And none of the other girls were approached by those Rose mingled with? As far as you're aware.'

'Not to our knowledge. No.'

It was possible, though. Something Taylor might not have wished to share with her family. Her being more involved than she had admitted to was also worth exploring. Had the young woman been mixed up in the drugs scene? Had she been lured into the seedy world of escorts?

If that was the case, his team would need to rely on the local unit for intelligence more than he had hoped. There wasn't much they didn't know about those kinds of services back in Peterborough, including the men and woman who ran the show. Up here, he wouldn't know where to start. The thought nudged out an idea.

'You ever worked this region?' he asked Frank Rogers.

Rogers shook his head. 'Not yet. I dare say I'll eventually cover every major county in the UK, but no, not North Yorkshire so far.'

'Fair enough. But the NCA will have intel on the gangs in the area.'

'Naturally.'

Bliss turned back to the grieving couple, whose lives had been shattered so completely by their daughter's murder it was hard to understand how they were both still functioning. 'Thank you for your time. I gave you our condolences before we began, but I just want you to know that wasn't merely part of how we handle the family of victims in such cases. It was genuine. Nobody should lose a child in such a dreadful manner. All I can do is assure you that we will do our level best to find out who did this, and to bring them to justice.'

'Thank you,' Taylor's father said, looking down at his wringing hands. 'I can't help wondering if this was a case of mistaken identity. Either that or the man who took our Taylor's life is some twisted psychopath killing people at random. But if that were the case, wouldn't we have heard about other victims?'

'Not if Taylor was the first,' his wife said, reaching for his hand.

It was an insightful comment, though Bliss believed Mrs Sweeting to be wrong. He was convinced this was the work of their man. And the starting point for the next phase of his investigation was to locate Taylor's housemate, Rose.

TWENTY-ONE

THE OVERNIGHTER HAD GONE well. They'd found a charming B&B that came without a drinks licence, but stood less than a hundred feet from a quaint old pub with a thatched roof. Before joining Rogers and Chandler in the bar, Bliss had called Sandra Bannister.

'I thought you might still have the hump with me,' she said with a strained laugh.

He considered leading her on, but decided to be straight. 'No, you and I are fine. I'm not entirely unfamiliar with that kind of angry outburst myself. The fact is, the Commissioner blew his wad too soon. And because of that, our man may now be aware we're onto him.'

'I did wonder about that. It seemed pretty reckless.'

'It was bloody moronic. He has a point to prove, but he's going about it the wrong way.'

'Hmm. Listen, Jimmy, we're expecting an update briefing later today. I could follow up with a pointed question or two, if you like.'

Bliss smiled to himself. Putting Benning under pressure sounded good. 'If you get the opportunity, toss him a couple of googlies. I'd like to see his own error aired in public. As for the briefing itself, I wouldn't hold my breath if I were you. We're spinning a lot of plates, and we have a working hypothesis, but without any firm leads as yet. Today might throw us a few crumbs, but I'm doubtful. There's nothing I can give you at this stage, other than to say this goes much wider and deeper than we'd imagined.'

Bannister thanked him. When he ended the call, he smiled once more. The PCC had used the media to make vague promises, which in reality were less than subtle threats. Hopefully, the nest Bannister intended to stir up was full of vipers as opposed to hornets. It was time to put Benning on the back foot.

Following a pleasant dinner and several drinks, the three of them had called it a night not long after 10.30pm. The conversation had flowed, but in truth, he and Chandler had done most of the listening. Rogers spoke eloquently about the results his unit had delivered, before elaborating more in reference to his own daughter's case. He admitted to being surprised at how effective he'd found therapy. There were more scabs to pick at than he'd anticipated, the largest of them covering the wound left behind inside the darker regions of his mind.

Nietzsche had warned that those who fought monsters needed to take care lest they themselves became monsters. He'd come closer than most during the manhunt for his little girl and had stared long and hard into his own particular abyss. But he'd emerged intact, if not fully functional. His daughter, Laura, had suffered psychological trauma at the hands of two genuinely monstrous people, leaving her with emotional wounds infinitely worse than his own.

Bliss admired the way Rogers was able to discuss both the case and the turmoil of its aftermath. Yet there were a couple of times when the man's voice modulated, faltering on the point of breaking as he became consumed with both anger and, perhaps, just a little guilt. Bliss understood both all too well.

After leaving the Sweetings that morning, they stopped for a late breakfast at a café in Pickering, 15 minutes east of Sinnington. Ignoring the tables outside in favour of cool air-conditioning, over an all-day breakfast they discussed the best way to proceed. When they had reached an agreement, each of them made a phone call. Frank Rogers asked for help from his team in identifying Taylor Sweeting's housemate, Rose. Chandler spoke with Bishop to get an update on progress. Meanwhile, Bliss made contact with all relevant area forces for the latest developments. He drew a blank on all of them.

Chandler's report was less than enthusiastic. Back at HQ, the team had made little headway. They were running into problems finding anybody close to the Armstrongs willing to be spoken to again. She explained that Superintendent Haskel had already been in touch with previous interviewees, her questions confined to the investigation and the investigators.

'The DSI has unintentionally muddied the waters for us,' Chandler said to Bliss. 'We might find the odd one or two who are happy to go through it all again, but by and large people just want to forget about it. Oh, and Bish says to tell you Fletcher is on the war path.'

He winced. 'I've already ducked half a dozen calls from her. I know what it's about. She told me to stay put while Diane was off work, not to stray too far from HQ. I don't think a day and a half – and an overnighter at that – up in North Yorkshire was what she had in mind.'

'If you have to get back,' Rogers said, 'I can hire a car and travel onwards to speak with our girl Rose.'

Bliss was impressed. 'You found her already, eh? That was quick.'

'I have a good team doing the grunt work for me. Rose Martyn lives with a boyfriend in Doncaster.'

'Which happens to be on the way back. Straight run down the A1 afterwards. We're in, Frank.'

'If you're sure. Just because we're working together on this doesn't mean we're joined at the hip.'

'It's not a problem,' Bliss assured him. 'Besides, we're running on fumes with this bloody investigation, and this girl, Rose, may well have some vital information for us in respect of Taylor.'

'I hope so,' Rogers said. 'Because as things stand, the Sweeting girl doesn't fit. We need to establish a link between her and criminal enterprise. No matter how remote.'

*

If Rose Martyn's boyfriend had been at home and not at work tending bar in Sheffield, she might never have admitted to working as an escort. As it was, when Bliss pointed out that the truth would remain between them, but could be everything they needed in order to find Taylor Sweeting's killer, she relented and allowed them to question her fully without any legal representation.

'At first I was just a companion,' she said, head down, picking at her fingernail polish, unwilling to look any of them in the eye. She wore a T-shirt and shorts, her bare legs tucked up beneath her as she hugged herself in a small armchair. 'I swear that's all I ever intended to do. But then the people who make the bookings and drive you to homes or hotels or whatever, started putting the squeeze on me. A woman whose name I never learned, but who seemed to be close to those in charge, told me one of the companions had asked her after our night out together if the next time he booked me he could have me spend a few hours with him afterwards.'

'What was your initial reaction?' Chandler asked.

'I told them to get stuffed. I said I didn't mind playing the role of a girlfriend, but I wasn't a whore.'

'So what happened next?'

'I did a couple more bookings. Then a man asked me about taking it further. He said if I was bothered about what others thought of me having sex with men for money, I was being naïve. He told me if anybody discovered I was an escort, they'd think that was what I did, anyway.'

'In other words, he suggested you might as well get paid for it if you were going to be convicted in the minds of anyone who found out.'

'Exactly. I said there was still the little problem of actually having to have sex with these men. That it didn't matter what anybody else thought, it was more about my own self respect.'

'And their response?'

'I thought they'd accepted it. But then they told me one of my regulars had insisted he wouldn't choose me again if sex wasn't on the menu. And others were starting to grumble about the same thing. I stood to lose a few hundred quid a week if the agency dumped me, when, as they pointed out, I could be making a thousand or more.'

'At which point you gave in,' Chandler said, with no condemnation in her voice.

'Yes. In the end, I decided it was just… just sex, you know?'

'I do. And I understand. That kind of money can be very tempting.'

The girl snorted derisively. 'I bet you wouldn't be, though. I bet no amount of cash could buy your body.'

Chandler edged forward on the chair she had taken. 'I'm not you, Rose. I wasn't ever placed in that situation. The people making your bookings made it seem perfectly safe, perfectly reasonable. Respectable, even. And the money was good for something as simple as sleeping with your clients.'

'Fucking them, you mean. That is what this is all about. I had sex with them, so there's no point making out there was any sleep involved.'

Chandler had done a great job leading the girl this far, but Bliss wanted to pull them back on track. He knew precisely the right tactic to employ.

'At what stage did Taylor start doing the same thing?' he asked.

Unbuckled by the statement as opposed to another question, the young woman fell into step with it without a second thought. 'A month or so after I did. I think I'd had my third or fourth client by then –proper ones, not just dates. If I'm being honest, it hadn't felt as seedy as I'd imagined. The men were clean and kind and not entirely unattractive. Older, of course, but they were nice to me. I spilled my guts to Taylor, and it didn't exactly come as a shock when she said she wanted in.'

'So Taylor was less reluctant than you were,' Bliss said, not showing his surprise.

She nodded. 'Oh, very much so.'

'And how did she take to it once she was a part of it?'

'A lot better than I did. I wanted out just as she wanted further in. Our bosses started using her to deal. Mostly not hardcore gear, just some uppers, a bit of E, some poppers. Taylor didn't touch the stuff herself, but some men like to indulge, and the people who ran us got us to report back if our clients went in for that sort of thing.'

Bliss nodded thoughtfully. He'd been wondering what the difference was between the two young women, and this seemed to be the answer. 'Okay, Rose. You're doing well. But now we've reached the point of no return. We need to know who these people are. I promise you they'll never know where this came from, and I'm sure they run many girls. We'll require names and contact details, including any phone numbers and email addresses you have, as well as a location where they can be found.'

She sat back, horrified. 'They'll kill me if they find out.'

'They won't find out, Rose,' Chandler reassured her. 'DI Bliss doesn't tell lies when it comes to important things such as people's safety. If he says your name and details are protected, then they are.'

Bliss nodded, but cast his eyes to the left. Frank Rogers had not said a word, but he had taken in the entire conversation. The man's gleaming eyes were narrowed in concern, but it could just as easily have been feigned. He had not lied when he told the girl her name would never be officially revealed, but could he be certain it might not spill out of the NCA?

'Frank, do you have something to contribute?' he said, shifting the focus of attention. 'Before this brave young lady tells us anything, are you able to offer the same kind of guarantees regarding her safety?'

If Rogers was startled at being asked, he did not show it. He simply nodded, and said, 'Absolutely. As cast-iron as your own, Inspector. We can achieve a conviction without Ms Martyn's statement, and I'm more than willing to put that on record.'

Chandler shifted further forward until she was perched on the edge of the cushion. The movement snagged the girl's attention. 'Rose, there's no way we'd offer to protect you if we knew we couldn't do it. Whatever you tell us we will act upon, and if you choose not to make a formal statement, that's entirely up to you. We'd like it for our records, and those records will remain internal. But if you refuse, we can still act on the information. Just tell us and then go about your business as normal. By the way, have you stopped working for them?'

The girl looked up as if startled. 'No, why?'

'You mentioned earlier that Taylor started at around the time you were looking to quit. I just wondered if you'd done so.'

'Not... officially, like. But I haven't responded the last few times they tried to get hold of me. And I had already told them I'd had enough and was thinking of quitting. But the truth is, I can't risk working where I live or where I study, so I get taken to other locations around the wider Hull area. They knew I'd be doing nothing for them during the summer break while I'm living here.'

'All right. So, are you ready to tell us everything you know?'

Rose Martyn breathed out a steady blast of air. Nodded. 'As ready as I'll ever be,' she said.

TWENTY-TWO

'Do we have enough to go forward, or are we conning ourselves into believing we have a lead when, in fact, we have nothing?'

The question was brutally honest. As Bliss intended it to be. He studied the faces looking back at him, seeing a familiar desire and determination from officers working the investigation. Yet what he did not see in either their eyes or body language was conviction. He knew they had the foundations of a workable case, but the ground beneath their feet was loose, lacking stability. It needed something from him to galvanise the team, and he hoped what he had to tell them would do precisely that.

'I understand why you're all frustrated,' he said. 'But we've been here before. Everyone in this room is experienced enough to understand this is the way it goes if we don't get a quick and obvious result. All we need is the one breakthrough. I'm convinced it'll come – if it hasn't already.'

Bishop, who usually had to be invited to his feet, slipped off the desk he'd been perched on and stood to face Bliss. 'Boss, you're always asking us to challenge you if we're at odds.'

Bliss nodded and smiled. 'Oh-oh. I'm in trouble when even Bish wants to take me on.'

When the gentle laughter had died away, Bishop continued. 'The problem, as I see it is, we have too many possibilities. Our reasoning has been sound, but it's produced nothing conclusive so far. I can't help wondering if we're seeing what we want to see on this one.'

'Do you expect me to disagree?'

'To be honest with you, I don't know what to expect.'

'The truth is, I agree with everything you just said. With the sole exception of your conclusion. We're not seeing what we want to see. We're seeing what's there right in front of our noses. The reason I believe that is because of the aspects we're unable to explain. We may not fully understand them, and we're certainly no closer to identifying a prime suspect, but I'm convinced we're gaining ground.'

'Your team is going to need more than that,' Superintendent Fletcher said. Her usual position when attending a meeting of this nature was to lean back against the far wall by the door. Today she was standing by Bliss's side, his stand-in SIO making everybody aware that she was in this with them.

He accepted the task. 'All right. Let's take what we discovered during our trip up to Yorkshire. We know Taylor Sweeting's death was not an accident, because we have a witness. It was planned and executed perfectly, and her killer lingered long enough to watch her die. In London, Birmingham, Essex, and Dorset, people have died in questionable ways. And then we bring ourselves to our own area, in which suicides were staged.'

Bliss paused, making sure he had everyone's attention. He gave an emphatic nod. 'In the staging, we find a common theme, a connection running between these victims. That alone should tell us we have a series of murders carried out by the same perpetrator. Maybe with an accomplice, maybe not. Either way, these deaths are bound together. And if one link between them isn't enough for you, we can find another. In every one of those cases – other than our own so far as we're aware – a murder victim had some form of involvement with crime. Organised crime, in the main.'

'Does the fact that we've not yet found the same kind of criminal enterprise link to our own investigations concern you at all, Jimmy?' Fletcher asked.

'Yes, and no. Yes, because I'd like nothing more than to have that confirmed. No, because I feel it's only a matter of time before we do.'

'And the doer?' The question came from DC Ansari.

Bliss gestured towards Frank Rogers. 'Our man from the NCA can tell you more about that. And before you all pipe up at once, yes Frank *is* the man who caught up with the serial killer, Lawrence Swain.'

Rogers waited until the resulting hubbub had died away before stepping up to say his piece. 'If our sources are right – and we believe they are – these murders are almost certainly the work of a man known to us as the Lightning Rod. As we understand it, it's a term used by others about him, rather than by the man himself. His work has not gone unnoticed, but he has. The NCA has only been aware of him for about a year or so, but not a single informant has so much as laid eyes on him, let alone learned his real name.'

'Does he work for Marty Reid?' DC Virgil asked.

'Among others. But again, that's only hearsay at present. Everything points to him being freelance.'

'Which explains why these victims are tied to a variety of villains and their sordid businesses.'

'Possibly. And by that I mean, we think it's more likely that the same group of firms all lead back to a single major outfit.'

This was news even to Bliss. 'You kept that quiet, Frank,' he said, testily.

'It's still little more than a theory,' Rogers responded.

'Even so, it'd be a significant development if we were able to narrow down our search parameters to one crew.'

Rogers stood firm. 'And I didn't want you deviating from the course you were on. My team was working on it as each new scrap of news came through. Our trip north might well have provided us with the final piece of the puzzle, because the agency Taylor Sweeting and Rose Martyn worked for as escorts, are also known to the NCA. In addition, their links follow a trail back to London.'

'To Reid?'

'We have no definitive proof of that, but it's certainly in line with our thinking. We're working on the theory that all roads lead to his enterprise, even if some of the victims themselves are on the periphery with no direct connection.'

Sometimes it took just a single word, or phrase, or statement to unlock a notion lodged inside Bliss's head. This was just such a moment.

'I may know why our killer is attempting to work by stealth,' he said. He ran a thumb across his unshaven chin. 'It might yet prove to be a quirk of his, and perhaps he genuinely does get a kick out of it. But I think he was chosen deliberately not just to carry out these hits, but to do so in such a way as to make them appear to be tragic events and not the work of a lone madman.'

Frank Rogers folded his arms and turned to him. 'Explain that to us in more detail, Jimmy.'

'I will. So far with these cases we've discovered victims with relatively minor ties to crime. People who work on the fringes. We've all agreed on that, at least. I don't think it's coincidental. I mean, if you were a major crime syndicate looking to pull the plug, you wouldn't start with those closest to the centre, to those high up the ladder. You'd do it like you were peeling an onion, a layer at a time. Starting with the outer ring and working your way inwards. The people being removed are the least noticeable in a criminal organisation. But I'm guessing that's not going to continue for much longer. Once they're all gone, presumably men and women who knew too much to be allowed to live, who for some reason had information that might bring the police closer to Reid's door, our killer starts on the next ring and continues working his way towards the core.'

'That actually makes a great deal of sense.'

Bliss squinted at him. 'Try not to sound quite so surprised, Frank.'

Rogers grinned. 'Not at all. But it does.'

'And it's something my team and I discussed beforehand. We thought we knew what was going on, we just didn't know why. Why these particular people? If I'm right, then that must surely open up a door for us.'

'If Reid is responsible,' Rogers went on, picking up the thread, 'he clearly doesn't want to start a panic. However, his organisation covers such a wide area that he's forced to eradicate potential problems. So he begins with a level of people none of his inner circle is even aware of. A haulier, an accountant, a club manager, an escort who deals drugs… and so on. He genuinely is cleaning up. Not after the deed, but ahead of time. He's preparing for something significant. He's either getting out, selling up, or going to war.'

'Which of those is more preferable?' Chandler asked.

Rogers took a moment before answering. 'None of them. Because either way, we can expect more bodies.'

TWENTY-THREE

On a blazingly hot cloudless day without even the hint of a cooling breeze, Xavier Brent felt a chill brush against his neck and spread its way across his bare shoulder blades. He shuddered once and it was gone, but the sensation lingered far longer in his mind than upon his flesh. Since childhood, he'd been troubled by a sixth sense. In the beginning, recognition occurred in retrospect, long after whatever terrible event had occurred. He quickly came to understand the sensations he had overlooked, and to then recognise and appreciate the signs ahead of time. He never knew the precise nature of the incident his senses forewarned him of, only that something awful was about to happen.

So what did the sudden icy blast mean on this occasion?

Who was about to get hurt?

He lay back in a soft reclining garden chair, staring out across the expanse of his infinity pool. The still water's horizon overlooked the Number 1 pond at Hampstead Heath. On a calm and pleasant day with the reflective surface capturing his gaze, he felt foolish even contemplating doom and gloom. Yet he couldn't let it go, unsettled by that brief moment. He breathed deeply, allowing his eyes to wander, taking in his surroundings once more as the sun beat down. Only here in this spot was he ever truly at peace.

The chime of his phone startled him so much he almost dropped the glass he'd been holding. As it was, Brent spilled some of his gin and tonic, half-melted ice cubes splashing and clinking in alarm. The specific tone told him somebody was at the front door. He jabbed an app icon and the doorbell camera winked into life. A figure stood on the top step, their back to the door. He activated the speaker and said, 'Yes? Who is it?'

The man turned. His face was set firm, neither friendly nor inimical. He glanced around before identifying the source of both the sound and visual component. He took something from his breast pocket and held it up for closer inspection.

'Mr Brent? Mr Xavier Brent?'

'That depends. Pull back whatever you're holding up just a fraction, please. It's out of focus.'

The man did as he was asked. Brent read the details on the inside of the wallet the man had opened.

'What can I do for you today, Sergeant?' he asked, troubled by the presence of a Met detective at his front door.

'Am I speaking to Xavier Brent, sir?'

'You are, yes. What is this about, please?'

'Sir, if you want me to stand here and explain for your neighbours and passing pedestrians to hear your business, I will. Personally, I'd rather have words privately inside. Either way, you're going to want to come to the door.'

Brent licked his lips in mild trepidation and put his glass down on a nearby table. These days, he was insulated. This couldn't have anything to do with how he earned much of his income. That simply wasn't possible, not with his connections. It had to be something personal, not professional. 'Give me a moment,' he said uncertainly. 'I'm out back, but I'll buzz you in and meet you in the entrance hallway.'

He jabbed another icon to free the front door lock. It was an easy life when you could do most things from your poolside just by using a phone, but face-to-face meetings required a little more effort. He pulled a vest over his head and stepped through the doorway that led into his living room. Shuffling barefoot along the short marble-tiled corridor, he wound his way down a tight spiral staircase to the ground floor.

The police officer Brent had allowed inside his home was not where he'd expected to find him. Juddering to a halt, he looked around. 'Detective?' he queried, glancing at his phone to see the doorstep now vacant. 'Sergeant Crews?'

From out of the dining room towards the rear of the house came a voice, deep and steady. 'Did you ever watch an American TV show called *Life*, Mr Brent?' the visitor asked.

When he appeared in the entrance hall, he looked larger and infinitely more menacing than he'd seemed via the doorbell camera.

'I'm sorry?' Brent said, turning an ear towards the man. 'What did you ask me?'

'I asked if you'd ever watched a TV show called *Life*. It featured an LA detective by the name of Charlie Crews. Played by an English actor, but sounding much like an American. Anyhow, that's where I got the name.'

'The name?' Brent still wasn't getting it.

'The name you saw on my warrant card. Detective Sergeant Charles Crews. I thought that was a nice touch, but clearly it was wasted on you.'

'So your name isn't Crews?'

'No. Well done.'

'And you're not a detective?'

'Oh, you are fast improving. Not the brightest bulb on the Christmas tree, but I can see the penny is finally dropping.'

'Who sent you?' Brent asked, now fully aware of what that earlier passing chill had been a precursor to.

'A friend.'

'A friend would call ahead. A friend would come in person.'

'Not for this, he wouldn't.'

'Not for what?'

The man smiled. He jerked his head. 'Join me outside by your pool, Xavier. Let me show you.'

*

In one of Kevin Spacey's least known films, he plays movie mogul Buddy Ackerman. Guy, played by a youthful Frank Whaley, is his downtrodden personal assistant. It's a thankless job, involving daily and almost ritual humiliation. Eventually, Guy can take it no longer and he takes Buddy prisoner in his own home. As the viewer witnesses the mental breakdown of the young subordinate, he deploys a delicious method of torture. In a most enchanting scene, he slices Buddy's face apart with the unsealed flap of an envelope.

He remembers watching that film with his father. They seldom spent any time together, so the moment stood out. The old man was sober to begin with, his mood tolerable. As the drama had unwound, he'd held his breath, slowing the flow of excitement ripping through his veins. He couldn't let on how much he enjoyed that part of the film, how thrilling he found both the act and method of torture depicted. He'd adored every Spacey film since, but none had touched him in quite the same way. Not even *Se7en*.

His most fervent wish after seeing the film had been to use the exact same technique on some poor soul. Fixing things was his usual job, but taking people apart was often a necessary act. Why not get a rush from both?

For the present, he was finding more practical ways in which to enjoy himself. An accidental drowning was a simple thing to stage, and Brent hadn't put up much of a fight. A weak and simple man, he died a weak and simple death. Imagining him to be an actor being forcibly drowned in a yet to be made movie provided an element of detachment. Nonetheless, by the time he was done, he felt unfulfilled and more than a little disappointed.

He told himself that the papercut scene from *Swimming With Sharks* was his to re-enact at some point in the near future. The thought elevated his spirits and cheered him no end.

TWENTY-FOUR

For the third time that morning, Penny Chandler checked her phone. Squinting hard, she called Bliss's work number. When it went to voicemail, she tried his personal mobile. After getting the same result, she shifted across to his landline. No answer. She looked over at Ansari, who sat using a laptop on the opposite side of the room.

'I don't suppose you've heard from Jimmy this morning, have you, Gul?'

The young DC peered around the office before shaking her head. 'I haven't. I just assumed he was here. He's always here.'

That told its own story. But Chandler's frown narrowed further. 'He asked me to come in early so's we could prioritise our own actions and go over the policy book entries.'

'I wonder if he's had a bad turn.'

Which was where her own mind had taken her. Bliss suffered from Meniere's Disease, a chronic illness that occasionally gave him various degrees of vertigo, leaving him unbalanced and fatigued. On rare mornings when he was too incapacitated to work, he always texted her first. And she couldn't remember the last time he'd not made it in while they were knee deep in a new investigation.

Chandler reached a decision. 'Cover for us, please, Gul,' she said before dashing out of the room heading towards the stairs.

It took her less than ten minutes to reach Bliss's home in the Ortons on an estate of similar looking houses made from brick the colour of sand. As she pulled into his road, she noticed the Ford Mondeo wasn't parked in the bay outside his house. About to turn around and drive back to work, on a sudden impulse she decided to stop and knock on the front door. There were times when Bliss had more than a couple of drinks and ended up leaving his motor in a pub car park. He might have had to grab a taxi the night before.

Chandler tried his doorbell, but got no luck. She pushed up the flap of the letterbox and put her ear to it, followed by her mouth to call out his name. She headed around to the back alley, but the gate was bolted. As she returned to the front of the house, a slim woman wearing a floral summer dress walked by carrying a small bag of shopping.

'You looking for the policeman, love?' she asked Chandler.

'Actually, I am. He and I are colleagues. I think we must have got our wires crossed. I don't suppose you've laid eyes on him today...?'

'No. Sorry, love. Mind you, that's nothing unusual. He keeps irregular hours. I remember his car not being there when I walked the dog last night shortly after eleven.' The woman paused, stroked her chin. 'You know, come to think of it, when it's hot like this and it gets light early, I take Patch out for his morning walk just after dawn because it's cooler. Most of the time I see your man's car there, and more recently we've run across each other while he's out with Max. But not today.'

'And what time did you go out earlier?' Chandler asked, feeling another jab of anxiety.

'A little after five. The sun wasn't quite up, but it wasn't dark out.'

Something felt wrong, adding to an increasing sense of unease. She thanked the neighbour and jumped back into her car, where she put a call in to DC Ansari.

'Gul. I need a favour. Look up the plate of the pool car assigned to Jimmy. Text it to me, then get hold of your go-to techie at Hinchingbrooke and have him trace the vehicle's GPS. I want to know where that car is right now.'

Chandler sucked in a deep breath, trying to slow her heart rate. Her thoughts went in search of reasons why Bliss might be neither at work nor at home. It was out of character, and she could think of no reasonable explanation to explain his absence. It seemed an age, but less than ten minutes later, Ansari called her back. Bliss's Mondeo was stationary in the Holiday Inn car park.

As she pointed her own Ford in the direction of the hotel, her mind formed a number of new scenarios based on this fresh information. There were several reasons why Bliss might be at the hotel, ranging from having had a few too many drinks in their bar and deciding to get himself a room, to having met somebody there and getting lucky. None of them explained why he was late for work, nor why he had not been in contact.

At the entrance to the hotel's car park, Chandler paused at the barrier while its camera scanned her car's number plate. Once inside, she drove slowly up and down the lanes, keeping an eye out for a Mondeo with a registration matching the one Ansari had texted her. It brought to mind an incident several years ago, in which she had been abducted from a different hotel in the city. The memory was enough to send a chill through her bones. It also made her more fearful regarding her partner's fate.

When she spotted Bliss's motor, she half expected to find him asleep at the wheel. She got out from behind her own to inspect the Mondeo, but saw no sign of him. The doors were locked, nothing inside seemed out of place. She took out her phone, called both his mobiles again, listening intently. Voicemail kicked in on both after ringing, but if either phone was inside the car, it was switched to silent.

Chandler breathed deeply. She didn't know what to make of the situation. But the NPR-style barrier gave her an idea. She jumped back into her car and drove to the hotel entrance, parking in the turning circle out of the way of a shuttle bus decanting and collecting passengers.

At reception she asked if a James or Jimmy Bliss was a guest of the hotel. Following a flurry of fingers and the harsh clattering of a computer keyboard, the answer came back in the negative. She then asked to speak with the on-duty manager. Hesitant at first, the receptionist became galvanised upon the production of Chandler's warrant card. Moments later, a surprisingly young woman appeared from a room close by.

'Good morning, officer. My name is Yana Stepanova. How may I assist you?'

Her English was excellent, accent eastern European. Chandler put the woman at no more than early twenties. 'I need to know how your car park system works,' she said. 'I noticed that it uses number plate recognition. Tell me, how does it differentiate between guests and visitors?'

'Hotel guests provide us with their vehicle details, at which point their car parking is designated free. The system recognises this so that guests may come and go as they please. A visitor must use one of the payment machines, which can be found both inside and outside the main entrance doors. But not if they are only dropping off or collecting, as the system allows for a twenty-minute period without charge.'

Chandler nodded. 'How about if a visitor stayed overnight with a guest? Might their vehicle be added to the guest's bill so's the visitor didn't have to bother with your machines?'

'That is permissible, yes. Also, if the guest does not have their own vehicle, their visitor can park for free instead.'

'Provided the vehicle details are logged into the system.'

'That's correct.'

'Tell me, is your software capable of being queried by the number plate, or is it by guest name and room number only?'

'No, no. We are able to query by vehicle.'

With a smile of satisfaction, Chandler gave the manager Bliss's plate details and asked if it was listed in the system with a hotel guest. She then thought of something else and asked for all details relating to that vehicle, itemising the initial time of arrival and also including times of exit and entry since – if applicable.

Stepanova slipped away with a brief nod. If she was flustered by the volley of questions or even mildly intrigued by them, neither her expression nor demeanour showed it. Chandler was impressed by the professionalism and slick manner of one so young. More so when she reappeared after less than five minutes and handed over a printed sheet, saying, 'I think this will have everything you asked for.'

Chandler thanked the woman and took the sheet of paper from her. The first thing she noticed was a guest name: Pamela Daniels. Reading further down, she noted just the one time code of 7.23pm. Her initial reaction was to hurry away before Bliss came bustling out of a lift, angry with himself for having missed an alarm. Clearly he had stayed overnight with a woman, though she was surprised her friend and colleague had not mentioned it. She had long since accepted his reticence when it came to discussing personal matters, especially where his love life was concerned. But if a new relationship had reached this point, then how had she not noticed? What kind of detective did that make her?

One who had failed to see through Jimmy Bliss; which made her one of many.

Yet while the hotel records offered the explanation she had sought, his continued absence from work bothered her. He was now close to ninety-minutes late. No call. No text. In all the years she had known him, he had never been this tardy for anything without notifying first her and then the office. Too unprecedented to ignore, Chandler decided.

'Would you please find out for me if Pamela Daniels is in her room?' she asked.

For the first time, the manager appeared to falter. 'You wish to talk to our guest about police business?'

'Yes. Why? Oh, I see. You think perhaps… no, trust me, this is not a personal issue. The fact is, I have to locate the owner of this vehicle.' She didn't offer up the information about Bliss also being a police officer. That was a piece of gossip the young woman did not need to be aware of.

'I'll see what I can do.'

Stepanova disappeared again, returning minutes later. 'I am sorry. Our guest checked out early this morning. And before you ask, I am not permitted to provide you with her details without further authorisation.'

Chandler bit her tongue. Protest was useless, as the manager was well within her rights. 'There is another way you might be able to help,' she said instead. 'Please tell me you have CCTV covering the car park area.'

'Of course.'

'In that case, I'd like to see footage starting when this vehicle entered through the barrier, and if necessary right up to the point at which my own car came through.'

This request took some time to arrange, during which Chandler made another call to DC Ansari. Still no word from Bliss, so by the time she sat down to spool through the hours of digital footage, her fear had turned to the kind of dread that felt physical. One of the security officers helped her with the equipment, pointing out the relevant camera numbers she'd need to track the Mondeo from point of entry to its parking slot, and from there taking the most direct path to the hotel entrance on foot. She dug in, expecting to find Bliss at least making his way towards the hotel.

Only that was not what happened.

She watched as he entered and found a spare parking space, which he backed into. A transit van had entered immediately after the pool car and reappeared on camera just as Bliss started to walk across to the entrance. Chandler paid close attention to the monitor as he paused, seemingly to speak to the van driver. Then he turned and walked across to it. When he reached the van, apparently to continue his conversation, the side door slid open and three men burst out. Each of them brandished a weapon – two carried pickaxe handles, the other a metallic baseball bat.

'Oh, my God,' she gasped, as she saw Bliss rear back and throw a punch just as the first weapon was raised. He got in a few more, sending two of his attackers sprawling to the ground. But the volume of blows raining down on him eventually took their toll. His arms warding off strikes aimed at his head, he fell to his knees, and then curled up in a protective ball on the floor as the three men continued to lay into him.

Chandler gave a horrified cry as each blow landed, a hand to her chest, mouth bone dry. Horror-stricken, she kept her eyes on the screen as the men finally ended their attack. They then picked up the fallen figure, bundled him into the van, climbed in behind him, before taking off at speed. She remembered the manager's words about the twenty-minute free entry allowance, so after a slight pause at the exit barrier the van passed through and beyond the scope of the on-site CCTV cameras.

She knew the car parking software would have captured the van's registration plate. She also assumed it would prove to be either fake or stolen. Bliss had been beaten and snatched. He was gone. The woman he had visited the hotel to see was now also gone. Chandler was in shock, and for a moment continued to sit upright and rigid in her chair in the hotel security office. Then, as if the enormity of what she had just seen hit her with force, she jerked once and turned to the security officer sitting alongside her.

'I want that footage,' she said. 'And I now need to know everything you have on Pamela Daniels.'

TWENTY-FIVE

DETECTIVE SUPERINTENDENT MARION FLETCHER had seldom seen the major crimes area busier or more determined in their efforts. In her experience, each officer, whether in plain clothes or wearing standard uniform, gave it their all irrespective of the case. Even so, it was perfectly understandable for them to strain every sinew a little more when one of their own was the victim.

With DCI Warburton absent and Bliss abducted, she stepped up to lead the team from the moment Chandler reported the shocking news. A fellow officer was in trouble, and that took precedence over Operation Insulate. The sense of urgency within the squad was palpable, and Fletcher did everything in her power to keep up the momentum by having every member of the team thinking positively. Every call, every conversation, was geared towards finding Bliss and getting him back without further injury.

Nobody spoke of the worst-case scenario.

The moment they had intel, Fletcher took Chandler and Bishop to one side to discuss their findings. It was Chandler who had the first break with the hotel guest.

'Pamela Daniels runs her own high-end fashion garment business,' she said, reading from a sheaf of paper still warm from the laser printer. 'According to her PA, Daniels was here in the city to attend a conference and a series of seminars. The event was held in one of the function rooms at the Holiday Inn.'

'Any prior connection between this woman and Jimmy?' Fletcher asked, considering the permutations.

'Nothing obvious, although at one time they did live in the same area of east London. Perhaps they were friends back in the day and happened to run into each other this week.'

'Okay. Let's try to firm up on that. I want to know more about their relationship.'

'On that note,' Bishop said, 'We have DCs Gratton and Virgil at the hotel asking questions. Seems Jimmy's motor was parked up there on a couple of occasions earlier in the week. Entry and exit times suggest he was there for a few hours each time.'

'Can't be a coincidence,' Chandler remarked. 'He had to have been spending time with this woman.'

'That doesn't prove a direct link between her and what happened to the boss last night,' Bishop said. 'The two things might be entirely unconnected.'

'Do we have Pamela Daniels' mobile number?' Fletcher asked.

Chandler nodded. 'From hotel records. I've called twice already. Straight to voicemail. She may be driving with her phone switched off.'

'Keep trying. Anything further on the van?'

'Other than confirming the fake plate, the PNC check gave us nothing else to go on. The reg was legit, but it belongs to a motor scrapped three years ago. Scrapped and crushed.'

The Superintendent was unsurprised. The police national computer lived off a diet of data input. Checking a vehicle registration number on the system led to a wealth of additional information about the vehicle itself, but also its owners. The system only worked when the plate was valid, however.

'Who do we have on CCTV, ANPR, and road cameras?' she asked.

'DC Ansari and a uniform, PC Randell, ma'am,' Bishop responded quickly. 'They're attempting to follow the van's progress, but the initial problem was we had no idea if it turned left or right when exiting the car park. Each of them began their checks going in a different direction, but once they located the vehicle, they switched to working in harness.'

By this time, Fletcher had viewed the hotel footage for herself. It was shocking to witness, but worse still, she expected their hunt for the van to be in vain. 'If whoever did this has anything about them, they'll have reached a camera blind spot as swiftly as possible and ditched the van in favour of a secondary vehicle. Continue to run it down, but don't get your hopes up.'

'We'll carry on doing what we do until we reach dead ends. I had the hotel room locked down until CSI can get in there. They're working on the car park at the moment. I don't expect to get any joy from the van, either. That leaves us with Pamela Daniels. If we can find no connection between her and what happened to the boss, then to be honest with you, I don't know where to start next. If we're looking for a motive for somebody snatching him, we have his entire work record to sift through.'

Fletcher turned to Chandler. 'Penny, you're closer to Jimmy than any of us are. Has he mentioned any concerns in recent days or weeks? Anybody in particular threatening him with retribution? Has he made a nuisance of himself with a local villain off the books?'

'Not to my knowledge,' Chandler said. 'That sort of thing is always a possibility when you rub shoulders with that kind of element. But if there was anything bothering him, he never mentioned it to me.'

'Me neither,' Bishop confirmed. 'But that doesn't mean it wasn't related to somebody he's helped put away.'

'Most likely candidates?' Fletcher asked.

'Lewis Drake and Neil Watson come to mind,' Chandler said.

'Convince me.'

'Drake's pure organised crime. Among a litany of other things, he was responsible for trafficking young women, one of whom he murdered. Or ordered it, at the very least. Made threats to both me and Jimmy when we visited him in Belmarsh. His last appeal failed not so long ago, so he might be feeling particularly vindictive at the moment.'

'And Watson?'

'Neil Watson was the man who got away with beating to death a young kid, his girlfriend at the time taking the blame for it because she was terrified of being next. Jimmy wound him up and when he cracked, the two of them had a scrap. Jimmy ended up going over a balcony railing, but Watson got hammered over the head and put into a coma by the woman he was attempting to beat when Jimmy showed up at her flat.'

'I remember it well. I also remember Watson surviving against all the odds. But I was under the impressions he wasn't mobile.'

'He's not. Lost a few marbles as well, which was catastrophic as by all accounts he didn't have many to spare. But he pulled through. As I understand it, he can remember some things, and is capable of reacting to that kind of stimulus. If he eventually remembered what happened between him and Jimmy, he might have enough thuggish friends to do the dirty work for him.'

'Two real possibilities there, then,' Fletcher said.

'There are others in the frame,' Bishop added. 'Nick Nevin is the ex-cop who murdered Jimmy's wife. Jimmy confronted him just over three years ago and managed to record him confessing to Hazel's murder. The bloke continues to tell anybody who'll listen how much he's going to make the boss pay.'

'Does he have reach outside of prison life?' Fletcher asked.

'We believe so, yes, but it's unconfirmed. Then there's the Thompson family from Sawtry. They blame him for one of their own going over the edge of a cliff, which they claim led to the lad's mother committing suicide. There are more than a few hotheads to go round with that incestuous bunch. Oh, and we can't forget Ryan Endicott.'

'The drug dealer, correct?'

'Indeed. Neither him nor his main supplier, Eric McManus, are happy with Jimmy still walking the earth. And those are just the obvious names.'

As a DI for major crimes, it was Bliss's duty to rattle cages and put bad people behind bars. How he went about it certainly antagonised criminals more than might be expected, and his reputation had earned him a target on his back.

'Jimmy Bliss has more than his fair share of enemies,' she said. 'Let's start talking to them if this relationship with Pamela Daniels doesn't pan out.'

As Fletcher spoke, Chandler's mobile vibrated with an incoming message. When she read it, her eyes widened in horror. 'Oh, my God,' she said in a dry, fearful voice close to breaking. 'We don't have to look any further than Pam Daniels.'

'Penny, what is it? What's happened?' Fletcher shot back.

'It's Daniels, ma'am. Four years ago, she reverted to her maiden name. You're never going to believe who she was married to.'

TWENTY-SIX

T HE RUSTING AIRSTREAM RECREATION vehicle smelled like stale fried food, warm motor oil, and a basic toilet unflushed in decades. Bliss had spotted its exterior the night before, when the hood he'd had draped over his head was removed and exchanged for a blindfold as he was dragged across to the RV and heaved inside. He saw little beyond the dense cloth wrapped over his eyes, but when he cast his gaze down, he noted the claret-coloured leatherette bench seat he was dumped upon.

He was still somewhat lightheaded, which was concerning. He knew the dangers associated with having been knocked unconscious by one of the heavier blows that had whacked him on the head after he'd failed to parry them successfully with his arms. Concussion might easily cause a lack of cognitive awareness, in addition to imbalance, nausea, and possible memory loss. Symptoms could lie dormant for hours or even days, and although temporary, they were unpleasant at best.

He had swum in and out of consciousness during the night, which was clearly not a good sign. He tried dismissing those short periods as him needing to sleep, but there was no fooling himself. He had slept, though only after failing to engage his captors in conversation. As darkness fell, he heard them playing cards and becoming increasingly boisterous. Later came the inevitable silence, punctuated by the occasional sound of men farting and snoring. He assumed they had taken turns watching over him in case he tried to struggle free, but in truth he'd been in too much pain to move.

It was now morning and light out, a moist heat already causing him to sweat. He felt better than he had at any point since the abduction. Able to think sufficiently clearly, despite the fierce headache forming across the bridge of his nose. The throbbing distracted him, but he remained sharp enough to gather his wits. Other than the stabbing pain in his head, he felt the lumps he'd acquired during the beating. Most of the blows he'd absorbed with his forearms, and those that had got through his defences didn't appear to have done any lasting damage. No breaks thankfully, as far as he could tell. He'd be purple and yellow for a while, and jabs of pain would act as reminders for days to come. Overall, it could have been worse, and that was the buoy he clung to.

If these men had wanted him dead, he'd never have woken up. The fact that they had stopped giving him a hiding and then driven him elsewhere before transporting him into the RV suggested they needed him alive.

But for what?

Or for whom?

The blindfold was large enough to cover his ears, but just as he could detect daylight bleeding through the rough cloth, so he was also able to make out muffled sounds. Since coming around, he'd picked out three, possibly four different voices. He only managed to discern the odd word, but the men sounded about as unhappy as he was to be stashed away inside the sweltering hulk of a vehicle long past its better days.

Every so often a welcome breeze brushed against his skin, telling him the windows were open, perhaps even the door as well. He heard heavy traffic rushing by in the distance, suggesting they were close to one of the parkways encircling the city. He'd been out fewer than thirty seconds that first time, and he knew they hadn't travelled far. He strained to hear familiar sounds, hoping to pinpoint a more precise location. Not that it would do him any good in his current situation, which he could think of no way to improve.

'Do you… do you people know who I am?' he said, having difficulty swallowing.

This time somebody replied, though their words were indistinct. When he shrugged by way of a response, he felt the blindfold tugged up to free his right ear.

'I asked if we ought to know who you were,' one of the men said, barking a crisp, humourless laugh. 'What, you some kind of celebrity?'

Bliss thought quickly. Surely by now they had searched him. Even if only to ascertain whether he had any weapons on him. If they had, they would have discovered his warrant card. If they hadn't, would telling them what he did for a living make any difference? He shook his head, silently admonishing himself for woolly thinking. Of course they knew who he was. Why else was he here?

'You know I'm a police officer, right? So you must also know my team is scorching the earth looking for me. That won't go well for any of you when I'm found and firearms officers arrive.'

More laughter. 'Nobody is finding you here, pal. So shut the fuck up.' A different voice this time.

'You'd be surprised.'

'I'd be fucking amazed.'

This seemed riotously amusing to them, resulting in real belly laughs. It was clear they had no problem snatching a police officer off the street. No threat of armed law enforcement was going to force them to rethink their position.

'Who are we waiting for?' he said, abruptly changing tack.

A third voice said, 'Who says we're waiting for anybody?'

'We have to be. You abducted me for a reason. You have me secure, but you're leaving me be. That tells me somebody else is on their way here.'

'Clever fucker, ain't you?'

'It wasn't difficult to suss out.'

'Well, you won't be feeling so shrewd by the time we're done with you, mate. When we get the word, we're going to lay into you so brutally you'll be begging us to kill you.'

'I don't see that happening,' Bliss said, more convincingly than he felt.

'You know what, pal, beg or don't beg. I don't give a flying fuck. It'll end the same way, whatever.'

Bliss said nothing for a while, then, 'So who *are* we waiting for?'

'You'll find out soon enough.'

'What do they want with me? What did I do to them?'

One of the men sniggered like a child. The others remained silent.

He let the moment slide, but only seconds later heard tyres crunching and slewing to a halt outside. He licked his lips and felt his heart kick up a notch or two. He had no clue as to who might have wanted him this way, but as his abductors had suggested, this wasn't going to end well. He hadn't lied when he said his team would be busting a gut to find him, but unless these men had been sloppy, the chances of that happening were remote at best.

Seconds later came the muffled sound of footsteps and the RV rocking slightly. The footfall grew louder, and then without warning the blindfold was torn from his head. In a defensive response, Bliss held up a hand, blinking rapidly to clear his vision. He'd expected to know the man now looming over him, but instead drew a blank. He stared hard but said nothing, pulling back against the bench seat and keeping his hand raised to ward off an immediate attack.

The man, considerably older than Bliss had imagined, turned to one of the four goons gathered around him. 'You sure this is him?'

'Absolutely. Clocked him the other night.'

'And he's definitely Old Bill, not some geriatric civilian?'

'He's a DI. No doubt whatsoever.'

The man sighed and shifted back into position over Bliss. His frown deepened, the leathery unshaven face sprouting wrinkles. 'How's it going, Jimmy-boy? Clearly you don't recognise me, and I have to say I'm struggling to remember the young, wet behind the ears tearaway from back in the day.'

The man had to be in his late seventies or early eighties, Bliss estimated. In decent enough condition for his age, and with a good head of white hair, though the watery eyes and liver spots on his hands gave the game away. Not a villain he had encountered before, he didn't think. At that moment, something alerted him to consider the case he was currently working on. At least this couldn't be the Lightning Rod. Or could it? He thought better of asking, but decided he could not remain silent.

'I don't think we know one another, pal.' His throat was parched, voice croaky. 'Pretty sure you and I have never met before. So, I have to assume this is all a big mistake. Whatever the reason, I get the impression some wires have been crossed somewhere along the way. I have no beef with you, nor you with me.'

The man leaned further forward, bending at the waist with some difficulty. He rested his hands on his legs. 'That's where you're wrong, old son. You're also wrong about us not having bumped into each other before, so already I'm thinking you ain't up to much. And yes, I do have beef with you.'

Bliss stared him down. 'Do you think I'm looking for you? Is that it? You think my team and I are hunting you down for some reason? I can assure you that's not the case.'

'Didn't we just agree you have no idea who I am? So why would you be looking for me? What could you possibly want from me?'

'There you go, then. You answered your own question. So what do you think I've done to you? How have I harmed you enough to warrant this? To snatch up a copper in the way these lads did is fucking madness.'

'You think I give a flying fuck about the Filth?' Spittle flew from a mouth filled with small teeth yellowed by tobacco. 'You're nothing to me. None of you. Flies for me to squash. I swallow up and shit out wankers like you every day. But let me say this much: before my lads make you piss blood and turn your bones to jelly, you and I are going to chat.'

Bliss sucked in a deep breath. If his time was up, he wanted to end it quickly. Not the way these madmen had in mind. 'A chat? Nothing I'd like more. What's it going to be? Andrew being a nonce, climate change?' he made a show of looking the man up and down, before sneering. 'No. With your sort it's bound to be bloody immigration.'

The man laughed. Not what Bliss had expected. The sound was wet and laboured. 'You think you can wind me up? You reckon you can succeed where others have failed so miserably before?'

'Mate, I think you're an old codger and not very bright. So yeah, I reckon I have half a chance with a halfwit.'

This time, the man merely nodded and stood up straight. He turned to the others. 'Fellah thinks he's a joker. Having a giraffe at my expense. Tell you what, lads, make him last an extra hour when I've finished with him. Sixty minutes of pure pain. See how funny he thinks he is then when he's rolling around in agony. Oh, and when you do bury him, make sure he's still breathing when he goes in the ground.'

Bliss swallowed, tasting bile. He'd not taken his eyes off the man, and now he was asking himself if the face was familiar after all. Not somebody he knew, not somebody involved in Operation Insulate, but quite possibly an associated, peripheral figure.

And then something at the back of his mind threw up the answer. He ought to have recognised the man's laugh right from the off. It was distinctive, but a sound he'd not heard in many a moon.

'Harry?' he said uncertainly. 'Is that you wearing an old fucker mask? With those smoke-stained railings and the pungent stink of piss all over you?'

'Oh, so you got there at last. About time, Sherlock. How's tricks, boy?'

Bliss winced. 'Been better, Harry. Your blokes smacked me around pretty good. I'm going to have to pay somebody back for that at some point.'

'Is that right? Tell it to someone who gives a shit. So, Jimmy-boy, how's mum and dad these days?'

'Not so good. Both dead, as it happens.'

The man spent a second or two reframing his face into a picture of sympathy, but gave up the pretence before it was fully formed. 'Good,' he said. 'Glad to hear it. Your old man was nothing but trouble.'

'He could be if you were a wrong'un, which made him ten times the man you ever were. But what did my mum ever do to you?'

'She married a copper. Ain't that enough? Then again, you were the biggest disappointment of them all. From the first time

I met you, I could tell you were on the cusp. Could've gone one way or the other at the time. I really thought we had a decent crack at bringing you over to the dark side. But look at you now. Old-fucking-Bill. You disgust me.'

His words scattered and flew like birds taking flight inside Bliss's head. He tried to claw them back in, but it was as if they were on a pulley system: the closer he came to reeling one in, another was let out far beyond his reach. He then realised that in striving to slot the pieces together, he'd almost missed something: the sound of another vehicle pulling up outside.

Harry's thugs inside the RV hadn't. Each of them reacted by reaching for a weapon, while the man gave the nod for one of them to check outside the door.

'What the fuck?' the man gasped as he peered out into the yard. A look of bemusement on his face, he glanced back over his shoulder at his boss. 'It's… it's someone you're going to need to deal with, H.'

That was when Bliss heard another distinctive voice.

Loud.

Pissed off.

And one he recognised so well.

TWENTY-SEVEN

MIRACULOUSLY, PAM DANIELS NOW stood in the doorway, her face creased with fury. 'You better have a damned good reason for this, Dad,' she snapped at him.

Her father didn't even alter his expression. 'Your bloody awful taste in men is the reason, sweetheart. First this tosser, who you had the sense to drop like the stinking turd he is before he tubbed you. Then you lumber yourself with that fucking loud and obnoxious ex of yours. And now I hear you're screwing this twat again. I mean, if my daughter can't do better than Marty Reid and shit-for-brains Jimmy Bliss, I have to do the worrying for her.'

'I can never get it right for you, can I, Dad?' Pam said, sneering at him. 'A decent, law-abiding bloke on the one hand, a bent-nosed criminal like you on the other, and neither of them good enough. Well, fuck you. I don't need your approval, so tell me what the fuck is going on here.'

Bliss blinked and felt his flesh turn cold. Had he heard correctly? Marty Reid? Pam knew Reid? And had her father mentioned something about an ex…?

'First, how the fuck did you find me here?' Daniels snapped back at his daughter.

She gave a self-satisfied grin. 'Oh, I still have my hooks where they need to be, Pops. I hear more shit about you now than I did when I lived at home under your roof.'

'I'll skin the fucker coughing up information to you if I catch the bastard.'

'If you say so. Now, you have that reason I asked for?'

The man stood his ground. 'All the fucking reason I need, sweetheart. You've been shagging this prick, which automatically puts him in my bad books. On top of that, he's Old Bill, you stupid cow. Just like his fucking old man. Why are you arse-slapping a fucking copper, Pam? What's that all about?'

She closed the gap between them until the two were virtually nose to nose. 'I'll tell you what it's about. None of your fucking business, that's what. It became none of your business a few years back when I left home. And since I am no longer part of *your* business, I'll see who I like, and shag who I like.'

'Not a fucking copper you don't. That's bang out of order.'

Pam prodded his chest with a perfectly manicured finger. 'I'll fuck the entire UK police force if I choose to, Daddy-dearest. Do I need to remind you that I know where the bodies are buried? Literally, in some cases. Do I also need to remind you that I am protected from you and your malevolent grubby mitts? You can't do fuck all to me without a mountain of shit sliding down on your head. That gold-digger you replaced mum with will go down, too. So, for the last time, you malignant fuck, leave me be. You let me live my life.'

Daniels took half a step back to avoid the jabbing finger. 'I can't do that, Pam. And the reason I can't is because you *do* know too much. So, I need to be aware of what you're doing and who you're seeing at all times. Because if you ever get the urge to shaft me, then I want to be two moves ahead.'

'I turn you in, I might as well slit my own throat. Don't you see that's my only leverage, you fucking moron? It's my protection, not a weapon. It's our cold war. Guaranteed mutual destruction, you daft old bastard.'

Daniels raised a hand as if to slap her, but thought better of it. 'I know that, you daft bitch. But am I not supposed to worry when you're sleeping with a fucking detective? I'm supposed to just let that slide?'

Pam wedged her hands into her hips and nodded, feet splayed. 'That's exactly what you're going to do. Because I'm leaving with him. And you're going to have to trust that I slept with him because I wanted to, not because I have some devious plan in mind to hit you or anybody else where it hurts.'

Furiously, Harry Daniels slammed a balled fist into one of the cabinets built into the RV. He punched it twice more before relenting. 'Well, ain't this a fucking two-and-eight we find ourselves in? How can I let him go now? I do that and tomorrow I'm having my collar felt.'

'No,' Pam shook her head. She looked over at Bliss. 'Tell him, Jimmy. Tell him you won't identify him.'

'Why the fuck should I?' Bliss asked defiantly. He was still barely able to grasp all that he had seen and heard, clinging on by his fingernails. 'Those bastards laid into me with their weapons on his orders. I can't turn a blind eye to that.'

She came across and squatted in front of him. Tears welled in both eyes, and swimming in them was a look of both terror and desperation. 'Jimmy. Just think about the situation you find yourself in. That we're both in. I want you to walk out of here with me. My father will let us go if I say so. I know he will. You're a copper, and it's your job to turn him in. But I'm asking you to set that aside. Your wounded pride doesn't want him to get away with what his men did. I understand that, too. But either you convince him you won't tell anybody about what happened here, or he ain't letting you drive off with me. If you're not worried about yourself, think about me, Jimmy. Think about the position that puts me in. Despite what I have over him, you're not the only one who might not leave here if you can't make that promise.'

'Your father's not a monster, Pam,' Bliss said confidently.

'Well, of course he ain't. I know he won't hurt me physically. We've fallen out, we're not enemies. But he might well find a good reason to keep us both here while he decides what to do with us, and you know me, Jimmy. Some old junked RV isn't for me, not even for a few hours, let alone days.'

Bliss reined in his panic. He couldn't let on that he knew who Marty Reid was, nor how or why. That door was closed to him. Quite where Pam fitted in he had no idea, but he could tell none of this was being staged for his benefit. The inside of the RV had become thick with tension. Harry Daniels's thugs were on edge and keen to take action. There was only one route still available to him, however unpalatable he found it.

'For your sake,' he said, eyes only on Pam. 'I'll let this go for you.'

'How touching,' Daniels snapped, scorn virtually dripping from his lips. 'And I'm supposed to just believe that?'

Bliss scowled at the man, unable to prevent righteous anger from spilling over. 'Obviously you consider yourself to be a hard bastard, Harry, especially when you have these four arseholes of the apocalypse doing your bidding. But you have good instincts, because you're right not to trust me.'

He felt genuine menace emanating from Daniels. Shaking his head, he said, 'No, I'm not going to name you and turn you in for what your blokes did to me last night. But the fact is, if you and I ever meet again after today, I'm going to have you. One way or another.'

'Is that so? You sure this is the right time and place to threaten me, boy?'

'Probably not. The thing is, while I get the feeling that you'd very much like to kill me here and now, I'm pretty sure you don't intend Pam any harm. And I think you realise you'd probably have to do something pretty extreme to keep her quiet if you take me out. Plus, you'll do well to remember that Pam and I have been seen together at the hotel. My team will have traced her by now, which means they'll trace you as well. And this ex-husband of hers. But the only way they get to learn of this encounter is if I let them. I can tell them I was taken and held by people I never got to see. I can stop them looking into your daughter, and you, as well as this Marty Reid. Only I can prevent that chain reaction now, Harry. That's the only way this works out for all of us.'

'Let it go, Dad,' Pam beseeched her father. 'Let's call it unfinished business and have done with it. Even if it's only for now. I have a feeling you two will run into each other again at some point in the future. You can sort out your differences then if you like. But let's all take a breath and step back from the brink here. Okay?'

With obvious reluctance, Harry Daniels nodded. Bliss locked eyes with him. He nodded as well. They were enemies now. But they would both live to fight another day.

TWENTY-EIGHT

If anybody suspected or even sensed Bliss was being unco-operative, they didn't let it show. He thought he'd done a good job of convincing them, and they seemed to buy his story in its entirety.

His captors were masked when he was attacked. He was forced to wear a hood at all times. Only two of them spoke, and then on just the one occasion. They told him this was proof he could be reached, could be whisked away whenever they decided to, perhaps next time never to be seen again. They uttered no specific warnings on behalf of anybody else, nor were any demands made of him in other ways. After a single night of captivity, he was released at an industrial estate on the edge of the city.

'What about when the van first approached you in the car park?' Fletcher asked. 'You must have got a clear look at the driver then.'

'I didn't,' he said, feigning regret. 'The window was tinted and partially wound down. I could see only the top of his head, plus he wore a peaked cap and sunglasses. The others, as you'll have seen on the security footage, they had masks on when they rushed at me out of the van. After the hood went on it didn't come off again until they dropped me off.'

'That makes no sense,' Chandler said, clearly bewildered.

Bliss didn't think she was questioning his story, more the point of the actions taken against him. 'I know, I know. If they're going to all the trouble of beating me and snatching me up, you'd think they'd continue their scare tactics afterwards. Or at the very least, ask me questions and make specific demands. For all I know, they might have had something else planned for me but were forced to change their minds. Either that or they were just trying to put a fright into me by making me doubt my own security.'

'Did you get the impression they'd be back? That what happened yesterday was only a taster?'

'No. Not from anything they said or did. But I can't rule it out. I can't rule anything out.'

'Could it be something to do with this woman you've been seeing?'

He and Pam had discussed different versions of the same essential story. She'd apologised on several occasions for her father's behaviour, pleading with him to keep his name out of it. Her ex-husband's, too. He assured her that by the time he contacted the office, his team would know who she was. From there it was only a short haul to discovering who she'd once been married to and who her father was.

He had no choice but to ignore the huge coincidence – if indeed that's what it was – of her appearing not only in his city, but right there in the pub he'd chosen on a whim, at the same time as her ex-husband featured high on their list of possible suspects. He was unable to raise these concerns with her because he couldn't afford to let her know the police were on Marty Reid's trail. It was a complex web of lies, omissions, and subterfuge, as if woven by an army of drunken spiders.

He was only now finding out from his team that Pam had booked her place at the convention and her hotel room long before the Sperling family were murdered. It looked as if Harry Daniels' men had followed her north and reported back on who she had hooked up with. The old gangster's own visit seemed to be that of a suspicious man, not one fearful of any current police investigation. The guilt Bliss felt at not being able to mention any of this to his colleagues stabbed at him like a fine blade. He believed he had made the right decision at the time, but found it hard to imagine how long he'd be able to keep up the pretence.

He shook his head. 'Sorry, what did you say, Pen? My head's a bit fuzzy.'

'Then you should have let me take you to hospital like I suggested, you doughnut.'

'That's Detective Inspector Doughnut to you.'

If Chandler was amused by him, she needed to tell her face. 'Yeah, laugh it off, chuckles. You've had a concussion before from a blow to the head when you were run over. This one could be even worse for all you know.'

He gestured for her to calm down. 'Like I told you, I'll make my own way over to A&E when we're done here. In all honesty, I was more worried about Max than my own condition. The second call I made was to one of his weekend minders. Now, again, what did you ask me?'

'I asked if you being snatched up could be something to do with Pam Daniels. I tell you, Jimmy, when her name came up as having been married to Marty Reid, Gul and I were confident she had lured you into a trap of some sort. But after running all the usual checks, she does appear to have been here in Peterborough for a legitimate reason this week. So, I'm not saying this was anything deliberate on her part. But if Reid caught wind of who she was seeing, there's no telling how he might have reacted.'

Bliss opted to show a lack of interest in the suggestion. He had to get his team off the Reid connection. 'That might've explained the beating. Might have. But snatching me up, keeping me overnight, only to offer vague threats and then dump me by the roadside this morning… *that* makes no sense, either. Not if it was Reid.'

Chandler blew out her lips. 'I suppose you're right. If he did all that because you were sleeping with his ex-wife, he wouldn't have left it alone. And he certainly wouldn't have let you go. But if not him, then who?'

'Once again, I have no idea. Believe me, I want to find out who is responsible way more than you do. I'm the one who was laid into, stuck in some dump wearing a hood all night, no food and little water. I have the bruises and the fatigue to prove it. But the simple fact is, I'm clueless on this one, and I think it's time we switched back to our case.'

'Agreed,' she said. 'We'll put it to one side for now. But we're not done with it, Jimmy. And I still have my eye on you in case you got banged up worse than you're letting on.'

Snapping his thumb and fingers together to simulate a mouth yapping away, Bliss said, 'Yeah, yeah. Nag, nag. Meanwhile, what happened to Frank? When we broke up the meeting yesterday evening, I got the distinct impression he was sticking around for the duration.'

Bishop, who had been listening intently, used his forefinger to draw a line across his throat. 'That was the plan. But plans change. He joined me and Penny for a drink, but just as we were about to order a second round, he took a call from his wife. Afterwards, he told us he was going home to spend the weekend with her and his daughter.'

Bliss grinned. 'Ah, yes. We've all had one of those calls before, right?'

Superintendent Fletcher had been sitting at a desk, hands clasped behind her head, but now got to her feet and stretched out her back. 'Jimmy, I called everybody in the moment we knew you were missing. Now that you're back and there appears to be no lasting damage or further immediate threat, I think it's time we gave people the time off they deserve. You still need to get yourself checked out, so I'm in favour of sending everyone home other than Gul, who is still on duty. That sound all right to you?'

Chandler looked over at Bliss. 'You asked me in this morning to discuss the case. We never got round to it. You want to do that now?'

He groaned and flexed his neck muscles. 'What I want more than anything right now is a beer and something to eat,' he said. He looked up at Fletcher. 'Ma'am, I think you have the right idea. Let everyone go. Gul has our numbers if something urgent comes in. Me, after I'm fed and watered, I could do with a rest and a decent night's kip.'

'After you've been to the hospital?'

'Naturally. Wouldn't have it any other way.'

'You're lying to me, aren't you?' Fletcher said sceptically.

Bliss winked. 'Naturally. Wouldn't have it any other way.'

Fletcher sighed and shook her head at him before turning to the group. 'In that case, everybody can bugger off. Thank you all, especially those of you who dragged yourself in from a day off. Gul, if anything does crop up, I'm your first call. And Jimmy… we're not forgetting what you went through. Not any of us. You're absolutely right to prioritise Operation Insulate, and I commend you for it, but the moment this investigation is over we're going to knuckle down and set our sights on finding out who was responsible for what happened to you, and why. That's my promise.'

'Thank you,' he said, guilt wrapping itself around him like a cocoon. 'And thanks to every single one of you. I'm more grateful than you'll ever know.'

Bliss felt another stab of remorse. This one the most cutting so far.

TWENTY-NINE

Chandler insisted on driving him to A&E. Bliss insisted on going straight home. She reminded him his car was still at the Holiday Inn and therefore he was in her playground for the time being. He reminded her there were taxis willing to take him wherever he told them to go, provided he had the wherewithal to pay them. She caved, as he had known she would. After working things out at the hotel, Chandler followed him back to his house. He stopped off at a shop just round the corner from his home to buy four small crusty rolls.

Chandler and Max made a fuss of each other while Bliss thanked a shy teen by the name of Lucinda for taking care of the dog's walk and food and for keeping him company. He took a twenty-pound note from his wallet and offered it to the girl, which she refused. 'I keep telling you, Mr Bliss, ours is a voluntary service. Besides, I love being with Max. He's adorable, and so much better than anything I have waiting for me at home.'

'And I keep telling you to call me Jimmy. Are you sure you won't take something for your trouble? The agency doesn't need to know.'

'It's not about them. And it's no trouble. I can't have a dog of my own, so by allowing me to spend time with yours, you're really doing me a massive favour.'

She won the argument. As he closed the front door behind her, Chandler gave Max one last stroke before standing upright. 'Cute kid,' she said. 'Hard to imagine her being stuck for things to do at the weekend.'

'Yeah. She's bright, so in today's world that probably marks her down as being different. She's getting better, though. That's the most she's said to me since she's been coming here. Listen, I'd still like to get her a little something. What can I buy that doesn't scream stalker?'

'I'm not sure. What does she like?'

'Dogs. Like I said, we don't talk much. She's obviously shy, and because she's cute I don't want to come across as an old perv.'

'Too late for that. You used to perv over me all the time.'

'That's when you weren't past your sell-by date.'

Chandler blew a raspberry. 'Up yours. As for the gift, it's a nice idea, but the usual chocolates or flowers will have the precise effect you're looking to avoid. She'll think you're after more than a minder for Max. How about a gift card? Amazon voucher?'

Bliss sneered at the suggestion. 'Too impersonal.'

'Ooh, how about sponsoring a dog on her behalf?'

'Now, that is a cracking idea. Wood Green runs a scheme. They'll keep in touch with her about the dog's welfare, and if somebody adopts it, we can just move on to another one. Well done, Detective Sergeant Chandler. I knew you weren't as dumb as you look.'

'I'm as dumb as you are handsome.'

He couldn't decide which of them had won that particular exchange. In the kitchen he pulled two bottles of Peroni from the fridge, then made them each a cheese spread and peanut butter roll. They sat together on the wooden bench out in his garden, saying nothing at first.

'This gets a bit… claggy after a while,' Chandler complained between mouthfuls of her food.

Bliss held a bottle to his lips. 'That's what the beer is for,' he said. 'Wash it all down with something light and refreshing. It'll do before the Guinness comes out.'

'You not going to the Windmill later?'

He considered it for a moment. It had been his local boozer for the past few years, and being within easy walking distance made it hard to resist. A few beers, perhaps a Chinese takeaway on the way home, sounded pretty good after the night he'd endured.

'You up for it?' he asked.

'Me? No, I'll probably go home after this one.'

'Shrek missing you?'

'He's still away on business.'

'Well, then. Don't be Billy No Mates. Come and have a few drinks with me.'

'You have beer in the fridge, don't you?'

'Of course. But in bottles or cans, Pen. Not draught. You can't beat a pint of draught.'

'I'll take your word for it. So, why are you refusing to go to hospital?'

Bliss reared back. 'Woah! That was a rapid swerve if ever there was one.'

'I like to keep you off balance.'

'Which isn't difficult given my chronic illness.'

Slapping a hand to her head, Chandler grimaced and said, 'Ouch! Sorry about that.'

He brushed her apology away. 'I'm joshing. Look, like you said, I've had a concussion before. This ain't that. No imbalance, no nausea, no confusion, no loss of… of… what was I going to say? Oh, yes… memory.'

Her two-finger reply was not entirely unexpected. 'What's with the fishing wire strung up over the pond?' she asked, switching the conversation back to a more mundane topic.

Growling beneath his breath, Bliss said, 'There's a bloody heron on the prowl. The pond design and the planting help to keep most of them at bay, but this one is a bit more determined. I didn't want any of my fish being snapped up, so I had the wire done.'

'It's the circle of life, Jimmy. Herons need to eat, too.'

'Yeah, well, they can keep their ugly pointy beaks off my koi and goldfish. Because if I catch the little shit, I'll wring its scrawny neck.'

Chandler chuckled, stretched out her legs, and released a languid sigh. 'It's nice just sitting here and relaxing in the sunshine. I can't tell you how worried we all were this morning. It was bad enough knowing you were missing, but seeing you beaten and abducted in that way… it gave me the chills. I have to say, I never once thought you might be a goner, but I did wonder if we'd get you back minus a few digits or bearing a few ugly scars.'

'Charming.'

'I know, right? It's a horrible thought, but not unwarranted given what happened.'

'It could definitely have been worse. But it wasn't, so we move on.'

'I'll drink to that. So now we have that out of the way, isn't it time you told me more about your big secret?'

Bliss froze. *What did she know? Had he slipped up?* 'What secret is that?' he asked.

'Pam Daniels.'

'Oh. Pam.' Relieved, he finished his beer and explained their chance meeting in the Woodman, how one thing had led to another after a tasty Italian meal in Stamford. A welcome night of passion. Two isolated souls making each other a little less lonely.

'And now she's gone back down to London?'

He nodded. 'Yep. I called her while I was waiting for you to come and get me.'

'And she answered? I kept getting her voicemail.'

'She probably ignored yours because the number was not recognised. Anyhow, she was under the impression I'd chickened out of our last night together. She was obviously shocked by what happened to me, but happy to know I was okay and that I'd been on my way to see her again.'

Chandler took a sip of her lager. 'And was it genuinely going to be your last night together?'

'Absolutely. It's only natural to consider the future, and we did. We chatted about it, discussed options. But in the end we called it a day. She and I were a serious item once, but that was four decades ago. We were just company this time around. She has her life down in London, I have my life up here. We agreed, and nothing that's happened since has changed that. We'll keep in touch for a while, I'm sure. But then without either of us meaning to, the calls will drop off and we'll probably exchange the odd text instead. Until we reach the stage where neither of us can be arsed or can remember why we were writing them in the first place.'

'Bloody hell. That sounds so pessimistic and cynical, Jimmy.'

He glanced across at his partner, genuinely surprised by her observation. 'Does it? I think it's the reality of the situation, Pen. She is not the next great love of my life.'

'Nor you hers?'

'No. Me and Pam were inseparable when we were in our midteens. It lasted a few years, too, and believe me, it was against the odds. You remember me telling you about how my neighbourhood was a mixture of both the good and bad side of the tracks?

Well, Pam's family was firmly stuck on the bad side. We were geographically close, but far enough across the border to count for something. Her old man had no time for me at all, and while my mum and dad liked Pam, they weren't entirely unhappy when we broke up. Hazel was much more to their liking.'

'Fair enough, I suppose. How many people end up married to their teenage love? All right, then, how about *her* big secret? Marty Reid. Sounds as if she did the sensible thing getting away from him, but what an incredible coincidence.'

'Which is all it was,' Bliss said more strenuously than he'd intended. 'We know this because of when she arranged her trip up here.'

Chandler said nothing, staring off into the distance.

'What?' he prompted, more than warm air prickling his flesh. 'What are you trying so hard not to say?'

'Nothing much. Only that, all we actually know is she booked her convention months in advance, so her being here in the city last week was a complete coincidence.'

'My point exactly.'

'But we don't know if her bumping into you at the pub was.'

'So what are you suggesting?' Bliss asked.

Chandler shook her head. She leaned to one side and ran her fingernails across Max's back. 'Nothing specific. Just that we can prove one thing, but not the other. So maybe you two meeting up wasn't the chance encounter you seem so convinced it was.'

THIRTY

Monday morning. Thorpe Wood police station. Bliss was delighted to see Diane Warburton in her office when he walked in. He rapped his knuckles on the doorframe and poked his head inside.

'How's Ava?' he asked.

Not wishing to intrude into a family matter, Bliss had texted rather than phoned to express his concern and wish his boss's daughter well. Following an initial generic reply to thank him, Warburton had telephoned on Sunday morning to elaborate further. Ava had been rushed to hospital with a ruptured appendix and had subsequently been diagnosed with peritonitis. Bliss was aware of how serious an infection it could be, but the hospital had caught it early and the young woman was recovering with the aid of an intravenous drip of strong antibiotics.

Warburton looked up from a file she was reading. Her face was drawn and pale, days of worry and stress evident beneath a layer of makeup clearly applied without enthusiasm. She nodded once. 'Well on the road to a full recovery, thank you. They'll keep her for another week or so, but Andy and I are now swapping bedside duties, so make the most of me today.'

'I'm glad to hear she's on the mend. Scary times, I bet?'

'The scariest, Jimmy. She may be in her twenties and off living her own life, but when she's laying curled up in that hospital bed and suffering, she's just your child again and you feel so bloody helpless.' The final four words were squeezed out together with tears and a thinly disguised sob. Bliss made to go to his boss, but she waved him away. 'I'm all right. It's okay. Ava's okay. Or at least, she will be. She was lucky, so I'm going to focus on that rather than what might have been.'

'That's the best way. And Diane, if you feel you need to be with her, just pick up and get out of here. You don't need for me to tell you family is more important than anything.'

'I know. And thank you for that. I've spoken to Marion, and she pretty much said the same thing. Anyhow, back to today. I've brought myself up to date with the case file and policy book. HOLMES, too. I'll work on tying them all together so that we start from a single baseline again tomorrow. Which brings me to the first order of the day: Jimmy, as soon as we're done here, you'll be seeing the on-call Force Medical Examiner. Doctor Gillespie happens to be in the building, so I've arranged for her to examine you in respect of a concussion.'

Bliss snorted in exasperation. 'There's no need to waste her time on me, Diane. If I had a concussion, I would have felt the effects yesterday. I didn't, so I don't. Can we just get on with what I fully expect to be a busy day?'

'Are you done?' Warburton's eyebrows arched.

'I don't know. Am I?'

'You might as well be for all the good your bluster will do. It wasn't a request. And until her examination of you is complete, you will be going nowhere. Have I made myself clear?'

'Crystal,' he muttered, setting his jaw.

'Stamp your feet and throw your toys out of the pram all you like. This is happening. Before it does, I have to say how sorry I was to learn about what happened to you on Friday evening. Where's your head at about it? Any further thoughts on who might be responsible?'

He hadn't had to think about that, but his mind had seldom strayed far from Harry Daniels and the bunch of scumbags who worked for him. Neither the beating nor the abduction sat well with him, and at some point he hoped to settle the score. Otherwise, his Sunday had passed off peacefully. He'd spent a couple of hours over at Ferry Meadows with Max, who was indefatigable when it came to fetching a ball. Fresh air and sunshine were all he'd needed to reinvent himself.

'Not really,' he said in answer to his DCI's question. He reflexively touched a hand to the worst of his head injuries: a large bump at the base of the crown. 'I'm sure it was no more than a warning shot across my bow.'

'What leads you to that conclusion?'

'For a start, they used bats and pickaxe handles. No sharps. That tells me the weapons were meant to subdue, no permanent harm intended. Then there's the fact they let me go the following day.'

Warburton leaned forward, peering up at him. 'And what do you make of that? Because here's the thing, Jimmy: how is it a warning if they don't tell you who is issuing it? Surely, a threat is too vague without identifying the source?'

'To the contrary, I actually think that was a major part of their tactics,' Bliss said, remembering what he had rehearsed the previous day while out walking. 'A name would give me clarity and a narrow focus. A target to set my sights on and be wary of in the future. The purpose of a more general warning is to create a greater and wider apprehension. This way, I might fear everyone and everything. I think it was done to put me off my stride.'

'To what end? In connection to Operation Insulate?'

'That I've yet to figure out, though it's doubtful. I'm putting up a theory here, Diane. It's about the only thing that makes sense to me.'

Warburton made no reply, easing back into her chair. 'Okay, but if anything else occurs, you tell me. Now, while I don't like to intrude upon your personal life, what's the story with this woman you've been seeing? Marty Reid's ex-wife?'

He thought he'd got away with it. Not so, it seemed. He cast an eye over her desk, noting she was snowed under. He admired her ability to concentrate at such an emotional time. 'Diane, I genuinely had no idea about that until I spoke to Pen when she picked me up after they let me go. Pam Daniels, as she was and as I understand she is again, was a girlfriend back in my teens. We lived in the same neck of the woods, hung around together, went to the same school, and eventually started going out. It ended, and I literally had not seen her since then until she spotted me in the boozer last Tuesday.'

'And what about that? An amazing coincidence, wouldn't you say?'

'I would. But that's what I believe it was. You've read the latest. It can't possibly have anything to do with Marty Reid. The timing bears that out.'

'Hmm. You'll have to forgive my scepticism, Jimmy. Something about it doesn't smell right, and I'm struggling to understand why your senses aren't picking up the same stench. Either way, your renewed relationship with Pamela Daniels cannot prevent us from continuing our inquiries. Marty Reid is on your list of suspects to talk to, so that still has to happen. I'm not going to instruct you on this, but you might consider having Bish and Gul interview him instead of you and Penny. However, we can't ignore the apparent coincidence, so we'll also need to speak to

Pamela Daniels. Now, here I will instruct you, and I will insist on somebody other than you interviewing her.'

Bliss realised there was no point in fighting his DCI on this. She had left the door open for him to confront Reid, but his personal connection to Pam meant he could not touch that aspect of the investigation. He thought of calling her to discuss her testimony, but decided it was too risky. The pair of them had developed the story and he had no doubt she would stick to it, irrespective of who asked the questions.

When he left Warburton's office, he felt as if he were walking on cotton wool. Nothing beneath his feet felt stable or secure. He'd done nothing wrong in reconnecting with Pam. The same could not be said for anything he had done since being rescued by her from her father and his thugs. He had lied to his team, potentially adversely influencing a major investigation. He didn't believe Pam was in any way involved with either the murders or the op, nor her husband, for that matter. Even so, the lies he'd told about Friday night and Saturday morning could be regarded as impeding their case. If anybody found out, it would mean the end of his career.

He'd spoken to Sandra Bannister on Sunday, and had arranged to call her again this morning. The media briefing late on Friday evening had taken an ugly turn as a result of her grilling the PCC about his tactics in potentially exposing an ongoing investigation to the perpetrator. Benning had not reacted well, surprising the gathering of journalists with a vitriolic retort. Bannister had concerns as to the response from her editors, and unless something had gone badly wrong, she'd now be free to talk.

She picked up on the second ring. 'Well?' he asked. 'You still have a job?'

'Very much so.' He heard the relief in her voice and assumed her morning meeting had turned out better than expected.

'See, I told you. Editors love that sort of stuff. You put that pompous oaf in his place, and then he wounded himself even further by the way he behaved. I do hope they told you to follow up on it.'

'That's exactly what they want me to do. He's shown he has a weak spot, and my job today is to burrow down into it. My article for later will ask if Benning is fit to be Commissioner when, in his desire to stamp his authority, he put at risk an ongoing murder investigation. I'll ask how that is serving the people of Cambridgeshire, and how it can possibly align with his own plans for improvement.'

Bliss sucked air between his teeth. 'Ouch. I can feel the burn from here.'

'You said he deserves it.'

'He does. And the rest. Tear him apart, Sandra. Then pick his bones clean.'

The journalist laughed. 'Now who's the ruthless one?'

'I just want that idiot to stop talking shit. Is that too much to ask?'

They agreed it was not. He wished her well, and was feeling a lot happier for having spoken to her.

*

He woke early that morning. Not struggling through the fog of sleep, but immediately alert and eager to face a new day. Sunlight bled through the window blinds, birds sang out in their individual voices. Leaving his wife snoring softly beneath a thin cotton sheet, he rose, exercised for thirty minutes in the room he'd turned into a well-equipped gym, showered, and then dressed in casual clothing. It was the summer holidays, so there was no need to get the kids ready for school. In fact, he had no plans at all for the entire day.

No list of fresh victims to work his way through existed as far as he was aware, so until he received a new text from his employer he was free to do as he pleased. Theirs was a simple enough arrangement, although every so often another name would appear while he was still making preparations for the previous one. He was meticulous in his planning, so an occasional overlap was inevitable. Nobody appeared to care provided he succeeded – and he never failed them.

Much of the time, his work did not require him to take lives. If he was asked to fix a problem without resorting to the ultimate punishment, that was precisely what he did. He did it well, too. He could be extremely persuasive when he needed to be. Many of the people he dealt with considered themselves to be tough, but he always managed to find at least one major weakness to exploit.

The burner phone sprang to life as he sat down to breakfast at the table on the patio.

He took a sip of coffee before checking the incoming message. The name surprised him. The rest of the text did not.

Just a strong word required. Details in place.

His orders were usually specific, an instruction as to what was required of him. His services ranged from having a quiet chat in the right ear at the right time, to committing murder; from an aggressive and mildly harmful initial approach, to putting someone in hospital. The names came via his phone, but the finer details of the job and the expected outcome were always left in an email account to which his contact also had access. No mail was ever sent or received, the information simply left in a draft message which was read and then removed in a neat exchange that was never transmitted. He had precisely thirty minutes to study the details, at which time if he didn't remove them, somebody else did.

Though no signatures or blood oaths were required, it was a contract of sorts. One he respected and believed in. He took his job seriously and expected those he dealt with to treat him in the exact same way. It was an effective procedure, one he was more than happy to comply with.

Seeing the name of Marty Reid's ex-wife on his screen, however, had momentarily startled him. As he read the details via his email app, he began to understand. Pam Daniels was known to be untouchable… for the time being. Nobody ever actually was, of course, not even Reid himself.

It was a dangerous world, and gradually becoming more so right under people's noses. The world of drugs and whores had never been quite so fluid. Long-standing peaceful arrangements over territory were starting to unravel. County lines and cuckooing had taken the drugs trade in a completely different direction, and established prostitution rings were threatened by those willing to traffic young men and women in from Europe and Africa. To their abject fury, one-time major players had become marginalised. Some were fighting back, resulting in a vicious and often bloody war that only on occasion exploded into the public domain. Others were packing their bags and heading for sunnier climes. Either way, problems needed resolving.

Then there were those who decided to join forces and take the battle to the newcomers. In these instances, the necessary solutions were often permanent ones. He regarded it as the circle of death, a destructive pattern of behaviour with no end in sight. Times of great upheaval and fear were good for business.

His business.

There were times when modern criminal enterprise required a man to speak to people, a man capable of applying pressure in a variety of ways. A man out front to absorb vengeful responses and protect the overall structure. He enjoyed being that man.

But in seeing the name of Pam Daniels, he had to wonder if the underworld he inhabited might be unravelling in a way and at a pace nobody had foreseen.

THIRTY-ONE

It hurt to have to sit out the interviews, but Bliss bit down on it and worked doubly hard with Chandler and DCI Warburton to disentangle additional threads in their investigation. They got stuck in together the moment he returned to the office after having his examination – which he'd passed with flying colours. The bruising on his arms, shoulders, and upper back was as extensive as expected, but the doctor confirmed he had no broken bones. Having not sustained a concussion or anything more serious came as an immense relief, though he refused to admit as much in the presence of his colleagues. He was simply glad to be focussed on the case.

The murder of Taylor Sweeting had significantly widened the scope of their HOLMES searches, transforming their entire approach. With individual victims now part of the search criteria, there were far too many possibilities to choose from, leaving Bliss to suggest they pause to reflect before moving forward again in careful stages.

'I think we limit ourselves for the time being to the cases we identified during our first sweep – except for one that came in just today. That stands out because the victim, Xavier Brent, was a known dealer who supposedly drowned in his own pool. The connections there are too obvious to ignore. The reason why I want to put a foot on the brake with the additional cases coming in is because we've not exhausted those we're already looking into. If it helps to persuade you, I spoke to Frank Rogers a short while ago and he agreed with me. He sends his apologies, but he's attending the interviews down in London. I've had Bish and Phil stagger their respective chats so that Frank can be at both. His insight might well give us an edge.'

Bliss hoped he had played his cards well. Rogers was a perceptive investigator, and there was a danger of him sniffing something out during these interviews. The kind of thing neither Bliss nor Pam Daniels wanted him to. He'd had to weigh the potential consequences of being pro-active against not suggesting it, which might have caused greater suspicion given it was the most obvious move in light of his own absence.

'I have two follow-up questions before we move on,' Warburton said. 'First, how much more do you hope to squeeze from these cases? After all, we've been working them for days, as have the original investigation teams. And second, what comes next if they offer up nothing we don't already know?'

'I honestly don't have an answer to the first of those,' Bliss replied. He flushed down two paracetamol tablets with hot chocolate from the vending machine before continuing. 'In my opinion, we're stretched too thin with all these HOLMES cases, and concentrating all our efforts on a smaller group of investigations might unearth something we've so far overlooked. There's more to be done, so I think it's worth squeezing every last drop out of them. As for the second, I'd suggest we initially pay attention to cases involving families. Widening the search parameters to include individuals was absolutely necessary, but it backfired and ended up breaking the banks, Diane. We've been flooded with cases and information and it's become unwieldy. If I were SIO, it's what I'd be writing up as a policy, and I'm happy to do so as your deputy if you're uncertain.'

Warburton fixed him with a heated glare. 'I'm quite capable of making my own decisions, thank you.'

He understood her resentment. She was vulnerable, and might think he was challenging her ability to think straight at a time when her daughter was hospitalised. He let it slide without challenge.

'No offence intended, boss,' he said, equably. 'I realise it's a major call, and I wanted you to know I stand by it. The truth is, we're swamped. We have neither the staff nor the budget to action all these cases coming in. I admit I got excited at first by having other investigations to look at, thinking the more we had the more they would confirm my theory. But the reality is, it's too much. We have to prune back.'

'I do understand, Jimmy. What's more, I agree with you. Go on… what else?'

He finished off his drink, buying time to gather his thoughts. 'I began the day with two cases in mind for me and Pen to stick with until we'd exhausted all current and potential leads. They were Mr and Mrs Worsley from Poole, and Taylor Sweeting from North Yorkshire.'

'I thought you wanted us to focus on families,' Chandler said pointedly. 'Isn't that what you just told us?'

'Only if neither of these pans out. And in addition to our ongoing op, of course.'

'All right. So why those?'

Bliss considered his words carefully before laying it out for both Chandler and their DCI. His partner worked her way through a finger of Twix as suggestively and inappropriately as possible, slowly sucking and licking off the chocolate while forming bulges in her cheek with her tongue. He did his best to ignore her, while their boss appeared to be genuinely oblivious.

'Regarding the Worsleys,' he said, 'they're a priority because so far they are the only victims with a confirmed link to this London villain, Marty Reid. That association matches our thinking as to why these murders are taking place at all. And with Taylor Sweeting apparently turning tricks and pushing for a firm up in Hull, we can't ignore a drug connection that might also lead us to the same bloke.'

'Forgive me for pointing out the obvious,' Warburton said, 'but we still have no confirmation that Reid is at the centre of this. Frank Rogers didn't even put this… this Lightning Rod person together with Reid, did he?'

'Not officially, no. He was interested in it as a theory, though. And he certainly didn't rule it out.'

'Fair enough. But what I'm saying is, aren't you putting an awful lot of faith, not to mention time and resources, into making this connection to Marty Reid? I'm not talking out of turn here, Jimmy, when I say that's not the way you usually work. You're starting with the assumption that Reid is involved and trying to build the rest of the puzzle around him, as opposed to slotting the pieces together and finding they end up with an image of Reid.'

Bliss took a deep breath. His boss wasn't wrong. This was not his normal way of building an investigation. Earlier, he'd asked himself if his renewed myopic view of the case had come about as a result of Reid having once been married to Pam Daniels. He gave the notion its due consideration, but was satisfied when the answer came back the same way: Reid had been an obvious suspect before Bliss knew about the gangster's past relationship with Pam. In many ways, ignoring that would be worse than now elevating him to main suspect.

'I accept it's arse-backwards,' he admitted. 'I hold my hands up to that. And if you have something better, another suspect for us to take a close look at, another course of action for us to follow, I'll happily listen. I'm not blinkered, and I'm open to any and all suggestions.'

Warburton gave a chagrined scowl. 'Unfortunately, I don't have anything else to offer at this time. Okay, you've explained your interest in Mr and Mrs Worsley. What about the Sweeting girl? Surely even you can see that's a stretch.'

'Of course I can. But there are a couple of reasons other than those I've already mentioned. As an individual, she is another anomaly, which is enough to grab my attention. But there's also considerably more room for us to nose around in when it comes to her case. As an escort and pusher, she had ties to a criminal enterprise, which gives us something to work with. But the main point is it's fresh. It can be difficult to rebuild momentum with a stale case, but hers is very much ongoing. I think there's more to be discovered.'

Nodding, the DCI made several notations on a pad lying open on the desk at which she sat. She paused with a fingertip to her lips for a moment before going on. 'Okay. I'm assuming Xavier Brent is in your top three for the same reason.'

Happy to defend his decision, Bliss also nodded. 'More so, in fact. He wasn't pushing a few relaxation drugs to clients in Hull like Taylor Sweeting. He was a genuine dealer of considerable weight. Details are sketchy at the moment, but there has to be something there for us to build on. Being in London, Brent may well have had provable connections to Reid. If they're there, I want to find them.'

Warburton sat back in her chair and ran both hands through her hair. Wavy with a copper tint, it was thick when she wore it down and her fingers inevitably got caught up in a tangle.

She closed her eyes, causing Bliss to wonder if fatigue might be catching up.

'Diane,' he said gently. 'Please don't take this the wrong way, but why don't you bugger off? Either go home and get some sleep, or go sit by your daughter's bedside. There's nothing here that can't wait.'

She looked at him with red-rimmed eyes. 'You mean besides a possible serial killer?'

'Marion is more than willing to fill in for you. I can run the SIO side of things. If you stress yourself too much, you might make yourself sick and end up having more time off as a result. We've got this. Trust your team to take care of it for you.'

With a resigned sigh, Warburton nodded. She stood, placed both hands on the desk and said, 'Everything we've discussed here makes sense. They're genuine lines of inquiry. I'll co-sign any decisions you make.' She let her eyes wander across to Chandler. 'Penny, I'm relying on you to keep him on a tight lead. He doesn't go anywhere near Pamela Daniels until such time as she is officially cleared. And I still would rather he didn't get himself involved with Marty Reid at this fragile stage, either. Do I have your word?'

Chandler smiled. 'It'll be my pleasure, boss. But you know, I don't think even Jimmy will want to add to your stress levels at the moment. So I think he'll keep himself in check.'

'I would hope so. But you're my plan B.'

*

Five minutes later, it was just the two of them in the office. Bishop and Ansari were in London interviewing Marty Reid, who had agreed to being spoken to under caution, albeit in the presence of his solicitor. Meanwhile, Gratton and Virgil were preparing to speak with Pamela Daniels in her own home. They would also do so under caution in case she slipped up, but Pam had offered to talk without legal representation. Bliss was secretly glad of that; to have requested a brief when being interviewed as a witness would have raised alarm bells for the team. As it was, she was playing it cool, just as they had planned. It was up to her now.

Meanwhile, he and Chandler pulled three new boards into the incident room, separating the Worsley, Sweeting, and Brent cases. Being the most recent, the latter clearly had a great deal yet to be discovered, so they agreed to tackle it first and bring it to a point at which they'd be satisfied to reassess the merits of each. Chandler suggested she call the investigation team in north London while he studied Xavier Brent's criminal record, and he was happy to comply.

Brent had been arrested on three separate occasions, each for possession of class A drugs with the intent to supply. All three arrests led to charges being made. The Crown Prosecution Service pulled out of the first due to a lack of evidence, the second had led to a trial from which Brent had walked away with a not guilty verdict, but he'd served a five-year stint in prison for the third arrestable offence.

Case files and HOLMES records contained more than the naked details of a crime. Reading between the lines, Brent was a man determined to live a lifestyle way beyond his natural means. If the occasional run-in with the police was the price he had to pay, it was one he did not seem unduly bothered by. Intel suggested he had, upon release from Wandsworth, immediately returned to his chosen life of crime. The same sources also revealed a complete lack of knowledge when it came to identifying the man's supplier. That alone kept Marty Reid in the frame, because few in the drugs trade kept their noses clean enough to continue supplying for any length of time without being mentioned in connection with a whole range of dealers.

When Chandler came off the phone, she was less than animated. 'Given who and what Xavier Brent was, a busy team is not busting a gut to get this one solved. It's one more piece of shit being murdered by another piece of shit as far as they're concerned. That's if it's even investigated as a murder. Currently, they're regarding it as an accidental drowning because that's where the evidence – or lack of – is pointing them. That said, a witness has today come forward to say they saw a man on Brent's doorstep last Friday showing some kind of identification to the security camera.'

Bliss perked up at that final snippet. 'What made them think this man was offering up his ID?'

'They observed him pulling something from his breast pocket and holding it up at the door. Said they assumed it was a business card of some kind. The bloke was suited and booted, looked like he might be selling something. And no, hardly any description as the witness saw only his back.'

'Presumably the camera records, yes?'

'It does. The local team is having a problem getting into the system, though. It's password protected. No sign of the password being written down, and the security company is demanding a warrant before releasing the cloud backups. The DCI running things down there was told access might be available by mid-afternoon today. However, there's a bloody big cloud hovering over this lead. The company reckons our victim's system had been playing up for days prior to his death, so it's anyone's guess as to whether it actually recorded our man at the door.'

Bliss pondered this for a few moments. Just as their killer knew Taylor Sweeting's running route, and that the Armstrong family had a dog, had he also known about Brent's security system and ensured it had no record of his visit?

'A monkey and my left nut says there'll be no evidence,' he said. 'In which case, we'll know for sure it's our man.'

'Why is everything all about testicles with you?' Chandler asked, giving him a withering look.

'Sometimes, Pen, it's all a man has left to offer.'

'What's that when it's at home? Some kind of ancient wisdom?'

'Not that I'm aware of. I'm a modern day sage in my own right.'

'Yeah, you're right up there with Confucius and Yoda.'

'You mock, but if I'm right and we don't get a decent security shot of our killer, then we have to press on looking for some kind of link between Brent and Reid, and…' Bliss lost his train of thought for a moment, before boarding another. 'Or do we?'

Chandler raised her chin. 'What do you mean?'

Bliss shoved the contents of his desk top to one side and rested his elbows on it. 'We've been working under the assumption that any link to criminal enterprise will do. Brent is in it up to his neck, but that doesn't mean he had any agreement with Marty Reid. Spending time searching for one might use up too many resources, including our time. I think we've reached the point at which we can now reassess the merits of three established cases. So to my mind, the next question we have to answer is, do we drill down into Taylor's dealings with the mob in Hull, Brent's supplier, or Hugh Worsley's rumoured association with Reid?'

THIRTY-TWO

Although Marty Reid was a known quantity, and the more obvious person to be pulling the Lightning Rod's strings, Frank Rogers was far more interested in his ex-wife. He had been since being told about Bliss's recent dalliances with her. He could not dismiss the highly likely association between the pair seeing each other again and the inspector's brutal abduction. The only question for him was whether she had been in on it.

As agreed with DS Bishop and DC Ansari, he could attend the Marty Reid interview but take no part in it. If he had observations or questions, he'd discuss them with the detectives during breaks. They were right to insist on this; Reid had to understand who was running the show. He hoped that knowing the NCA were also in attendance might provide its own level of discomfort.

They'd arranged to use an interview room at Charing Cross police station just off the Strand. The building's impressive exterior gleamed in the bright sunshine, but inside the old walls and floors creaked and groaned as befitting its age. The structure looked and smelled as if it were hanging together with duct tape and WD40, though Rogers had to admit the staff made a decent brew.

From a purely observational standpoint, he found the process fascinating. The more senior officer allowed his partner to take the lead. Both Bishop and Ansari were clearly comfortable working that way, the DC having received specialist interview training. She was good at it, too. Prior to the interview, Reid's solicitor spent a few minutes going over the ground rules. Bishop stated the intention to speak to Reid as a person of interest. The whole point of Reid agreeing in the first place was to answer all questions put to him, though the solicitor insisted on making an objection if he thought lines were being crossed. Rogers knew what that meant: essentially, the moment Reid was treated as a suspect, the police would be told to back off.

Ansari skilfully prodded and poked, came right up to the established boundary lines but never once crossed over. In the main, she focussed on Reid's character and associations, steering well clear of his actual alleged misdemeanours. The man disowned his poor reputation as being the result of a vindictive campaign against him based on the legacy of his father's days ruling the roost in the capital's underworld. When it came to people he knew and mingled with, he became more reticent. Some he admitted to socialising with, others he refused to comment on.

The first contentious moment came when Ansari asked Reid about the identity of the man known as the Lightning Rod. She, Bishop, and Rogers had discussed this approach prior to the interview. The hefty sergeant was against it, unwilling to let Reid know they were even aware of the gangster. Having provided the lead to the investigation team, Rogers was happy for it to be out there. Even if this lone wolf idea was nothing more than smoke and mirrors, he'd argued, law enforcement would be aware of the name. He'd gone as far as to suggest that it might seem odd if it were not brought up. That left DC Ansari with the deciding vote, and she confirmed her mettle by going against her partner's advice.

As anticipated, Reid claimed to have no knowledge of any crimes being committed by a person bearing that name. If that was the sobriquet being used by one of his known associates, then he was unaware of it. Rogers had expected nothing different from this blank statement. However, he was watching the man closely when the question was asked and answered, and noted a clear indication of a lie being told. He felt that achieved as much as they were going to get, but he had earlier suggested a second prickly topic, which Ansari moved to just as they were about to wrap things up.

'Tell me, Mr Reid, do you still have any influence over who your ex-wife sleeps with?'

Rogers's lips twitched as he hid his smile. The young DC had used the precise wording he'd recommended.

'What kind of fucking question is that?' Reid snapped at her, his body jerking to attention. Alongside him, his expensive solicitor turned and shook his head in admonishment.

'It's not outside the scope of our agreement, Mr Reid,' she shot back. 'I ask because we have colleagues on their way to interview Pam Daniels. Your marriage ended some time ago, and with some enmity between you. Despite that, our intel suggests she remains part of your organisation.'

'And what organisation would that be?' Reid asked, sitting back and folding his arms.

'Careful, detective,' the solicitor warned.

'Apologies. A slip of the tongue. I meant, of course, your father's organisation. Let's not pretend *that* doesn't still exist. You may claim to play no role in it, Mr Reid, but we believe your wife did. We suspect she still does now that you two are divorced. In turn, that leads us to wonder how closely you are involved in her daily life.'

Just as he had seen a reaction a short time ago, Rogers spotted several tics and facial spasms, each of which told him Reid was uncomfortable with the turn the interview had taken. Any open display of aggression beyond that initial outburst would do the man a disservice, and to call an immediate halt to proceedings was not something he would surely even consider. Ultimately, Reid held it together well, which Rogers found admirable. But it was already too late. The man's body language had answered the staged question.

*

'What's your relationship to Detective Inspector Bliss?' Rogers asked Pamela Daniels. He and DC Gratton had agreed on him getting the first crack at the woman. He deliberately employed the most direct, tactless approach to see if it rattled her.

To her credit, the woman did not flinch. 'We have no relationship,' she said dismissively. 'We were a couple several decades ago. It ended, and that was that.'

'Did he object to the way your family earned a crust?'

'You'd have to ask him that?'

'Did your family object to him because of what his father did for a living?'

'You'd have to ask them that.'

Rogers nodded. 'So why did your relationship end?'

Daniels absently brushed a speck from her skirt, smoothing down the material around her lap. 'I genuinely don't know the answer to that. I suppose it just ran out of steam.'

'I see. How, then, did it start up again?'

Still no change in her blank expression. 'We met by chance last week. I was having lunch in a pub, where I spotted him sitting at a table all by his lonesome. We had dinner and drinks on a couple of occasions after that.'

'That all?' Rogers asked, throwing a little scepticism her way.

'What more do you need?'

'Did you sleep with him?'

This time, she did react. She was an attractive woman except for when she scowled, as she did in response to his tasteless question. 'How is that any of your business, sunshine? I was led to believe I was being interviewed as a witness. If that's changed, then so will my own approach.'

'You agreed to answering questions about both your ex-husband and DI Bliss in connection with the latter's beating and abduction. That occurred in the car park of the hotel in which you were staying. He was on his way to see you that evening. I think it's not only fair but also pertinent for us to know how close you two were, because when looking for motive, we can't rule out a jealous ex.'

'You think Marty was involved?' she scoffed, then chuckled to herself. She was good, Rogers thought. But he was better.

'I do now.'

'What do you mean by that?'

'Your reaction. You can say all the right words in the right order, you can shape your features to express them in just the right way, but it's those micro-expressions we hear so much about these days that give the game away.'

Anger blazed in Pamela Daniels' eyes. She shook her head and puffed out her already pouty lips. 'Such bollocks you people talk. Micro-this and micro-that. I'm betting the only micro thing about you is your dick. That, or your brain. It's pure invention, trashy nonsense to drum up trade, or used by snake oil salesmen like you to suit any old agenda. Counts for fuck all in the real world when push comes to shove, old son. Now, forget all about your new-age shit and listen to what I have to say. Marty wasn't involved, and I'll tell you why. First, he doesn't have a clue about me and Jimmy. Second, even if he did, he wouldn't give a toss. Third, Marty never misses his Friday night poker game, and I can absolutely guarantee that's where he was when Jimmy was assaulted.'

Rogers forced down a smile. He enjoyed a battle of wits and found her response humorous. 'How about later that night?' he asked. 'Or the following morning, come to that? Can you point to his whereabouts at the time?'

'I dare say he was at home, tucked up nice and cosy with his slapper and their bastard child. Either way, I was on my way back down to London by then, so how the fuck would I know? The simple fact is, my ex has no interest in me these days, nor what I do or who I see.'

'I don't believe you,' Rogers stated firmly.

'And I don't give a monkey's what you believe. I'm a witness, right? So here's all I have to say on the subject: I met Jimmy for the first time in yonks, we spent some time together. He didn't turn up on Friday night. I called him a couple of times, left messages, but then let it go. I assumed he was busy at work and owed me no explanation. I drove home the following morning completely unaware of what had gone off. That's it. That's all I know. Other than one thing for certain: whatever happened to Jimmy had absolutely nothing to do with me. You lot are barking up the wrong tree like a blind dog with a cat fetish.'

She was telling the truth about the phone calls. Bliss had mentioned them, both coming in to his personal mobile. The voicemails she left were innocuous, but suggestive of the fact that she had no idea what had happened to him. The calls could have been staged, of course, but Bliss had dismissed Daniels as a suspect from the beginning. Right now, Rogers was asking himself if he could do the same.

THIRTY-THREE

THE AFTERNOON HAD TAKEN a frustrating turn for Bliss and his partner. As a result of their deliberations, he and Chandler had chosen to take a closer look at the Worsley case, hoping to make further inroads. Travelling all the way down to Poole was out of the question, and to his immense irritation, nor was he able to speak to any of the detectives working the operation. As a consequence, all they had to go on was the case file and HOLMES updates, neither of which provided them with a fresh lead. Worse still, they fared no better with the cases in either North Yorkshire or London.

This left Bliss again questioning his motives in pursuing a link between Marty Reid and these three investigations, in particular the one in which his name had already cropped up. But as before, he convinced himself he had it right. The connection to Reid had been proven in respect of Hugh Worsley. For Reid to become a firm suspect, all they needed was to confirm one more, yet they were making no headway at all. His mood low, he'd turned to his partner for inspiration.

'Here's a novel idea,' she said brightly, tapping her pen on a notepad. 'I realise this might seem a bit old-fashioned, and I could well be thinking too far outside the box here, Jimmy, but why don't we spend some time working on our own investigation?'

Despite himself, Bliss smiled. Beneath the sarcasm lurked a valid point. It was the one case requiring no assistance from other area forces. Without any further discussion, he agreed. Together they went back over the information, actions taken, policy decisions, the Sperlings' finances, social media, and phone data. Bliss paid particular attention to the couple's family, friends, and acquaintances. Everything he read told him they were solid and squeaky clean.

Until he came upon a name he recognised in Donald Sperling's contact list.

The world around him disappeared as he used a variety of online tools to research more diligently. Jocelyn Parker was a solicitor he had never sat across the table from, but her reputation spread far beyond the boundaries of the city. When he ran a cross match between Parker and Donald Sperling, he came across a number of articles describing the solicitor's defence of Sperling in a trial relating to alleged tachograph misuse and reporting. This was shortly before the requirement to replace analogue devices with digital. The case was dismissed due to lack of evidence, but one link led to a piece in the *Peterborough Telegraph* that mentioned Sperling having leased a fleet of smaller vehicles for his haulage business. The significant factor in the article was the weight limit: a transportation vehicle up to 3.5 tonnes, like a Ford Transit or Mercedes Sprinter, did not require the installation and use of a tachograph.

Hands poised over the keyboard, Bliss took a breath and asked himself what, if anything, this shift meant. Even if Sperling had been guilty of tachograph abuse, it didn't mean he was concealing anything other than shady business practices. But had he subsequently introduced a different kind of vehicle simply in order to overcome the necessity to have an electronic device monitoring the vehicles and, by association, their drivers? If so, then Sperling clearly wanted to keep part of his business away from prying eyes. The team had previously discussed the possibility of the haulage company running drugs on the side, and this news appeared to align itself with that theory.

Excusing himself, Bliss had slipped out into the corridor to make a call to Sandra Bannister. Relieved to discover she continued to be oblivious to his abduction on Friday night, he asked about the item he had seen and whether the newspaper held a file on Mr and Mrs Sperling. The journalist told him she didn't know, but to hold on while she checked through the *PT* archives. When she came back a couple of minutes later, it was clear there was no more to be gleaned from that particular aspect of the case.

'How's it coming?' she asked.

'Grudgingly,' he admitted. 'It's like pulling teeth. But if I were you, I'd start working on a background piece for the Sperling family. I can't tell you specifically what our interest is, but I have a feeling we're close to breaking the back of it. If we do, there's a story in it for you.'

'Thanks. I look forward to it. And while I have you, my piece on your Commissioner is shaping up well. He's going to regret everything he said on Friday evening.'

'Good to hear. He has it coming. And I hope the result of the review makes it an even worse week for him. I have a feeling it will.'

As he headed back into the incident room, he gave more thought to the likelihood of Sperling being involved in running drugs. If it were true, they'd be raking in a great deal more money than was evident from their bank statements and stock portfolios. His mind ran on and arrived at a logical solution.

'What if they were paid in product?' he said as he reached the desk at which his partner sat.

Chandler glanced away from her monitor, popping a Ricola herbal sweet into her mouth. 'What?'

'The Sperlings. If their haulage company was transporting drugs, Donald Sperling could easily have negotiated payment in gear rather than money. Bricks of cocaine, hidden away until the time comes to put them up for sale. Think about it, Pen. These days, with the international co-operation of the banking industry, it's more difficult – though not impossible – to hide large amounts of cash. Plus, it must always be in the back of your mind that if an offshore bank folds or is discovered breaching all manner of laws, your readies might disappear overnight. But stashing away the product and then selling up come retirement time while you're sunning yourself on a beach in the Turks and Caicos, is a tasty way around the problem.'

'Okay. Makes sense. But we already came up with the notion of him running drugs. How does this bring us any further down the road?'

'I don't know that it does. But if we can get a warrant to search his home and his business property, we might be able to find his stash. We do that and it could take us a step closer.'

Chandler seemed unconvinced. 'What, you think the bricks will have Reid's fingerprints all over them?'

Bliss brushed away her point. 'No. I'm not saying that. But we might find something else hidden away with them. Some kind of ledger, perhaps. Something incriminating, pugged away as leverage should it all go tits up. And if not, at the very least the payment in product will confirm what we suspect.'

Chandler shrugged. 'It's better than anything I've come up with so far. You want me to sort the warrants?'

'Please. We need to find a way in. I can't see anywhere else to go with the Sperlings. That leaves the Armstrongs, which means I need a word with Naomi Haskel.'

That was the stage they had reached when first Bishop and Ansari, and later Gratton and Virgil, arrived back from London. Keen to get a sense of their respective interviews, Bliss fetched each of them a hot drink before debriefing the four detectives involved. He was still digesting the results when Frank Rogers intruded.

'We need to talk,' Rogers said to Bliss as he marched into the incident room. He wore the heavy frown of a man struggling with the weight of knowledge he carried.

'My office?' Bliss suggested, concerned that the NSA man might have pierced Pam Daniels' armour.

'How about over a drink, instead? Finish what you're doing, then call time for the day and I'll treat you to a nice pint. We'll have a lad's night out.'

Chandler looked up from her notepad. 'Can I come?'

'Are you a lad?' Bliss asked her.

'I'm flat-chested enough to be. Will that do?'

'That doesn't count, no. And although I haven't checked them out recently, because apparently it's no longer acceptable to sneak a peek, if I'm remembering correctly, you're by no means flat, Pen. Even if you were, small boobs don't make you one of us.'

'Not one of you, that's for sure. Your tits are like a porn star's.'

He feigned outrage, forming a wide 'O' with his mouth. 'I can't decide if that's sexist or misogynistic. And before you give me some old flannel, they are not the same thing.'

'Actually,' Rogers interjected before Chandler could reply, 'I need to speak to Jimmy alone if that's okay.'

Bliss squinted at him. If his actions were about to be revealed, he'd front up to them. It was the only way he knew how. 'There's nothing you can't say to me in the presence of my oppo, Frank. Nothing I wouldn't tell her afterwards, anyway.' He swivelled in his chair. 'Pen, you're in. So bind up those pups of yours, and the first round is on you.'

They saved the serious stuff for later in the evening. Bliss enjoyed Rogers's company, and the two of them proved to have a lot in common, sharing a love of sport and music. Over dinner, Chandler rolled her eyes on more than one occasion as the pair discussed TV shows and films. All three laughed along together as Bliss shared his favourite Disney and Pixar movie moments.

'You have any sprogs, Jimmy?' Rogers asked when they'd all settled.

'Nope.'

'How about you, Penny?'

'Just the one. A daughter. She's with her father in Turkey at the moment, but she goes to Cambridge, so I get to see her quite often.'

'That's nice. My kid, Laura, loves all the same stuff we do. She's a walking Disney encyclopaedia. Sings along with all the songs, knows every lyric and melody. My son wasn't a huge fan. He was more of a football nut.'

'You grew up in the east-end like me,' Bliss said. 'Please don't tell me he was a Hammers boy.'

Rogers shook his head as if horrified. 'Oh, no bloody way. A Gooner through and through.'

Bliss winced. 'Ouch. Sorry, but I'm a Blues man.'

'We each have our own cross to bear, Jimmy. I know you'll remind me they're the champions of Europe, but your owner's luck is running out, mate. One of these days, his ties to Putin are going to come home to roost.'

'Not that we're mixing metaphors,' Bliss said with a grin.

'Please, not football,' Chandler complained. 'Anything but that.'

'How about music?' Bliss offered.

'No, anything but that, as well. Knowing my luck he'll like that bloody awful Steely Dan mob, too.'

Laughing, Rogers said, 'As it happens, I'm a huge fan.'

As the two men shook hands on a shared appreciation, Chandler put hers to her head and groaned. 'Please, if there is a God, help me,' she implored.

This served only to make them laugh harder still.

'I mean it!' she snapped. 'One more word about them and I'll scream.'

After a somewhat ominous silence, it was Rogers who brought them back on point.

'I spoke with your friend Pamela Daniels today, Jimmy. Have to admit, I liked her. Nice enough lady when she wasn't being quite so bolshy.'

Bliss met his gaze, ignoring the facial scar. 'That's something she always had going for her. It was a trait I admired even when I was on the receiving end of it. Never took a backward step, that girl. Never suffered fools gladly.'

'It was an interesting conversation, that's for sure. The reason I wanted to speak to you, actually, is to tell you I think you were wrong to dismiss her as being associated with what happened to you last Friday. I also think there's more to her relationship with her ex.'

Feeling awkward and exposed for a moment, Bliss now understood why Rogers had asked for them to talk alone. He took a pull from his pint glass and said, 'Okay. I'll take your word for it on the second of those statements. I don't doubt the possibility, though I certainly don't believe the two of them are close. Nor working together, for that matter. You're going to have to explain the first part to me, though.'

'I intend to. Before I do, please believe me when I say I have no skin in this game. My interest lies in the man we refer to as the Lightning Rod. My interest in Marty Reid lies in the possible connection between the two. As part of my NCA investigation,

I became aware of your… of Pamela Daniels. I have a pretty good grasp of her background, and her involvement in various enterprises, including her own business.'

'And all this leads you to conclude…?'

'Not much, really. Not until I got to speak to her today for the first time. But here's what bothers me: the fact that she signed up to this week-long event in Peterborough so long ago suggests that her subsequent approach to you and everything that followed was purely coincidental. A chance happening. The timing tells us this must be the case. Except, what if it doesn't?'

'Go on,' Bliss urged, offering a single nod.

'What if Daniels used the event as cover to seek you out? You might think of it as an extreme case of long-term planning, but that doesn't preclude it from being the case. What if her intention was always to find the right time and place to bump into you last week? What if her intention was to lull you, making you somewhat more vulnerable to a surprise attack?'

'What if her intention was to get to know me again because she had something she wanted to share with me?' Bliss countered. 'Something she wanted to confess to?'

Rogers shook his head. 'No. I don't believe that to be the case. If it were, I don't think she'd have left it until your final meeting.'

Bliss licked his lips. He could not fault the man's logic. 'That's an awful lot of speculation, Frank. I'm not going to sit here and insist you must be wrong, but I do wonder how you came to ask yourself these questions.'

'Because I looked into her eyes, Jimmy,' Rogers said in a flat, even tone. 'And I have to tell you, I did not like what I saw there.'

THIRTY-FOUR

It was the first day of a new hosepipe ban, so naturally the weather changed for the worse. Dark, roiling clouds formed overhead, and not long after dawn broke, they unleashed a torrent of rain as if the sky had been saving it up for weeks and its bladder could no longer hold it in. Fortunately for Bliss, the worst of it fell after he'd taken Max for his morning walk. Not that the Golden Lab didn't seem to enjoy shaking drizzle from his coat all over the hi-fi system when they reached the dry sanctuary of home.

'You expect a treat after doing that, do you?' he said, taking care not to raise his voice or make the dog feel as if it had done something wrong. Max was a changed animal, but the roots of his previous owner's behaviour went deep and were in no hurry to be killed off. Instead, he fetched a meat stick from a variety pack, got Max to sit while he stroked his head and allowed the dog to take the food from his open hand. Building a trusting relationship was slow going, but Bliss was determined to get it right.

Arriving on time for the unit's morning meeting, he thought long and hard before addressing his colleagues. He was operating on only two hours' sleep, and had risen early to sit out in his garden where he often did his best thinking. Taking sips from a mug of tea, his mind had churned in uneven circles. Finally, he accepted he'd been fixated on a single pathway, and having closed both his eyes and ears to it, he now understood what he had to do.

'First on the agenda today is an apology from me,' he said. 'I've allowed myself to be all-consumed by Marty Reid's involvement in our case. Actually, not even our case. The fact is, his connection to Hugh Worsley down in Dorset is the only proven tie to any of the investigations we've been analysing up to this point. There remains a strong argument for continuing to identify victims involved at some level with criminal enterprise. That has been established in respect of recent additions, Taylor Sweeting and Xavier Brent. However, yesterday, Pen and I came to the conclusion that we'd be better off concentrating on our own cases – both the ongoing investigation and the op from four years ago. Any arguments there?'

Bishop, who had already managed to stain his tie with yolk from an egg McMuffin, scratched behind his ear and said, 'Not an argument as such, boss, but are you telling us to forget all about the interviews we did yesterday?'

'No. Definitely not. When it comes to Marty Reid, we know he paid Hugh Worsley to cook his books. There's a strong feeling that Worsley was murdered by the man known to us as the Lightning Rod. And as Frank Rogers has yet to arrive, I'll speak for him and remind you that he and his team are convinced Reid and our killer are connected in some way. Reid, then, remains a legitimate suspect, most likely to have at the very least ordered and paid for the hit on Worsley.'

'And Pamela Daniels?' DC Gratton asked.

Silence hung in the air, all faces turned to Bliss, who was ready. 'She's a person of interest owing to her close association with Reid. Now, I want you to think back to last week. I said then that I believed we'd find our way through this mess via our victims.

Not to blow my own trumpet, but I think that was proven correct every time we discovered a link between the victims and criminal behaviour. But I also allowed those minor victories to sidetrack us, leaning too heavily on our suspicions relating to Reid. He's in it up to his neck. He just may not be the main player. Being his ex-wife, Pam Daniels comes into the reckoning. Even so, I strongly suspect we will be better off focusing on the targets in our own two cases.'

Bliss glanced around the room. Nobody seemed unduly put out, so he continued.

'Today, in line with that decision, we'll be carrying out search and seizure warrants at the home and business premises owned by Mr Sperling. Obviously, we're looking for anything remotely incriminating, but our primary objective is to find a stash of the product I suspect Sperling was shipping around the country. I could be wrong, but I have the nagging feeling that he was compensated for his work with drugs and not cash. Although, if you do happen upon a few million quid in used notes tucked away in a duffel bag, I won't be unhappy.'

He smiled at his own joke, but he felt curiously anxious. Often he was driven by a desperate need to find some kind of justice for victims and their families. Every so often, that determination came from an unnerving fear of failure. Here, he was looking at numerous victims and multiple families. He could not afford to get this one wrong. Not out of some selfish desire to protect his own reputation, but simply because there had already been too much suffering for him and his team not to get a result.

'So,' he said, pulling himself together. 'While you lot are out on location armed only with your fine-toothed combs, Pen and I are going to take another look at the Armstrong investigation.'

'Ooh, I have incoming intel on the Sperlings, boss,' Ansari said, looking away from her laptop monitor. 'A local resident left the area on the day the Sperlings were murdered. He was away all week and only heard about it when he arrived home again. Thing is, when he did it reminded him of something. He claims to have seen a motor pulling into the Sperlings' driveway that afternoon. In fact, this chap stopped to allow the vehicle to turn across the road and into the drive.'

Bliss flushed beneath the giddy rush of adrenaline. 'Was he able to tell us the make and model? Registration plate? Could he describe the driver?'

'Sadly not. It was one of many motoring encounters during his journey. But here's the cherry on top of the icing: his car is fitted with a dash-cam. He checked it and sent us footage on a microSD card. A dappled glare on the driver's window and windscreen makes it difficult to see the interior, but the make and model of the car have been identified from that video. And… it also shows the plate.'

Bliss beamed at his DC, but he sensed there was more to come. 'I'm guessing that's where the good news ends, Gul. Pound to a penny our killer didn't use genuine plates.'

'Ah, no. But it's still decent intel, boss. Thought you might want to know before we went any further.'

'Yes, of course. Thank you. I didn't mean to sound unappreciative. Every scrap of intel is useful. It's amazing how it begins. One minute you're looking at a single flake of snow falling from a frigid sky, and the next you're being broadsided by a bloody massive avalanche. We'll go back to the dash-cam footage and see what we can make of it, okay?'

Delighted with her intervention, Ansari beamed. 'Okey-dokey. By the way, the motor was a silver Land Rover Defender. Big beast of a thing, so our witness said.'

Bliss thanked her again, then knuckled down to the job in hand. 'The Armstrongs,' he said dolefully. 'Once again, we have our suspicions. Could their business, ostensibly selling flowers and plants on a grand scale, have been a cover for drug running? Either supply or distribution. We don't yet know. What we do know is that the family was murdered by the same man who took out the Sperlings. If that man is this Lightning Rod chancer, then the Armstrongs were up to no good, and I want to know how. Any questions?'

His colleagues read the room well. He was in no mood to play games. Too much time had already been wasted. Getting back on track was his only ambition, and to move forward he had to stop thinking about Pamela Daniels and whether she had played him all along.

*

He found Detective Superintendent Haskel in the third-floor conference room. Her Thorpe Wood counterpart was on her way out as they made their way in.

'How's everything shaping up?' Fletcher asked him outside in the corridor.

'As well as can be expected,' Bliss replied. 'You know how it goes.'

'Anything in particular I need to know about?'

'Not at this stage, ma'am.'

'Okay. Find me when you're done here, Jimmy. I want to know more about these warrants.'

Haskel had files and printed A4 sheets of paper strewn across the large wooden table. She looked up as he entered, easing her laptop lid shut and pulling an open file closer. Her movements were furtive, but Bliss clocked them.

'Welcome to the paperless workplace,' she said. 'I make no apologies. Staring at a screen for too long gives me a blinding headache. If I have to plant a tree to compensate for all this paper and the electricity to run the printer, so be it. Now, what can I do for you, Inspector?'

'We've reached the point where we could do with taking a good look at the Armstrong op,' Bliss told her. 'I was told to speak to you ahead of polishing my spade and planting it in the soil, so here I am.'

'And I thank you for that small courtesy. You find me collating material and completing the initial draft of my report. I don't foresee my having to retrace my footsteps, so that investigation is all yours, Inspector.'

'Thanks for that.' He allowed his gaze to fall first upon the laptop, and then the file. Wanting her to know he had seen, and that he understood her caution. 'I know you can't discuss your findings, but is there anything of note that we should be looking for?'

Haskel breathed out through her nostrils, cheeks pinking. 'My remit was limited, as you know. In reference to your current operation, you'll obviously be searching for overlap between the two families. My only dealings with relatives and friends pertained strictly to the investigation. There's much I can't say about that for obvious reasons, but what I can tell you is that I encountered reticence from one or two individuals. If it were my case, I'd be narrowing my focus to those closest to Mr Armstrong.'

The two of them exchanged nods. Without telling him anything, Haskel had given Bliss a steer. He was grateful, and told her so with his eyes. On his way to Superintendent Fletcher's office, he placed a call to Neil Abbott, the forensics crime scene manager.

'I'm calling about the comparison checks between the two cases,' he said. 'I'm about to plunge into the Armstrong one, so whatever you can tell me now will be useful.'

'I only wish that were true, Jimmy,' came the CSI man's reply. 'I am able to confirm some cross-contamination. I've ruled out both my team and yours, Nancy Drinkwater as well. We have matching hairs and fibres from both scenes. Loose hairs, I'm afraid, so no roots.'

'I thought you could now obtain DNA from hairs without their roots.'

'It's technically possible, but hideously expensive. No way we're going to be given the go-ahead to take it to that level. If you catch your man, we'll be able to match the hairs and, hopefully, some fibres to him. Until then, I have nothing of use to you, I'm afraid.'

'Are you receiving forensics from investigators in other areas?'

'It's started flowing in. Don't hold your breath, though.'

'Okay. Thanks, Neil.'

Bliss ended the call. In Fletcher's office moments later, he explained the purpose of the warrants.

'You're fishing,' she said on the back of a wry smile. 'But you might just land yourself something. Why are you thinking product and not bundles of cash?'

'Maybe it's just the latent criminal in me,' he joked. 'If I were hiding away a stash, it's what I'd choose. Cash devalues over time. Cocaine rarely does. More often than not, its worth only increases.'

Eyeing him suspiciously, Fletcher said, 'I think we're going to have to keep tabs on you in your retirement, Jimmy.'

'I think you're right. After all, I won't be around to catch me.'

Back in the major incident room, he spotted Frank Rogers sitting quietly at a desk, scrolling through something on his phone. Chandler sat close by, talking into her mobile. As Bliss entered, both looked up at him and raised their eyebrows.

'While my team is picking apart the Sperlings, Pen and I are going to take a closer look at the Armstrongs,' Bliss told Rogers. 'That's the case my team investigated four years ago.'

'Okay. And…?'

'There's still no obvious connection between any of them and crime, organised or otherwise. But a little bird told us we might want to have words with those closest to Kevin Armstrong. Evidently, his family is reluctant to talk. It'd be interesting to know why. See if we can cajole or even provoke them into saying more than they have.'

Chandler had ended her call and was now studying the case file. 'Bob and Kieran Armstrong are favourites,' she said. 'Kieran was Kevin's brother, Bob their father. Neither had a great deal to say during the original investigation, either.'

'Where do they live?' Bliss asked.

'The dad in… Wisbech. The brother here in Peterborough.'

'Good. Let's not make appointments. I'd rather they didn't talk to each other between interviews, though. Frank, you want to take one of them on their own?'

Rogers nodded. 'Happy to.'

'Cheers. We'll have a chat with the brother, leave his father to you.'

'Okay. You want the brother because if Kevin Armstrong was running some kind of criminal and clandestine business on the side, he's more likely to talk about it with his sibling than he is with his old man, right?'

Bliss felt himself blush. Was he really that transparent? Frank Rogers was good. Too good to put one past without any stealth or subtlety. 'I think that's likely, yes. You still all right with the arrangement?'

'Of course.' The NCA man flashed a quick, amiable smile. 'No problem. Like I said, I'm happy to help.'

THIRTY-FIVE

Kieran Armstrong's detached house in Westwood Park Road had to be worth somewhere around the £1million mark, Bliss thought. Not bad going for a builder. His suspicious nature made him wonder if something other than the man's declared income had been invested in the property, which came with substantial gardens to the rear. The landscaping looked new, the lawn neatly manicured. A year-old Jaguar SUV sat outside a three-car garage.

The man was not a happy camper discovering two detectives standing inside the porched entrance when he opened the chunky wooden door. He stood in the open doorway wearing a lightweight robe and scratching a chest matted with thick greying hair. Clocking their credentials, he let out a plaintive sigh and said, 'Can't you people leave us alone? I have nothing more to say. Nothing new to offer.'

'I'm sorry you feel that way, sir,' Chandler said at her most agreeable self. 'But the fact is, everything we thought we knew about what happened to your brother and his family was wrong. Surely you can find some comfort knowing he didn't take his own life?'

'Comfort?' Armstrong peered at her as if she were deranged. 'If you were telling me it was accidental, then yes, I might be able to live with that. But I struggle to see how murder is better than suicide.'

'Perhaps because the latter would have been by choice, the former definitely not. Also, you have to be relieved to know he wasn't a murderer. Mr Armstrong, however you decide to look at what happened four years ago, the fact is your brother did not kill his family and he did not kill himself. Our hope is that you want to find out who did every bit as much as we do. Possibly more so.'

It was an approach she and Bliss had agreed upon during the short drive over. Judging by the shifting expression on the man's face, it was the right one. Bliss decided to press home the small advantage.

'Sir, we do realise this news will have come as a shock. Even four years on, you might still be struggling to understand what took place that night. But there's some light being shed on it now. You no longer have to ask yourself how you missed Kevin's pain, nor his intent. Because he didn't do it. None of it. And we want your help in finding out who did.'

Chandler had created the gap through which Bliss had stepped. It opened it wide enough for Kieran Armstrong to allow them through the door and into a vast living room, separated into three sections for TV viewing, listening to music, and also playing – if the piano was more than a talking point or ornamental feature. He told them his wife was out, which Bliss regarded as a positive. Her absence might compel her husband to speak more freely.

'I don't know what you might have seen, heard, or read,' Bliss continued. 'But I am able to confirm that we have good reason to suspect the murders of your family members and those of another north of the city are connected. If only by their killer.'

'I'd heard about it, of course,' Armstrong muttered. 'But you know what the sodding media are like these days. All doom and gloom and scare tactics. It comes as a shock to know that it's all true.'

Armstrong threw himself down into an armchair. As he and Chandler lowered themselves onto a settee, Bliss continued. 'I can only imagine. The problem for us is that we're now four years down the road, and starting a fresh murder investigation at this late stage means we can't hang about. Especially now that we know the same man has just taken more lives.'

'I understand. Though I still can't think what else I can tell you.'

'You may be surprised. What we're looking to establish is a clear motive for the murders. We believe we've done so during our current investigation. We now need to look harder still at your brother and his family. We have to ask why somebody would target them. And in doing so, we also have to ask if you're aware of any reason why someone might want them dead. Your brother in particular.'

Armstrong's face screwed up as if he'd bitten into something sour. 'Of course not. Nobody would want that.'

'And yet somebody did,' Bliss reminded him. 'And my gut tells me if anybody has a clue as to why, it's you. His brother. Now, before I continue, let me make it clear that I have no interest in you or any association with whatever your brother was into. Our position is this: we believe Kevin was mixed up with some bad people. The kind of people who don't think twice or even blink before ordering a murder. I'll be brutally honest, we think your brother was moving drugs for a dealer. Using his florist business to move gear around the country. We don't consider him to have been either the supplier or the seller, more the middle man. The man who shifted things from point A to point B. What's more, if I had to guess, I'd say you knew of his involvement.'

'That's absurd,' Armstrong said, seemingly outraged by the suggestion. He folded his robe tighter still. 'Utter nonsense. All of it.'

If words were the only guiding factor, his protestation might have worked. They sounded genuine enough. But Kieran Armstrong's face was an open book, and the man looked absolutely terrified. Bliss read this and decided to switch tack. He hadn't intended to make the interview confrontational, but the time was ripe for a more direct approach.

'Kieran,' he said, more familiar now and gently spoken. Bliss hoped it came across as sympathetic. 'Let's both be honest, shall we? You knew what your brother was doing, and to what extent. The reason being, you were involved. I don't know how, nor why, and to a degree I don't much care at this point. But I drew back the curtains for you, Kieran. I saw all that it revealed to you. You're frightened now. I can see it in your every mannerism, from the dry lips you keep licking, to the halting breaths. You're sitting there wondering if the man who murdered your brother and his family is going to come for you and yours. But I don't reckon you have anything to worry about on that score. If they'd wanted you dead, you would be by now. I'm certain they didn't know about you, because you helped Kevin out indirectly.'

Armstrong said nothing for a while, then his nostrils flared. 'Even if what you just said was true, wouldn't I now have even less reason to talk to you than I did before? Why would I put myself in the frame, exposing my own wife and kids to this bloody nightmare image you've painted?'

Bliss had prepared an answer for him. 'Because I don't think you've had long enough to think it through, Kieran. See, if we leave here without the information we're looking for, then we have no alternative but to report back and begin investigative proceedings against you. The truth will come out, that much I can guarantee. And where until now your name was unknown to these people, it will suddenly light up on their radar like a beacon. However, you talk to us, you tell us everything you know, and I will personally see to it that, provided you haven't physically or financially hurt anyone, we won't arrest you.'

'You'd seriously put me and my family at risk if I don't co-operate?' The man looked at him in disgust.

Bliss nodded. He wouldn't, of course. But Kieran Armstrong didn't have to know that.

'But you'll leave us be if I answer your questions?'

'Provided you answer them honestly and in full, yes.'

Another pause. Bliss looked on as the man's shoulders collapsed beneath the weight of his fears. 'All right,' he said softly. 'I'll tell you everything I know.'

THIRTY-SIX

Bishop and Ansari were still conducting a search of the Sperling home and grounds when DCs Gratton and Virgil delivered within minutes of arriving at the haulage firm on the outskirts of the city. With a drugs find being the primary expectation, a trained sniffer dog had attended each scene. The bricks had been hidden cleverly, but the German Shepherd by the name of Caesar was not to be fooled.

To the rear of the yard stood two Scania lorries, still attached to their trailers. A sign affixed to the brick wall behind them revealed they were the first fleet vehicles purchased by Donald Sperling in the early nineties. Now out of commission, they had been retained as part of the company history and kept on display. Held on a short lead by his handler, Caesar scampered around one. He showed only a passing interest in it, even when he was hauled up into the cab. When he came to the second trailer, he immediately began to paw at the ground. His handler crawled beneath the container, throwing a torch beam over the underside of the entire unit. On finding nothing untoward, he directed the animal to join him below. No sooner had Caesar done so than he lay flat and again started to scratch at the dirt beneath his paws.

Looking on with increasing fascination, Gratton turned to the yard manager who'd chosen to observe proceedings. 'You have keys for the vehicle?'

The man shook his head. 'Neither of them runs any more. Be no point in having keys.'

The manager had been uncooperative since their arrival, and Gratton didn't believe him. Moments later, he summoned a mechanic from the Hinchingbrooke vehicle yard. Within two minutes of arriving, he'd broken the lock and had the engine turned over and running. He shifted it into gear and edged the lorry forward until Virgil gave him a shout. Only then was the sealed compartment in the ground revealed, its lid covered in a layer of dirt and gravel from the yard. It was also locked, but it proved no match for the mechanic or his tools. When DC Gratton finally pulled the lid open, he stood back and whistled. Beside him, Virgil had precisely the same response.

*

'Sixty four bricks, which means sixty-four kilos,' he said after describing the find to Bliss and Chandler back at Thorpe Wood. 'About 2.5 million quid. There was room for another thirty-two bricks, I'd say. The search team are still looking, but I reckon that's his only hidey-hole.'

'Where's the gear now?' Bliss asked, delighted with the find.

'Awaiting forensics and requisite transportation.'

'That's a bloody good job, you two.'

'You're the one who called it, boss,' Virgil said. 'We were just on the plot.'

'You got the job done, and done well. Trusting the dog was the right move. Nothing else in amongst the stash, I take it?'

'No. What were you hoping for?'

Bliss shrugged and gave a yearning sigh. 'I don't know. A note saying, *Dear Mr Plod. This is my payment for drug running on behalf of... Mr Bad Guy.* That sort of thing.'

'No, sorry. Nothing like that. Just the haul.'

'Which is plenty good enough. It proves his links to the drugs. We now have the same regards the Armstrongs. Well, Kevin Armstrong. He ran the business on his own, so his wife may not have been implicated. Either way, he shipped drugs just as we thought. The father was oblivious, according to Frank. And although the brother coughed, he's no more than an accomplice. I don't think he did enough for us to concern ourselves with at the moment, but once this is all squared away we'll revisit his involvement and possibly give him a tug to see what he has to say for himself. Kieran Armstrong is small-time as far as I'm concerned. His brother was the real deal. Up to his neck in it. No idea how he was paid for his services, but somewhere there's booty to be found.'

'Do we know who he did business with?' Gratton asked.

Bliss gave a nod. 'We do. Armstrong ran drugs for a gang out of Leicester. The Mahmood family. The name rings a bell, but I've had no personal dealings with them. Thing is, the boss of that family went missing back in the spring and the entire enterprise went dark. I spoke to a DI based at the Enderby HQ and he reckons border control has no record of Mahmood leaving the country, though obviously he could have scarpered with fake ID. Nobody on the street has any firm idea, just rumours ranging from an early demise to the man having it on his toes.'

Gratton's expression changed to one of bemusement. 'So if this Mahmood was employing Armstrong to shift his gear, why would he take out a hit on the man four years ago?'

Head angled to one side, Bliss said, 'We don't know that he did. Leicester CID has intel suggesting Mahmood started using somebody else around about the time of Armstrong's death, and doing so until shortly before he disappeared. Man goes by the name of Mark Fredericks. And here's where it gets very interesting, because Fredericks is a known associate of Pamela Daniels.'

'Who in turn is a known associate of Marty Reid.'

'Precisely.' Bliss's lips curled. 'It's all a little bit... not quite incestuous, but you know what I mean?'

Chandler, who'd been listening close by, said, 'Mahmood could have had a falling out with Armstrong and decided not to take any risks. That's definitely a possibility.'

'Equally, Reid could have taken him out in order to slip his own man in. However it happened, whoever ordered it done, it's all very murky.'

'So, what is the situation with Reid, boss?' Virgil asked. 'Are the Met watching him?'

'Up to a point. But he's no idiot. He's survived until now because he keeps his hands clean. It's not as if he's going to be caught in the same room as this Lightning Rod character.'

'Who we're no closer to identifying, let alone catching,' Gratton snapped.

'Hold on to that anger,' Bliss told him as his mobile rang. 'It can be useful in the right circumstances.' When he was done with the call, he turned to his colleagues with a huge smile written large across his face.

'Jimmy?' Chandler said, getting to her feet. Her eyes gleamed. 'What is it? What have you got?'

'Didn't I tell you this man we're after is only human? He's made mistakes before, and he may do so again before we catch up to him. But the one he made in Hampstead is the breakthrough we've been looking for.'

'What did he do? Or not do?'

Bliss was like a cat who'd dined well on a plump canary. Buoyed by the phone call, he took his time delivering the news.

'Remember Frank Rogers talking about our killer's hubris? He must have thought he was so damned clever interfering with Xavier Brent's security cameras. But that was our liaison at West Hampstead nick on the blower. The security company got back to them, confirming they have no useable footage from last Friday.'

His colleagues exchanged puzzled glances. 'On what planet is that good news?' Chandler asked.

'It isn't. But our killer overlooked one minor detail. The doorbell camera isn't on the main system. It runs off a simple mobile app. They got into Brent's phone, found the app, and checked the footage for the day in question. Our killer is on it, standing out like a mortuary assistant's nipples. They're sending the best quality still images through to us now, together with the relevant video file. We may not know who he is or where he is, but in just a few minutes we're going to know what he looks like.'

The others punched the air or handed out high-fives, whooping with joy, barely able to contain their excitement. 'Fucking brilliant!' Chandler said with both hands clenched.

Bliss nodded and pumped a fist, thumb raised. 'Oh, there is one more thing I almost forgot to mention.' He waited until his team had settled, the room silent once again before he gave up the most intriguing news of all. 'That ID he's holding up to the camera… it's a warrant card.'

*

Pamela Daniels' offices on New Bond Street were small, yet lavishly stylish. A lot of glass and shining chrome, large framed photographs of models wearing clothes from her own range adorning the walls. Having posed as a buyer in order to arrange an appointment with her, it was just the two of them in her office overlooking the bustling shoppers three-storeys below.

He had declined the offer of a drink, so while Daniels reeled off the anticipated spiel about her, the company, and the quality and style of their garments, he made mental notes while silently scrutinising her. A fine looking woman, well put together, albeit dressed a little inappropriately for her age. She had the bust and legs for the dress she wore, but they were definitely in mutton territory. Now she was looking at him expectantly. He wondered how she might react over the next few minutes, though he was prepared for either fight or flight.

'Do you ever wonder how many psychological disorders one person can have?' he asked without inflection.

For a few seconds, Daniels sat quite still in her chair just staring at him. Questioning if she had heard him correctly, perhaps. She then licked her lips – uneasily, he thought. She cleared her throat before speaking. 'That was an unexpected turn in the conversation, if I may say so. Are we still talking fashion here, Mr Malvo?'

'You tell me. It's said that leaders, whether running countries or businesses, often crave validation and recognition from others, tend to be self-centred, but achieve high levels of attainment. Their charm is superficial, they lack empathy, and most are narcissists. Think Donald Trump or Steve Jobs. In short, they display psychopathic tendencies. I, myself, have been described as emotionally stunted. I lack the capacity to be either sympathetic or empathetic. But the thing is, Pam, I'm also able to be that person only while I'm working. It's as if I pull on that personality along with my suit, shirt, and tie. At home, I'm a cuddly teddy bear, I promise you. My wife and kids think the sun shines out of every single one of my orifices. And my soulmate has never, ever been in my presence when another of my psychological disorders overtakes me. Would you care to guess what that is?'

Daniels visibly withdrew from him. 'No, I wouldn't. To be perfectly honest with you, Mr Malvo, I think it would be best all round if you left. I don't know what this is all about, but it's unprofessional and just a little too weird for my liking.'

'Aw, and here was I thinking I might be in the presence of a kindred spirit. You are a business owner, a leader, after all.'

'Mr Malvo. Please…' Daniels gestured towards the door. Clearly frightened now, but keeping her composure.

He smiled. 'That's three times you've used that name without a sign of recognition. Have you ever seen the television series, *Fargo*? Not the movie, which was superb in its own right, but the first series with Billy Bob Thorton?'

'No, I can't say I have.'

'I thought not. You see, he played a character by the name of Lorne Malvo. Now, there was a serious psychopath. I so admired him. He had a certain… panache. But most of the time he killed out of necessity. It wasn't that he got a kick out of it. Unlike me. You know what they call my particular psychological… malady, Pam?'

She stood abruptly, sending her chair skidding backwards. 'I'd like you to leave,' she said, still in control of her emotions. Barely. 'I'd rather not call the police, but I will if I have to.'

'It's called sexual sadism disorder,' he ploughed on, ignoring her. 'In other words, I can only get turned on when I'm inflicting pain on another person. The sole exception to this condition is my wife who, if you asked her, would describe our sex life as perfectly normal. Odd, don't you think?'

'Mr… whatever your name is. What is this all about? What are you doing here? Why are you telling me all this?'

'I was getting around to that, Pam. You are impatient. What I'm trying to tell you is that, whilst that side of me exists, you don't need to see it. You won't have to endure it. I'm not about to inflict any pain upon you, is what I'm saying. Not today, not here, and not now.'

'And what the fuck does any of that mean?' Daniels' voice became strident.

'Hmm, you're slipping a bit there, Pamela. Losing your composure. Revealing your hard underbelly to me. Look, it's a good thing. Please see it that way. It means I'm here to talk. Just talk. I can't predict the future, of course. Circumstances have been known to change. But as things stand, I intend you no harm.'

'Why would you? Who are you?'

'Asking who sent me would be the better question.'

'So who did send you?'

'I can't tell you that, Pam.'

'Then why did you suggest I asked you?'

'I didn't. I said it would be the better question. I said nothing about answering you.'

Daniels threw her arms up in the air then clapped her hands together with a resounding slap. 'All right. This has gone on long enough. You've had your fun at my expense. I've humoured you up until now, but no more. So, let me tell you something. You are not the only one with another side to their nature. Nor are you the only one who wears a mask like a second skin. You don't know me, so you have no idea what I am capable of. Whatever this was about, it's over. Do you understand me?'

He smiled and nodded. 'I do. But you're wrong. I'm the one who says when this is over, and it is not. Not quite. First, I have a message to pass on. Are you ready to listen?'

'Not really, but go the fuck ahead. I'm weary of this now.'

'Stay away from the policeman, Pamela. That's the first part of the message.'

If she was startled by his words, she did well not to show it. Instead, she rolled her eyes and said, 'Suggesting there are more parts left unsaid?'

'Just the one. Now, here you need to fully understand the seriousness of what I am about to say, and I will emphasise every word so that we are both clear. Is that understood?'

She nodded.

'I'm going to need to hear your words.'

'Yes! Yes, I understand. Serious… emphasis…'

'Excellent.' He stood and buttoned his suit jacket. With a wry smile, he paid tribute to James Bond and shot his cuffs. 'I apologise for repeating myself. But I will, all the same. Stay away from the policeman, Pam. If you don't, if I have to come back here again, or seek you out elsewhere, then your world may well turn very dark indeed. You're a good looking woman, so I can easily see why the policeman is interested in you. But I can undo what God gave you. You have a great body, but I can dismember it. I can also do so slowly, keeping you awake and alert long enough to feel every nerve-ending burn as if I were pouring acid on it. It's of no consequence to me if I never see you again, Pam. But it will be of the gravest significance to you if I do.'

He sighed as she trembled. A bone-jarring judder ripped through her body. Her bottom lip quivered. He had been told this woman was as hard as nails. Frankly, he wasn't seeing it.

'Oh, and just one more thing,' he said as he turned to leave.

'What's that?' she said with all the strength she could muster.

He favoured her with his most charming smile. 'Do you validate parking?'

THIRTY-SEVEN

The use of facial recognition software by the UK police was nowhere near as widespread as many of its citizens believe. Movies and contemporary TV shows implied 'Big Brother' was everywhere, yet even in the nation's capital its use was restricted and limited in scope. The Metropolitan police were awaiting news of a significant expansion of its capabilities, enabling them to process historical images from CCTV, social media, and any number of other sources in a bid to track down suspects. The counter-terrorism budget was taking a hit, but these new facilities were set to increase dramatically the Met's ability to tackle all manner of crime-related activities.

The reason Bliss and his team were discussing it that day was because the warrant card lead that had so invigorated them had been yet another dead end. The man's photograph was genuine enough, but they'd discovered the rest of the identification to be fake. The warrant number had never existed, and nobody by the name of Charles Crews had ever worked for the UK police. With the team's initial euphoria having been diminished by this news, it was Frank Rogers who had alerted them to the possibilities of FR.

'What if that photo is not even a true likeness?' Chandler

had argued. 'He could have disguised himself before creating the fake ID.'

'That's possible,' Rogers shot back. 'But what if you're wrong? Come on, Penny, think more positively.'

'She's only saying what I would say,' Bliss pointed out. 'But you're right, Frank. The forged ID is a pisser, but facial recognition might still come to our rescue.'

Critics of the system had already submitted their outraged protests, claiming it would further entrench discriminatory policing and increase the opportunities for abuse. Bliss genuinely believed people's fears were wildly exaggerated; hyperbole in predicting chaos seemed to be not only tolerated but encouraged in today's society. He regarded the noise created by protestors as camouflage, designed to hide away their hidden agendas and lack of verifiable evidence.

'It's all feelings over facts,' he said to the gathered team. 'If you denounce something loud enough and often enough, even before it's truly begun, then you stand a good chance of making sure you get your own way.'

'You saying the old days were better?' Ansari asked. 'Before social media and the twenty-four-hour news cycle started providing us with these stories.'

'Yes, I am, but I'd describe it as bombarding us, Gul. And whatever happened to the news being a truthful account of events? At least back in the day, you had to have genuine and multiple sources. Nowadays, any old wild speculation makes it to our screens. I'm not saying people ought to just accept what the establishment tells them and foists upon them. But let's have an adult and well-reasoned debate, not blatant scaremongering.'

'So how is facial recognition going to help us with our case?' Chandler asked, perhaps hoping to take the heat out of the subject.

'In two ways,' Frank Rogers said, picking up a nod from Bliss. 'First of all, the best quality image from that doorbell camera footage will be used to compare against a number of databases. It works by taking precise measurements of and between our features, and then searching for the closest match. If our man is in the system, it'll pick him out. Then we have LFR, which is the live version of facial recognition. The program will be instructed to search for that image on the systems currently in operation.'

'Good job he's not black,' DC Ansari said with more than a hint of scorn. 'All of these systems are weak when it comes to non-caucasian faces.'

'They are, but they're improving.'

'Hold on a moment,' Bliss interjected, irritated by the negative connotations. 'Look, the system is legitimately available, and if the Met do sign this deal with the NEC Corporation, it's going to be used more widely and, hopefully, more effectively. If it's a tool we can use to help find our killer, then I'm in favour of it. Go on, Frank.'

Rogers folded his arms and widened his stance. 'I won't stand here and tell you the system is perfect. Nor may it ever be. But it has proven to be useful so far, and if it gives us our man's name and address, will any of you ignore the intel because of how we arrived at it? If it then goes on to locate him walking along a street in London, will you be disappointed by his arrest?'

Mere seconds before, the room had echoed to a low muttering. Now you could hear the proverbial pin drop.

'Let me finish,' Rogers continued, 'by saying this: if the man at Xavier Brent's door is identified, the Met will get the first crack at him if he lives somewhere in the Greater London area. If he lives anywhere else, then it's me and my team at the NCA. I know that won't go down well here, because of the current and previous cases being worked. That said, you all know this series of murders stretches way beyond your own region, and every area will feel the exact same way you do. We're the only national crime agency, so it is our job whether you like it or not.'

'Will we be involved at all?' Bishop asked.

'That depends on where we find him. First up will be the locals. You'd want that if he lived in Cambridgeshire, and it's procedure. Believe me, I understand how frustrated you'll all be if you play no further part. But your great work will not go unappreciated. I'll see to that.'

His colleagues were not exactly turning cartwheels at the news, but Bliss was proud of the way they accepted the situation without dissent. 'How long before we have answers?' he asked Rogers.

'Unknown. The current technology has limitations, among them speed. While we're waiting, why not go over where we are following today's revelations?'

Bliss nodded. 'We now have a firm connection between Sperling, Armstrong, and the drugs business. No link as yet to Reid where Sperling is concerned, but something tangible when it comes to Kevin Armstrong. Even so, we do hit another wall. Did Reid get shot of Armstrong to make room for one of his own people? If so, why? Looking for an in with Mahmood's operation? But if not and Mahmood contracted the hit, we don't have any idea why he did so. However, we have to ask if answering these questions takes us any closer to our Lightning Rod, and I don't see how it would. Whoever employed him, and for whatever reasons, I'm confident he did it. What I'm far less certain about is finding evidence to back that up.'

'If we grab him up, we're going to need a confession,' Chandler said. 'We could pull at these strands we have all day and all night for the next year and still not find enough to charge him with.'

'Not even with this Xavier Brent bloke?' Virgil asked.

'Not so far,' Bliss replied. 'Say we ID our target. We prove he was there, that he went inside, and later left. If nothing at the scene proves he drowned Brent, then all he has to do is find a reason for his presence. No, with this geezer, he's either going to have to cough, or we catch him in the act. That's it.'

Frank Rogers had been paying close attention. He cleared his throat and said, 'Jimmy and Penny are absolutely right. Our killer has made plenty of mistakes, and being caught on camera at Xavier Brent's house is a real balls-up. But proving he and the killer are one and the same is not possible with what we have. Ask yourself, if you pull him in now, do you have enough to convince the CPS to charge him? Do you have enough to apply pressure to him in the room? Clearly you don't. Hairs, fibres, DNA, witnesses, GPS data, mobile texts… where is any of that in his case?'

Bliss remembered he had not informed any of his colleagues about his conversation with the crime scene manager. 'Apologies for not mentioning this sooner, but Neil Abbott and his team discovered a couple of cross-contaminants when they ran comparison tests. We're unlikely to pull any DNA, and we all know fibres can be so widely available as to be virtually useless in terms of hard evidence.'

'Well, that's fucking depressing,' Ansari said. This prompted some gentle laughter; she was not prone to swearing, so this was extreme for her.

'It won't be the first nor last time this happens,' Bishop said stoically. 'We've all been there, and it hurts. When you know, just know, someone is guilty but you can't find that evidence and you can't break them, it's like a knife to the guts. Please tell me this isn't going to be one of those cases.'

Having given the matter due consideration, Bliss had something in mind. He turned to Rogers, saying, 'I want to be thorough. I'd like to think the Met are still trying to pick up our killer's trail. They have him in a fixed position at Brent's house, but he had to get there, and he had to leave again. There'll be plenty of CCTV in and around that area of London to sift through. But if that's not happening due to lack of staff or budget or they just have too much on their plates, then somebody else has to run that trace on their behalf. If it is, I want to know what they find. I'm happy to spare two of our team to handle it if necessary.'

Rogers agreed. 'I'll pass your thoughts on.'

'To someone who will take them seriously, please.'

'The Met do employ good coppers as well, Jimmy,' Rogers said. 'You were once one of them. I'm sure they know what they're doing, and if they're not doing it fast enough, I'll try prising it out of their sweaty palms. That good enough for you?'

'It's going to have to be,' Bliss said reluctantly. 'Oh, and while I have your attention, Frank, what do you think about the notion of not arresting him if we get a hit on his ID?'

'You mean deliberately? Choosing not to?' Rogers's frown was deep.

Bliss understood why. Having a bird in the hand was a common enough model for the police to work by, but there were occasions when sitting on that knowledge drew greater dividends.

'Yeah,' he said. 'It stands to reason that if the Met ID him, they'll want to pick him up for questioning. Bloke like this, I'm pretty sure they'll have to arrest him to do so. They can make a case for that, given he was at Brent's house that day. But if it plays out like we think, he'll walk away from it when the clock runs down, extensions or not. Only then he'll know we're onto him. He'll take greater care, perhaps even lie low for as long as it takes for us to lose interest. Meanwhile, his paymasters bring in a replacement who we know nothing about. It's lose-lose. On the other hand, if we don't pull him, but instead put the watchers on him, we might learn a lot more about the man and those handing out the orders.'

While Rogers considered, Chandler revealed her concerns. 'I'm not so sure about that, Jimmy. What if he gives them the slip and kills somebody else? There will be hell to pay if we give him enough rope to do that while we could have had him in a room throwing questions at him.'

'I'm well aware of the risks,' Bliss acknowledged. 'Even the Met watchers are not immune from the occasional lapse. But look at it the other way. What if the next time he pays a visit to kill somebody, the Met are all over him and stop it from happening?'

'Yeah, that sounds fine in theory. But how will they know for sure? You take the Sperlings, for instance. If he found his way to them the way we think, then surveillance would see he was up to no good and would be on the spot to prevent it. But Taylor Sweeting? No way they could have reacted in time, even if they were only twenty yards away. We might've ended up with him behind bars, but she'd be just as dead. Same deal with Brent. Close surveillance doesn't give us a racing certainty, so I'm against this idea.'

Bliss hung his head. He was used to Chandler having her say. He encouraged his colleagues to challenge him. Her argument was sound, but he had another side to address. He took a step back to look out at his entire team and their NCA colleague.

'Penny is right,' he said. 'I accept that. It could all go tits up. But tell me, in reference to everything we just discussed, do any of you think we have sufficient evidence to charge him with murder?'

DS Bishop spoke up immediately. 'At the moment? No.'

'And I think we can agree there's no way this man is going to hold up his hands to any of it.'

'Yes, we can,' Gratton said. 'He's not going to talk.'

Bliss started to feel more confident in his approach. 'Then the only advantage we have in arresting him is in taking him off the streets for a short time, after which he'll most likely go to ground.'

'Again yes.'

'So what about my earlier argument? With him on the back burner, his bosses bring somebody else into play. Somebody who may be as unknown to us as this bloke was. As Penny quite rightly pointed out, if we let our man go about his business, he might slip through the net. But the way I see it, we can absolutely guarantee the killings will continue if we pull him in.'

Chandler shook her head, firm and resolute. 'Guarantee? No, I disagree.'

'Pen, these people are clearing house. Whoever they are. That much we can be certain of. Why would they stop? We're clearly not onto them, only their fixer and pet hitman, whose identity we've yet to discover. They can go about their business freely. There might not be much more of it to do, after all. A couple, few more kills, and then it could all be over.'

'But that's just it. We're making educated guesses. At this point, we don't know anything for sure. But if this ID comes up and he can be located, it's an opportunity to take him off the board. Do we really want to pass up on that?'

Bliss hated having to defend himself from a position of weakness. There were times – plenty of them – when swimming upstream had garnered results they might otherwise not have achieved. Here, both he and Chandler were right. The trouble was, she was more right than he was. He couldn't shake the feeling of dissatisfaction. Going to all this trouble in finding their man only to bring him in knowing full well he'd walk out again the moment his time was up was no reward at all for their efforts. Yet could they really take the risk of allowing him to function as he pleased?

He felt trapped and saw no way out. The decision would not be his, but falling back on that was the coward's way out. The Met had the first option, and their word was final. Yet knowing that didn't deter him from speaking his mind.

'Either way is a risk,' he said finally. 'I just happen to think that leaving him be and following his every move is the lesser of the two.'

'I don't suppose this helps,' Rogers said quickly, 'but you're a long way down the list of potential decision-makers, Jimmy. It'll fall on me before you, and most likely not you at all.'

'You're right,' Bliss said. 'It doesn't help. Not me, not this unit, not our victims, nor their families.' He'd said it a little more aggressively than he'd intended, but he let it hang there.

Rogers took a beat or two before responding. 'I realise that, Jimmy. But at this stage, we don't even know if the Met will obtain an ID.'

That wasn't what Bliss wanted, either. Although they had no firm evidence to offer in respect of the killer, what they had done was build a case. The op was struggling, but today they knew more than they had twenty-four hours ago, and a similar progression over the next day might bring them closer to nailing the bastard. His mouth felt dry, tasted sour. He was both exhilarated and disheartened by developments. He'd told his team that finding out more about the victims would lead them to their man. That wasn't the case, and his pride was wounded by the failure.

'I feel as if I've let you all down,' he admitted. 'I put my faith in victimology, but all it really achieved was proving the links to crime. In my head, once we had that it'd inevitably lead us to why they were killed, which in turn would point us in the direction of their killer. I hadn't anticipated him being so insulated. At best, what we have is a disparate bunch of rogues using the services of a freelancer. When you boil it all down, it's going to be a simple piece of technology that gives us our man.'

'That's a harsh judgement,' Rogers observed. 'And I also think it's unfair. Let me remind you, the only reason the investigating officers in Hampstead took a hard look at Brent, was because of the work you and your team have put in. Yes, I had this Lightning Rod on my radar, but it was silent and had been for a while. You brought it back to life, Jimmy. You saw the connection to crime even when it was obscured. You put those pieces together. We know what we know because of this unit. Proving it… that's just another stage of the investigation.'

Bliss remained unhappy about the situation, but he acknowledged the fact that their efforts had not been entirely in vain. The Lightning Rod had been hiding his work in plain sight until Bliss and Major Crimes had come along. Whatever happened from this point on, that was something nobody could take away from them.

THIRTY-EIGHT

When eventually the Met contacted Frank Rogers, they had both bad and good news to relay. Facial recognition had compared images with its own banks of databases, but found no match, leaving the man on Xavier Brent's doorstep unidentified. However, the pilot system for analysing historical imagery allowed for case-centric testing, and to the admitted astonishment of its chief operator, this time they got a hit.

'A short while ago,' Rogers told the major crimes team, 'FR found a matching image. The trial scheme is limited to central London and is currently monitoring the entrances and exits to selected underground stations. There's a better than 97% chance that the man who showed the fake warrant card at the Brent property on Friday was also seen emerging from Bond Street tube station earlier today. The Met research experts swept for anybody with even a remote connection to our investigations who lived or worked in that area, and one name popped up.'

He paused, scanning the room until his gaze fell upon Bliss. 'Pamela Daniels has her main offices in New Bond Street. I ask you, are we to believe this is yet another coincidence?'

Unprepared, Bliss took his time answering. He chased potential answers around in circles. 'If it's not, then we need to work out how the two of them are connected. She may well be familiar with this man from her time with Marty Reid. But even if that's the case, the visit today is highly suspicious.'

'We can't entirely discount a social visit,' Chandler said, looking around at the rest of the group. 'I mean, it happens. People do go to see other people just to catch up over a coffee or have lunch together.'

'True. However unlikely it sounds. We're speculating again, of course. Let's look at what we do know about this man for certain. He shields those who pay him well by fixing their problems so they don't have to get their own hands dirty. Maybe Pam has become a problem for one of them.'

'Has to be the ex-husband,' Bishop said. 'But how can we know for sure?'

'The obvious way is to ask her. But do we want her knowing we're interested in him?'

Superintendent Fletcher had been called down to join in with the discussion, and she stood centre stage firmly shaking her head. 'Our first duty here is to prevent further loss of life. We know our killer studies his victims before he acts, so this visit might be his initial recce. Jimmy, I think you have to call her. Unofficial to begin with. Sound her out. You needn't tell her everything. Just ask if she's seen or spoken to anybody this week who might have set alarm bells ringing.'

'She won't let that slide,' Bliss said. 'She'll want to know why I'm asking.'

'Just tell her you're concerned. That you've been feeling uneasy about the attack last week and the possible fallout landing in her direction, given you were on your way to see her at the time.'

She looked across at Rogers. 'How does that sit with you and the NCA, Frank?'

'I'm fine with whatever you decide. I'm more worried about the Met. If you run the suggestion by them, I'm sure they'll pass. Having taken the step of including our operations in their FR pilot scheme, they're going to want to run with this one.'

'So we don't mention it to them,' Bliss said. He shrugged. 'We're not duty bound to. We already agreed they had first shot at our killer if they got the ID. They didn't. That was all we signed up for. Operation Insulate is still very much ongoing, and if there's even a small danger of this man having Pam Daniels in his crosshairs, then we need to react.'

'I don't mean to be the arsehole in the room,' Bishop said, 'but doesn't this fall under your own *watch and wait* policy, Jimmy? You said if we identified our man we ought to sit on him and watch his every move. We're not quite in that same territory here, but I'd say it was close enough to be relevant.'

'You think we endanger that by me having a word with her?' Bliss asked.

'I think it might worry her enough to change her patterns of behaviour. We don't know how long our man has been watching her – or if he is at all. But if it's been longer than just his visit today, any significant changes on her part may not go unnoticed.'

Bliss wasn't used to having his own plans come back to bite him, but they had, and now he was placed in an unfortunate position. There was only one right way to play it, and he conceded the point. 'You're probably right, Bish. I confess, I wasn't thinking about that angle. I briefly wondered if there was a way to gain intel without alerting her, but she's too smart for that to work. She'll know something's up and she may react badly.'

'And please, let's not forget all that we don't yet know,' Fletcher pointed out. 'This man exited Bond Street tube station, and that's where FR lost him. He could have headed off in any direction, for entirely innocent reasons. Granted, Pamela Daniels having an office just a few streets away does raise all kinds of red flags, but we don't know for certain what he was doing in that area. If we jump the gun on this, we may blow the op completely.'

'Is the Met scouring CCTV to see if he can be followed from the tube station?' Chandler asked.

'They are,' Rogers said. 'But it's going to take time. Time we're potentially running short of.'

'Then we have to make our own decisions.'

'You're all agreed?' Rogers said, eyeing Fletcher.

The DSI nodded. 'I don't like it. I do feel we ought to be warning this woman. I just don't see a way to do that without it having a domino effect.'

Rogers frowned, forming creases hampered by his scar. 'Warning her about what? That a man we've failed to identify, who rang the doorbell at a house in which a man later drowned, was seen at a tube station in the same vicinity as her offices? Although I would have spoken out against telling her, I am in favour of Jimmy having a private chat. Who knows, if he keeps it low key she might blurt something out that we can use. But if we're not even going down that route, then I'll ask the Met watchers to keep an eye on her.'

'I think Frank has the right idea,' Bliss said, stabbing the air with a finger. 'Just a brief conversation between old friends. That's all I intended it to be. Checking in to see how she is. Allowing her to approach me if she feels the need to.'

Fletcher sighed heavily and said, 'We're going around in circles again. It's a tough call either way, but I'm making it. Jimmy, you give her a bell, but you keep your concerns to yourself. If she tells you she received a visit or has noticed something off, then you react as if you know nothing about this man. Frank, you speak to your Met liaison. Pamela Daniels must be considered a potential target, and as such, I want to know every move she makes.'

*

Bliss felt an itch all the way down to the bone. Several other area forces were now either reinvestigating cases or, at the very least, re-examining their operations. All roads did not appear to lead to Marty Reid, but they did terminate in criminal enterprise. However many organisations or crews were involved, they were all using the services of the Lightning Rod. This explanation failed to satisfy him, and the niggle was something he'd been scratching at for a few days.

DC Virgil had been his team's point man when it came to gathering intelligence. Results feeding back into the system were positive, but left many questions unanswered. Reports from covert sources suggested they were aware of a presence out there; a man rumoured to be doing the bidding of anybody in need of a fixer or contract killer and able to afford his services. The police had only recently woken up to the possibility. Yet at the same time there was no certainty, no word from anyone who had actually laid eyes on the man or even heard people discuss employing him to clean up behind them. Many believed the stories were inventions, promoting the notion of this shadowy figure in order to keep criminals in check. Few considered him to be real, and only the NCA in the shape of Frank Rogers and his team had taken more than a passing interest in the rumour.

The idea of such a figure gave Bliss an uncomfortable feeling in the pit of his stomach. He had no problem believing in the Lightning Rod's existence. Where he struggled was in accepting that all of these various criminals left no trace of having used his services. No observed or known contact, no reported sightings, no financial traces, no unexplained or unidentified characters suddenly appearing on the scene. More importantly, their killer clearly thrived on his anonymity. Would he leave himself open to discovery by spreading himself so widely?

Much more likely, in Bliss's view, was a scenario by which their man worked in conjunction with just one other. Somebody seated at the high table, who gave the instructions on behalf of everybody else beneath them, often introducing their own dirty work into the bargain. Suspicion naturally veered back towards Marty Reid, and he understood how dangerous that was. His own feelings, emotions, and general outlook were compromised when it came to Pam's ex-husband. It was difficult to disassociate himself from that.

While Rogers made temporary camp in the major crime area to continue his dialogue with the Met, Bliss spoke to his own team. 'I'm open to suggestions,' he said, trying hard not to look as weary and dispirited as he felt. 'Does anybody here think Operation Insulate has more to tell or give?'

'I think we've exhausted all possibilities, boss,' Bishop said. 'We've uncovered Sperling's side business, and although there's no way of tracing those drugs to a specific supplier, it was a bloody good haul to bring in. I realise that was never part of the investigation, but we did good. Despite the lack of evidence, I'm satisfied that we are on the right track. This Lightning Rod character is our killer, and I just don't see how Insulate brings us any closer to identifying him. Most we can do is start building our case for the CPS by bringing the policy book, case file, and HOLMES up to date.'

'And the Armstrong case?'

'Same answer.'

Bliss looked around. 'Any arguments?'

There were none.

He nodded once and said, 'I don't know about the rest of you, but this leaves a bad taste in my mouth. As a team, we're unused to being on the fringes. We've worked joint task forces before, but we've previously headed them up. This time we're left to wrap up our op, seeing to it that the Armstrong case is given a decent burial, and all without having our suspect identified, let alone behind bars.'

'It's the job,' Chandler said with a grudging hike of the shoulders. 'At least, it is the way this one worked out. We can be content knowing we got the ball rolling. We did the spade work. If the Met or some other force grabs him up and finds enough to arrest, charge, and prosecute him, then I can live with that. Anything that takes the bastard off the streets.'

Live with but not be happy with, Bliss thought. Taking a killer out of play was the common goal, irrespective of who slapped the cuffs on. Knowing the chances were slim that it would be him and his team stung a little, but he'd cheer the right result just as much. The difference was, when it was his unit involved, he felt more confident of the outcome. It had nothing to do with seeking praise or glory, nor the inevitable back-slapping that would soon follow. It was about the pursuit and final take down. Working at his desk compiling reports while others took over was something he found impossible to contemplate.

The Sperlings and Armstrongs were just a few of this madman's total number of victims. But they were still victims in need of justice, and Bliss felt every bit as responsible for delivering it as he had before.

*

Bliss sipped decent coffee from a proper mug, both of which he'd purloined from CID. He toggled between the open case file and the electronic version of the policy book, copying and pasting specific phrases from one to the other. The knuckles of his fingers ached, and every few minutes he had to stop in order to flex his hands and rub warmth into the joints. During one of those pauses, a text came in from Sandra Bannister. It was a link that took him to her article in the Peterborough Telegraph.

He worked his way through the contents of the mug while he read, offering a grunt of satisfaction when he had finished reading. She had eviscerated the Commissioner, branding him ill-suited for such an office. In conclusion, Bannister posited the theory that Benning had put his own ambition above that of a serial murder investigation. The reporter had written the piece so that it left the reader in no doubt as to who the villain was in this battle of good and evil.

He texted a reply.

Love it. You held nothing back. I'm proud of you. Thanks. I owe you a large G&T.

The article elevated his spirits, soothing his troubled mind. He continued his mundane tasks with greater alacrity. Twenty minutes later, Rogers visited his office, finding him still hard at it. The NCA man's expression told him something was wrong, the scowl he wore creased with tight edges hardened by anger. Bliss felt his happier mood evaporate in an instant.

'The Met's watchers blew it somehow,' he said.

Bliss looked up from his computer keyboard. 'You mean they located him and then lost him?'

'Looks that way. They're circling the wagons, of course. Nobody actually accepting blame. Another team surveilling Pam Daniels' office followed her when she left the building. No problem there, and they still have eyes on. But the team watching her home in Streatham thought they might have spotted the target. They chose to break ranks and follow. The target made a couple of obvious evasive manoeuvres, but then a not so obvious one

– he just disappeared. Because they were splintered at this point, the watchers were short on ideal numbers and left vulnerable as a result. Word has it that the target managed to slip through the cordon right where two officers had been stationed before they started to follow him.'

'Damn! So, either he was fortunate, or he spotted the tail and found a way to lose it. We have to know which, Frank.'

Rogers agreed. 'If they're blown, then he's not going back to Daniels' place. Nor her office.'

'Right. And if they're not, they have to sit tight. He may well have been overly cautious and lost them without even knowing they were back there. Frank, make sure they don't get pulled out unless they are positive.'

'I'll do what I can. But I have no authority over them, Jimmy.'

'Sorry. I understand that. Please, just do your best.'

'Will do. I'm going back home myself tonight, leaving in a few minutes. Before I do, what happened when you made the call to Daniels?'

Bliss sucked air between his teeth. 'In effect, sweet FA. She didn't mention being visited, and I couldn't push.'

'How did she sound?'

'Her usual bullish self. But I get the feeling she'd act that way irrespective of who might have rattled her cage. I'm half wondering if we have it all wrong. Maybe our man was in that area on other business, after all.'

'That would be good, wouldn't it?' Rogers raised both eyebrows. 'For Pamela Daniels, I mean. If he wasn't there for her, then she's in no danger.'

'Yeah, but we kind of want her to be, don't we? We want him to be stalking her because it's the only way we're going to grab the murdering bastard.'

'True enough. I can't tell if we got lucky or unlucky having him turn up on the FR system. Either way, I suspect we'll find out soon enough.'

Bliss shook his head. 'It can never be soon enough as far as I'm concerned.'

The team was long gone for the evening by the time he decided to head out. By then, Pam Daniels was at home and under surveillance for at least a further day and night. He couldn't help but wonder where their man was now. Had he been spooked by the watchers? If so, he was too smart to fall into the same trap. If not, there was still a good chance of him going after her. Perhaps by the time his alarm went off in the morning it would all be over.

THIRTY-NINE

Bliss woke with a start, his head reeling. He blinked rapidly in darkness punctuated by a muted glow, trying to shut out the shrill noise raging in his ears. Moments later, when the world realigned, he realised the source of both the sound and lightshow was the mobile phone on his bedside cabinet. It had woken him from a tense moment in a dream in which he was being pounded by a cartoon fist the size of a wrecking ball. He took a second or two to gather himself before answering the call, noting it was 3.07am.

'Jimmy, it's Pam. Please don't hang up.'

He hadn't even noticed it was his personal phone, having assumed he was being called into work. He sat up straight, knuckling his eyes. 'Pam? What's wrong? Why are you calling?'

'I'm in trouble. At least, I think I am. I didn't mention it yesterday when we spoke, but a man came to visit me. He said he was there just to warn me off having any dealings with you again. He told me exactly what he'd do to me if I didn't listen. I was mad as fuck over it, so I called Marty. He denied knowing anything about it, but when I spoke to my son afterwards, there was something in his tone. It's like he was fending me off, Jimmy.

Keeping me at a distance so's he didn't have to think about what was going on. I got scared. Terrified. I never felt so frightened before in my whole life.'

'Okay, okay.' He thought for a moment. He couldn't tell her she was under observation, but felt sure he could finesse his way around it. 'Do you want me to drive down, keep you company? Or might that make things worse? I could have a car come by to pick you up, take you somewhere safe.'

'That won't do any good. I'm not at home. I wasn't about to risk hanging around waiting for something to happen. I slipped out the back way in case the bastard had somebody on me at my drum. I've had another motor stored in a lock-up for a while, so I made my way there and did a runner.'

The Met watchers were going to be fuming at having dropped another bollock on this one. 'Okay. If you were that frightened, it sounds like you did the right thing. So, tell me, where are you now, Pam?'

'Close.'

'To where? Home?'

'No, to you. Jimmy, I need to know I can trust you. I feel as if my whole miserable life has turned upside down. It's bad enough my ex wants to control my every move, but my own son? I knew I'd lost him to Marty and that world of his, but I never once imagined he'd turn his back on me so completely. He didn't even come to me himself with a warning, Jimmy. Just sent some animal in to scare me into silence.'

'I've nothing to lose or gain, Pam. You can trust me, I promise you that. You want me to call in some back-up?'

'No, Just you, Jimmy. For now. I need some time and space to clear my head, but I also have to feel safe. Just come and sit with me for a while.'

'Tell me where you are.'

Ten minutes later, he was leaving the house. He reached his car and slowly looked around. The street was empty, houses dark. A soft glow from the streetlamps lit the way. For a moment he wondered if Marty Reid had somebody watching him, but it was a tough ask in this neighbourhood, with few places in which to hide while still having an unobstructed view. He climbed inside the Mondeo, turned the engine over and eased his way out of the estate taking every opportunity to check his mirrors.

The Verve looked more like a young offender's home or YMCA hostel than a hotel. Located in the Boongate district industrial park and surrounded by home improvement warehouses and car dealerships, it didn't look at all out of place. Bliss imagined Pam had chosen it because she'd be able to persuade whoever had to be nudged awake behind the reception desk to let her pay with cash. The room Pam let him into was small and perfunctory, passably clean and tidy for what he assumed had to be a low budget price.

The conversation that followed was more difficult than he had imagined. Juggling so many balls in the air was never easy, but when you were with somebody seeking assurances, it was hard to hold on to the truths among the litany of lies. Quite who was meant to know what by this stage almost proved too much for him after being woken in the middle of the night. He was not at his best, but he thought he'd held it together.

Even when she dressed down, Pam Daniels looked amazing. Skin-tight jeans clung to every contour, while her pale silk blouse left little to the imagination. If clothes make a man, they also had the ability to create a man's vision of the perfect woman. But she was visibly different from the last time he had seen her. Stripped of all her confidence, she was now a timid creature, fearful and nervous, perhaps also bereft, having been abandoned to the baying pack by her own flesh and blood. Bliss held her tight for a short while before taking a seat in the room's only chair. She sat on the edge of the bed, hands intertwined in her lap, loosely fumbling.

'I don't think I've ever felt so completely alone,' she said, wiping away a fresh welling of tears. 'I've always considered myself to be strong and independent. To be here, now, having to rely on a man I've seen only a couple of times since I was eighteen, is humiliating. I realise how shallow my life has been, Jimmy. And, what's worse is… the man I'm relying on isn't even aware that I set him up.'

Immediately alert, Bliss's eyes flashed across to the door. Pam read the look and shook her head. 'No, not this time. Not tonight. But I couldn't ask you to come here to help me and not tell you what I did. I just couldn't.'

He looked her up and down as if seeing her clearly for the first time. 'So I'm guessing our meeting at the Woodman last week wasn't a coincidence after all, then?' he said tentatively.

'No, it wasn't. Not at all. It all came about when my boy approached me. He said he and his dad might have a bit of business up in this neck of the woods, and that it would be nice to have an in with the local police. Somebody told him about me and you, you know, back in the day. He looked you up. Came to me with a half-formed idea. I'd read about the convention at the Holiday Inn and thought it might be my way in. It was never meant to be anything other than an initial approach to sound you out. We thought there was a chance you'd be willing to take money in return for information, or turn a blind eye when we needed you to. What better opportunity to exploit that possibility than when I was close by on legit business?'

'You thought I might be on the take? A bent copper? Me?'

'We thought it was worth finding out.'

Bliss felt a quick pulse in his cheek. 'So what went wrong?'

'Donald Sperling. I got a call from my boy on the day after the Sperlings were murdered. He wanted to call the whole thing off because you'd been assigned the case and would be working flat out. I told him I'd already travelled up and taken my room, so it would be better if I saw it through. If you were the type to talk about your day, I might get something out of you that they could use. So that's what I did.'

'Was sleeping with me part of the plan?' he asked.

Her head snapped up. She blinked back a few more tears. 'I suppose I deserve that. And no, that was never my intention. I can't honestly say I didn't have one or two fanciful notions before the trip. There's always a bit of a thrill when you anticipate meeting up with your first love again, don't you find?'

'I wouldn't know, Pam. From my side, it happened unexpectedly, remember?'

'Of course. But I never imagined you and me ending up in bed together. I think I assumed you'd be married, couple of kids, that sort of thing. Even if that weren't the case, it never occurred to me that we might still fancy each other. Finding out about us didn't go down well with Marty, though. I don't flatter myself enough to think he was in any way jealous. He'd wanted us to meet, to talk, even over dinner and a drink. But nothing as intimate as sleeping together. In his head, a one-way street of information was suddenly in danger of becoming a two-way flow.'

Her explanation sounded plausible. Apart from one thing. Bliss fixed her with a hard stare and said, 'The thing I don't understand, Pam, is why you did it at all. You and he are no longer married. Why would you still do his bidding?'

For the first time, Pam looked a little hurt by his question. 'I didn't just obey a command, Jimmy. And it was my son, Angus, who asked me, remember? To be honest, it didn't sound like a taxing way to spend the week. By day I'd be networking with people from my line of work, and by night I'd hopefully be spending some time with you.'

'Pumping me for information.'

'Something like that. I was excited by the thought of seeing you again. Is that so bad?'

Bliss ignored the question. 'Okay, so that's why you did as he asked. But what I still don't get is why he did. If you two were living such different and separate lives, why would he assume he could waltz back into yours and ask such a thing of you? And don't give me all that guff about your son, because we both know it had to have been his father's idea.'

'I suppose because he knows me too bloody well,' she snapped. 'Jimmy, I make no bones about it. My dad's a criminal, my ex-husband is a criminal, and now so is my son. And I won't insult your intelligence by leaving myself out. We led separate lives, but we lived those lives in the same world.'

He let it go and moved on. 'All right. Tell me about this bloke who threatened you.'

Pam went over the man's visit, recalling their meeting minute by minute, word for word. He frowned when she was done talking. 'Okay, so he warned you how things would go if you didn't keep away from me. Sorry if I'm being a bit thick, but I'm not seeing how we got from there to here. Surely this is the worst possible thing for you to have done? If you'd just stayed away, never called or taken a call from me, you wouldn't have had to run.'

Following a stifled, scornful laugh, she said, 'Once again, you don't know my ex as well as I do. He's not the kind of man to act on impulse, because that's a cut-and-dried moment in time, and all too rapid for Marty Reid. The thing with him is, he always has the threat made first. It psyches people out, because you can never tell when a warning is precisely that, or when it's much, much more. In some cases, provided you don't transgress again, you're left to go about your business. In others, you live with that cloud over your head, do nothing to provoke him again, and still he does a job on you. It's not always terminal, either. Might be a broken kneecap, a few nails ripped from your fingers and toes, or it might end up with a few days and nights in a hospital bed sucking food and fluids through a tube.'

'And you assumed yours was the latter kind of threat?'

'In all honesty, probably not. But I wasn't about to hang around to find out.'

Bliss felt himself calming down. He remained suspicious, wondering if the door was going to burst open at any moment. Yet he felt Pam was being sincere. She had confessed her role in duping him, although that could have been part of her plan to lull him. Even so, he decided to give her the benefit of the doubt. Fool him again, shame on him.

'So what now?' he asked.

'I couldn't bring a great deal with me. Only what I could stuff into an overnight bag. I may need to replace my wheels, buy some clothes, and although I have a decent amount of cash with me, I'm going to need a hand getting things done.'

'Done in readiness for what?' He glanced pointedly around the room. 'This can't be your final destination.'

Pam smiled for the first time since he'd arrived. 'Not even in my worst nightmares. I have fake ID I can use to travel with. I'll find somewhere to go. Somewhere nobody can find me, not even somebody with Marty's reach.'

'How many days do you need?'

'A couple. Maybe three. I've thought about it ever since me and Marty broke up, but there was always Angus to anchor me. Now it seems like I don't have him keeping me here, either. I expect I must come across as pretty pathetic to you, Jimmy.'

Bliss shook his head, softening his gaze. 'Not in the least. On the contrary, you're still a strong and determined woman, only in a different way. The woman I always thought you'd be, as it goes.

We chose different paths, Pam. I could have gone your way, but I don't think I ever had it in me to be a hardened criminal. Yeah, when I was younger and didn't know any better, I'd benefit from some moody clobber from time to time, and I was handy with my fists so I could look after myself. But what I learned from my old man was by far the greater pull. No, you chose your way of life and that's all there is to it. What's happened to you is sad, but you're not. Things have turned against you, is all. If I felt sad for you, I'd never have slept with you.'

She blinked slowly, like a cat showing its trust. 'Thank you for that. Will you stay?'

He checked his watch. 'I can't, Pam. I have Max to think of. I made plans for him on the nights I saw you, but I need to get back and get him sorted for what promises to be another long day. Have to psyche myself up for a tilt at another windmill, too. Before I go, you'd better give me your mobile.'

'I left it at home. I called you from the room phone.' Pam nodded towards the bedside cabinet.

'That was good thinking. I'll pick you up a pay-as-you-go cheapie later today. But I am very busy at work, plus I need time to think about the best way to keep you secure until you're ready to leave. I'll come back as soon as I can, though. Okay?'

'Absolutely. I'll be fine. Nobody would even think of looking for me here,' she said with a light laugh. 'They all know – or think they know – that I'm far too up my own arse for a place like this. When they do look for me, it'll be in swanky hotels on swankier resorts.'

He smiled and gave a nod of encouragement. 'Okay. I'll get back to you the moment I'm free. I'll call the room before I come, so if anybody knocks on that door, it ain't me. Understand?'

*

She did. More than anything, she wanted him to stay. Had come close to pleading with him to lie down on the bed, holding her close until the first light of dawn broke through the flimsy curtains. She was not above using her full array of feminine wiles, but on this occasion the thought of it left her feeling queasy. Jimmy had offered a helping hand, despite the pair of them being relative strangers. He had a job to do, but he was still willing to help her out of the mess she found herself in, although he must have felt so betrayed.

So yes, she understood.

When he got to his feet to leave, she did so, too. She accompanied him down a flight of stairs, out of the reception area and into the car park. As he opened the door of his vehicle, she tugged at his shoulder. He turned. She held out her arms and he stepped into them. He held her until she felt brave enough to break away, his strong arms leaving her feeling protected and safe in a way she hadn't in many years. She watched in silence as he drove away, waved until his car disappeared from view.

Happy that she had told him the truth, yet still confused in respect of her feelings for him, Pam sighed and ambled slowly back to her room. She was not a child. She knew there was no chance of her and Jimmy having any kind of future together. Just because they'd screwed didn't mean either of them was emotionally involved. She might get there given time, but time was not something she had in reserve. Moving on and away had to be her sole focus.

Her thoughts turned once more to her ex-husband and son. She had always known that if Marty found out about her doing more with Jimmy than just hooking him to provide her with information, he would be furious. But going so far as to send his pet attack dog to threaten her? That was a step too far. Especially as she knew the man's reputation. What's more, Marty had to be aware that she would regard the threat as more like a death sentence. He wanted to inflict that kind of emotional pain on her, a painful realisation to acknowledge. She wished she found it impossible to believe, but sadly, it summed up their entire relationship.

But not Angus. Not her son. That betrayal bit deep enough to break her heart.

With a sense of deep foreboding and the bitter sting of loss causing her to weep once again, Pam entered the hotel room and shut the door behind her.

At the same time as the man from the day before stepped out of her bathroom.

FORTY

Bliss took Max for his first walk of the day, which gave him time to think. Grey skies and fine drizzle were what he could expect from the next seventy-two hours. He didn't mind, though he much preferred days when he could dress light and feel warm. Off his lead, the dog tore across open stretches of land no matter what the weather. He kept one eye on his keeper at all times, never straying completely out of sight. For a few weeks at the beginning he'd stayed closer still, fear of abandonment probably lingering in the animal's thoughts. The greater freedom gave Bliss longer periods in which to clear his head.

Although he barely knew the woman Pam Daniels had become, the girl he had dated click-clacked along the corridors of his mind in high-heeled shoes and mini skirts. Prior to her deliberately running into him at the pub, he hadn't thought about her in years. Perhaps even decades. They say you always remember your first real love, and in that context, he could. A myriad of memories flooded his senses to the point of overflowing. Yet they served only to indicate how little she meant to him now. They were strangers as adults, albeit strangers with benefits. Despite that, her believing she was being hunted by the Lightning Rod put an entirely different complexion on the police operation.

She could no longer be used to lure their killer out; she would never go for it, even if he could bring himself to suggest such a dangerous plan. Aware of this man's terrible reputation – if not the name he was known by – Pam was clearly terrified. Bliss could only imagine how much deeper that terror would run if she knew what he was fully capable of.

No. Using her as bait was out of the question. Keeping her away from the man was now the main goal, but could he offer her the kind of protection she needed? The budget for the Met watchers down in London – not that they had been at all effective – was considerable, but couldn't simply be switched across to the Cambridgeshire police. He might be able to persuade Superintendent Fletcher to provide Pam with a safe house, perhaps put her up in a slightly better hotel in exchange for information. But that depended entirely on what and how much she was willing to tell them. If she volunteered to say anything at all.

Dawn encroached over to his right, the damp morning air pushed into his body by a steady breeze. When Max started to hover closer, Bliss threw the dog's tennis ball, smiling as the animal hurled himself after it, appearing to be in no hurry at all to return once the toy was clamped securely between his teeth. *Doggy Day Care* was going to have an exhausted and wet, but happy, client on their hands.

As for Pam, he wasn't sure what to do. The nature and tone of their conversation earlier implied she wanted to keep things between the two of them until she'd had time and space to think things through. Her notion of obtaining a change of clothes and lying low for a few days before making off with fake ID and whatever cash she was carrying suited her. Did that mean he had to go along with it?

She was currently neither suspect nor victim, so he had nothing to hold her on, even if he did inform his team. Yet he now had knowledge of a crime about to be committed, in the shape of her using forged documents. The fact that she carried them was enough to warrant a more in-depth conversation, in addition to removing them from her person. Could he ignore all that and stand aside while she went ahead with her plan?

He walked Max home, showered and dressed for another working day. Over a cup of tea and a slice of buttered toast, he ruminated further. By the time he'd consumed his small breakfast, he'd made up his mind. He would try to convince her to come in, to discuss options with him and Superintendent Fletcher.

He called the hotel and asked to be put through to her room. The voice at the other end told him there was no answer and to try again later. Pam might well be asleep, perhaps having turned the ringer off on the room's phone. Yet Bliss wondered if, in her current mental state of distress, she was capable of sleeping soundly? Sleeping at all, for that matter. Also, surely she would prefer to keep the ringer on knowing it was the only way he could contact her without actually driving over with no advance notice, something he said he wouldn't do.

A knot of anxiety swelled behind his ribs. According to Pam, nobody else knew about her stashed car, and she'd left her mobile at home. There was no way of tracing her movements without either of them leaving behind a trail of GPS breadcrumbs. So why, then, was he still fretting? Could she have been followed all the way from London? Unlikely, considering the Met's watchers had been oblivious. Or had they? Just because he'd heard nothing from them didn't mean they hadn't stuck to her like glue.

Bliss puffed out his cheeks, patted Max's head, and headed back out the front door. 'Lucinda will be here soon, boy,' he said over his shoulder. 'She'll take care of you. Oh, and if you've got nothing better to do, have dinner waiting for me when I get home, will you?'

It took him less than ten minutes to hit the Boongate roundabout. The roads were quiet, the pavements equally so. The hotel car park was half empty – or half full, depending on your point of view. There was nobody at the reception desk when he entered, so he found the stairs and took them two at a time. He walked along the corridor until he reached Pam's room.

Shit!

The door was ajar.

Bliss hated that. He much preferred them wide open or even closed. Ajar conjured up all kinds of possibilities, none of them good. Tensing, he pushed the door and it swung all the way in. He caught a muffled sound, and he instinctively knew it had come from inside. He licked his lips and realised stealth wasn't going to be a factor here. Instead, he drew in a deep breath and stepped into the room.

He didn't know what he had expected to find, but it wasn't two wildly undernourished youths. The pair stood frozen to the spot, poised over Pam's overnight bag. The female had been rifling through it, the male moving from foot to foot by her side. Two pale faces now turned to Bliss, eyes wide.

'What the fuck are you two doing here?' he snapped at them. He clocked the situation once more and shook his head. 'Never mind. You're turning the room over. That's what you're doing here. That stops now. Instead, tell me where the woman whose room this was went to.'

The lad weighed him up, seeing if he fancied his chances. He had almost forty years on Bliss, but rather than puff himself out he shrank back into the shadows. Beaten before the first punch was thrown. The girl removed her hand from the leather holdall and stood straighter.

'What you going to do to us?' she asked, her voice cracking.

Keeping a watchful eye on the pair of them, Bliss said, 'Nothing, provided you tell me the truth.'

'We don't know nothing.'

'Which tells me you know something.'

'I said we didn't see nothing.'

'That's not what you said at all. And it means you did. Tell me what you saw, what you know, and I'll stand aside so long as you leave behind anything you've already taken. And before you say another word, I'm a police officer. This won't end up with a clipped ear and a sore arse from the toe-end of my boot. It'll be hours inside a cell back at the factory. By the look of you two, how jumpy you both are, I reckon you can't go that long before your next fix. So, what do you say?'

He was banking on neither of them having heard of the Police and Criminal Evidence Act.

'We heard her.' Still the girl, her boyfriend mute. 'First, there was a big bump against the wall. Then she cried out. A couple more crashes. Then it all went quiet. We're in the room next door, so it woke us up. I peeked out through the curtains, but the landing was empty and quiet. I didn't see nothing for ages. Then two of them came out of the room. I didn't really get a look, but I could tell one was big, the other smaller. We gave it a while – I don't know how long. Then I crept out to check, saw the door was open. We waited and waited, then risked coming in to have a look around.'

Bliss looked down his nose at her. 'So you saw and heard all that, and rather than call the police, you decided to rob the place instead.'

Her face became a twisted snarl of defiance. 'We weren't going to call you lot, were we? We're not stupid.'

'I'd argue otherwise,' Bliss scoffed, 'but I'm not sure your defence would hold water. So you claim you didn't see them go, just knew they had.'

'Yeah. I was looking from behind the curtain, not through the gap. I saw… shapes, I suppose. Two of them. Like I say, one small, the other much bigger.'

'Did either of them say anything as they passed by?'

'Not that we heard.'

'Did you get a look at a vehicle?'

'I told you, we waited ages before we left our room. They were long gone by then.'

Bliss jerked his thumb towards the open doorway. 'Fine. Now fuck the fuck off.'

They didn't need to be told a second time. He heard their own door slam, followed by raised voices. Sounded like she was ripping into him for saying and doing nothing. Good for her. The prick deserved the fierce rebuke.

Bliss was torn as to what to do next. This was something he ought to be reporting. He couldn't imagine the man he and his team were searching for bungling this so badly that he'd leave behind any evidence, but if there was the slightest possibility, then Bliss couldn't ignore it. No way to keep it quiet if he did, either.

Chin slumped against his chest, he took out his phone and made the call.

FORTY-ONE

It was the shit show Bliss had anticipated. Following brief conversations with both his sergeants, he then ensured the crime scene investigators were ordered out to the hotel. His next call was to Detective Superintendent Fletcher, who immediately summoned him back to Thorpe Wood. Upon arrival, he was instructed to carry out necessary case admin in his office until such time as he could be officially spoken to. He didn't believe he'd done a great deal wrong, certain he had answers for any questions Fletcher and perhaps Feeley might throw at him. Still, he was on edge until finally receiving the summons to attend a meeting in the conference room.

On either side of Fletcher, both DCS Feeley and the PCC were also seated at the table. Benning in particular wore a smug, almost contemptuous expression that Bliss wanted to wipe off with his bare hands.

'Please explain your actions to us, Inspector,' Benning began.

Bliss made a point of looking at his boss, who nodded for him to do as asked. 'No problem,' he said. 'In the early hours of this morning, I was contacted by Pamela Daniels. In short, she told me she was in Peterborough and asked if I would meet her at her hotel. I did, and we talked. We were right about our man visiting her yesterday. Whatever he said scared her enough to make her think she had no option but to flee. I don't know what her plans were, other than to get away from London and simply be elsewhere. I'm not certain she knew, either. She asked me for advice and help. I told her to spend the night thinking about her next move and said I'd be in touch later on today. When I woke up, I had an uneasy feeling, wondering if she might have been followed. I called her room but got no answer. I drove over to the hotel, found her door ajar, so I went in fearing she might be hurt… or worse. I was confronted by a couple of druggies from the room next door. They told me they'd heard an argument, a scuffle, and shortly afterwards two people left the room together. That's when I called it in.'

Feeley had his hands clasped together on the table, his thumbs pressed together and moving in a steady rocking motion. He made a show of shaking his head admonishingly. 'There's a lot in that explanation not to like, Inspector Bliss.'

'Really? I'm happy to answer any questions you might have, sir?'

'How gracious of you,' Benning hissed. 'You say that as if you have any choice in the matter.'

Bliss ignored him. 'Sir?' he said to Feeley.

'Very well, let's begin by asking why you didn't call it in the moment you became aware Pamela Daniels was in Peterborough.'

'My apologies, sir, but what exactly would I have called in at that stage?' He thought back over his own arguments, justifying his approach. 'Pamela Daniels is not a suspect. Neither was she the victim of any crime that I knew of at the time. Yes, she'd slipped the surveillance believing if she was being watched it would be either by the man who'd visited her office or her ex-husband. But she didn't ask to be under observation. She'd done nothing wrong. She was asking for my help. I can't see that I had any reason to call it in.'

'And the hours following your conversation with her? You say it occurred to you later that she might have been followed, but why didn't that cross your mind at the time?'

'Regarding her being followed, I felt if she'd managed to slip away from the Met's watchers, it was unlikely that anybody else had stuck close to her. She was using a vehicle nobody else knew about, and had left her mobile at home. That ruled out a GPS trace. She seemed free and clear. If it hadn't been for an uneasy feeling, I wouldn't have even driven over there again so soon after my last visit.'

Feeley studied him. If he thought Bliss was being evasive, he didn't show any irritation. In fact, he was behaving remarkably calm. 'Inspector,' he said. 'I'm sure you'll be able to explain all of it away. After all, you've had plenty of time to consider your responses. There's no doubt you walk a fine line, but I've never known you to deliberately hurt a case before.'

'Never have and never will, sir.'

'Are you saying you've done nothing wrong here, Bliss?' the Commissioner sniped, raising his voice. 'Because I would and will argue otherwise.'

Again, Bliss looked to Feeley for guidance. If the DCS wanted to throw him to the wolves, this was the ideal opportunity. Fletcher started to say something, but was interrupted by the Chief Superintendent.

'I'm satisfied,' he said. 'For now. I think we can all look back and say we might have acted differently in the same situation, but aside from perhaps a lapse of judgement there's nothing here to warrant sticking you on the bench. Your… relationship with Pamela Daniels is something we may have to revisit if, upon reflection, it clouded your judgement. But I think you've clarified everything we wanted to know.'

'I strongly disagree!' Benning said, his cheeks burning.

Feeley turned to him. 'Then perhaps you can take it up with the Chief Constable, Commissioner. I'd advise against it, because there's nothing obviously incorrect about anything Inspector Bliss did in terms of procedure. He's right when he says Daniels was neither a suspect nor a victim.'

'How does that in any way explain her abduction?'

'I'd like to answer that,' Bliss said. He did not wait for permission. 'Mr Benning, I should point out that we don't have any evidence to say for certain that Pamela Daniels was abducted. She might well have left of her own volition with this other person. If I'm being honest, I doubt that's true. But we don't know for sure one way or the other. And secondly, if she has become a victim, I could hardly be expected to have predicted it. She had been in that hotel room for quite some time before she called me. If anybody had followed her there, I would have expected them to react sooner rather than later. I regret not staying with her, but she told me she needed space and time to think. We arranged to talk later… we just never got around to it.'

'That's all very well, Inspector,' Benning said. 'But somebody seemingly tussled with her in that hotel room. According to witness testimony, she then left with that person. If nobody followed Pamela Daniels to this city, and no GPS tracking devices were either on her person or in her vehicle, how did they locate her in the first place?'

Bliss made no reply. He had none. It was the question now bothering him most of all.

*

'How did you find me? How did you even know I'd left home?' Daniels asked him. Although in fear for her life, she refused to be cowed by this man and his brooding presence.

The building she now found herself in smelled dank and stale, and while it was relatively free of clutter, it was nonetheless grubby with an air of abandonment about it. She had no idea where they were, but she'd heard the intermittent clatter of trains on a track close by. He'd bound her to a chair with tape, leaving only her head freely able to move. He'd also placed a strip of tape over her mouth, removing it only after she agreed not to cry out. The threat he'd made was enough for Pam to keep her promise.

'I shadowed you pretty closely throughout the afternoon. Though I wasn't the only one watching you,' he said. His eyes bored into hers, forcing her to look away. 'I almost stumbled into a police surveillance team.'

'I wish you had.' Her words had the bitter taste of defeat about them.

His shrug was emphatic. 'All the wishes in the world won't do you any good now. But it was close there for a moment. If I'd been even a fraction off my game, I'd probably be sitting in a holding cell right now. But I spotted them, evaded them, and then shifted emphasis. I considered what your reaction might be to our earlier meeting. Fight or flight responses are usually easy to gauge, but you're a bit of an enigma, Pam. I couldn't decide which way you'd go, but erred on the side of caution.'

'So you followed me from my house?'

He shook his head before removing something from his jacket pocket and tossing it onto the desk by her side. The square box meant nothing to her, but he was clearly making a point.

'No, no. I prefer to be one step ahead if at all possible. See, you thought nobody knew about the wheels you had stashed away in that lockup, but you were wrong. I broke in and put that GPS tracking device underneath your car long before you got there. When that moved, so did I. At my leisure, several miles behind you. After you arrived in Peterborough, it was easy enough to get your room number once you'd checked in. I even had the presence of mind to remove the tracker before we left.'

'So, what? You want a medal?'

He closed his eyes. Took a deep breath. Opened them again. 'You asked a question. I replied.'

'So if you knew where I was, why didn't you come for me straight away?'

'Because I'm nobody's fool. I thought I'd sit back for a while to see what you did next. Calling your police friend was an obvious move, so I wasn't surprised when he turned up. If you'd tried to leave the hotel with him, I'd've taken you there and then. Be glad you didn't, because he'd be lying dead in a pool of blood as we speak. I knew he'd be back at some point, though, so I decided to slip up the stairs while you two were outside getting all loved up. But I was right to wait in the first place.'

'Why? What difference does it make now? You should've killed me there and then. Got it over and done with.'

He took a step closer, almost into the light. A large man with indistinct features. Somebody you'd pass by without a second thought. 'I have no intention of killing you, Pam. Did you think somebody wanted you dead? Don't bother to answer. I can see by the sheer terror in your eyes that you did, and still do. So let me put your mind to rest. All I wanted from you were answers to some questions. Now that you've spent more time with your boyfriend, I have additional questions. I'll ask, you'll answer. If I think you're lying to me, or even holding something back, then things won't go so well for you.'

She stuck out her chin as her eyes flared. 'Oh, really? What are you going to do to me, big man? You going to beat me? You going to lay into me with those meaty fists of yours?'

He flashed a thin smile. 'Nothing so crude, Pam. If you knew anything about me at all, you'd know I have more flair than that.'

'What then? Torch me? Pull my fingernails out? I know the kind of strokes you people pull. Whoever you are, I'm sure your methods are limited.'

'Oh, I beg to differ.' This time he removed something from the inside pocket of his lightweight jacket and held it in front of her face. 'To you, I'm sure this must look like an ordinary envelope. Which, in fact, it is. On the surface, then, not much of a threat. But you've given yourself papercuts before, right, Pam? Sting like a bugger, don't they?' He raised the flap and looked along its fine edge. 'I wouldn't want to carve the Sunday roast with this,' he went on. 'But I can assure you it's plenty sharp enough to take your face apart one slice at a time.'

FORTY-TWO

Organising a three-way video conference between himself, the NCA in the form of Frank Rogers, and the Met's Strategic Firearms Commander, Chief Superintendent Alan Wylie, took less time than Bliss had imagined. Following brief introductions, the focus of their conversation was Marty Reid.

'He's hardly unknown to us,' Wylie said. A neat, closely shaven man with salt-and-pepper hair, and a deep baritone of a voice. 'A number of our more high-profile operations have led to the arrests of men and women with suspected ties to that toe-rag. Just a fortnight ago we had four ARV units put a stop on a vehicle coming in off the A4 carrying three of his known associates. The problem is, none of them so far have admitted to working for the slippery bugger. I have to say I'm surprised you managed to persuade a magistrate to issue a warrant for his arrest.'

Bliss allowed himself a brief smile of satisfaction. 'My DCs can use persuasive language when it's needed most. We could have asked for him to be arrested without one, but I thought the warrant would be good to have in our back pockets. Additional ammunition, if you like when we enter his home.'

'Can't ever hurt, Inspector. There must be high confidence

of him having committed a crime in this instance. Frank has already explained to me your reasons for requesting firearms authorisation, and I have to agree with you both. If Reid ordered the abduction of his ex-wife with the intent to harm her, he's unlikely to come quietly. We know he's gone armed on a number of occasions, but unfortunately we've only managed to discover these incidents in retrospect.'

'I'd never heard of the man before our investigation connected a victim to him,' Bliss admitted. 'But I know Frank and the NCA have taken an interest.'

Rogers nodded. 'They say if you're a known face, then you're not top of the pile, but that may not be true in Marty Reid's case. He has just the right number of degrees of separation from the mugs on the street to be king of his particular hill. He's come to the attention of my agency by reputation only, but the teams working organised crime had previously decided to make him a priority in the weeks and months ahead.'

'Let's hope the NCA won't have to go anywhere near him after today,' Wylie said. 'But I won't hold my breath. Tell me, both of you, have you considered the possibility of his ex-wife being inside the house with him?'

'Considered and dismissed,' Rogers told him. 'The man we believe Reid instructed to take her works alone. He'd want no direct contact. In fact, neither of them would. No, if Pamela Daniels is still alive – which we have every reason to believe she is – then the man who snatched her from the hotel is keeping her elsewhere. The arrest of Reid is necessary to gain further intel on where that might be, or at the very least to provide us with a way of contacting him.'

'Reid is not going to talk. You do know that?'

'He won't want to,' Bliss said. 'We just have to come up with a plan to convince him it's in his best interests. Right now, he's our only way in.'

'And if you get what you want from him, I gather we'll be required to attend a second location?'

'Yes. We'd assume so.'

'All right. How much time do we have to surveil Reid's home?'

Rogers shook his head. 'We can't know. I'm confident Reid doesn't have Pamela Daniels with him, but I'm equally confident that our man does. To my mind, her life is in danger either way, because all it takes is a single call or text message from Reid to our killer.'

'Which is why you'd be looking for a dynamic entry, I assume?'

'Yes. If we bowl up and knock on his door, he has time to make that call or send that text. A dynamic entry gives him little or no time to react… we hope.'

'In other words, the need is urgent.'

'Extremely so.'

'Which means we have little time for surveillance. Consequently, we may have to go in without any idea if he is even at home.'

'I'm sorry, Chief Superintendent,' Bliss said. 'I wish we could be presenting you with a more favourable scenario. The best I can offer you is the intel we have coming in live, which is that the only mobile we can find registered to Reid is currently shaking hands with towers close to his home, and the GPS associated with his Mercedes has it sitting on his driveway.'

Chief Superintendent Wylie took a deep breath. 'In that case, I think I have all I need from you two for the time being. I'll speak to my TFC about his preferred tactics, and have my OFC gather a team together. Reid's home is in Surrey, but I don't think we can afford to involve them at this strategic stage. Perhaps once we have the op in hand, we can let them know we're going in and ask for a local response on the fringes to help with containment.'

'That's the Met's call,' Rogers said. 'Are you sure that's the way you want to go?'

'It is. Have to admit, I'm concerned about leaks if this gets too big, so that's another good reason to inform them once we're already on the plot.'

Bliss struggled not to grin. The Met were notoriously slow at advising other force areas of their presence, but while Wylie's reasoning appeared sound, it was the Tactical and Operational Firearms Commanders he'd mentioned who'd be in the firing line from angry and humiliated local police.

'You'll keep us in the loop?' Rogers asked.

'At every significant juncture, Frank. We go in at your request, but with the highest authorisation. Equally, whatever you learn you funnel through us. Especially if you discover he's on the move.'

They wound up the video call a couple of minutes later and, now sitting alone in his office, Bliss was left to wait and hope, all the while anticipating the many things that might yet go wrong.

FORTY-THREE

The armed dynamic entry on Marty Reid's home went like clockwork. All assembled units would have preferred going in at either dusk or dawn, but with a woman's life potentially at stake they had no option but to act as soon as they were fully briefed and prepared. Command officers spent two hours discussing plans with the various unit heads. The entry team consisted of officers from the Met's elite SCO19 specialist firearms unit and tactical support team, leaving Surrey's own Godstone-based unit on standby to offer backup should Marty Reid decide to run.

Surrey police were naturally angered at being told about the op only after the teams were already in place. But the Met were used to taking command of their spontaneous or unpredictable planned deployments irrespective of where they took place, and while the local forces justifiably complained, they usually lacked the levels of immediate resources to run the play at such short notice.

After settling into various locations surrounding the property, the first officers due in were given the word to go. In addition to the traditional big red key enforcer – essentially a heavy metallic tube with carry handles – they took with them a hydraulic tactical breaching kit, including a spreader and cutting tools, light enough to be carried by a single officer but powerful enough to take out high-security doors and windows.

Silent and stealthy until the breach itself, firearms officers piled in through the doorway making a big noise, identifying themselves as armed police and barking out instructions for anybody within earshot to get down on their knees with their hands behind their head. Further actual barking followed in the shape of two German Shepherds, both held on short leads. It was a textbook entry and domicile search, but as each 'all clear' rang out across the Airwave devices tuned to a specific channel, so everybody involved in the raid began to have doubts about the result.

In one of the outlying unmarked police vehicles crewed by two of Surrey police's finest, the officer behind the wheel cursed and slammed a balled fist on the steering wheel. 'I fucking told you,' he snarled, looking across at his partner as the radio transmissions continued to pour in. 'Those wankers from the Met's goon squad naused it up. It's all very well for our own Roads Police Command to stick us out here on fringes and pretend we've got the sweet end of the dead, but we should have had overall Gold command here on our own patch. We had a chance to nail that fucker Reid, and now we're left holding our dicks in our hand.'

'To be fair, that's not unusual for you,' his colleague joked.

'Don't! Just don't. I'm not in the fucking mood.'

His partner turned to mutter quietly at his reflection in the side window. As he did so, he spotted a figure rushing along the pavement outside a row of shops. The man wore a peaked cap, but the uniformed officer recognised him immediately.

'Fuck me, it's him!' he said, wrestling with the door release. 'It's Reid.'

The gangster was no whelp, but he took off like an Olympic sprinter. He was known to keep himself in shape, with regular circuit training and visits to the gym, and he was virtually out of sight before the two police officers had cleared their vehicle.

Lagging behind his colleague by a good ten yards, the driver called it in, informing command that he and his partner were in pursuit on foot. He fed them the name of the road they were in and the direction in which they were headed. By the time he'd delivered the message, he was panting and could feel the burn in his thighs and calf muscles. He was fit enough, but the weight of equipment he carried, including the bulky stab vest, held him back.

Up ahead, Reid turned into an alleyway towards the end of the parade of shops. It emerged into a road running parallel to the one on which the unmarked police car was parked. To the right, more shops with a large open park at the end. To the left, the shops led to a square on which a bandstand stood gleaming with new paintwork. Beyond the square lay the entrance to a small shopping centre. Neither of the two uniformed officers were gaining on Reid when he disappeared into it.

*

In response to the driver's urgent call, backup arrived swiftly, lights and sirens. Detectives, additional uniforms, and firearms officers clad in black clothing rapidly flooded the area, clearing out shoppers as they went. Even with only two levels and a single outdoor car park, the centre was a warren of linking corridors, stores, alleyways, and vehicles. The two officers who first gave chase lost sight of their quarry from the moment he entered the structure and did not lay eyes on him again.

In communication with his Tactical Firearms Commander at all times, Operational Firearms Commander Sergeant Paul Groves took responsibility for deploying resources on the ground.

About to bark out his instructions, his eyes were drawn to a more senior figure cutting through the throng of police officers.

'Who's in charge here?' she demanded. The epaulettes on her shoulders told Groves this was the Deputy Chief Constable for Surrey police. He stepped forward. 'That would be me, ma'am.'

The newcomer looked him up and down and seemed not to like what she saw. 'This deployment has now become a static scene, wouldn't you agree?'

'I suppose so.' He knew what was coming next.

'Good. Therefore, I think it best if our command structure took over from this point on. I have our own OFC on his way here as we speak. Our firearms units are already part of this deployment, so the changeover process ought to be reasonably seamless.'

'With respect, ma'am,' Groves said, standing his ground, 'I've never experienced a seamless change of command in all my years in the job. We have a dangerous man loose inside that shopping centre, and as we stand here deliberating we're wasting time we don't have a great deal of to spare. The Met's command structure is already in place, SCO19 is here and fully prepared to go in. We also have plainclothes officers, both ours and yours to accompany them on the search. I think to mess with that now would be foolish.'

'I don't intend to *mess* with anything,' the DCC snapped, eyes becoming slits. 'Are you suggesting we're not up to the Met's high standards officer…?'

'Groves. Sergeant Groves, ma'am. And no, that's not what I'm saying. I was simply pointing out that we're ready to go in as soon as I give the word, and I think changing command, tactics, and operational involvement at this important phase of the deployment is likely to be detrimental to the outcome. An outcome you'll have to explain away, if you decide to go ahead.'

He thought he'd perhaps overreached with that final line, but as soon as he saw the impact of his words reach her eyes, he knew he'd won the argument. Rather than waste more time, he chose to jump in with both feet.

'Ma'am. I'm more than happy to bring your people in to the operational side. After all, it was your two officers who spotted him and followed him here. I'm not interested in making a power play, I'm just looking for the right result. As I'm sure we all are.'

He left it there, hoping it was good enough.

Surrey's Deputy Chief Constable closed her eyes and then nodded. 'Very well. I'll inform our firearms commanders.'

After speaking with the two officers who had chased Reid on foot into the mall, Groves contacted the centre's security manager. On being alerted to the possibility of an armed man loose in the centre, the guard had dashed across to the small CCTV suite. He and the three members of security staff on duty at the time proceeded to manipulate the cameras spread across the site and scan the monitors for a man acting furtively, perhaps hurrying while sneaking looks over his shoulder. As Reid's description filtered through, they began to focus more intently on men of the right age, build, and colour, wearing the described clothing.

Delighted to learn that the mall subscribed to the local Shopwatch scheme, which meant every store had access to a two-way radio system, Groves instructed the security manager to put out a message directing all store officials to steer shoppers calmly out of emergency exits, where police officers would be waiting for them. Cleaners and mall maintenance staff were then to be told to seek their nearest emergency exits as well. He also told the security staff to concentrate on the cameras and monitors and to report back anything they considered to be suspicious.

A short while later, police fanned out and converged steadily towards the central food court from each of the four main entrances, clearing and securing each store as they went. Some of the larger shops took twice as long to search than their smaller neighbours. It was both time-consuming and tense for all involved, officers not knowing if Reid was carrying a gun, but aware they might walk into a firearm every time they turned a corner or opened up a door.

And in the back of their minds the whole time, the knowledge that their suspect might have slipped away before the police cordon had even been established.

FORTY-FOUR

Dejected by the news concerning the raid on Marty Reid's home and the subsequent chase into a nearby shopping centre, Bliss turned to his team to ask for one final push. 'This was always going to be a shot in the dark,' he said. 'Even if they'd pulled Reid, we can't know he would have talked. Rather than sitting here with faces like slapped arses, or pissing off down the pub to get mullered, I'm all for having another crack at finding our killer.'

'Where do you suggest we begin, boss?' Bishop asked. He did his best to sound game, but the disappointment in his voice was obvious. Bliss felt his colleague's anxiety.

'I say we go back to what we know about him. We have his mug, but that doesn't seem to be helping us much. We might also have his wheels. There's that dash-cam video, remember? Which reminds me, do we have that CCTV footage in from Hampstead, yet? The one they pieced together tracing our man to and from Xavier Brent's place.'

'What exactly are we looking for? We already know the cameras follow him out of a parking garage and back to it again afterwards.'

'Yeah, so what I'm interested in is what happens later on.

He walks from the car park, visits Brent's house, goes inside the house, and when he comes out again, he heads straight back to where he came from. That probably means he parked there, in which case he must have driven out again.'

'I doubt that footage will be on the same clip they sent us,' Ansari said, wincing with each word as if they caused her physical pain. 'That file was edited, and only included the relevant moments from when he first shows to when he vanished again.'

'Okay, that's somewhere else to start. So do we have access to the unedited version? The CCTV outside that parking structure?'

'Yes, boss. I'll dig it out and bring it up on the smartboard.' Although Bliss steered clear, his DCs were dab hands at using the technology fitted in the major inquiry room. He'd been offered courses aimed at familiarising him with the equipment, but he was happy for others to demonstrate their expertise.

While they waited for the DC to find and cue the film, Chandler challenged him as to what purpose he hoped to achieve by running it. 'Even if he's using the same motor as the one he drove when he murdered the Sperlings, what does that give us that we don't already have?' she asked.

'I'm still processing that,' Bliss confessed. 'But we'll know two things more at the very least. First, we'll confirm if it's the same vehicle or not. Second, we'll confirm whether he uses the same licence plate… or not.'

'And what will that tell us?'

'Wait and see.'

Ansari raised a hand to indicate she was ready. On the large flatscreen monitor attached to the wall, time and date stamped video footage appeared. 'Thanks, Gul,' Bliss said. 'Fast-forward from the point at which our man disappears into the bowels of the parking structure, but not so fast we miss something if we blink. If the motor shown in our dash-cam footage is our killer's, and if he uses it on a regular basis, then we should see it come out of that multi-storey car park any time soon.'

The time on the screen had moved on by almost twenty minutes when DC Virgil called out, 'There!'

Ansari stopped the fast-forward, rewound until the vehicle that had just exited was in full view.

It provided them with no clear shot of the driver, but the vehicle was the silver Land Rover Defender they had been hoping to see.

Bishop was the first to speak. 'It's a different plate from the one in the dash-cam footage, but that has to be our man.'

Bliss felt the first stirrings of heat warming his neck and cheeks, and the fizz of excitement slipping through his veins. 'Run it,' he told Ansari.

Her hands danced on the keys. Moments later she shook her head, saying, 'The registration does come back as a Defender, boss, but an earlier model and different colour.'

'That's him, all right,' Bishop said excitedly. 'That's our killer.'

Bliss calmed everybody down before addressing them. 'Okay, settle please. I was hoping for the same plate, but our killer is no fool. I'm not too disappointed, though. We have to assume this man is sent to do a number of jobs, many of them minor. He's not going to risk nicking a different motor for every one, and someone of his calibre is bound to change plates on a regular basis. But here's what's stirring in the back of my mind: is he likely to have a stock large enough to use a different one for every job he does? It's much harder now than it used to be to obtain false plates. And remember, this fixer or killer or whatever you want to call him, was under the impression that he was operating way beneath our radar. Yes, he still took precautions, but having a different set of plates for every single job…? I don't see that happening.'

'So what are you thinking, Jimmy?' Chandler asked.

By way of an answer, Bliss turned once more to DC Ansari. 'Gul, pull up the ANPR site and log in. Run both of the plates we now have for this vehicle. Begin with data collected just this month – we can expand on that if necessary. I want to know where those plates have been. Moreover, I want to see if they have ever been picked up on numerous occasions by the same camera. If we can find a significant overlap, then we might just have the general location of our Lightning Rod.'

'ANPR search parameters are wide-ranging,' Ansari explained. 'Even so, an exploration of the entire country will take time.'

'Then you best get cracking, Gul.'

Leaving Ansari slogging away at the computer terminal, Bliss concentrated on the remaining members of his team. 'Is there anything else we can be doing?' he asked. 'The results we're after may not appear for a while yet, so rather than sit here with our thumbs up our arses, let's discuss alternative leads.'

'We know several other areas he's visited,' Gratton said eagerly. 'We can run a CCTV scan now that we know the vehicle he most likely used. That might throw up a few additional number plates for us to add to the ANPR search.'

'Good. Thanks for volunteering.'

The young DC put his head back and groaned. 'Oh, fuck me! Not cake detail?'

The others laughed and jeered while Bliss nodded gleefully.

'Surely coming up with a good idea negates the implied volunteering,' Gratton complained. 'At the very least, it shouldn't be a punishable offence.'

Bliss gestured with his hands. 'I don't make the rules, Phil.'

'Well, if you don't, who does?'

'It's tradition.'

'I know. *Your* tradition.'

An increased whine in his voice elicited additional laughter.

When they settled, Bishop had another suggestion. 'Boss, all along you said we ought to look at victimology, right?'

'I did, but I was wrong.'

'We don't know that for sure. But what I'm thinking is, we now have a new victim. Pamela Daniels may not be dead, but she is a victim all the same. We have a good idea who took her, but what we don't know is why? What is it about her that made her a target?'

'I have no idea.'

'All right, so then why now? Whatever she's been involved with down in London, she's been at it for a long time. Yet they choose to do something now? What's different? What's changed? She spent time with you. That's what.'

Bliss instinctively knew his sergeant was right. Their focus had been on who had taken her and how, but they had not asked themselves why. 'There is one possibility we've yet to explore,' he said. 'We know our target has other skills. He's also a fixer. When he intends to kill, his victims wind up dead. No messing around. He didn't do that in this case. He subdued Pam and then he drove away with her. Why? What could he possibly want from her that he couldn't get there and then in that hotel room?'

'He needed the solitude,' Chandler said tentatively.

'Exactly. And for what purpose? What did he want from her specifically?'

'Information,' Chandler said. It wasn't a question.

'There you go. He wants to know what she told me. How much information she coughed up. That's why he took her alive. That's why he needed her on her own with all the time in the world on his side. And he'd've wanted to do so in comfort, on home soil. Somewhere familiar to him. One way or another, he intends to get answers out of her. And if Pam is anything like she was as a teenager, he'll have to extract it the hard way.'

FORTY-FIVE

HER FACE WAS A patchwork of lurid crimson hatchings, the work of a master artist caught in the downward spiral of their final despair. He was delighted with the results of his experiment, but with this experience he realised the character in *Swimming with Sharks* had underplayed the sheer ecstasy obtained from the ruination of another person's appearance. From her widow's peak to the point of her chin, no aspect had been left untouched; even her ears had felt the deliberate viciousness of the envelope's touch.

A number of the precise incisions were shallow. Some were not. Not all of them bled profusely, but he had blotted much of the blood with tissues to keep his creation relatively unobscured. He had threatened her with one slice of the envelope for every question unanswered or not answered to his satisfaction, and he had delivered on that threat. In many ways, he reasoned, Pamela Daniels' disfigurement was her own fault for not being straight with him. She had brought it upon herself.

A single strip of harsh LED lighting spot-lit his victim, the tragic figure slumped in the chair to which he had bound her. Dirt and grime and grease lurked in the shadows, as if kept at bay by the fierce glow from the ceiling. Bathed in its radiance,

Daniels looked for all the world like an actor on the stage of some terrible rendition of a modern horror story.

He loomed over her, admiring his handiwork. 'You know one of the benefits of this method of inflicting pain?' he said. 'It's the lack of physical exertion on my part. I could literally keep this up all day and night.' He paused, a finger poised against his lips as he pondered. 'I wonder how long you can last. Now, that might be an interesting development to explore.'

'You're sick!' she spat, flecks of blood flying from her lips as she raised her head. She glared up at him through puffy eyes, the physical trauma of her wounds causing her face to swell.

'Hmm, so you've said. And frankly, you've become a bit of a bore, Pam. I'm rapidly losing interest in you, if not the job at hand.'

Her wretched features contorted. 'You call this a job? You think this is any way to make a living? By torturing a person for information.'

She amused him. Her question surely couldn't be a serious one. He idly scratched at his chin. 'I do. It's a calling, one I've worked hard to be the very best at in my profession. And, if we're being honest here, you're the one stretching it out.'

'How?' Her face became taut with fury and incomprehension. 'By not giving you the answers you want to hear? All I can tell you is the truth as I know it.'

'But I have to be certain, so please, tell me again. And this time keep a few things in mind: I can move down to your neck, your breasts, and all ports further south. But sticking with your head for the time being, I've heard a papercut on the tongue can be crushingly painful. Before I begin that journey, however, there are two other facial items I've yet to touch… your eyes.'

Daniels hung her head and whimpered, stifling a louder sob of both pain and fear, a thick ribbon of mucus hanging from her nose. As much as he admired her willpower and determination not to break, she had to know it couldn't possibly last.

'Tell me then, Pam. Tell me about you and Detective Inspector Bliss. What secrets did you spill during your coupling? Or perhaps while basking in the afterglow? I'm guessing when you came you weren't exactly thinking clearly, but afterwards you might have wanted to reward him. What I want to know is, did you play him or did he play you?'

Her head came up again slowly. Hate burned in her eyes. She swallowed thickly and said, 'You tell Marty he sent the wrong man to do the job. He could have used Angus, or even asked me himself. I would have told either of them.'

'Told them what?'

'Every word I've already said to you. Because every word has been the truth. The difference is, either of them would have known it. They would have seen it in my eyes, because they know me better than any man. And neither of them are anywhere near as deranged as you.'

He smiled. 'But neither of them can do what I do without risking everything. I protect people's interests. I protect their reputation. I protect them by insulating them from the police, and from the likes of you. But what I don't quite understand, Pam, is… what does any of this have to do with either Marty or Angus Reid?'

FORTY-SIX

When word came from a colleague embedded with the building security team in the CCTV room that movement had been spotted close to the JDSports store, two firearms officers known to their colleagues as Dawn and Jennifer despite both being male, eased forward at pace in pursuit of their suspect. Usually they travelled in threes, but some trios had been reduced to pairs in order to cover more ground more quickly.

Counter Terrorism Specialist Firearms Officer French took the lead with his carbine cradled across his chest pointing down, right index finger stretched out straight alongside the trigger guard. He wore full body armour and a peaked cap bearing the Metropolitan Police insignia. No more than a pace behind him at all times, SFO Saunders wore dark plain clothes beneath his protective gear and carried a Glock, his own rifle clipped to a belt and ready for action whenever it was required.

CTSFO French spoke quietly into his Airwave. 'Any more movement to report? We're approaching JDSports.'

The reply came back immediately. 'He's in there. Not all staff made it out as swiftly as others, and one of them spotted a man matching our suspect's description sneaking in and heading for the back of the unit. We have all exits covered and internal store cameras currently searching. Get the remaining members of staff out of there, seal the entrance door, and I'll let you know when we have him in shot.'

The two men did as they were instructed, methodically and without the slightest trace of panic. By the time they heard back, they were itching to go in. 'You're a go, go, go, Blue One. Head towards the stock room which is at the far end to your right. Containment only if at all possible, as suspect is wanted for questioning. Be advised we do not have a confirmed ID, but if it is our suspect then consider him armed.'

French snorted humourlessly. Off comms, he said to his colleague, 'Usual arse-covering. It's him but we won't confirm, he's likely carrying but we want him taken down, not out.'

'There's no longer a threat to civilians,' his partner reminded him. 'We've got this.'

'Too bloody right, mate. Let's go. But if he is holding and so much as twitches, I won't hesitate.'

He'd only ever discharged his weapon once before at a live scene, a suspected terrorist wearing what proved to be a fake bomb vest taken out in an incident not widely reported on any form of media. He'd done his job, but unless you were a psychopath, you couldn't help but feel emotional at having taken another life. That didn't mean he would even pause in pulling the trigger again if it meant saving himself or his partner. The number one rule of the job was to go home at night.

The two officers eased their way through the store, heads on swivels. Opening a door presented them with a moment of acute tension. Entering the room beyond left them exposed and vulnerable, and being the experienced firearms officer he was, French paused to speak into his radio once more.

'Do you have the stockroom on your monitor?'

'Yes, we have it, Blue One. Suspect is currently out of camera range, but he passed through the stockroom onto the loading bay. You're clear to move.'

Warily, they advanced, senses heightened, prepared for anything their suspect might throw their way. All the many hours of training were geared towards this moment. Their Airwave devices squawked with an incoming message. 'Blue One, hold at double doors leading to loading dock. Suspect is still not in view. He must have found somewhere out of shot to hide. You're clear to move in when you're ready, but approach with utmost caution.'

French entered first, covering the corners and all higher elevations to his left. Saunders followed to his right. The loading dock was only part of a much larger area, but at first sight there were few places in which to hide. They checked out an office, closing the door behind them when they exited. Moving around the perimeter, weapons at the ready, the pair cleared four aisles of empty shelves, plus half a dozen packing crates, and behind a huge tower of wooden pallets.

French exchanged puzzled glances with Saunders. Had they missed him? Had he doubled back somehow before they'd had a chance to reach the bay? Then he felt a tap on his shoulder. He followed the direction of his partner's pointing finger. At the foot of a small flight of steps leading towards the bay into which vehicles reversed to unload, stood two blue industrial-sized waste containers.

Taking one slow and steady step at a time, French advanced into the bay and down the steps, indicating his partner should remain above to provide cover. He reached the first container and tapped against its side with the barrel of his firearm.

'You inside,' he called out, ensuring he could be heard. 'We know you're in there. If you are armed, leave your weapon inside before raising the lid. Climb out slowly. Once you do so, keep your hands where we can see them and make sure they are empty at all times. When your feet touch the ground, you drop to your knees. Then follow my commands. Do you hear me?'

Silence.

'If your name is not Marty Reid, you have nothing to fear from us. Just come on out, do exactly as you are told, and no harm will come to you. Marty... if that is you inside, provided you follow my instructions you also have nothing to worry about. Do you hear and understand me?'

Still nothing.

French tapped the container one more time. 'Listen to me, scumbag. Don't make us have to come in after you. If we have to raise the lid, we're going to assume the worst. Today, that ends only one way.'

For what seemed the longest time, the only sounds French could hear were his own breathing patterns and those of Saunders. Then, with a high-pitched squeal, the lid raised up by a couple of inches. 'Okay, okay. I'm coming out. I'm unarmed. You got that? I am unarmed.'

CTSFO French took a couple of paces back. Standing above him and to the right, SFO Saunders stood with his pistol raised and aimed at the moving lid. When it was fully open, Marty Reid climbed up and over the side, easing himself down to the concrete floor.

'Put your hands behind your head and get to your knees,' French bellowed at him. As soon as Reid had complied, he continued. 'Good. Lay yourself face down on the ground and slide your hands down behind your back. Do it now, but do it slowly.'

'All right, all right. I'm not carrying. Don't shoot me.'

'I won't, provided you don't give me a reason to.'

While Saunders continued to cover their suspect from a secure distance, French approached him cautiously before carrying out the arrest. After cuffing him, he conducted a thorough search. Other than a wallet, a mobile phone, some cash, and a set of keys, the only other item in Reid's possession was a small penknife.

Tightening his grip, French leaned in and said, 'I thought you weren't armed.'

'What, that?' Reid said, staring at the penknife. 'It's nothing. Fuck all. Couldn't kill a fly with that.'

'Is that so? We'll see what a jury thinks about that.'

Hoisting their suspect to his feet and clutching him by the throat, French backed Reid up past the waste container and slammed him hard against a painted breezeblock wall. He knew they were out of the security camera's reach, so he let the carbine hang at a shallower angle, pointing it at the man's groin.

'I'll forget all about the knife if you tell me where she is,' he said with an urgent rasp.

'Where who is?' Reid roared back, adrenaline possibly getting the better of him.

'Pamela Daniels. Who has her, and where?'

Reid squinted at the armed police officer. 'Pam? What do you mean? Somebody's taken her?'

The man his colleagues called Dawn released his grip and then jabbed his forearm hard into the man's chest. The tip of his carbine moved a couple of inches closer. 'Don't give me that old pony, Reid. We've been dying to make your acquaintance, pal. Now that we've met, you can always become a statistic; another hardened criminal gunned down while resisting arrest.'

'But I'm not resisting. I'm not!' Panic caused his voice to climb and break at the same time. 'I don't know what the fuck is going on, but if you think I've done anything to Pam, you're off your trolley. Is that why you lot were lying in wait for me at my gaff?'

'Don't lie to me, you piece of shit. You ordered her to be taken. We know you did, so there's no point in denying it. Just tell me who took her and where they're keeping her. Do that, and you get to keep your crown jewels.'

'I didn't have anything to do with it! I didn't! You have to believe me.'

The firearms officer looked over at his colleague. Saunders shrugged and shook his head. French cast his gaze down to the floor. A moment later, he activated comms and spoke into the Airwave. 'Command, this is Blue One. We have one under arrest. I can confirm it is Marty Reid. We're bringing him out of the loading dock, so call up transport and advise the custody manager.'

He took his finger off the Airwave button. Put his face closer. 'If you're lying to us, Reid, I'll have you. You hear me? I'll fucking well have you.'

Reid said nothing. But French didn't like what he saw in the man's eyes.

It was innocence.

FORTY-SEVEN

They took two pool cars. Bliss and Chandler in the Mondeo, Bishop and Ansari in a Volvo. From the moment DC Ansari discovered a single ANPR camera picking up the separate vehicle registration plates on multiple occasions, they were all action.

The camera was located in Whetstone, a north London suburb in the borough of Barnet. The road it stood on was a direct run up from Islington to the M25 motorway, well used on a daily basis by any number of unsavoury characters. The same camera had led to a huge volume of number plates being automatically recognised and flagged as vehicles headed both into and out of central London. On this occasion, it might just have steered them towards a killer.

Superintendent Fletcher agreed to run things from a temporary command post in the major incident room. DC Gratton took over computer duties from Ansari, his job now to identify all relevant CCTV camera feeds in the area and scour them for any sight of the silver Land Rover Defender. Alan Virgil was tasked to contact bus, coach, and taxi companies in the vicinity to request security and dash-cam footage as appropriate. The pair set to work with enthusiasm, leaving aside their disappointment at not going mobile with their colleagues.

Bliss called Frank Rogers just as he slipped on to the A1(M). 'Tell me what you know, Frank,' he said. 'We're heading your way. I need to bring you up to speed as things stand from our end, but don't want to muddy the waters with second-hand intel.'

'And hello to you, too, Jimmy. Did you just say you were on the way down here? How come?'

'I'll get to that. Are you going to update me or not?'

'Hold your horses. Before I begin, let me turn that around: what do you know about the takedown of Reid?'

'Only that it failed. He wasn't at home, then he was spotted but managed to get away. That's what makes this next move so fraught, mate. He might feel he now has no option but to give our man the order to end it and do a runner.'

The NCA man's voice came back crackly, but Bliss could just about make out what he was saying. 'Old news, Jimmy. I did wonder if the Met would keep you in the loop as they promised, and it seems I was right to doubt them. Listen up, the firearms lads eventually took him down. Reid is having none of it, though. Says he has no idea where Pam is. Didn't know she'd been snatched up until he was questioned following his arrest and definitely didn't order it done.'

'Well, he was hardly going to admit to it, was he?'

'Those were my sentiments exactly. Only, the two FOs who collared him said they were as persuasive as they dared to be in the short time they had, and both of them reckon he was being legit. He gave the same story when they got him back to the nick. They can't know for sure, Jimmy, but they are currently operating under the assumption that Marty Reid did not order the Lightning Rod to abduct Pam Daniels.'

'Fuck!' Bliss said, adding weight to his accelerator foot, ignoring the road surface made slick by showers. 'Mate, I need to give that some thought. Meanwhile, let me tell you where we're at.'

He outlined his team's progress in potentially narrowing down their suspect's location to Whetstone. Rogers was impressed. 'That's some great thinking. If he lives there or is based there operationally, we might just be in with a chance.'

'Yeah. So that's why we're on our way. We got the break, I think that means we should be in on any takedown. Plus, I have Phil and Alan still working on it back at the ranch. With so much security coverage these days, between CCTV, on-board, and dash-cams, there has to be a good chance of locating him.'

'Sounds like a plan, Jimmy. What do you want me to do in terms of backup?'

Bliss had given the matter some thought before making his call. 'I'd say we rendezvous somewhere close to Whetstone. Let Chief Superintendent Wylie and his Met firearms command team know the where and when, arrange to have a few ARVs and other firearms units on standby. We might be looking at another dynamic entry, but at all costs we have to avoid it becoming a hostage situation.'

After a few moments, during which Bliss assumed Rogers was hurriedly making notes, he heard, 'Got it. How about Boreham Wood nick as a staging area? It's right by the Elstree film and TV studios, so you can't miss it. Close enough to Whetstone without being right in the mix. Twenty minutes door-to-door. I can call ahead and arrange it.'

Pleased with the suggestion, Bliss said, 'Sounds good, Frank. Get back to me with details when you can. I'll give you a bell as soon as I get more info.'

He asked Chandler to relay the rendezvous details through to Bishop and Ansari in the following car. As happy as he could be with the arrangements, Bliss nonetheless yearned for a different play. He'd love nothing more than for his team alone to handle this stage of the op. Not because he wanted to cowboy it, and it certainly wasn't an ego thing. The problem was, the more people you have involved, the more components you set in motion that need to work together in a single, fluid manner. Experience had taught him to be sceptical when too many moving parts attempted to mesh together flawlessly.

Despite his anxiety, he was also knowledgeable enough to understand the nature of the man they were hopefully about to confront. The Lightning Rod was a killer, had murdered numerous men, women, and children on multiple occasions. He was devious, cunning, and unpredictable. Having him and the police on the same plot made for a highly combustible mixture, with Pam Daniels at its core. The presence of armed police was essential, although an operation in Met territory would inevitably see them running the show. A bitter pill for Bliss and his team to swallow, but it was necessary. As he had told Frank Rogers, whatever tactics they employed they could not afford for their target to consider Pam as a hostage and use her as such to negotiate a way out.

'Do we know enough about our killer to predict his reaction to any given circumstances?' he asked Chandler when she was off the phone.

She thought about it for a second or two. 'Depends. What are we talking about?'

'Say we don't manage to take him by surprise. He spots us, or we give ourselves away before we can take the doors off their hinges. Does he try having it on his toes? Does he shoot it out like Butch and Sundance not caring if he goes down? Or does he barter for Pam's life?'

Chandler fixed a band on her hair, tidying her ponytail. 'Hmm. Tough one. He's managed to remain unknown to us all this time, so he's unlikely to come in without a fight. Which means the shootout is a definite possibility. That said, Pam Daniels is a pretty decent shield and liable to slow down the process from our end. He's no mug, though, so he'll eventually come to the conclusion that his chances of walking out of there are almost zero once the place is surrounded. No car, bus, chopper, or plane to whisk him away to a country with no extradition. No, he'll realise that path is taking him nowhere other than a cell or a grave.'

Bliss followed the progression to its logical conclusion. 'So, if you're him, you take the chance and leg it?'

Chandler nodded.

'Me, too. I just ran the same permutations and came up with the exact same result. In which case, the moment we find out where he is, we'll need to take a good close look at the plot. If he's going to run, I want to know in which direction.'

Making good time in the outside lane of the dual carriageway, they were south of Biggleswade when Chandler took a call from DC Gratton. She put him on speaker. 'What have you got for us, Phil?'

'I can't promise you anything, but I might just have his whereabouts.'

Bliss licked his lips, switched hands on the steering wheel, and ran a finger over the scar on his brow. 'Okay. You officially have my interest, Phil. Tell me more.'

'CCTV caught a silver Defender heading south on the High Street in Whetstone and taking a right into Totteridge Lane shortly after 7.00am this morning. Different plates again, but that surely has to be him returning from Peterborough, boss.'

'I'd say there's a better than evens chance of that. How close are you to narrowing that down for us, Phil?'

'We literally got this break five minutes ago, boss. We're working on it is all I can tell you.'

'Then you best stop nattering to us and get back to it,' Bliss said, giving Chandler the nod to end the call.

'That's a bloody terrific break,' she said. 'I know people complain about Big Brother and the surveillance society, but when it comes to something like this, we'd be nowhere without it.'

'I know. How did they ever solve crimes in the old days before technology came to save us?' He was being facetious, yet there was an element of regret in what he'd said. In some ways there was an over-reliance on technology, but CCTV, phone data, and GPS were vital tools for all law-enforcement officers. A significantly large number of crimes would not have been solved without the tech, and Bliss didn't know how he felt about that.

Superfluous was one description, perhaps.

They drove on in silence for a number of miles, each lost in their own thoughts. Wipers intermittently batted rain away from the windscreen, but the sky was starting to look less threatening. A pale-yellow sun had begun to poke its way through the grey blanket of clouds as they dispersed. Bliss wondered if his colleague used their silent times to examine herself to see if she was up to the fresh challenge ahead. He knew he did. Every time.

Lao Tzu had insisted that knowing others was wisdom, but knowing the self was enlightenment. Bliss believed in that philosophy. You had to know your own strengths and weaknesses well enough before entering the fray alongside your partner. To fail yourself was one thing, but to fail them…? No, it was unimaginable to him. Not that mistakes couldn't still happen no matter how well prepared you were. Failure and the resulting self-recrimination went with the job, but he thought only poor coppers didn't question themselves before and after a moment of extreme tension.

At a steady 70mph and now running with the blues and twos, they had just emerged from the tunnel beneath the Galleria shopping Centre at Hatfield when Gratton called for a second time. On this occasion, his voice was high-pitched and almost screaming. 'You're never going to believe this. An on-board bus camera caught the Defender turning off Totteridge Lane into Allum Way at 7.07am. Best of all, that road leads to only two places: the Totteridge and Whetstone tube station car park, and a single-track lane off to the right that Google Maps says leads to a garage.'

'All right, all right,' Bliss said, feeling Gratton's exhilaration, but needing his DC to remain calm and collected. 'Take it easy, Phil. Now, I'm sensing there's more. So spill.'

'Sorry. Okay. So, on street view I spotted the car park CCTV. At first I thought our target might've taken a train – after all, we don't know if he still has Pamela Daniels with him. Anyway, I contacted them and they checked out their footage. They sent it across to us. Boss, on that video, we can clearly see the same silver Defender taking the right-hand fork.'

'That's excellent news. Great work.'

'Cheers, boss. So, we dug around a bit. There's a sign suggesting the garage is somewhere along that track, and when you follow it, you can see it runs along the back of a row of houses. There are a couple of parking spaces along there, too. The houses are possibilities, naturally, but here's something interesting about the garage: there's a building and a yard up there right at the far end, but it has a padlocked wrought-iron gate securing it. Thing is, Alan found out that the garage owner died five years ago, and the place has been non-operational since. Dead end, you might think. But you know DC Virgil, boss. Dog with a bone and all that. Anyhow, he contacted the local utility providers. I don't know about you, but I'm struggling to think why a defunct business doing no trade at all over the past five years is still using and paying for water, electricity and gas supplies.'

FORTY-EIGHT

Patience not being one of his virtues, Bliss found the waiting game interminable. He understood and accepted the benefits in this instance, but that didn't prevent him from becoming increasingly frustrated and irritable.

'Keep your fingers still,' Chandler snapped at him.

He flashed her a puzzled look.

'Your mitts are always tapping on something when we're inactive. Honestly, you're like a bloody child.'

He dropped both hands from the steering wheel. 'I can't decide if you sound more like my mother or my wife,' he muttered.

Muted laughter came from the back seat of the Mondeo. Bliss eyed Frank Rogers in the rear-view mirror. 'Glad someone finds it funny,' he said, his dour expression not changing.

Rogers grinned. 'You two are welcome light relief. To tell the truth, I could use the distraction.'

'You're not the only one,' Bliss grumbled.

They were settled in a car park behind a Waitrose, some 150 yards away from the garage in which they believed The Lightning Rod was holding Pam Daniels. Inconveniently, they had entered the outskirts of London during the height of rush hour. Lights and sirens helped forge a path through, but their progress was slowed all the same. They were the last to arrive at the staging point, which Bliss felt did them no favours.

At the briefing between him, Rogers, and the various Met team leaders, the Peterborough Major Crimes Unit were well and truly put in their place by the more senior command officers. That did not sit well with Bliss, but he had no choice but to swallow it. He and his team were guests in the city in which he'd been born and raised, observing the Metropolitan Police at work and lacking any genuine authority. The same went for Frank Rogers of the NCA, who appeared equally frustrated.

They'd listened intently as the plan of attack was pieced together by the Strategic Firearms Commander and his more tactical colleague. When Chief Superintendent Wylie asked if there were any questions, Bliss spoke for the first time since they'd huddled down over maps of the main plot and its surrounding area.

'I'm uneasy about this idea,' he said. 'If it goes wrong and we lose the advantage of a surprise entry, we leave him with only two choices.' Bliss counted them off on his fingers. 'He responds with gunfire or he takes Pam Daniels hostage. I made this clear to Frank when we spoke earlier, but he may not have clarified the point as forcefully as I would have.'

SCO19s Operational Firearms Commander, Sergeant Paul Groves, nodded. 'No, he did. And we listened to what he had to say. But when you scrutinise the location, the element of surprise is negligible no matter how we go in. Taking it head on has us moving in along that dirt road, so that's not a great option. To the left is the station car park, which is at a lower elevation. We can use ladders to get up and over, but there's dense vegetation and tightly packed trees between the fence and the garage building itself, so the final stage will be both cumbersome and less stealthy than we'd prefer. As for the other side, we could persuade a homeowner to allow us through their property and proceed via the garden, but again it's hard to do unheard and there are two fences to overcome. Beyond the chain-link fence at the back of the property is a good amount of wasteland, so once again our approach could not be entirely undercover. The command team therefore believe it's worth risking a closer look at those front gates before we commit to anything.'

'But you're sending up a drone to get a live overview of the plot. Won't that tell you what you need to know?'

'That we can't be certain of until it's up there. First and foremost, if the drone shows us the silver Land Rover parked up in the yard, then we can be reasonably confident of him being inside. But the sign at the bottom of the lane says Taylor & Son Garage, the kind of place that does repairs and maintenance, so if he's got even half a brain, he'll have tucked his motor inside out of the way. Now, if the drone can get us a good look at the gates and the padlock, we can make a decision on the fly. Having a couple of our people get closer still is a last resort, but one we may need to action. Okay?'

'I suppose it's going to have to be.'

Groves blew out a steady breath. 'Look, I've already had a barney with the DCC of Surrey Police today. I mean no offence to you or your team, DI Bliss, but as operational command, I can't waste time debating every single decision me and my TFO make. It's my job to carry out these tactical measures, and I will. Believe me, I appreciate how crucial a role you and your colleagues played in bringing us this far. You tracked our man to Whetstone, and without your efforts none of us would be here. It's pretty much the only reason I'm allowing you to be involved at all, albeit not as a direct-action team. It's up to you, of course, but we can do this with or without your help.'

Bliss had sucked it up and found himself with nothing more to add. Google StreetView showed a padlocked gate, but they had no way of knowing how reliable the images were. The view was likely to be several years old, the padlock possibly now rusty due to lack of use. On the other hand, if they were able to confirm its good condition having supposedly been shut down for the past five years, they could then start to feel more confident about their target being there.

Staring out through the windscreen as Waitrose shoppers came and went, Bliss reflected on his disappointment at the results sent back by the drone. It had confirmed many of their worst fears, such as the overgrown vegetation, the many obstacles, the open wasteland to the rear, and no Defender occupying space out in the yard. But to avoid being seen by anybody inside the garage itself, the drone had to remain at a height from which it could obtain no quality images of the padlocked gate.

He checked the time on the Ford's dashboard.

Less than a minute to go before the first phase of the operation got the go-ahead.

FORTY-NINE

He was done with her. She hadn't broken, insisting no matter what he did or threatened that she was telling him the truth. Her resolve left him feeling disappointed. The woman was no fun. It was time to move on to other things. The message he sent was brusque and to the point.

Getting nowhere. Same responses every time. Hit or quit?

He didn't care what answer he received. If she was lying, she was either extraordinarily brave or extraordinarily stupid. He'd left her face a ruinous mask of deliberate slashes, and he'd be astonished if she wasn't blind in one eye. He was of the opinion that few people were resilient enough to resist the physical and emotional pain of the torture he had inflicted, and Pam Daniels was neither martyr nor dummy. If he had to guess, he'd say she'd been telling him the truth all along.

Not that her responses mattered to him in the slightest. He'd been asked to do a job. No guidance had been provided as to how he might best achieve the expected result, nor any boundaries beyond which he should not cross specifically indicated. Left to his own inventive devices, he'd done as requested and had taken it as far as he could while keeping her alive.

Looking at her as she sat scared and alone and continuing to shudder spasmodically, he felt it would perhaps be a kindness to take the job to its logical conclusion. A striking woman who cared about her appearance would almost certainly prefer to die rather than live with the horror staring back at her from every mirror she stood in front of. Plastic surgery might rescue her from several of the more minor lacerations, but the majority were beyond even the most skilful repair. All she was good for now was scaring children at Halloween.

The final decision rested with another. If her future hung in the balance, it was not for him to rest a thumb on the scales.

He walked over and crouched down in front of the woman. 'It's okay,' he whispered. 'It won't be long now. One way or another, I'll put you out of your misery.' He turned his head, taking in the familiar surroundings. 'See this dirty, grubby little place, Pam? This… this was my old man's kingdom. He worked bloody hard to build up the business, wanted me to join him when it picked up enough trade to provide a living for two families. It never did, of course. Five years ago, he was sitting right where you are now in that chair when he keeled over with a heart attack. No second chance for him. Not like you're being given. One and out. I inherited this shithole, but never had it in me to follow his lead. Didn't have the heart to sell the place, either, which I'm now glad of. Must say, it's come in handy at times. Times like this, in fact, when I need to be discreet.'

The sound of a vehicle approaching from somewhere along the track disturbed his muse. Curious, he walked across to the front-facing window and peered out between the dusty vanes of a closed blind. Beyond the gates, by the two-car parking area, a Yaris he had not seen before sat with its engine running. A man and a woman clambered out. The woman, attractive and most likely in her thirties, stood in a puddle by the passenger door while the man she was with walked around the vehicle appraising it. He was about the same age as her, only Asian, with deep-set eyes and a seemingly permanent frown. The man sank to his haunches to look along the bodywork. Finally, he stood back a couple of paces, surveying the Toyota in its entirety.

'It drives well, right?' the woman said. 'Just like I told you on the blower. I think your girlfriend is going to love it.'

'It did have a nice feel to it. I'll give her a bell.' The man took out his phone, jabbed at the screen, and proceeded to talk into it.

From his position inside the garage, he was able to hear the conversation clearly. He listened as the man described the car, the way it steered and ran, how it looked in ideal condition for the money being asked. He then paused to take a series of photographs from all four sides. It seemed like an innocuous enough transaction. The woman was selling the Yaris, the man considering the purchase on behalf of a female friend. Their presence left its mark on his consciousness, but he was losing interest in such a mundane deal.

But then, just as he turned away from the grimy window, unwashed for half a decade, he stopped dead in his tracks when the phone the man was supposedly speaking into started to ring.

FIFTY

Having exploded through the rear door as quickly as his legs would carry him, he'd gone only half a dozen paces when he became aware of several figures dressed in black out on the scrubland beyond the property line, each of them frozen in place like participants in a child's game of Statues. Juddering to a halt, he swiftly weighed up his options, spun on his heels, and bolted back to the garage just as rapidly as he had fled.

Ignoring the many strident cries ordering him to stand still, he returned to the gloomy interior and shut the back door with a clatter behind him. In the chair by the desk, Pam Daniels jerked as if electrocuted; no doubt startled by his unexpected reappearance. Dismissing her from his thoughts, he set his mind to two separate issues: how had they found him, and how was he going to evade them?

Like a machine his brain rattled through every option available to him. His gaze fell upon the Land Rover currently occupying space where the hydraulic ramp had once stood. Could he jab the button to roll up the bay doors, dash across to the Defender and fling himself in behind the wheel, stamp his right foot down and build up enough speed at the precise angle required to spin the vehicle around inside the yard before bursting through the padlocked gates?

Perhaps.

If absolutely everything went his way.

But if the police had firearms out back, they were bound to have him surrounded. If they had rifle officers among their number, then at least one trained sniper was going to take him out before he could reach the main road.

Discounting the vehicle left him trapped inside the building.

He had leverage in the form of the woman. Her presence would buy him time, provided he made sure those lying in wait knew she was in there with him and that he was willing and able to end her life at any given moment.

And yet, he was not naïve enough to regard taking Daniels hostage as anything but a short-term solution. At most, having her trapped inside the garage with him would give those waiting outside pause for thought. They had no knowledge of her condition, nor what lengths he would go to. Even he couldn't be certain if he was willing to die rather than surrender.

He couldn't imagine how they had found him, but if the police were here, then they must already know enough about the way he made a living to put him away for life. Prison was always a risk for people in his line of work, but the idea of spending the next thirty or forty years behind bars was overwhelming.

His stash of arms and ammunition sitting on the shelves inside the storeroom was considerable, but the police were better equipped in every conceivable way. They also outnumbered him by a significant amount.

If he opted to fight, they would win.

It was that simple.

And that complex.

FIFTY-ONE

Bliss turned the air blue inside the pool car, his anger and choice of language unrefined. He and his colleagues had heard armed officers react to the target's sudden and dramatic appearance to the rear of the garage. Tension crackled across the communication devices. Moments later came the chatter discussing the error that had triggered it.

'Do you believe that?' he said furiously, holding his head as if tearing out what little remained of his hair. 'It was a decent enough idea dropping a couple of plain-clothes officers in closer to take sneaky shots of the padlock. But what sort of idiot doesn't turn the volume off on their mobile while they're on a covert op?'

'What sort of idiot called him?' Chandler scoffed. 'Had to be a work phone, so who wouldn't know he was on a job?'

Frank Rogers huffed and shook his head, a sour expression on his face. 'They've ballsed that right up. Heads will roll, and I would not want to be them right now.'

Bliss agreed, his mind alive with possibilities. 'Now there's no element of surprise. He knows we're positioned outside. Has to realise we have him in the pocket. But now suddenly the advantage lies with him. He still has Pam, and that's a pretty good card to play.'

Chandler turned in her seat to face him. 'She was already top of SCO19s list of priorities, Jimmy. Going in heavy with flashbangs and smoke might have given them a chance of getting her out of there alive. But now... I reckon they've just blown that out of the water.'

He noticed "we" had rapidly become "they", but he couldn't help but agree. 'I said right from the beginning that if he's not taken by surprise, it'll take only seconds for him to realise how serious his situation is. He has to know he can't blag his way out by using her as a shield. It's going to come down to the two worst choices imaginable for him. There's only one way this can end well now, and all kinds of ways for it to go wrong.'

'There has to be another option,' Rogers said firmly. 'Something we haven't yet considered.'

Chandler looked over her shoulder and shook her head. 'You have to be kidding, Frank. Unless he has a tunnel or a way to access the sewer from where he is, he has no exit. Unless those same two options are available to us, we have no entry. It's a stalemate. If he chooses not to come quietly, it will all go to shit before it's hardly begun.'

Bliss made no comment. He thought about what Rogers had said. Recollected his own views on the case he and the team had built. To his mind, it all boiled down to people and personalities. With all the major players now condensed into a single tiny part of a London suburb, what or who else was there to consider?

That was when a solitary phrase repeated itself silently inside his head.

If not Marty Reid, then who?
If not Marty Reid, then who?
If not Marty Reid, then who?

If Reid had not contacted The Lightning Rod to fix his Pam Daniels problem, then who had? The suspect, now in custody, had also ruled out their son, Angus. Bliss tasted defeat on his tongue as he moistened his lips. He wanted to spit it out, but instead grimaced as he swallowed it down. His head spun, his thoughts a blur.

Let's say it wasn't either of the Reids, just as Marty claimed. Who exactly did that leave…?

FIFTY-TWO

Having yanked the front door open so incautiously, the man looked thoroughly shocked to see DI Jimmy Bliss, together with two complete strangers, standing in the porchway entrance to his house.

Bliss removed his finger from the bell. 'Your own daughter, Harry?' he said in a voice dripping with incredulity. 'You put a contract out on your own daughter? How the fuck could you?'

'I don't have the foggiest idea what you're talking about, boy,' Daniels snapped back, regaining a measure of composure.

Bliss forced his way past and entered a long passageway in which a collection of coats and jackets hung from hooks fastened above a wooden shoe stand. He turned to face Pam's father, leaving Chandler and Rogers blocking the route out. 'We don't have time to play these childish games, Harry. It's all gone Pete Tong, mate, and you may have only minutes to save Pam's life. If you want to, that is.'

The man's eyes narrowed, and Bliss recognised a look of genuine concern coupled with the first faint threads of fear. 'What do you mean?' Daniels demanded to know. 'What are you telling me, boy?'

Bliss took a step closer, eyes locked on the older man. 'Pam's in real trouble, Harry. Your fixer, this Lightning Rod or whatever it is you call him, is trapped inside a small garage not too far from here. He's like Saddam caught in his spider-hole, and with the same result on the cards. The difference being, your only daughter is in there with him.'

A tic pulsed in Harry Daniels's cheek. 'I still don't know who the fuck you're talking about, Jimmy. But *if* my Pam happens to be with an acquaintance of mine, then she couldn't be more secure or in better hands.'

'Was,' Bliss growled, ramming his point home. 'She *was* safe, she *was* secure, Harry. But then you set your man on her, and now the pair of them are surrounded by armed police. Believe me when I tell you he has no way out.'

'What of it? Sounds to me as if a bloke like that is resourceful enough to cope with just about any situation that arises.'

'Is that what you think? Really? Or do you simply not care? Man like him… he's not built for prison. No danger of that. I don't know him, but I do know his type. You tell a man who exists the way he does that he has to spend the rest of his life in a cell, he's going to look for a quicker exit. And you, Harry, have no way of knowing if he'll take your daughter out seconds before he tops himself.'

This time, he got a sense his words had struck a nerve. Daniels bit into his lower lip while he stood shivering as if he'd been dipped into a pool of ice. Bliss hoped the old villain was quietly contemplating the end of the line for the wheels he had set in motion.

'There's no contract for that,' Harry muttered softly, shaking his head. 'It's just a job, a problem in need of fixing.'

'What job?' Bliss snapped back. 'What kind of problem?'

'I… I had to know what she'd told you about us, that's all.'

'And you couldn't just have asked her?'

'I did. Of course, I did. But I knew she was holding something back. Something about you. No way I could take the chance that it wasn't something ruinous for me and my people.'

Bliss got in his face. 'Well, whatever she kept from you, I'm telling you it didn't relate to anything about you or your business. But Harry, I don't care how deeply you distrusted her, you don't go setting a man like that on your own flesh and blood.'

'He doesn't... look, I have to be careful what I say here. I'm not about to order my own cell by spilling my guts. If – and I do mean if – there's a man out there holding my daughter, he has specific orders. Topping her isn't one of the outcomes.'

'Harry, you've already confessed to employing him to do the job for you, so don't dick me around. Tell me about him. Who is he? How does he operate? I want to find some leverage we can use against him.'

Daniels visibly paled, shaking his head dismally. 'I can't,' he said, his voice now weakened and pitiful if you were being charitable.

'Can't or won't?' Bliss demanded. 'This is Pam, for fuck's sake.'

'I can't tell you what I don't know. This man he's... he's everything they say about him, only more so. I don't know his name. Fact is, I don't know a damned thing about him other than he's the best at what he does. We do business, that's all. We've never met. I promise you, I can't give you anything on him.'

Bliss wasn't sure if he believed Daniels, but he knew he'd get nowhere firing more questions at him. 'Okay. Even if you didn't tell him to kill her when he was done with the questions, things have changed out of all recognition. He's surrounded by dozens of armed coppers, each of them eager to take him out. If it all kicks off, Pam could just as easily get caught in the crossfire.'

'He won't go that far without being told to. He's just not built that way.'

'Are you for real?' Rogers snapped, taking a stride closer as he confronted the man for the first time. 'The very same man murdered innocent women and children just because he could. Because he chose to. Not built that way? It's coded into his fucking DNA, you bloody fool.'

'Not my Pam, he won't,' Daniels shot back. He shook his head, desperate now. 'I'm telling you, when he's asked to fix something in a certain way, that's what he does. Questions and answers are all this particular job is about. He might lean on her, might do so a bit heavily. But he won't take the ultimate step without… getting the nod from me.'

'If that's the case, how do you contact him?' Bliss asked.

'Phone. I text him, then we move to an email account.'

'You mean the old terrorist ruse of leaving draft messages only, never sending them anywhere?'

'Yeah, that's it. If it ain't sent, it can't be intercepted. Not foolproof, but it gets the job done without too much fuss.'

'When did he last send you an update?'

'A short while ago, as it happens. He's done with her. Wants to know where things stand. But I'm guessing that was before your lot got involved.'

'So send him a reply. Make sure he knows he's to leave Pam alive regardless of what else happens.'

'I can do that, but I'm telling you he already knows not to go any further.'

Bliss leaned in, their heads now no more than six inches apart. 'And I'm telling you he's now improvising. With half the Met's firearms units having circled the wagons around him, his first concern is no longer his reputation, nor what you and others might do to him if he steps out of line. This is not just another day at the office for him, Harry. Get that into your thick head.

He's fucked. And the moment he realises that, what does it matter to him if his job gets fixed for good?'

Daniels closed his eyes. Left them closed for several seconds that felt as if they lasted several lifetimes. Finally, he sucked in some air, and on release said, 'I'll send the text.'

FIFTY-THREE

The chilling caress of realisation brushed against his skin. He'd received no further instructions regarding Pam Daniels, so he put her out of his mind for the time being. His only concern now was himself.

Prison or death?

Not much of a choice. Not at his age. Not with all he had going for him outside of this way of life. But was prison a foregone conclusion if he gave himself up? Everybody deserved their day in court, and with the right legal representation, just about anything was possible. What did they have on him when it came to Daniels? He bitterly regretted using the envelope on her now. Without that, it would have been a straightforward abduction, and only then if he couldn't persuade her to lie. He could do that kind of time standing on his head. But torture, slicing her open like he had… no, that would earn him a decade or more banged up. Better than a life sentence, but almost as hard to contemplate. And that was if they weren't able to pin something else on him. The fact that they'd found him suggested there had to be more evidence of other, more severe crimes.

Pacing the floor with its ingrained residue of oil and grease stains, he began babbling to himself. 'You've had a good run. Enjoyed a good life. You won't have time to miss your wife or kids. You step outside now and it'll all be over before you can snap your fingers. The only real question is whether you do it yourself or let the police slot you.'

The more he thought about it, the more he liked that idea. The officer, or more likely the dozen or so officers, who pulled the trigger would suffer many a sleepless night afterwards. They were normal people, not monsters. They had consciences, doubts ready to eat away at them. Bit of luck one or more would retire, perhaps even put a bullet in their own brain as PTSD tore them apart from the inside.

'Yes, that's the way to go,' he muttered breathlessly, his shoes squealing on the floor as he came to a sudden halt.

His mind made up, he breathed deeply and went to fetch a pistol that he'd been holding back for just such an occasion. His thoughts turned to a movie he had enjoyed. A Coen brothers remake of the old John Wayne western, *True Grit*. The scene he pictured featured Jeff Bridges as Rooster Cogburn. In response to a taunt from a character by the name of Lucky Red Pepper, who had called him a 'one-eyed fat man', Cogburn had responded with all the ire he could muster, 'Fill your hand, you son of a bitch!'

Standing absolutely still, he nodded to himself.

Yes. It was all so perfect.

He'd make them fill their hands, the sons and daughters of bitches. And just like old Rooster, he might take a few of his enemies down before they could slot him, and maybe even find a way to escape into the badlands.

He slapped a full magazine into the pistol, chambered a round, turned and headed towards the back door.

He'd taken two steps when his phone chimed, stopping him in his tracks.

Only one person would send him a text today. Given the circumstances, could he afford to ignore it? He decided he had time to see the job through. If he was instructed to release Pam, that's what he would do. He took out his mobile and, ignoring the text message, went straight to the shared email account instead.

As expected, there was a message in the drafts folder.

Just three little words. The last he would ever read in his life.

Caught in the moment, they made him smile. He looked across at Pam Daniels, then back at the screen. This time, he laughed. He carried on laughing as he stared down at the message on the phone.

END IT NOW.

FIFTY-FOUR

Bliss looked at the expression on Harry Daniels' face and immediately knew something was horribly wrong. 'What did you tell him to do?' he cried, snatching the phone from the man's hand. With his flesh feeling as if it were tightening across his skull, he read the words on the screen.

END IT NOW.

He looked back up, his gaze hardening. With his heart thumping behind his ribs, he thrust the phone out. 'Message him back, Harry.'

Hands raised as if surrendering, Daniels said, 'It doesn't happen that way.'

'Call it off!'

'I'm telling you I can't,' Daniels said with a snarl. 'Not even if I wanted to. That's not the way it works. We set it up in such a way for this precise reason. He won't accept a change in instructions within an hour of receiving the previous one.' He shrugged and shook his head. 'It was our agreed safety net. It's done. Let her go.'

'Like you have, you evil fucker?'

Bliss took out his Airwave and activated the call button. 'It's DI Bliss,' he virtually screamed into the communication device.

'Suspect has orders to take out Pam Daniels. I say again, he's going to kill her if you don't do something about it right now.'

Barely able to make eye contact with the man who had just ordered the execution of his own daughter, Bliss shook his head and said, 'Why? She gave me nothing, Harry. I have no reason to lie to you, and I'm telling you she never once mentioned the business.'

Daniels heaved a sigh. 'I believe you, boy. I genuinely do. It's nice to know she remained loyal to the end.'

'Then what on earth were you thinking? She didn't give you up to me, so why did you just push the button on her?'

It took a few moments before the man replied. When he did, his voice was filled with pain but not a trace of regret. 'Because if she'd walked out of there, she would have given you everything. Honestly, Jimmy, can you see Pam in prison greys or blues or oranges? That's a slow death for her right there. No, old son, she would have done a deal. She'd've thought about me setting my man on her, and she would have burned down my empire out of revenge and to save her own neck.'

'But there are flames licking all around your damned empire as we speak. You're done, Harry. Finished. We have enough on you now to bang you up for the rest of your natural. You go down, your business gets dragged down with you. There's nothing left to save. Nothing other than your own daughter. You can still do that, Harry. You have time for one final decent act with just a single phone call.'

'I already told you I can't do that.'

'You could at least try,' Bliss told him.

Daniels sniffed, shook his head, and drew himself up to his full height. 'I don't think so, Jimmy-boy. I'll take my chances the way they are. If Pam walks, she talks. This way, well, I suppose we'll see how it turns out.'

When he next stepped out of the garage to the rear, he had one arm wrapped around a struggling Pamela Daniels, the other extended, hand gripping his gun. He stood quite still for a moment, surveying the rear of the yard and the open ground beyond the fence. Then he took two strides, hoisting his hostage along with him, her bare feet scraping along the ground recently softened by rainfall.

'You lot might as well come out from beneath whatever rocks you crawled under,' he cried out. 'I know you're out there. Might as well show yourselves.'

He waited, but saw no obvious movement. There wasn't a great deal of cover out on the wasteland, but they were using it well to secrete themselves away from his sharp eyes.

Wriggling his hand back and forth to draw their attention to the weapon, he shouted, 'I don't suppose you'd consider letting me go, would you? I promise I'll leave her somewhere safe.'

No reply, no movement.

'I know how this ends,' he hollered. 'I put one in her head, you put a dozen in mine. That's not a fair trade-off, but it is what will happen. And she'll be just as dead.'

He lingered, knowing that eventually they would have to at least pretend to negotiate with him. At that moment, his phone rang. No incoming text chime, no email ping. An actual phone call. Making sure to keep behind his hostage, he whispered in her ear, 'I'm going to have to let you go for a moment while I take this call. You run, I'll kill you. You try to fight me off, I'll kill you. You so much as look at me funny, I'll kill you. That's just the kind of mood I'm in, Pam.'

'I… I won't do anything,' she stammered, staring down at her feet. Whatever spirit she had once had, it was long gone. If he'd cared enough about his captive, he would have pitied her.

'Good girl. That's what I want to hear. Besides, it could be the warden giving you a last-minute pardon.' He chuckled to himself, then released his grip on her arm. The phone continued to ring. He slipped it out of his pocket and pressed the button to receive.

'Who is this?' he demanded of the unidentified caller.

*

'Who I am is not important,' Bliss said, blood rushing in his ears. 'What is of great importance is the message I have for you from Harry Daniels. He's calling you off. He no longer wants you to end it. Let Pam go. Those are your new instructions.'

The response was not long in coming. 'I need to hear it from him.'

'You're hearing it from me. Harry's… well, he's not doing too well right now. I'm speaking on his behalf. I'm using his burner. Isn't that good enough for you?'

'No, it isn't. And Harry would know that better than anybody. If he gives me the original instruction, he has to give me any changes to those instructions. And in the prescribed manner.'

Bliss thought quickly, desperate to turn this around. 'Listen to me. I apologise. I tried it on with you, but now I'm going to tell you the truth. Harry didn't send you that email. Yes, it came from his account, but it was Marty Reid who sent it. You know who he is?'

'I do.'

Doubtful now. A little less confident. Bliss heard it in the man's voice before he continued. 'It's him who wants his ex-wife killed, not her father. Ask yourself, why would he? A father wanting his own daughter dead? You must know that can't possibly be the case. But Reid, on the other hand, he has plenty of reasons. Think about it. That's all I ask. Just think about it. I'm telling you the truth this time. I'm pleading with you to spare her life and end this.'

Bliss hoped for a delay, time enough for the man to at least consider what he'd been told, but there was none.

'We have our arrangements for a reason, me and Harry. A good, sound reason. I can't deal with any other possibilities. You could be anybody. I have no way of knowing if I can trust you.'

Play to his ego, Bliss thought. *This man doesn't know what it is not to succeed.*

'You're right. You don't. But you'll be making the biggest mistake of your life if you pull that trigger. You'll have failed. A miserable disaster ending in unnecessary – and unwanted – murder. You want a botched job to be your last?'

This time, there was a pause. Bliss felt a flicker of hope vying for air in his chest. It was extinguished just as suddenly when the man said, 'You ever seen the movie *True Grit*? The Coen brothers remake.'

'The… what the hell are you banging on about?' The man was close to the edge. He wasn't right in the head, and now he was slow walking into oblivion. Bliss had to stop him from taking that final last step. 'In case you hadn't noticed, this is real life. And you hold an innocent one in your hands right now. Let her go. Just let her go. You do what you need to do for you, but leave her alive.'

This time the reply was instantaneous, as if the man had heard nothing. 'Look out for it. It's a good film. If you get around to watching it, remember me and my final words when you do. Bye.'

The call did not disconnect. There was a loud thump and a skittering sound, as if the phone had fallen to the ground.

'Hey!' Bliss bellowed. 'Hey! Listen to me! Listen to me!'

Nothing. Then the same voice, only more distant this time.

'Fill your hands, you sons of bitches.'

And then the shooting began.

FIFTY-FIVE

Post-op briefings were often lengthy and drawn-out affairs. Operations involving discharged firearms dragged on far longer, though often with justification. When a person died as a result of that gunfire, all bets were off. Bliss had been sitting alone in a room at Boreham Wood police station for almost four hours when Frank Rogers entered.

'Where's my team?' he asked sharply, looking up with a scowl. 'Are they being taken care of?'

Rogers raised a hand. The NCA man looked a little dishevelled and awkward. 'Easy, Jimmy. They're fine. All three are on their way home.'

'They've been debriefed?'

'Yes, they have. I've been asked to collect you for yours. Before I do, I need to know if you'll want to see Pam later?'

Bliss blinked. Once. Twice. Shook his head. 'You mean the bullet hole in her head? Or maybe her sliced up face? No, thank you. I think I'll spare myself that if it's all the same to you.'

'I meant, did you want to visit her in hospital before… well, you know?'

'Yes, I know. Before they pull the plug, you mean?'

'She's brain dead, Jimmy. The only thing keeping her alive is a machine. Her son has already given them permission to stop treatment and shut everything down.'

'Then let him deal with it. I want no part of it.'

Rogers hung his head. 'I'm sorry, mate. I really am.'

Bliss puffed out a quick breath. 'Yeah. I know. Me, too.' He dragged himself to his feet. 'Come on, let's get this over with.'

Hesitating, Rogers said, 'Before we go, Jimmy, I just wanted to say it's been a genuine pleasure working with you. You and your team. They're a credit to you.'

Bliss reached out and the two men shook hands. 'I've had my eyes opened watching you work, Frank. I admire what you do.'

'If that's the case, why not come and join us?' Rogers said. 'You'd be a good fit for my team. You might want to consider that when the time comes.'

'Can you give me an extra two years if my lot won't?'

'I'd certainly be willing to try. If we base you in Bedford, you'll get to work our Peterborough cases. And you won't necessarily have to move home.'

It was a good pitch, catching Bliss at a vulnerable time. 'How about an extension of your unit up in my city?' he asked. 'Thorpe Wood can make room for it.'

Rogers twisted his mouth. 'Hmm. I'm good, my friend, but not that good. Sounds like a big ask.'

Bliss was happy enough to be considered, irrespective of where he might fit in. With no idea how his future might unfold, he was willing to consider all offers. 'The ball's in your corner, Frank. But if you're not bullshitting me about the move, don't leave it too long. Let me know by the end of the year and give it your best shot.'

'So you'd come over? You'd leave the MCU to join us?'

Bliss clapped him on the shoulder. 'Put it this way, Frank, you've given me something to think about if they no longer want me come next May.'

'That's good enough for me.'

Bliss wasn't finished. He had a question that had been gnawing away at him. 'You've spoken with Daniels since his arrest. Were we right about his reasons for cleaning up after himself? Was he selling up, moving on…?'

Rogers nodded. 'Kind of. He was putting business matters in order ahead of migrating to the Algarve. Apparently, he doesn't have a great deal of time. Advanced liver disease. He wanted to live out the rest of his days by a pool, basking in the sunshine. So yes, he was tidying up behind him, getting shot of those he felt he couldn't rely on to stay schtum.'

Bliss took a beat. At least Pam had been telling him the truth about that. 'And Reid?' he asked. 'Any mention of him?'

'Indirectly. There was no love lost between the two of them, but we got the distinct impression that Reid was picking up some of Harry's business.'

'Which included using his fixer.'

'Looks like it, yes. Seems to have been more an arrangement of convenience because of Pam and Marty's son than anything else.'

It made sense. As much as any of it did.

They left the room together, still discussing the possibility of him re-joining the NCA. Upon entering the briefing room one floor above, Bliss felt like a dying creature being observed by birds of prey eager to pick apart the carrion, clean down to the bone. Chief Superintendent Wylie's gaze was impassive. His man on the ground, OFC Groves, glanced away, which Jimmy took to be a bad sign. A sturdy, po-faced woman sat between them. Bliss clocked the epaulettes on both shoulders; two small diamonds sandwiched between the insignia and the crown.

Nodding once, he said, 'Good evening, Deputy Commissioner.'

Julia Wallace responded with a single nod of her own. 'Inspector. Please take a seat.'

In the Metropolitan Police, Commissioner was a rank you earned, not a title bestowed upon you if you won a vote. It was the highest of them all, one rung above Wallace. Bliss didn't regard ambition as a negative trait, but it could lead to bad decisions being made in the pursuit of loftier goals. How Wallace reacted in this moment to a police-involved shootout that claimed two lives, would be scrutinised in great detail should the opportunity arise for her to make that final step up. Bliss worried about her presence, because in addition to being the most senior individual in the room, her position also made her the most unpredictable.

'I don't have many questions for you, Inspector Bliss,' she began, her tone as solemn as her manner. 'I've heard from the majority of officers involved in today's operations, and I believe I have a clear idea of what took place across the three main locations. Obviously, there will be a full internal investigation ahead of my convening an independent panel. To that end, we're looking for answers concerning your own involvement.'

'Yes, ma'am,' he said. 'I understand.'

'Good. Then let's get started. We're interested in two significant aspects. To begin with, please tell us what led you to visiting the home of Harry Daniels.'

It was the question he had been preparing himself to answer for the past few hours. One he had silently put to himself on numerous occasions. He asked whether the leap he had taken from discovering Marty Reid's lack of involvement in Pam's abduction, to realising her father was responsible, could solely be the result of applied thinking and gut instinct. Nobody else in the room knew of his prior encounter with Harry Daniels on Saturday morning, and nobody could learn of it. The problem for him now was whether he was able to explain away his decision successfully.

'I took a chance I thought I had no option but to take,' he finally said. 'We were previously convinced of Marty Reid's guilt. We felt he had reacted adversely after learning his ex had spent time with me, a serving police officer. No villain of his stature is going to take kindly to such an arrangement, however fleeting. To say we were flummoxed when we learned Reid had nothing to do with it would be an understatement. But we couldn't just sit there and curse ourselves for having got it so badly wrong. Some quick thinking was required.'

'I understand that aspect,' Wallace said. 'But how did you then get from Pamela Daniels' ex-husband to her father? You say you took a chance, but this seems to me more like divine providence.'

'Not really, ma'am. For me, it was a process of elimination. The more I thought about it, the more I knew we were right. Wrong about the who, but right about the why. And if we were, who else would want to question Pam about her meetings with me? Had to be another criminal of some note. Someone close enough to her to know she'd spent time with me.'

'So… a leap of faith, at the very least?'

'Perhaps,' Bliss acknowledged. 'I come back to what I said at the beginning. I took a chance. Somebody was pulling the strings of the man holding Pam. I thought if we could get to them, we might turn things around in her favour. In the end, I didn't think we had anything to lose by questioning him.'

'Okay. I'm with you so far, Inspector.' Wallace sucked in her cheeks as she gave credence to his words. 'Which leads us neatly to our second main area of concern. You've had ample time to think about the way things went down with Harry Daniels. With the benefit of hindsight, would you have done anything differently? Before you answer, let me be a little more specific. Would you have still allowed him to use his phone to contact the man holding his daughter, and would you subsequently still have used that phone to call that same man afterwards?'

Bliss cleared his throat before responding. 'Yes. To both. At all times, we knew what was going down at that garage. It was a tense situation in which a known killer was trapped. He had to choose between a prison cell and his own extinction. We… I believed he'd go with the latter. If that happened, there was a clear danger of him either taking Pam down with him, or of her getting caught in the crossfire if the man opted to fight his way out. Having Harry Daniels use that phone to contact his man was the only way I could see of us gaining something positive from an op that had turned out so disastrously.'

'With respect, Deputy Commissioner,' Frank Rogers interrupted. 'I was with Inspector Bliss throughout. It was a fraught state of affairs, one that demanded quick thinking and decision-making. If I'd felt at any point that the Inspector had lost the plot, I would have stepped in. He was right about Pamela Daniels' father being involved in her abduction, and in my opinion, he was right to allow the man to use his phone. I genuinely thought DI Bliss had got through to Daniels and was as surprised as anyone by the content of the message he sent.'

'Your comments are noted,' Wallace said, somewhat dismissively, Bliss thought. 'I've no doubt the NCA will want to run its own inquiry, given your presence. Now,' she said, turning to Bliss once again, 'tell us more about that final phone call, Inspector.'

If he closed his eyes, he could imagine it all ending so differently. Harry Daniels sending a message instructing the Lightning Rod to let Pam go was one way it could have gone. Bliss persuading the man not to take her life was another. Instead, he had quoted from the film, raised his weapon, and without further pause, shot Pam Daniels once in the head. The other shots they'd heard through the phone all came from SCO19 officers. He closed his eyes again, only this time he saw the truth.

'It was a last resort,' he admitted, his voice little more than a whisper at this point. 'The last throw of the dice. Last gasp. Eleventh-hour. Call it what you will, my only way of communicating with him was to use the phone.' He huffed dejectedly and shook his head. 'Let's settle for do-or-die, shall we? That probably sums it up best of all.'

'Why didn't you wait for a trained hostage negotiator to intervene?'

'Because I knew we had no time for that. This man we hunted down was a hardened criminal, not some naïve thug with a lust for the kill but a greater desire to save his own neck. He knew what his chances were, and he also knew it was too late in the day for negotiation.'

'Perhaps. We'll never know for certain. Even so, Inspector, why did you not run it by the operational commander?'

Bliss drew in some much-needed air. 'I refer you again to the lack of time.'

'You couldn't possibly know how much time you had.'

His eyes hardened. 'Have you worked the streets, ma'am? Have you been involved in active situations like that in terms of tension and the potential for the worst of all outcomes?'

Wallace met his gaze. 'As a matter of fact, I have.'

'Then you know. You know there comes a time when all your training and experience tells you what the protocols and procedures say you ought to do, yet you go instead with your instinct.'

'Because your instinct tells you this is an individual situation which no procedure could ever make allowances for.'

Bliss closed his eyes and nodded. 'Your brain is telling you to wait, to make sure everything is in order, but your gut is screaming at you to act before it's too late…' He stopped talking, almost choking on his words. He swallowed back a sob before continuing. 'That was the position we were in at the time. I acted because I knew Pamela Daniels would lose her life if I didn't.'

'And you'd do nothing different if you encountered the exact same circumstances again tomorrow?'

He sniffed and smiled crookedly. 'I can't answer that. All I can speak about is what happened today. Would I act differently if I could go back in time? No. No, I don't believe I would.'

The three Met officers exchanged glances. Wallace eventually nodded and regarded him with a little more empathy this time. 'That concludes our business here, Inspector. Unless you have questions of your own?'

Bliss shook his head. 'Not at the moment, thank you. I'll save them for when I have a clear head.'

'Very well. You understand the nature of these post-op briefings, I'm sure. While we like to have a first impression as soon as possible following an incident of this nature, we also appreciate we're asking questions of people at their lowest ebb, with adrenaline still pumping hard and thoughts unusually scattered. You mentioned needing a clear head, but in my opinion, you've handled yourself remarkably well given everything that occurred today. My report will reflect that. It will not single you out when it comes to the formal inquiry. I'm of the opinion that you did your very best in the most trying of circumstances. At the end of the day, it's all we can ask of our officers.'

FIFTY-SIX

Bliss arrived home in the early hours of Thursday morning. His dog minder had left long ago, and if the jumping up and down, spinning in circles, and furious tail-wagging was anything to go by, Max was delighted to see him. He fussed over the animal for a good twenty minutes before rolling back onto the sofa, exhausted yet at the same time fizzing with the kind of vibrant energy that comes at the conclusion of an investigation. His eyes were drawn to a note on the coffee table, telling him that Max had been fed and walked and played with until 11.00pm. He smiled and stroked the dog's head, which now rested on his chest, feeling a welcoming hot breath on his face.

Before leaving London, he'd listened to several voicemails. One from Sandra Bannister referred to a media briefing from the PCC, during which he vowed to launch his own inquiry into Bliss's actions ahead of what would undoubtedly be a controversial formal version conducted by the Met. He couldn't even be bothered to be angry. In fact, he thought it might just work against Benning, given the Deputy Commissioner of the Met's own findings. The man would be made to look every inch the fool he was. Thinking about the message, Bliss took out his phone to send the journalist a text.

I have some good stuff for you. Will call tomorrow.

Penny Chandler had left him two voicemails. She had travelled back to the city with Bishop and Ansari. In both of her short messages, she sounded concerned about him. Anxious to know how things had gone at the post-op. He composed a short text for her as well.

Home. Knackered. Post-Op went better than expected. See you tomorrow.

No sooner had he sent the message than his phone rang. He smiled. He might have known his partner wouldn't have been able to switch off without hearing from him.

'I said tomorrow, Pen,' he answered with a grin. 'Go to sleep.'

'Check your watch. It is tomorrow.'

With a groan, Bliss heaved himself into a sitting position. Max took that as a sign to climb up and settle on his lap, pawing at him for attention. 'I meant work hours,' he said.

'Then you should have specified. Anyway, you're up, you're talking, I'm up, I'm listening. So tell me how it went.'

He walked her through it, swallowing thickly as he revealed Wallace's final words to him.

'Wow, that's a turn up for the books.' She sounded impressed. 'So Wallace is more than just a pretty face, then?'

Stifling a laugh, he said, 'To tell you the truth, I didn't even notice.'

'What? Jimmy Bliss fails to spot an attractive sort – that could easily be tomorrow's headline.'

He smiled to himself. 'Oh, I think they'll have other stories to focus on.'

'Yeah. Of course. Did you get to see Pam before you left London?'

'I chose not to. Besides, she's gone. Died before they could shut everything down.'

'I'm so sorry, Jimmy.'

'Don't be,' he told her. 'Pam… well, she was a fling. Nothing more than that. I'm not even sure if she counts as a fling. What's shorter and less significant than that? A dalliance?'

Chandler's voice became softer. 'Don't do that. Don't belittle it. Whatever it was, it was something. Even if all it amounted to was a couple of nights of comfort.'

He rested the phone against his head for a few seconds. Max looked up at him and whimpered as if knowing he was troubled. He ruffled the dog's head once more.

'Yeah, I know. All I'm saying is don't get all… Penny on me. I'm sad she's gone. It pains me to think of her final hours. But that's it. No brooding, no climbing inside a bottle. I don't think I'll ever know what her role was in all this, but I enjoyed my short time with her. No regrets. I just wish we could have saved her at the end there.'

'You did your best, Jimmy.'

'Funnily enough, that's what Deputy Commissioner Wallace told me. Said it was all any of us could expect.'

'And she's right,' Chandler said urgently. 'Occasionally we rise above it, but only if the circumstances allow. This time, they went against us. Anyway, are we now taking it as a done deal that Harry Daniels was the go-between, the man in the middle taking requests from various criminal figures and passing them on to the Lightning Rod?'

Bliss felt a wave of exhaustion wash over him. He almost told her he was done talking, but his colleague deserved better having waited up for his return. 'It certainly looks that way. Frank had him arrested, and the NCA took the first crack at interviewing him as his reach extended far beyond the Met. I also understand they found a number of burner phones in his house, so the data on those will make for interesting reading. I reckon there'll be a few dawn knocks on front doors around the country over the following days and weeks.'

'How could anybody do that to his own flesh and blood, Jimmy? Do you understand it? You were there, same as I was. But I can't make sense of it.'

'No. Nor can I. But then, I'm neither a father nor a criminal. I'm hardly the best person to ask.'

'You told him Pam had never spoken to you about his business. Was that true?'

'Yeah. It was her ex and her son who suggested the visit to Peterborough. I'm guessing they were already planning to use Harry and his fixer to take out Donald Sperling, and must have thought it'd be a good idea to have a foot in our camp. I don't know if it's ironic, but they sent Pam up here looking to acquire information, yet her old man's fear was that she was busy doling it out. I genuinely think he believed me at the end there, but couldn't stand the thought of what she might say to keep her own neck off the block.'

'Families, eh?'

'Yeah. Some, anyway.'

'I don't suppose the Reids will walk away from this smelling of roses.'

'Certainly not Marty. I'm sure they'll find a way to connect him to some of this, though it'll be a tough old job. Not sure if Harry will give him up, but I wouldn't bank on it. Those degrees of separation are crucial, and proving they put the hit on Sperling and others won't be a simple task.'

'So what is the deal with our killer, Jimmy? The fabled Lightning Rod.'

'The Met are still picking apart his garage. So far, they've uncovered a stash of weapons and ammunition, but not a single lead. He had no ID on him whatsoever. All he carried was his phone and a bunch of keys, one of which was for the Defender. At first glance, the mobile gave them nothing to go on, either.'

'So all those murders and we still don't know the name of our killer?'

'Nope. We stopped him. We might even have shut down those who paid for and arranged his services. But as for the man himself… he died as he lived. A complete enigma.'

'You think we'll ever identify him, Jimmy?' Chandler asked.

'You know what, Pen?' Bliss replied, reflexively smoothing down Max's fur. 'I really don't know. The man was a ghost in life. Imagine how much more difficult it'll be to suss him out now he's actually dead. In the end we closed the case, so that has to count for something. It might be all we get, but perhaps it's all we need.'

'Hark at you, being all positive. Oh, and if you want some more of that in your life, I have news.'

'Okay. But that's it for the night. As some people keep telling me, I'm an old man and I need my rest. Have to admit, I'm feeling it right now.'

'You'll be happy to hear what I have to say,' she teased.

'Don't string it out. Just tell me, damnit!'

Chandler sniggered before clearing her throat. 'While we were out galivanting in London, Detective Superintendent Haskell filed her report. The boss made a point of telling me when I called to let her know what was going on with the post-op.'

'I'm guessing it's good news.'

'The best. She's cleared the investigation team of all wrongdoing. She says that based on all the evidence and intelligence gathered during the op, the team arrived at the only logical conclusion.'

Bliss allowed himself a small smile of victory. 'Ah. That explains the Commissioner's media briefing last night. He's coming after me because he failed to get what he wanted from Haskel.'

'But you're on firm ground, aren't you, Jimmy?' Chandler asked.

'Yes,' he said. 'As firm as it can ever be.'

And if not, working alongside Frank Rogers sounded like a pretty decent alternative.

FIFTY-SEVEN

Christine Taylor told her two children to scoot and watch television while she cleared away the breakfast dishes. Earlier that morning, she had enjoyed her first coffee of the day out on the back garden patio. The air was cool after the rains of the previous days, but a watery sun was climbing, and the sky carried only a few puffy cumuli. It was going to be a lovely day; she felt it in her bones.

Staring out of the window above the sink, the vibrant blue displayed in a panoramic view almost hurt her eyes. The garden was looking great this year, and she could already tell the autumn colours were going to be spectacular. She smiled to herself as she dipped gloved hands into the washing-up bowl. There was no point in using the washer for a couple of dishes and glasses and her own single mug. She became so lost in thought that it wasn't until her daughter tugged twice on her skirt that she realised the girl had been calling her.

'It's Daddy,' she said excitedly, eyes wide and gleeful. 'Come see, Mummy. Daddy's on the telly.'

'What?' Christine scrunched up her face, knowing her daughter had to be mistaken. 'Sweetheart, your father is not on the television. You know he can't be.'

'But it is him, Mummy.' More gentle tugs. 'It is. Come see.'

The child's mother gave a good-natured sigh, peeled off her gloves and draped them over the dish rack. She followed her daughter out of the kitchen and into the living room, the big flat screen busy with images and text scrolling across from right to left. For a moment she had no idea what her children were watching, only to realise she had left the station tuned to *Sky News* when she switched it off prior to heading up to bed the previous night.

'Okay, silly,' she said, hands planted on her hips. 'You show me which one's Daddy.'

'He's not on there now.' A sing-song voice dulled with vague disappointment. 'Just wait… he'll be back.'

Christine played along. Pretty soon somebody would appear, and the mistake would become obvious. She frowned when she realised what her children were watching. Reports had come in the previous evening of a shooting incident, resulting in the loss of one life, with another critical in hospital. Sky was running footage every half hour or so showing aerial shots of the scene, an update in bold yellow font currently running across the screen suggesting the critical patient had subsequently died. Such a terrible shame for their families, she thought. Whoever these people were, whatever they had done, it was always the poor families who were left behind to pick up the pieces.

Just then, the image changed. On screen now was a photo of a man, described as a contract killer responsible for several murders, including those of woman and children. The man had been shot dead by police but had yet to be identified.

'See,' Christine's daughter said, jumping up and down on the settee and pointing at the TV. 'I told you it was Daddy.'

AUTHOR'S NOTE

This book was a long time in the writing. The back end of 2021 and the first half of 2022 proved to be difficult periods for me in terms of my work. A protracted house move, a conveyer belt of tradespeople in and out working on our new home, a wedding trip to Hawaii, and a certain amount of poor health, all combined to ensure that *The Lightning Rod* got written in fits and starts. Don't get me wrong, much of what happened was joyous and overwhelmingly positive, but it consumed time with a voracious appetite. The negative elements did the same, only more so. The consequence was, I never managed to achieve a constant rhythm in producing this book until the editing stage, and all I can do is hope that phase pulled my arse out of the fire.

ACKNOWLEDGEMENTS

I NEED TO THANK MY wife for putting up with my moods while I struggled, and for not minding when I worked weekends to get this book finished. I also have to thank a large number of my Facebook group members for their support and good wishes during that period especially. To my beta readers, Dorothy Laney, Kath Middleton, and Lynda Checkley, I once again thank you for your honesty and integrity in addition to your blooper-spotting eyes. I'd also like to extend a warm thank you to the Facebook group, UK Crime Book Club, for their outstanding work in promoting and supporting authors. Word of mouth is hugely important for those of us splashing around in the shallow end, and the UKCBC admins allow us and our readers to spread that word. I hope book bloggers already know how much I value and respect them, but I need to put that in print here and now. I want to also thank fellow author and police advisor, Graham Bartlett, for his invaluable help and advice in respect of procedure, in particular with case reviews and the firearms scenes.

Finally, a special thank you to Donna Morfett for organising my ARC reads and blog tour, in addition to her dedication and hard work in supporting so many authors, of which I am proud to be just one. Her enthusiasm is only surpassed by her generosity of spirit, and I can only hope she goes on to achieve all that she dreams of.

Cheers – Tony

For more about me, please follow this link:
https://linktr.ee/TonyJForder

Printed in Great Britain
by Amazon